I0664007

OZoo

THE WICK CHRONICLES
BOOK TWO

BLUE BOX BOOKS

OZOO
THE WICK CHRONICLES
BOOK TWO

Published by Blue Box Books
www.blueboxbooks.com

ISBN 978-1-932461-48-0

Printed in the United States of America

THE WICK CHRONICLES

BOOK TWO

MAX THOMPSON

1

Slowly, deliberately, the King folded the white cloth in his hands. He folded until it was the size of human fist, and he held it there, pressed between his hands, until Midlam's Queen was visibly uncomfortable. He stared at her, the look on his own face a curious mix of anger and pity. Her eyes were fixed on that piece of fabric as she waited for him to respond to her surrender and abdication of Midlam's throne to him.

When it seemed as if she was going to speak again, perhaps to remind him she was there at all, he pressed it back into her hands, turned around, and walked across the roof of the royal house. We had been celebrating the return of Finn and the surprise that he was the Emperor's father, and that they'd managed to stop the end of the world two hundred years in the future.

Everyone—except perhaps for the Emperor, the Queen of Pacifica, and Prince Andrew—watched as the King made his way wordlessly to the roof door, and as he slammed it closed. It shut with a loud crack, and from the corner of my eye I could see Midlam's Queen startle. She looked from the door to the face of her son, who stood there with tears in his eyes and Oz's arms around him, and then to the Emperor, who very clearly felt the anger that the King had avoided displaying.

He wasn't the one who reacted. While he ground his teeth together, trying to compose his thoughts in a way that wouldn't make things worse, the Queen of Pacifica stomped toward the Queen of

Midlam and snapped, "What the hell is wrong with you, Shazia? Why would you put him on the spot like that?"

"I'm giving you Midlam," she said, still confused by the silent rejection of the King.

"That's not how it works." Drew—Prince Andrew of Midlam—sucked in a deep breath, pulled Oz's arms from his waist, though he kept hold of her hand, and swallowed the sudden slap of grief that had left him gutted when his mother hinted at the loss of his father. "We're not at war with Pacifica. You can't surrender to them. And if you abdicate—you abdicate to me. *Only* to me."

Now, the truth, and one I supposed Shazia Van Hoff already knew, is that Drew didn't really want the job. He was in San Francisco, Pacifica's capital, to finish his education and eventually—if they decided they wanted to—marry Oz. The plans they had been making since they were barely in their teens were simple: be friends, no matter what; get to know each other; fall in love; marry; merge Pacifica and Midlam. Two of the bullet points on their list that were chiseled into metaphorical stone were being friends forever, and merging the countries into one.

Drew moved to San Francisco at the start of summer in 2415; they told their families he wanted to spend more time there to get to know Oz better, but they fooled no one. They'd been talking nearly every day, either online or on the phone, for the better part of five years and had known each other all their lives. They knew each other well.

He did not want to be King; he wanted to be her Prince and for her to reign while he worked to make a difference in the lives of their people. He wasn't sure how, but knew now that he wanted to follow the Emperor's lead, minus the crushing loneliness, and help the disenfranchised. Oz wanted him to follow his bliss, whatever that might be.

Now his mother was standing on the roof of the Blackshear's royal home, trying to hand over an entire country to the King of Pacifica.

"We're at war, Andrew," she said to him. "The order of things has changed."

The Emperor finally spoke. "Jax walked away from you. What

does that tell you? He couldn't say anything, Shazia, not to accept, not to reject. Because anything he said might bite you both in your royal asses."

"Still impudent, aren't you, Emperor? Haven't yet learned your place?"

Drew let go of Oz's hand and stepped directly in front of his mother, with only a few inches between them. "Don't you dare. Not one word against him. And since when are you such an elitist?"

Anyone else would have set a hand on Drew's arm to get his attention and diffuse his anger, but the Emperor didn't touch people. He could hear inside their heads when he did, and often they could hear inside his, something he guarded against. "Ah, she's fine, Drew. She loves me."

Drew didn't move. He stood firm, glaring at his mother.

"It's a stupid little dance we do," she said softly. "I didn't mean anything by it. I tell him he's mouthy and impertinent, he calls me 'Princess.' I'm sorry, I know this isn't the time."

He didn't care. "Where's Dad?"

"Andrew—"

Angry, tiny flecks of spit leapt from his lips as he growled, *"Where is my father?"*

The Queen of Midlam broke. Right there on the roof, with her heavily guarded hover car behind her and her youngest son in front of her, everything inside her shattered. A breath in, a breath out, and she seemed to age twenty years in front of us, her face wilting under the strain of his anger and his fear, and from the stress of being abruptly dismissed by the one person she was sure she could count on to fix the war now being waged.

Her voice was thin, mixed with the tears she battled to hold inside. "I don't know."

Aubrey's anger slipped away with that, and Pacifica's Queen reached out for Shazia Van Hoff, enveloping her in a hug meant to take away some of the pain and to give her a chance to breathe for a moment, before facing Drew's rage again. He watched his mother fall against the Queen and he reached for Oz's hand, and then looked to the Emperor for help.

"Everyone off the roof," the Emperor said. "Jax is probably

waiting to speak to you informally, Shazia. But this time, don't surrender, not without gut-punching him first. Declare war, lose, *then* surrender."

She pulled away from Aubrey, puzzled, until Aubrey sighed. "He thinks he's funny."

As they filed into the stairway, the Emperor held Zed and his parents back. He told his parents to go to his apartment and relax—Finn knew the way, having spent a night there when he was forty years younger, though to the Emperor it had only been a few weeks—and asked Zed to run and get groceries for his apartment.

His mother, Jo, started to protest—it was too late and they would be fine until morning—but Zed laughed and said he would raid the staff kitchen, so it didn't matter how late it was. "I hope you don't mind a lot of bread and cheese and frozen pizza."

Finn hesitated at the roof door. "Don't tell me I'd be eating from a pizza I ate from forty years ago."

"Hey, not my fault you got old since I saw you all of, what, three days ago?"

I patted at the Emperor's leg to remind him I was still there. *Is Zed still his friend? Finn did get a lot older.*

He picked me up. "I don't know if they'll hang out, but they're still friends. You'd still be friends with him, wouldn't you?"

Yeah, but I like anyone who feeds me.

He put me on his shoulder and started down the stairs. It had been a while since I'd had to balance there; he and Drew had been carrying me around in sweatshirts that the Queen had modified for me by opening the top of the hand pouch so that I could ride without worrying about falling.

I never worried about it and I had never fallen, but everyone else seemed to enjoy not having my claws digging into their shoulders.

"Do me a favor and sleep in my room tonight," he said as we rounded the first turn on the stairwell. "My parents will be there, and my mother misses you. I know she wants to apologize for trying to send you through the portal."

I hadn't minded the idea of going into a portal headed for two hundred years in the future. She and Finn were trying to save the world, and I was their test subject; I was supposed to walk through to the other side, and if the world was still there, come back and tell them. Instead, the Emperor went in my place, reasoning that he could not survive without me—I am his anchor in this When—and that if Earth was gone and he didn't come back, it was a preferable way to go.

It took some work—Finn had to go back to a year before he left to tell himself how to fix the mistake he'd made in trying to save the world—and I went into the portal after the Emperor to keep him company while he was stuck inside it, but we both survived.

There was no reason for Jo to apologize; I was fine. The Emperor was fine. More importantly, because I was fine that meant he wouldn't die in a few months, and since he was her son, she had a huge stake in how that turned out.

I'll sleep with them unless there's bouncy stuff going on.

"Wick, they're in their seventies."

So? Old people bounce, too. And they have things to celebrate.

As we neared the royal apartment, he picked me off his shoulder and held me. "Well, now I know how Oz feels when confronted with her parents' love life."

Sleep on the balcony, dude. Your apartment might get loud tonight.

He sighed hard—either because he really did not want to think about it or because he was suddenly resigned to the idea that Finn and Jo were people, too—and carried me into the living room. Jax was in his favorite chair, near the dining room but not quite in it, and Shazia was in the less comfy chair across the room from him. Oz and Drew were on the sofa, and the Queen was in the kitchen.

That was no surprise. Aubrey Blackshear liked to feed people. I could hear her banging around, looking for snacks to bring out on plastic platters. The Emperor grabbed two chairs from the table and dragged them into the living room, places for him and for the Queen when she was ready to join them.

I jumped onto Drew's lap. If anyone needed to be purred on, I thought it was him.

After we'd stepped into the living room Jax asked Shazia for her phone, and while I got comfortable on Drew's lap, he was poking through it. I thought that was a bit rude; people were generally protective of the things on their phones, considering them to be as private as a diary, but she didn't seem upset with having to hand it over. Instead, she seemed eager to see what he would find.

After a few quiet minutes, he muttered, "There it is."

Aubrey came back with a plate loaded down with grapes and strawberries and cheese, and she set it on the coffee table in front of Drew and Oz. If anyone was going to dig into the snacks, it was Drew, and there was a good chance he would share the cheese with me.

"He was in the Dayton bunker," Jax said almost absently. "He's not sure it's safe to leave yet and will stay put until we give him an all clear." He poked at the screen a few more times. "Richard is fine, Shazia. You can exhale now."

She started to cry, more relieved than sad, but Drew's anger flared.

"What? You didn't even bother to check your messages? You just assumed he was dead and then ran? What the hell is wrong with you?"

I moved over to Oz's lap, just in case.

She wanted to explain, but the words would not come out. When she tried to answer him but couldn't, the Emperor leaned forward in his seat, elbows on his knees, and said, "She did exactly what she was supposed to, Drew. This is a plan that's been in place since you were a baby. If anything went wrong and she was separated from your father, she was to come here."

"Minus the surrendering," Jax grumbled. When it looked like Drew was about to protest he added, "This is not up for discussion."

Shazia was looking to Drew, pleading for understanding, but he stared at the coffee table instead. "Andrew, I can't do any of this without him, and I thought he was gone."

"You couldn't stay put long enough to make sure he was all right? He spends half his time in Dayton. More than half. He goes to work, jumps in the tube, and heads for Dayton at least three days a week. You *had* to know he was probably there."

Before she could explain any further, Jax stood up and said, "No more questions, not now. We need to get on top of this."

He asked the Emperor and Midlam's Queen to accompany him

to his office, and it was clear that no one else was invited to their party. Drew folded his arms, scowling, watching as they got into the elevator and as the doors closed behind them.

"Sweetheart, trust Jax," the Queen said. "He's always looked out for your mother and he knows what help she needs right now. But your father might need some reassurance that she made it here and is fine."

"I don't think I can call him when he's in the bunker. He can get texts but there's a delay." He leaned his head against the wall behind the sofa. "There's a delay. In both directions. I'm an idiot."

She took him into her little office nook off the kitchen. I heard the wall panel slide, and knew what she was doing. She had one of half a dozen communications systems in the building that could reach where regular phones could not and she plugged him into a line that would connect him with his father, then gently closed the door to give him privacy.

"That's not a phone call I ever want to have to make." Oz pulled some cheese apart, rolling it into tiny bites for me. "How do you tell your dad that not only are you at war, but there's a good chance you'll lose your country?"

"We won't let them lose, Oz."

"Then how do we explain to the people of Pacifica that we're sending our troops to possibly die for Midlam's war? We're allies, but they'll want a better reason than that."

"To crush Florida? Do we need a better reason?"

Oz waited for a better reason.

"We can't let Florida take Midlam, Ozzie. I would honestly die before I'd see that happen."

Hey, no dying.

"Fine, furball," Oz muttered, dropping a few pieces of cheese on the floor for me. "Hyperbole aside, Mom, we need a really good reason to enter into a war against Florida."

Aubrey considered her daughter for a moment, and then said, "It's not hyperbole. I would truly rather die than see the First Minister of Florida get his hands on anything more than he already has. And if he ever gets his hands on Pacifica…kill me."

2

Within days Jax had negotiated a temporary cease-fire—Florida's First Minister agreed to stop further attacks, though he refused to give up any ground taken—and a month later it was still holding. Large parts of Chicago were uninhabitable and the masses that had fled Florida weeks before the attack had rooted themselves in Kansas, effectively taking almost half the state. Pacifica's army surrounded the borders to keep them in place, and the only fighting consisted of odd skirmishes, though General Myers, head of the Department of Defense and de facto Secretary of State, thought it was an uneasy truce that could fail at any turn. He described Florida's military as twitchy as hell and thought they were more likely than not to shoot even in the middle of a cease-fire.

Many of Florida's civilians had been armed, and those most loyal to the First Minister were twitchier than the soldiers.

There was no place in Midlam where Jax felt Shazia would be safe. She governed from Pacifica, where she could easily consult with Jax, and she resided in Drew's tiny apartment while he slept on the couch. Drew's father came and went, unable to stay away from his lab in Dayton for more than a few days at a time.

"My work goes on," he explained to Drew, who was perhaps less concerned than his father wanted him to be. "And after spending time with Finn, I'm of the mind that it may be critical soon. We're working on similar theories, and if I can construct the hardware he needs, we might be able to push his research ahead by several years."

He wouldn't tell Drew what it was, but Drew knew Finn was trying to perfect long distance transporters. He could send himself from one point to another using his giant egg-shaped ship if it was nearby, but the distance he wanted—hundreds, leading to thousands, of miles—was still outside his grasp. He'd attempted to send inanimate objects only a few miles, but what transported to the arrival point was always reconstructed out of order, often inside-out.

"There will be no sending Wick through this," Finn promised.

Drew surmised that his engineer-father was working on the mechanics of it, helping re-build the framework of the gate that they both thought would be the eventual keystone.

"I don't really care," he told Oz. "I'm just tired. I need about twenty hours of solid sleep somewhere that's not my too-short sofa. It's five feet long. I'm a little over six feet tall. It just doesn't work."

We were on the balcony; it was their favorite place to do nothing, where their parents rarely bothered them. Oz pushed two of the chairs together and they sat holding hands, their fingers laced together, resting on the joined arms of the chairs. "You could sleep in the guest room up here again," she told him. "Under the circumstances, my dad would not mind."

"Oh, he'd mind. He would understand, but he would mind."

The Emperor stepped out onto the balcony and asked, "Who would mind what?"

Unlike the parents, the Emperor had not yielded the balcony. It was also his favorite place to sit quietly, often in the middle of the night when it was cold and damp and generally unpleasant as far as I was concerned. Drew did not mind his company and Oz treasured it, so his presence was not an intrusion.

"Mr. B would mind if I was two doors down from his daughter again," Drew said.

"Ah." He pulled up another chair and sat next to Drew. "Explain to me why your mother refuses to take residence in the guest suite. It's considerably more spacious and it's private, and the décor would better suit her tastes."

Drew's mother wanted to be close to her son, and on those nights when Richard was gone, she didn't want to be alone. He understood, mostly, but was ready for her to get a grip on her feelings, and, he admitted reluctantly, "grow up already."

"Your mother does not do well on her own," the Emperor said. "When you compare it to all her other qualities, it's a small flaw, don't you think?"

Oz snorted a tiny laugh through her nose. "Says the man who keeps calling her 'Princess.'"

"She would be disappointed if I didn't," he said.

"Oz, it's literally what her name means," Drew said. "And I get it, she's a good person and I love her, but come on. It's a small one-bedroom apartment and she has guards twenty-four hours a day. No matter how quiet they try to be at night, I still hear them and I just want one damned night alone. This is even worse than when I was a kid…at least then I could close my bedroom door and not have to hear the damned guard sniffing every three minutes."

"So sleep in the guest room. Dad really will not mind."

"Or," the Emperor offered, "use my spare room. You'd only be across the hall and close enough for your mother to not feel as if you're trying to get away from her, and you'll be able to close the bedroom door to be utterly alone if you choose."

Drew's mouth popped open a little and Oz's eyebrows tried to hide in her hairline. The Emperor rarely had guests; he'd allowed Finn to spend one night there while he was trying to regain his fried memory, and more recently his parents stayed with him while they looked for their own apartment nearby. For him to outright offer his private space to anyone other than family was unexpected enough to be worthy of their shock.

When the initial surprise wore off Drew sputtered, "I wouldn't want to get in your way."

"I won't be spending much time at home, so you won't be."

"But—"

"Andrew. I am comfortable with you. I no longer have anything to hide. You are more than welcome to sleep in my spare room, and you're both welcome to just hang out in my living room to watch videos or read or even to simply be away from everyone else. The kitchen is yours to use as well, just clean up after yourselves."

Before he could change his mind, Oz got up and pulled Drew with her. "Keep this up and not only won't he never be afraid of you again, he'll start to like you." She planted a kiss on his cheek. "I'll help him get a few of his things and then show him which room is your spare. My old room, I'm guessing?"

"Yes, your old room. Zed's is crammed full of books and an unhealthy amount of dust. But don't relax too much, Andrew," the Emperor said as they headed inside. "I know where you'll be sleeping."

I jumped up to the chair Drew vacated.

I'm not used to people touching you.

"Only Oz, really," he said. "She's helping me learn to not listen. She touches my arm frequently, and lately has taken to kissing me on the cheek and surprising me with hugs. I have to admit, I enjoy it."

The Queen touches you, too.

"She warns me before she does. She's very good at closing off her thoughts. The only things I ever hear are the things she wants me to know."

Zed?

"Soon, I hope. There are things I'm not ready to risk with him, and he has secrets that he isn't ready to share."

I knew Zed's secrets. So did the Emperor. I don't think he had any clue we knew of the things he'd been up to when he borrowed the Emperor's car, but we weren't about to embarrass him and the Emperor wanted Zed to come to him on his own timetable.

William?

He reached over and ruffled the fur on the top of my head.

When you get to where you can touch people without hearing inside their heads, will you still be able to hear me?

He patted his lap, inviting me over. "Mister Wick, I will always be able to hear you. I've never had to touch you to understand what you're saying. And I will never examine that too closely. I don't need to know why I can, I'm just happy that I can."

So am I. How else would you know how badly I need something dead and delicious to eat right now?

With an amused sigh, he picked me up as he got out of the chair. "When are you not hungry?"

What time is it?

*

After he fed me—in the staff kitchen so that Drew did not feel as if he was hovering while Oz showed him around the apartment—we walked down the stairs to the King's office. The Emperor was not a believer in taking the elevator at every opportunity; he favored the stairs, so much so that he sometimes ran up and down them for no reason other than to go up and down.

He had been joining the King on his afternoon runs—which honestly surprised me since I hadn't seen him really run in a couple of decades—and pushed Jax to lap Union Square faster and for longer than he was used to. I watched from a spot on the stairs directly across from the family's residence, grateful that I was not being taken along, bouncing in the Emperor's sweatshirt while he worked up an actual sweat.

"It would not hurt you to move more," he told me when I pointed out the futility in running when there was nothing chasing you. "If you start moving now, you'll be able to move faster if those pigeons ever really do decide to attack."

I'm counting on you to save me.

"What if I'm not around? They might pick you up and fly you all the way to Ocean Beach before anyone notices you're missing. What then, Mister Wick?"

It's not nice to play on my fears.

If those birds ever formed an association and actually did try to carry me off, it would probably be from the roof-top lawn, and they'd probably let go once they got me over the ledge.

Never trust a bird with the potential for gang alliances.

I've seen them strutting around Union Square, clustering in feathery little groups as they robbed people of their hot dogs and pretzels. Don't tell me they don't belong to a gang. Or at least a union.

The King was at his desk, watching news clips on the massive video monitor on the wall across the room. Without saying anything—not even grunting "hi" to Jax, which was a few kinds of rude—the Emperor sat in the comfy chair near the throne, and I jumped onto his lap. We watched as images of the detritus in Chicago played in front of us; weeks after the attack, it was still a smoldering pile of rubble and ash. Buildings that once stood twenty stories and more were reduced to broken boulders and stones, and spotty fires were still a problem. Half the city was gone; half its people were dead, and many bodies were still buried in the rubble.

Until they could get in with big equipment, I was afraid they'd stay buried.

The video footage Jax seemed most interested in focused on one building on the University of Chicago campus; it had taken a direct hit and was little more than soot, and was where Richard Van Hoff did most of his research. His office was there; one of his labs was there. There was a crater on the far end of the long building, where his workshop had been.

It was no wonder that his queen thought he was dead.

The idea was worse than the image, so the King switched video feeds. We were now watching an army mobilizing around and through Kansas. Many of the troops were from Midlam, but for the most part we were seeing Pacifica's uniforms, men and women marching through fields and down empty roads, boots covered in dust, laser rifles at the ready as they kept Florida penned in.

The majority of those who emigrated from Florida under the guise of fleeing for freedom wound up in Kansas City and in Topeka, but there was a large cluster that had pushed on to Salina, and among them were hundreds of members of their military. Their army had made its way into Midlam right on the heels of the bombing of Chicago, skirting around fractured Midlam troops while facing virtually no opposition.

Jax paused on an image of a teenaged boy in dark blue slacks and a white dress shirt, carrying an ancient and inefficient firearm. It was slung across his back and the strap that went across his chest pushed the collar of his shirt up on one side, making him look even younger than his likely thirteen or fourteen years. He was still baby-faced, his cheeks free from even the wispiest of whiskers, his hair cut with little-boy bangs.

Sixteen-year-old Zed looked like a grown man in comparison.

They were putting their youngest men—kids from fourteen to eighteen—in between their army and the clusters of citizens who were holding ground. Jax had balked and demanded they be withdrawn, only to be reminded by the General that the Church of Florida considered its people to be responsible for their own souls at age eight, upon baptism. Their teenaged boys were deemed to be men, and served at the order of the First Minister. He was not removing them from service, not without a direct order from God himself.

Jax's voice sliced through the silence. "I have to meet with the First Minister. None of this will be resolved until I do. We both know that even if Shazia was up to negotiating on her own behalf, he'll never deal with her, and he's deliberately ignoring overtures made by General Myers. He's holding out for a face to face with me."

"Indeed."

Jax clicked the monitor off and leaned back, the leather of his chair creaking while the springs under it squeaked, mimicking the turmoil in his eyes. "It can't be in Midlam or in Florida. New England won't allow a meeting on their soil, and the Governor of Texas would insert himself into any negotiations."

"You have to host the meeting here, in Pacifica."

Jax inhaled deeply and then exhaled sharply. "I promised Aubrey he would never step foot in Pacifica."

"No, you promised her he would never step foot into your house. And he won't. There will be guards at every entrance, and the only people who will get through any of those doors will be family."

"Will."

"You know what I mean, Jax. We can lock down the security so tightly that he won't even consider trying to get in. She never has to see him."

"It's still a betrayal."

"She'll be angry for a while, but she'll understand."

I jumped onto his desk and curled up in front of him. Without thinking, he reached out and began to scratch the top of my head with the tips of his fingers. "It won't be anger. Hell, I can deal with anger. If all she throws at me is rage, I let her yell until she's done. I can do that. But with this? She'll be deeply hurt, and I'm not sure I can handle that."

She likes chocolate when she's upset.

Maybe she'll still like it if her feelings are hurt. Bake some brownies.

"You have two choices. Hurt her, and potentially end a war that never should have been, or spare her feelings and allow thousands more to die. Many of them will be her own people. And for what? Which do you think she'd choose? Which would she forgive you for?" The Emperor pushed himself up from his chair. "Make the call. I'll arrange for reception space in the old Hyatt and reserve accommodations for Florida's contingency and for Texas and New England as well. I presume they'll want to be present for the start of talks."

Jax gave a very slight nod of his head and reached for the phone. When the Emperor left, I got up and head bonked the King gently, and then went to find someone less stressed out to pester, because if I stayed and he got even more upset, that nice scratching behind my ears could become a bruising massage.

Oz and Drew were always a safe bet. Drew no longer smelled like a dog, he was quite generous with the snacks, and he always seemed happy to see me. I went down the stairs to find them; his apartment door was closed, which meant his mom was probably inside and on her phone or a video chat or whatever else a queen does when she's not at home but still working. Directly across the hall, the Emperor's was open—Drew never closed the door if Oz was alone with him, because he didn't want the King to be upset—and they were sitting on the sofa together. The video monitor was off, but the lights over the bookcase were on, and I could see dust motes floating in the air just in front of all of those books.

Someone needs to clean up in here.

Drew was on one end of the sofa and Oz was on the other, and they faced each other with their legs tangled up. If either one needed to get up quickly, someone was going to get hurt. Judging from the proximity of Oz's bare foot, I guessed it would be Drew in the most pain. I saw her kick Zed there once, and it was a good half minute before he could even breathe, let alone cry.

They were discussing how long it would be before the Emperor regretted offering him the room; Oz didn't think he would, but Drew was certain it would only be a day or two, somewhere around the third time his mother came looking for him late at night. He was sorry, too, because his mother being there all the time had cut into time he had expected to spend with Oz.

"Not your fault," Oz said. "Not hers, either."

School started without them three weeks earlier. Oz should have been just getting over her first-year nerves and Drew should have been getting over his new-school stomach ache, but instead they were floundering, waiting to see what was going to happen. After the bombs hit Chicago, their classes were the last thing anyone thought about, so they missed the first few days and were dropped from the schedule.

Who they were didn't matter; miss the first day, get dropped from the class.

"We barely got our plans started, and they've gone all to hell," Drew said. "I really wanted to just, you know, date you like a normal person. I had this picture in my head. We'd go to classes, meet for lunch, maybe go somewhere after school a couple days a week."

"Hm, like borrowing the Emperor's car and making out at Ocean Beach?"

The notion did not disappoint him. "Something like that."

"Zed beat us to it. He's borrowing it every chance he gets and so far the Emperor hasn't told him no. We could use his air bike to go places and take a blanket along. Maybe go hide in the woods in the Presidio."

"Sure. You, me, and how many guards?"

"Well, in every biology class I took, we were told to always use protection, so…"

At that, he laughed. "We would be the most protected couple in Pacifica."

Her foot twitched toward him, but he grabbed her toes. "Let's not start something we can't even remotely finish," he said, nodding toward the door. "Between my mother and the Emperor? Yeah. No."

Should I leave? I'll leave if I have to.

"The Emperor would be amused if he walked in and I was doing nasty things to you with my foot. I'm not sure about your mom, but I think it's Zed you need to worry about. He did threaten to break your fingers."

I was there. I remember it. He totally did.

"I'm pretty sure I could take Zed. You, on the other hand…" He lifted her foot and swung her leg over his, and then sat up all the way, both of his feet on the floor and his groin safe from her wandering toes. "Oz, I really hate that we both missed out on all the stupid teenage stuff. Like dating. Going to the beach with friends. Hell, step it up a notch and dress up to go to the theater. I'd kind of like to experience at least some of that before we…you know."

She scooted closer to him, and kissed him on the cheek. "God, you're adorable. Fine, let's go on a date. Somewhere normal, like everyone else."

Can I go? There's usually food on a date. Jax took Aubrey to get food sometimes.

"There's an impressionists exhibit at the DeYoung," Drew said. "We could go tomorrow and get lunch after. Or walk around Golden Gate Park. I've never seen the Tea Gardens."

I jumped onto his lap and pawed at his stomach where my sweatshirt pouch usually lived.

He scratched under my chin. "Wick, I don't know if they'd let you in."

"Drew, they're not going to tell me no. I wouldn't even have to say anything, they'd just let me bring him. It's one of the few perks. If Wick wants to go on a date with us and see a bunch of paintings, why not?"

Tell them I'm your snoopervisor. I'll bite him if he touches things he shouldn't.

Drew shrugged. "Yeah, why not? If anything, he'll keep us in line."

"Sure he will."

"Oz…he can talk to the Emperor. Anything we do, he can report. And who knows in how much detail?"

Vivid detail, but I won't.

I don't even want to see it.

Besides, the Emperor knows about stupid teenage groping. He used to have to hear about it from Jax after his dates, even the ones before he met Aubrey. He doesn't want to hear about it again.

They weren't listening to me. Oz smashed her lips against his and I was about two seconds away from leaving, when the Emperor knocked on the door jamb to his own apartment and said, "Sorry to interrupt."

"Not half as sorry as I am," Oz grumbled.

"Your father wants to see you both upstairs. Family meeting."

I'm family; I followed them out and up the stairs, racing past their giant feet when it seemed as if they were taking their own sweet time getting there. The Queen was at her happiest when she had her entire family with her, and when she was happy, that meant meaty treats for me. It was the perfect circle of contentment: they're happy, I'm happy. We all win.

Jax was alone in the living room, but he didn't look any sort of happy and I felt my odds of beefy chunks or chicken nibbles slip away. Drew slowed down and I think he wanted to turn around and go back downstairs, but Oz pushed him all the way into the room and asked, "What'd we do now? Whatever it is, I blame Zed."

He gestured to the sofa—sit down—but didn't say anything. The Emperor took the other chair without being told to, and I had no idea what to do. Jax was upset, but I had a feeling that I couldn't do anything about it. The Emperor didn't seem any sort of distressed so he didn't need me, and I couldn't choose between Oz and Drew's laps. I jumped up onto the coffee table where I could see them all, and waited.

Someone's stomach growled but it didn't sound like hunger. It was the sound of unhappy insides. Gurgling, wheezing; Jax looked the most uncomfortable, and I thought he was starting to look a little nauseated. He fixated on the floor, that thousand-yard stare that people who are bored, scared, or about to erupt with violent barfing seem to do.

You should get him a bucket. He's gonna spew.

I know the Emperor heard me, but he didn't move.

Is that why you wanted everyone here? To watch him hork up his toenails?

He knotted his eyebrows together, and mouthed "Stop it."

The uneasy quiet was getting to Drew; after only a couple of minutes he was fidgety, and he started running his finger over the edge of the coffee table, trying to get me to pounce.

I humored him and took a swipe at his hand, but it didn't seem to help.

We sat in that uncomfortable quiet for a good five minutes, when the Emperor suddenly stood up. He'd heard the elevator settle just before the doors opened, and knew it was the Queen. She exited the elevator and came straight into the living room, nearly tossing her book bag onto Jax's chair without looking.

There was a small chance he would have caught the bag before it smacked him in the face.

Dude, get up.

She bent over to kiss him. "I'm sorry, sweetheart. I came home as soon as I could."

Finally, he got up and took the bag from her—and stole one more long kiss—to hang in her office. He was procrastinating, probably not on purpose but procrastinating all the same. When he came back, the Emperor was still standing and so was she.

"Just rip the bandage off, Jax," the Emperor said.

"Zed's not here yet," he argued.

"And Zed is not needed."

Aubrey waited, her hand on Jax's chest as she tried to soothe him from whatever was hurting inside.

He didn't have a choice. "The cease fire is about to break. The First Minister won't negotiate with Shazia, and Richard refuses to engage on her behalf without her participation because he feels that nothing he might agree to would be binding. General Myers is not an acceptable substitute for either, in the Minister's opinion."

Her hand dropped away.

"I am left in the untenable position of needing to step in and negotiate as Midlam's proxy. If I don't, the combat resumes, which would require we send thousands more of our troops to fight. And I don't relish the idea of what I would need to do in order to stop this war in its tracks."

"So you go lay the verbal smack down on him," Oz said.

He didn't look at Oz; his gaze was fixed on Aubrey's face. "I can't negotiate in either Midlam or Florida. Either of those locations puts the opposing party in an unfavorable position. The only reasonable neutral locations—Canada and Mexico—are places the First Minister is not welcome."

Aubrey took a step back. "Where, then?"

Jax closed his eyes for a moment, and then said, "I swore to you he would never step foot in this house, and I meant it. He won't. But there will be a reception at the Hyatt, and we'll host negotiations from there as well."

They stared at each other. I couldn't even read their expressions; it was just two people locked onto each other, purposely silent, and the unease I felt building came from Oz and Drew. Jax was waiting for Aubrey to explode, and she was waiting for him to cave in and change his mind.

When he didn't, she turned around and walked out of the room.

Jax didn't move. He didn't watch her leave, and he didn't look down or away. He was frozen in place, until the Emperor said, "Go after her, Jax. Don't wait."

I hadn't heard the elevator door open, and her shoes would have made clicking sounds on the stairs if she were going somewhere else. I jumped down and peeked around the entry way; they were on the balcony, and Aubrey looked wounded.

She wasn't angry and her feelings weren't hurt.

She was horribly, deeply wounded.

His mouth formed the words "I'm sorry" and he reached for her. She fell against him, and began crying harder than I had ever seen a grown person cry. I'd never seen that look on her face before, and I had never seen her that sad.

The Emperor called me back into the living room. "Give them privacy, Wick. There's nothing you can do for them right now."

"What's the deal?" Oz asked as I made my way back. "I know they don't like the First Minister, but just walking out on Dad is a little over the top. Why is she so upset?"

"She has her reasons."

There was a bit of space between her and Drew, so I wedged myself between them.

He went on to explain the bigger issue to them—there was no other safe place to hold initial negotiations with someone as volatile as the First Minister, and he could be contained in Pacifica—and briefly outlined some of the details they needed to know. There would be a formal reception in three days, one that would include not only Florida, but representatives from Texas and New England as well. Canada, France, and Japan expressed an interest in attending. When Oz asked him why, he told her that witnesses to the process were necessary, and they all had a stake in the outcome.

When he went on to tell them they would be fit for proper attire for the reception, Oz groaned. She hadn't worn a dress since she was a little girl and had convinced herself that she'd never need to again, and then grumbled that she would have to shave her legs for this.

"You don't *have* to," Drew said. "I'm not shaving mine."

She elbowed him, but not hard enough.

"You have appointments with the Kovlov's tomorrow morning at ten for your fittings," the Emperor went on. "And like it or not, your formal wear has already been chosen for you. The King wants to set a certain tone with the reception."

This time, it was Drew who groaned. "Aw, man. We had plans."

"Change them. And fair warning—you need to be prepared to roll with the punches during both the reception and the negotiations. You will undoubtedly hear things that are surprising and unsettling, but you cannot tip your hand to anything that's news to you. He needs to see you as being strong and resilient."

"So I can't throat punch him?" Oz asked.

The corner of his mouth twitched upward. "Not unless things go horribly wrong. I think it's safe to say there will be no family dinner tonight. Go downstairs, order a pizza, and put it on my account. Your parents need space tonight, Oz. This is not the time to ask them any questions. Just let them be."

Where should I go?

"Stay here, Wick. The Queen will need you, I think. The King as well."

And you?

"I should spend a few hours with my parents while I have some free time. Richard and my father are trying to roll a bowling ball between here and Dayton, and apparently Dad will explode if he doesn't get to tell me all about it soon. If you need me, get Oz. She can call me."

"Okay, I get the gist," Oz said. "How will I know if he needs you badly enough to interrupt the world's greatest bowling ball story, or if he just wants something to eat?"

"Put food in front of him. If he refuses to eat, he needs me. Call, and I'll come home."

And then I'll eat. I'm not wasting good food.

"It needs to be important, Wick. If I didn't want you to stay here, I'd take you with me."

Drew and Oz headed for the stairs, and when they were a few steps down he said, "I am never going to get used to that."

The Emperor wasn't used to it, either. He'd spent most of his life pretending to not understand me when we were in front of other people. He still felt somewhat judged when he answered me and often waited until we were alone unless someone else prompted him. The Queen, especially, wanted to know what I was saying. She worried that my needs weren't being met, and was happy that someone could tell her what I wanted.

"When in doubt, feed him," the Emperor told her. "Shrimp, beef, canned food, cheese, ham, chicken…in that order. He hates turkey, but I've never figured out why."

I was glad he'd fed me earlier, because Aubrey was probably not going to be in the mood to even register I was there, much less remember to open a can for me.

She'd cried when he told her how his father found me, tiny and dirty and starving in the nineteen-sixties, and how I had never felt full, always wanting more to eat, even when I was already eating. It broke her heart and he had to caution her: Wick gets more than he needs, so don't let that change anything. He's small, but he's not losing weight, either.

I didn't get more food than I had before, but I got more snuggles and head kisses from her, and that was just as good.

When the Emperor left, he made sure he turned to go down the stairs without looking toward the balcony. I followed to the entryway and sat down, looking out the glass door because people generally don't mind when the cat watches them. Truly, they rarely even notice, no matter how personal their activities happen to be. They were still holding onto each other, but she wasn't crying the way she had been. Her eyes were closed and she rested her head on his shoulder, her arms clutching him the way Oz used to grip her teddy bears.

Aubrey could wrap her arms around someone to soak up their pain; there was no one who could do the same thing for her. Not even Jax, no matter how badly he wanted to or how hard he tried. He could stand there with his arms around her all night, but it would only be an embrace. He couldn't heal her.

I couldn't either, but I could help him try to make her less sad. I pushed my way through the cat flap near the door and jumped onto the seat of the chair closest to them, and stood on my back legs, patting her arm with my paw. She didn't let go of him completely, but she reached one hand down and rubbed a finger under my chin.

"Sweet Wick," she whispered.

I dropped onto the seat and then got right back up, this time patting Jax's side. They finally pulled apart a bit, but they weren't getting it, so I jumped down, then back up, and then down again.

Jax kissed her, slowly and sweetly, and then sighed. "He wants us to sit down."

Now you get it.

They sat in the chairs Oz and Drew had pushed together, and he slipped his arm around her shoulders. I jumped onto Aubrey's lap, purring as hard for her as I could, and he reached over with his free hand to stroke the top of my head.

Neither told me I was a good boy, for which I was grateful.

They were quiet after that, until the sun started to go down and the cold began pricking at the tips of my ears. Jax didn't seem as if he was going to move at all, but then she heard his stomach growl, and this time it sounded like hunger. She reached over the arm of the chair and rubbed his leg, half-whispering when she said she would go make him some dinner.

"Not tonight," he said. "Let me cook for you. If you want to go soak in the tub, I'll try to not burn something and I'll keep it warm until you're ready."

I expected her to argue with him; food was her domain. The kitchen was hers and she only granted access when the kids were making sandwiches or wanted her to teach them how to cook something. When they were younger they sat at the breakfast bar and talked to her while she cooked dinner, but Jax was rarely part of that. I'd seen her chase him out before, threating to hit him with a plastic spatula, warning him against encroaching on her territory.

To Aubrey, cooking for people was love. It didn't matter if she'd worked all day; when she came home she went into the kitchen and crafted tasty meals, a lot of them meaty and made without things that could make me sick, because I was always going to get a bite or two. It didn't matter if it took half an hour or all afternoon; she was cooking for her family, and they were going to sit together at the table and eat. Whether she had to say it out loud or not, they didn't leave without hearing that she loved them.

Most of the time she said it.

She didn't argue this time. When he stood up and offered his hand, she tucked an arm under me and let him help her up, and didn't let go of him until we were in the living room. She set me on Jax's comfy chair and then lingered for a minute, slipping her arms around his waist before kissing him again.

It went on long enough that any other time I would have left the room, because sooner or later bouncy things would commence, and I'd had enough of that. I stayed because she was too sad and he was too upset for that. I waited until she stepped back, touching his cheek the way she did when she wanted to show someone a little affection. She went down the hall and into their bedroom, and I followed Jax into the kitchen.

When I jumped onto the breakfast bar, he didn't complain.

This is really serious, isn't it?

He wasn't looking for pots and pans or even food. He rested his elbows on the counter and for a moment held his head in his hands. When he looked up, he said, "I hate breaking her heart, Wick."

I'm sure she's not a fan, either.

Seeing the King cry was as rare as seeing the Emperor cry; I think he was about to, but the sound of the elevator doors sliding open brought him out of himself. Zed hurried in and was about to explain why he was late, when he realized the only one there was his father and he didn't look to be in that great of a mood.

"Go find your sister," Jax said, his voice uneven. "She's probably downstairs with Drew. You're on your own for dinner tonight."

"Um, yeah. Okay." Zed took a few steps closer. "Everything okay?"

"No one's dead, if that's what you're worried about."

"All right. But—"

"Zed." He almost sounded angry. "I need time alone with your mother. Just go find Oz."

Zed dug his phone out of his pocket as he backed away, and his voice faded from us as he made his way down the stair case. When we could no longer hear him, Jax began poking through the pantry, looking for anything he could make that would resemble edible food. He settled on macaroni and cheese and then found hamburger in the refrigerator, muttering to himself as he fried horribly misshapen burgers that he wished he'd paid more attention to how she managed feeding them all every night.

She'll like what you're making. There's meat and there's cheese. That's almost all the food groups.

When she saw what he'd cooked she managed a little bit of a smile, and thanked him for it. He made her sit down and he brought the food to the table, and then fetched drinks for them both before he joined her. "You know, I never thank you for doing this," he said. "And I'm sorry for that. I'm grateful every day—"

"I know you are, sweetheart. If you thanked me every night I think it would get a little old."

"Still."

"It's my joy. My comfort zone. It's not yours."

I jumped onto the chair across the table from her, and he didn't tell me to get down. They ate without much conversation and then cleared the table together, but before he could fill the sink with water to start washing dishes, she told him they could wait until morning. She was tired, and just wanted to go to bed.

"That's fine. I can do them," he said.

She reached for his hand and told him he was tired, too.

Don't argue with her, dude.

I followed them down the hall, waiting on the window seat while they brushed their teeth and gargled gross things. Jax came out of the bathroom first and kicked his shoes off, then sat on the foot of the bed to pull his socks off.

You better not leave those on the floor, not tonight.

Whether he understood me or not, he thought better of it and picked them up, taking them to the hamper on the other side of the room. Aubrey came out of the bathroom then and reached for him; I resigned myself to a lot of hugging for the rest of the night and figured they were going to sleep wrapped around each other, but I could still curl up near her and purr if she needed me to.

I was looking at the bed, trying to figure out where my best spot would be, when she took a step back and started pulling his shirt from the waist of his jeans.

"Aubrey, no, not if—"

She told him to be quiet; he was smart and shut up.

I wondered if that was my cue to leave. It was usually easy to tell: there was a lot of laughing, kisses that lasted a long time, and Jax often ripped his own clothes off and threw them everywhere. This felt different. They were slowly undressing each other, and I didn't know what to make of that. Their clothes fell to the floor like feathers, and instead of the loud laughter and groping that tended to send me running, they just stood there, locked together in one long kiss that went on until Jax's breath hitched.

Aubrey brushed tears off his cheeks with her thumbs and then ran her fingers down his arms, closing her hands around his. She led him over to the bed, and again I wondered if I should leave, even though the Emperor had told me to stay in case she needed me, but all they were doing was kissing and I saw that all the time. I liked it when they kissed and their clothes stayed on. It made them both happy and even when they were tired and sleepy or in a hurry, it made them smile.

No one was smiling. Without the laughing and touching that made me want to run, I wasn't sure what was going on. It didn't feel like something I had to get away from, even though I was pretty sure I knew where it was headed and thought that was private enough that I should go. But the Emperor wanted me to stay with Aubrey.

I decided to close my eyes and take a nap while they finished as quietly as they started, and when I heard her whisper "I will love you forever, no matter what happens" against his lips, I think I finally understood.

It wasn't loud and funny because it needed to be quiet and sweet; this was how she could let him soak up some of her pain. I didn't think he could heal her hurt, but no one was crying anymore, and with any luck when I woke from my nap they would be under the covers and asleep, and wouldn't need me until morning.

*

Somewhere around midnight I woke up and heard noise coming from the kitchen. Jax was still awake, propped up in bed with his pillows, and Aubrey's head was resting on his stomach; her eyes were closed but I didn't think she was asleep. Her breathing wasn't shallow enough, and even if she had wanted to sleep, he was running a finger over the outline of her ear and that's enough to keep anyone awake.

I got up and stretched, and then headed down the hall to see who was in the kitchen. If it was Zed, I could just turn around and go back, because he was not as free with food as everyone else. If it was Oz, I had a fifty-fifty chance of getting something to eat. If it was the Emperor, I felt duty-bound to tell him to go raid his own kitchen, but only after he'd gotten me something.

The lights were on in the kitchen and both Oz and Zed were there, standing near the sink. She was washing the dishes that Jax had left, and Zed was drying and putting them away.

That's nice of you.

Oz heard me and turned to see where I was. "I take it you didn't need the Emperor tonight, Wick?"

No. I don't think I needed to be here, either.

"You know he's probably just telling you the only thing he needed was someone to feed him," Zed said. "Mom and Dad obviously ate but if she was as upset as you said, would either of them have thought to get dinner for him?"

They did not. Something meaty would be nice. Do we have steak? I could go for some steak.

"Wouldn't hurt to give him something."

He tossed the dishtowel onto the counter and reached into the pantry for my food, and then grabbed a plate from the cupboard. "Do you think they were fighting?" he asked Oz while he scooped out the tuna-flavored gooshy food. "I didn't see Mom when I was up here but Dad, geez. It looked like he was trying not to cry."

"What I saw didn't look like fighting. Mom was crushed. Whatever's going on, it seriously crushed her."

Zed set the plate on the floor. It wasn't steak and it was in the wrong spot, plus he used a people-plate and not my special dish, but I wasn't going to complain.

"Drew's mom needs to go home," Zed decided. "He's basically kicked out of his own apartment. Mom and Dad are stressed out. You're not happy."

She rinsed off another dish, getting drops of water on my head when she handed it to him. "What makes you think I'm not happy?"

"You didn't get to start school. You've got no time alone with Drew. If she'd deal with her own crap at home, you guys would both be buried in homework and he'd have more time for you."

"We have plenty of time together."

"But not the kind of time you want." He reached for the next dish. "And I feel a little guilty because I still get to go to school, and I have time to work and hang with my friends."

"Hang," Oz snorted. "Is that what you're calling it? You've borrowed the Emperor's car like ten times in the past couple of weeks. You have a bike to get around on, but you take his car...a lot."

"It's more convenient. And I'm saving for my own car. I'm on the payroll now."

"What's her name?"

I looked up; Zed's cheeks turned a little bit red.

"Well?" Oz prompted.

Mostly mumbling, he answered, "Rhonda Jones."

"What, seriously?" Oz tossed the dish rag into the sink. "I know her, Zed. She's not exactly...nice."

He shrugged.

"You know she was supposed to graduate when I did? I had four classes with her last year. She always sat in the back, and if she wasn't asleep, she was snotty and really, really unpleasant. In English class when she was asked what the underlying theme to Mercutio's Queen Mab soliloquy was, she pretty much told the teacher to go screw himself. Only she wasn't that polite."

"She doesn't like school," he said. "She likes me, though."

"Yeah, I know what she likes, Zed." She reached back into the sink and started scrubbing the pan Jax had fried the burgers in. "I'm just surprised you're willing to give it to her."

"What, like you're not willing to give it to Drew?"

"We're not having sex. Not yet."

"Fine. I'm not exactly dating Rhonda, Oz, but she definitely likes me enough."

"Likes you enough to use you for sex."

He shrugged again. "That's all it is. I'm okay with that."

Oz made a face. "Yeah, but Rhonda? To lose it to her? Ugh."

"Who says I lost it to her?" He took the frying pan, and laughed. "Oz, I might be the quiet kid in the corner, but I'm not the innocent everyone probably thinks. I've had girlfriends before."

"Oh God, she's your girlfriend," Oz sighed.

"No, she's not. I didn't ask her to do anything. She asked me. Point blank. And that's all it is."

"Zed, she'll do every guy in your class. Why would you want to be anywhere in that line? Why not be the guy who tells her no, and just take her out for pizza or something? Be the one guy who treats her with some respect."

"I thought you didn't like her."

"I don't have to like her to want you to treat her like a human being."

I finished eating and left them to argue while they finished washing the dishes. Whatever Zed was doing wasn't any of my business. My job for the night wasn't done, so I went back into the King and Queen's bedroom, and jumped up onto the window seat where I'd been before. They were both awake; he was still propped up against his pillows, but she was sitting cross-legged on the bed next to him and holding one of his hands, tracing the lines on his palm with the tips of her fingers.

The only light in the room was coming through the window, and it twinkled off the moisture in his eyes.

"I never wanted him to be anywhere near our kids," she told him. Her voice was thin, as if she was trying to speak softly but not whisper, but it was getting all tangled up in her feelings. "I really don't want him near Ozzie. Every time I see him on the news a part of me wishes you'd picked Zed as your heir."

"By the time I hand the crown over, he'll be long gone. He won't be her problem."

"Is it too much to ask that you hold onto it until he's dead? Even if you want to retire as young as your father did? He's stubborn enough to live into his hundreds."

He sat up and scooted on the bed until he was just in front of her. "I'll hold on until the day I die, if that's what it takes. I swear. As long as he has a stranglehold on Florida, I'll remain King. I know she's smarter than he is and stronger in every way that matters, but I will never put her in the position of being alone in a room with him, for any reason, no matter how old she is."

She pulled his head down to hers, and kissed him. "I'm using you tonight, you know that."

Softly, "Aubrey. I don't mind."

"And yet, you would never use me like this."

"That's not what this is."

"I remember when you made me that promise, Jackson. The sweet boy who had just told me he loved me and wanted me, and understood when I couldn't—" Her voice caught, and he kissed her again, waiting. "You told me you would wait forever, and swore you would never use me like that. Because if I couldn't be with you that night, there would be another. We had all the time in the world and you would wait through every second of it."

"I still will."

"I know that. And here I am, trying to make myself feel better and using your body to do it."

She pushed on his chest, until he was on his back.

"I'm not sorry for it, Jax."

"Neither am I. I don't feel used. I feel needed."

I felt nauseated.

All right, not really, but the Emperor was wrong; the Queen was not going to need me at all. Whether she was mad or sad or crying or not, whatever she needed she was getting from the King. I left and headed for Oz's room. She was up late and had to be up in the morning, so I figured she might need a furry alarm clock in the morning, and until then, I didn't have to worry about what I was intruding upon.

3

The bedroom door at the end of the hall was still closed when Oz shuffled out of her room at nine the next morning. She stopped in the hall and muttered that it was odd; they never slept that late and she was pretty sure her father had meetings to get to. She considered knocking to make sure he wasn't late, but noticed me at her feet before she did.

"What do, Wick?" she asked. "I have no idea how late they stayed up. Should I wake him?"

No. Aubrey hugged him to death all night long. He's probably not done being dead.

"You'd know, right? If I should wake him, go to his door. Leave him alone, head to the kitchen."

Yeah, I went to the kitchen. That's where the food lived, and where my best chance of getting her to open a can was. Plus, Drew was already there, and he was making coffee.

"The Emperor thought this would be a good idea," he said when she sat down at the table, still not quite awake. "He figured they were up late last night and would appreciate having hot coffee and breakfast waiting." He gestured to the oven. "Blueberry muffins. From a mix, so don't be impressed. If we just leave a plate of them on the table, they'll notice, right?"

"Most likely. You'll make someone a good wife someday."

"Hey. I intend to be a spectacular wife."

He brought the plate of muffins to the table when they were ready and even grabbed her some orange juice, and in that, at least, he was a lot like Aubrey. He even kissed her before he sat down.

There's been entirely too much kissing going on.

"I didn't forget you, Wick," he said. "There's a plate with food for you on the counter. Just don't tell Mr. B that I let you eat up there."

Okay, he was a lot like Aubrey.

Oz perked up as she ate, and half an hour later we were in the elevator, headed for the King's tailors. They were the only ones he trusted to fit him for official clothes, but thought they were as Russian as the Emperor was Scottish. Mrs. Kovlov spoke in an accent with clipped sentences, but he'd heard her yell at Mr. Kovlov and when she was really mad, it disappeared and she could rip him a new one with perfect grammar and complete sentences.

"I'm not sure why Dad only trusts them, but he always looks good when he has to," Oz said as we approached the front door. "Anything special Mom needs, she has made here, too."

When we went inside, I had an idea why he didn't go to anyone else. No one passing by was going to be able to watch while he was measured all over. Just past the door was a privacy curtain that blocked any view to the back room, and Mr. Kovlov sat near it like a guard. He was older and grumpy-looking, with angry eyebrows that looked like they wanted to bite someone, and I was pretty sure he wouldn't take crap from anyone. He told Oz to go on back; the Emperor was already there and they were next, just find the Mrs. and she would get them all set up. He tickled the top of my head and asked if I was getting a new suit today, too, because if I was he would do the fitting personally.

I could use a new collar. I'd like a red one. Or a purple one. I think I'd look stunning in purple.

Oz pushed the curtain aside and we went in. The room was large and brightly lit, and lined up against the back wall were three tall, glass-walled cylinder-type containers, and one with dark glass that I couldn't see into. They looked like giant bell jars with doors, and the Emperor was in one right in front of us. He stood at its center with his feet just inches apart and his arms spread out with palms facing us. He was also nearly naked, wearing only skin-tight red shorts.

"Damn, he's ripped," Oz said.

"And that's way more of him than I ever wanted to see," Drew muttered.

Oz wasn't looking at things she didn't want to see. This was the first time she'd seen the Emperor without his shirt, even when he was teaching her to swim, and his chest and stomach were covered in tattoos. She wanted to step closer and ask if he minded if she looked, but before she could Mrs. Kovlov came out from behind a partition to our left and she handed them each the same type of red shorts the Emperor was wearing, plus a shirt for Oz.

"You," she said to Drew, "no underwear. Just this."

"Wait. What?"

To Oz she said, gesturing to her own chest, "You. Leave top undies on."

Oz was not thrown by it and took the clothes from her, but Drew was very hesitant.

"Seriously, what?"

Mrs. Kovlov let out an exaggerated sigh. "Shorts only. Makes suit fit better." She pointed to a door to the right. "Go. Change. Come back."

"*Together?*"

Oz laughed and pulled the door open. "There are stalls, Mister Modesty. Just pick one and get naked." She pulled the curtain back on the first stall to the right, and pointed to the one across from her. "I won't peek."

He ducked behind the curtain and she added, "Maybe."

I waited on the floor between them, listening to the rustling as they changed, and then Drew's flustered groan. "These things are really thin. And why do you get to keep your bra on? That doesn't seem fair."

Oz pulled the curtain open. "Because I'll be wearing one with the dress and she doesn't want to measure me with bouncing boobs and pointy nipples."

"Oh."

She jerked his curtain back; he had finished changing, but stood in the center of the stall, hands clasped over his groin.

"Seriously, Drew. I have a brother. You don't have anything I haven't seen before. Hell, Zed is *so* not shy that he stomped through my room bare-ass naked last week, looking for a clean towel."

If William can do this, so can you. He's super modest.

She opened the door, and Drew reluctantly followed, making sure it didn't close on me. The Emperor was just coming out of the jar, and Mrs. Kovlov pointed to Oz and told her to get in.

"What the hell is this?" Drew asked the Emperor.

He pulled a t-shirt over his head, covering the tattoos. "They use computer-controlled lasers to measure essentially every inch of you. You get a perfectly fit suit and no one has to touch you."

"Yeah, but…" He watched as Oz set up, planting her feet where Mrs. Kovlov told her to, spreading her arms out just so. "I don't think I can do this with her here. Not having to be pretty much naked. I mean, she's never—"

The Emperor laughed. "Don't look at Oz when you're in there. Just close your eyes and think of your mother, hovering over you in your apartment, watching everything you do. Nothing but your mother."

"Huh. Thank you. That actually helps."

"Don't even let the idea that Oz will be out here watching you closely, thinking of all the things she could be doing to you, enter your mind."

"Son of a—you're mean."

"Little bit, yeah."

Drew pointed to the darkened cylinder. "What's that?"

"The tailor, basically. As soon as your measurements are done, your suit is pieced together in there. By the time you've changed back into your clothes, it'll be ready."

"Last time I had to see a tailor, he practically manhandled me and it was like a month before I saw the suit, and by then it didn't fit. This thing you just get in and stand there, and then walk out with a custom fit suit?"

"Suit, dress, slacks, t-shirts, whatever you want."

"Huh."

"The Kovlov's inspired eighteen-year-old me to get in better shape for fitted custom shirts. Tight t-shirts, cut just right. Every damned one of them black."

Drew patted his own stomach. "Eh, I'm almost there. But, yeah. It'd be a new look."

"For Oz."

Drew half shrugged. "I don't mind when I catch her looking, no. But, you know, when I actually have clothes on. Not…Jesus, these are tight."

Oz stepped out of the machine, and Mrs. Kozlov waved Drew over.

"Well, she'll definitely be looking now. Intently. Taking mental measurements."

"I think I hate you a little bit right now," Drew grumbled as he took Oz's place.

The Emperor was laughing as he went into the dressing room. Oz waited and watched as Drew listened to Mrs. Kovlov's instructions, and snickered when he closed his eyes and began to mumble to himself.

I'm not getting that new collar today, am I?

She kneeled down and scratched under my collar. "This is boring for you, isn't it? I'm sorry. But you're being very patient."

I'm always patient. Meaty things come to those who wait.

A few minutes later the dressing room door swung open and the Emperor came back out fully dressed and holding a gym bag.

"You're making Drew very nervous, you know," he said to Oz.

"I know."

"That's not very nice."

"I know."

He set his bag down near me and went to talk to Mrs. Kovlov; from the smell wafting from the bag I was pretty sure he'd worked out before coming here and I hoped he'd showered because he was pretty close to her and that wouldn't be very polite.

By the time Drew was done being measured, I thought he was going to start hyperventilating. Oz hid a grin behind her hand, trying to not laugh outright, and then told him it was over. He could go put his clothes back on.

She followed him into the dressing room and I went into his stall to sit on the little chair in the corner while he changed. "You get to keep the shorts," she called out from the other side of the curtain, and he was staring down at them when she darted into the stall with him.

"Oz. Cripes."

He stepped back until he was against the wall, and his eyes were wide, like he was afraid of what she was going to do to him.

She laughed and pressed up against him. "Definitely keep the shorts." Her hands were on his hips, and his were plastered to the wall. "And I was wrong. You just might have something I haven't seen before. Hello."

"Oz."

"Oh, come on. I'm not going to rip them off you. Just give me a kiss or two."

"But—" He relaxed a little, and took his hands off the wall and put his arms around her. "You're a grabby little thing."

"No, if I were grabby, my hands would not be at your waist. And yours don't have to stay on my back." She reached behind herself and grabbed his wrists. "Live a little."

Zed's gonna break his fingers.

"Holy hell."

Really, Zed said he would break his fingers. I remember.

"Yeah, don't tell me you haven't wanted to do this."

STOP TOUCHING THOSE OR ZED WILL BREAK YOUR FINGERS!

"Oz—"

The dressing room door popped open. "What the hell are you doing to that cat?" the Emperor demanded, yanking the curtain open.

Oz stepped away from Drew, leaving his hands hanging there in the air.

"Ah, we weren't doing anything, really," Drew said.

The Emperor's head cocked to the left a little bit. "Clearly. And you're *not* thinking about your mother anymore, either. Get dressed, both of you. Your clothes are nearly ready."

The door clicked shut and Drew still hadn't moved. "Is he mad?"

Oz opened the curtain on the other side and started pulling her clothes on over the shorts and shirt. "No, he's not mad. And your mother? What?"

He finally took a normal breath and then reached for his jeans. "It was his advice while I was being measured. Sort of." He grimaced as he pulled them on. "Can you not watch me do this, Oz? I'm having a hard enough time as it is."

"I can see that."

She let him finished getting dressed alone, but his face was still more pink than usual when we left the dressing room. The Emperor was signing for his suit when Drew held the door open for me and he was nice enough to not mention how embarrassed Drew looked, but Mrs. Kovlov chuckled and told him he was adorable.

I don't know about either of them, but I was glad to get back outside where there was fresh air and sunshine, and no chance that anyone would be snapping Drew's fingers in half. I rode on his shoulder, wishing he had his sweatshirt pouch for me sit in, and they walked holding hands.

That was better than the groping, but a part of me wished for how they'd been earlier in the summer. They joked around a lot but there was no risk of broken fingers and inappropriate touching, and my sensibilities remained as unmolested as Oz's boobs.

When we were at Union Square, across the street from the royal house, Oz hopped up on the steps so that she was eye level with Drew. "I'm sorry if I embarrassed you back there. I really am. But you have to know, the shorts fit you *nicely*."

"I wasn't embarrassed. Exactly. Maybe a little. But it's probably a good thing the Emperor opened the door when he did. That was almost a…sticky…situation."

"Ah, I kind of regret that he opened the door when he did." She slid her arm over his free shoulder, her hand cupping his neck. "You know, I have this really hot boyfriend and he doesn't seem to want to sleep with me. It's a little confusing, because I know he loves me. And just a few minutes ago I was made aware that he's at least interested."

"Hey, I will find that hot boyfriend and kick his ass. I thought we had an exclusive thing going on."

"No, that's all right. He's sweet and adorable and wants to be a teenager again, though I have to admit I'm not really sure why. I'm a teenager, and let me tell you, it's frustrating as hell most of the time. I watched my friends go through all the teenaged crap…all they wanted was what the hot boyfriend and I have."

He leaned toward her and kissed her. "Oz, really, I want to in the worst way."

"Then what? Because you're not alone in that. I'd sleep with you in a heartbeat."

"Because," he sighed, stealing one more kiss. "A lot of reasons. I really do have more than one. But partly? It may actually *be* the worst way…it's gonna suck at first, and I don't want to hurt you."

"Suck how?"

"Honestly? I'm not going to be any good at it and it'll probably be over before you even really get started. Seriously. You might be able to count to three, but that's stretching it."

She smiled at him, the way Aubrey smiled to Jax when he was being sweet but dense. "We're both going to suck, Drew. I think the first few times we're just going to have to do it to do it, and if it's over too quickly? We get to keep trying. We get to keep getting better together."

"I still don't want to hurt you."

"Then we're never having sex because the first couple of times it probably will, and honestly…yeah, that's not gonna fly with me. I mean it's not a deal breaker for a while even if that means a year or two, but sooner or later, yeah, I want to. With you."

Oh, holy can of tuna will someone let me off his shoulder?

"My mom is still living in my apartment."

"She won't be there forever."

"And I don't want it happening in the back of the Emperor's car. Or even in his guest room."

"That would be rude," she agreed. And then as the thought hit her, "Wait, are you thinking about waiting until we're married?"

"It occurred to me. I mean, if that's what you wanted. I would wait."

"God, you really are adorable."

Very quietly, he said, "I have other reasons, but…I swear, I love you and I really want to be with you."

She brushed a finger across his cheek, the same way Aubrey liked to touch Jax when she wanted him to feel better. "Drew, it's all right. Hell, before we do, I should probably go see the doctor, anyway."

"What for? Are you all right?"

You're not all that bright sometimes.

"Seriously...I love you but I am not risking any little Oz or Drew clones running around. Not for a long time."

"Oh. Oh!" He untucked his shirt and peeled the waistband of jeans down a couple of inches. "About an inch below my belly button, to the right. Feel that."

She touched him with her pointy finger. "What is that?"

"I got an implant. Before I left Chicago. I mean, the thought occurred to me that sooner or later—"

The Emperor's voice made them both jump. "Sooner or later what? And why are we peeking into Drew's pants in the middle of downtown?"

"I'm looking for treasure," Oz said.

Drew turned pink again. "I just wanted to show her something."

"I'm sure you did."

"You know, Emperor," Oz said, "you're developing a knack for showing up at inopportune times. He was just showing me his implant."

"All right. And when did you get this implant?" he asked Drew.

"May. A few weeks before I came here."

"I presume you had high hopes, even then?"

"Emperor." Oz was laughing. "Come on."

"Hey, I'm not the one inviting women to peek into my pants. But I suggest that any further exploration not be done in public. Like it or not, someone may be taking pictures of you."

"People have been pretty respectful about that my entire life," Oz argued. "Of all of us."

"Traditionally, perhaps," he said as he dug around in his bag. He pulled his tablet out and turned it on, showing the screen to her when the picture he wanted to show her loaded. "Even a week ago, I would not have thought this would be on the front page."

Oz took the tablet. The picture was of the King and Queen standing on the balcony, holding onto each other. Her face was turned away from the camera so no one could see that she had been crying, and for that I was grateful. "Nice headline. 'King and Queen of Hearts.'"

"Swipe to the next page."

There was another picture of them, later in the evening when they had been sitting together on the balcony. Aubrey's head was on Jax's shoulder and her hand was on his leg. In the next picture, they were getting up, and he was kissing her.

To anyone else looking at the images, it was just a couple who still loved each other. I think Oz realized they'd been taken last night and something was wrong, but even knowing that, the images were still sweet.

"These aren't horrible."

"But they exist," the Emperor said. "And they were taken from a height that gave the photographer a clear line of sight to the King and the Queen in their own home."

He didn't know if they'd been taken using a drone, or if someone living directly across Union Square had taken them and had them published, but neither scenario was good.

"The barrier is going back on the balcony, isn't it?"

He shrugged. "If someone is taking pictures like these, then someone could set up a line of fire. I imagine your mother will want the barrier to protect you and Zed."

"Damn." She went on, explaining it to Drew, "There used to be a tall barrier around the balcony, that went from the ledge to just above the door line. It was clear acrylic and we could still see all around, but it really cuts down on how nice it is to sit out there."

"You'll still have the roof, if that helps."

The roof had a barrier around it, too, but at least it was big enough to still be nice, and high up enough that they would have privacy, unless someone really was using a drone.

"Do Mom and Dad know about this yet?"

He didn't know. "I haven't spoken to them yet."

"Yeah, they were still in bed when I left this morning. Should I tell them or do you want to?"

He took the tablet from her. "I have a meeting with your father in a bit. I'll tell him."

"If he's even up yet. For all I know Mom stapled him to the mattress and isn't letting him up today."

That made the Emperor smile. "Good for her if she did. If he doesn't show up for the meeting, I'll call him. But don't bother them today if you can avoid it."

He started to walk off.

"Emperor," Oz said. She took a few steps toward him. "Should I be worried? Are they okay?"

"They're fine, Oz. They know how to take care of each other."

"Yeah, that doesn't make me feel any better. Dad pretty much threw Zed out of the house last night and made him come downstairs to hang with us. We couldn't figure out if they were fighting, or what."

"Definitely 'or what,'" he said. "But give them space today, and please, don't ask them for an explanation. This falls firmly in the realm of being only their business."

"And yet, you know."

"Oz." He kissed her on the forehead. "I promise you, your parents are all right. They're allowed their private moments, the same as you are."

"So you're not going to tell them what you walked in on?" Drew asked.

"I am not."

"Thank you."

"Oh, make no mistake, I'll torture *you* as often as I can. But informing your parents or hers of what I see is not my job."

"What is?" Oz asked.

He touched the tip of her nose, and with a laugh turned to walk across the street. She watched him until he was inside, and then reached for Drew's hand.

"What was that?" he asked. "He's not usually that touchy-feely in front on me."

"The kiss was just a kiss. Touching my nose? It was an answer."

"And?"

"'To protect you.' That's how he sees his job now. To protect me."

4

If the King's mood improved over the next couple of days, we didn't see it. He left in the morning before everyone else was awake, and he came home late at night; the Queen waited up for him and they sat together at the table while he ate, but his mood was not easy to figure out. He was tired, that's all I could be sure of.

She was still sad; of that I was positive. When he was home, Jax made sandwiches and she didn't chase him out of the kitchen. She slept in. She didn't go to school to teach the sticky people; instead she stayed home to help plan the reception that she did not want. Jax told her he would make excuses and no one would think ill of her for not being there, but the Emperor still needed her help. There were caterers to secure with little notice, security to plan, and there needed to be some sort of décor. He could handle the particulars—hiring the right people, making sure the building was secure—but he preferred having her confirm or negate the choices he made about how the room would look and the food that would be served.

They sat together at the kitchen table with papers scattered across it, and she let go with an amused laugh. "This isn't a high school prom, William! Oh, lord no, no balloons."

She wanted classy. And despite the King's wishes, she wanted the official throne moved to the reception hall. He wouldn't need to use it, but its presence would make a point: this was Pacifica, a monarchy, and he not only reigned, he ruled.

He arched an eyebrow, half serious. "Do you want him to wear the crown?"

"If only it fit."

He was getting her to laugh and I liked that, but the details of the reception were starting to bore me so I went downstairs to find Oz and Drew. They were in the Emperor's apartment, and for once they were sitting on opposite sides of the room instead of wrapped around each other on the sofa. Oz was in the favored comfy chair and Drew was on the sofa, and they each had a computer tablet in hand.

"All right." Drew leaned forward so that his elbows rested on his knees. "The First Minister's name is Levi Munson. He's been married for fifty-three years to Valerie Keats Munson. The Second Minister is Redmond Munson, and is his fifty-two-year-old son. He's been married for thirty years to Darlene Kimball Munson. There's no mention of any kids that either of them have, other than Redmond being Levi's son."

Okay, this is pretty much like being upstairs.

"I don't know how true it is because it might be based on an old stereotype, but I'm pretty sure having as many kids as possible is routine in Florida. I wouldn't be surprised if they each had a dozen."

"I can't even imagine that."

"Seriously. The norm here is one kid per family. I mean, it's not law but I can only think of one of my friends who has siblings. She has four, but still…"

He looked up. "It's a little different in Midlam. Most of my friends have brothers and sisters, but not many. One or two each. Have you thought about that? Kids?"

She was still looking at her tablet, flipping through pages. "Abstractly. We're more or less expected to have kids, Drew. If that's a problem, tell me now."

"I'll have whatever you want. What about the Texas Governor? He's on his third or fourth wife, I think."

"Yeah, I don't want to have the Governor."

"You sure about that? He has horses and lets people ride them. He put me on a really beautiful black horse when I was four, but it bucked me off and I landed in mud. At least I hope it was mud."

Snickering, she said, "I'm sure. And he's married to his third wife, Maria. She's fifteen years younger than he is, no kids together, but he had two with his first wife. Zed has insulted them both, even. The kids, not the governor and his wife."

"Easy to do. Who else important will be there?"

"New England," she said. There was more, too, I think, but the Emperor came in and sat next to Drew.

"Whatever you're doing, it's time to stop. The King wants to see you."

They both turned their tablets off and started to get up.

"Not you, Oz. Just Drew."

"Just me?" His voice squeaked a little. "What did I do?"

He shrugged. "All I know is that you need to be prepared for some tough personal questions. He's waiting in his living room. I wouldn't make him wait long if I were you."

"That was mean," Oz said when Drew was out of the room.

"Nah, mean would have been warning him that your father is waiting with a shotgun."

Dude, no way!

"No, Wick, he's not. But you could go up there and keep an eye on him. Drew might be a little less stressed out if he has you to pet."

"You're using the cat to spy on them," Oz said.

"I don't need to spy. I'm supposed to follow in ten minutes, after he's had time to get Drew rattled. Go on, Wick. Drew's nervous."

I ran up the stairs after him; Drew often shared his bacon with me, so I had a vested interest in his survival. I caught up as he was heading into the living room and darted past his giant feet; he was slowing down, and I could feel the dread radiate off him like little rays of unhappy heat.

Jax won't hurt you.

He was in the kitchen and when he heard Drew, he reached into the refrigerator for a soft drink bottle and told Drew to sit at the table. I jumped onto the Queen's chair so that I was right across from him and could see him swallow hard as Jax handed him the bottle and then sat in his seat at the head of the table.

I sniffed the air to see if I could figure out what was in his glass. It looked like beer, but it was too early for that. Tea, maybe. It smelled kind of sweet and when the Queen wasn't there to stop him, he liked to dump enough sugar in it to make sludge at the bottom of the glass. When she was there, he added sugar when she wasn't looking, and just kept stirring it because clearly she would not notice all the little glucose bombs spinning around in his glass.

"I wanted to ask you about your intentions—"

"I'm not sleeping with Oz, I swear."

I don't think Jax knew whether to be angry or not; he was shocked at first, and then his eyebrows knotted together while he ran through all the impulse thoughts in his head, until he finally said, "All right. I'm a little relieved, but it's not any of my business." Before Drew could say anything else he added, "I'm not stupid and I'm not naïve. I won't give either of you a hard time when it does happen, but don't shove it in my face, either. It'll be a long time before I'm comfortable with the idea."

Drew started fiddling with the soda bottle, running his fingernail over the lettering on the label. "Yeah. Okay. I get it."

Jax watched him work hard to avoid looking up. "Jesus, I have to ask. Strictly out of curiosity, why not? I know you love her. I see how she looks at you. You haven't been that annoying little boy always picking on her for a very long time and I swear to God, your hormones enter the room before you do."

Drew took a sip of the soda, delaying.

"Come on. I won't bite your head off."

I'd like to see that. Well, the effort of it. Not the blood and stuff if you actually did it.

He didn't want to answer.

"Look, I know it's inevitable. I'm just surprised—"

"It's not that I don't want to. I do. She does, too. We're starting to talk about it and I think we should probably do that first. Talking about it, I mean. So we're both on the same page." He took a deep breath. "We have to really talk about it first because I want her to be more sure of me than anything else."

"She trusts you."

"Yeah, but…" he trailed off, staring at the bottle again, and Jax let him think through it. When he was ready to answer, he sat up a little straighter and didn't focus on the bottle so much. "You know my brother. He's not exactly…nice…to women."

"Carter isn't exactly nice, period. He's still more than a little immature."

"No, it's a lot worse than immaturity. He's like the ultimate man slut, and he's mean about it." The Emperor came in and sat down at the table with them, but Drew barely seemed to notice. "All right, like my first year at Northwest. I spent a couple hours in the cafeteria between morning and afternoon classes, and there was this one girl who was always there. She sat in the same place at the same table every day, near the manager's office. She was always alone—you know that one girl who always seems lonely and tries to hide inside herself? That was her. She'd eat her lunch and then study, and never sat with anyone else. Or she didn't until Carter noticed and locked in on her."

He was staring at the bottle again. The King glanced at the Emperor and it felt like he wanted to say something, but knew Drew needed to get this out.

"He spent like three or four weeks working her over. He'd get her to smile, then to laugh, and then it was like he didn't want to spend his lunch hour with anyone else. He'd touch her hands and laugh at the things she said, then was holding her hand. I mean, I could tell, she started thinking he really liked her. Then one day he's there with a bunch of his friends, and they sit a few tables over and he starts making her laugh and convinces her to sneak into the manager's office with him. I sat there too stupid to realize what was going on, and his friends were laughing their asses off. Ten minutes later Carter came out of the office raising both his arms like, victory or whatever, and they all jumped up and high-fived him…and he walked out of the cafeteria like some kind of star. And then everyone in there just stared at that door, waiting for her to come out. Five minutes later, she tried sneaking—"

His voice broke, and he finally looked up. "Her hair was all messed up and her lips were puffy, and she froze in place when she realized he wasn't there. I mean, she looked for him and expected him…and she just broke, right there. She was crying and had blood running down her leg, and she didn't know what to do."

"Drew."

"Carter traded that girl's dignity for an orgasm. And he didn't care. She was just…there, and as far as he was concerned that made her available to use."

"You're not Carter." Jax nudged the soft drink bottle to get Drew to look at him. "You are nothing like him."

"No, but I swore I would never forget that girl and what he did to her. I already knew then that I loved Oz and I was determined that I would be the complete opposite of my jackass brother. I want her to know that I mean it to be forever and not something we're doing just because we're both curious and horny."

"Forever is a long time, son."

Son. You approve.

"You knew. You were Oz's age and you knew."

Ha.

"All right, that's fair. So I'll ask you the same thing my father asked me when I told him I was marrying Aubrey. Do you really want to be tied down so young? Think of all the things you might want to do while you're still young. Travel. Jump out of an old airplane. Race a classic motorcycle across the salt flats in Utah. There's a lot of living you could do before you commit to that last relationship."

Drew looked confused. "There are a thousand things I want to do, Mr. B. But I want to do them with Oz. I want to see Paris, and walk around the Eiffel Tower holding her hand. I want to visit all the old castles in Europe. And yeah, I do want to ride an old motorcycle at stupid fast speeds, but with her on a bike racing next to me. It's not being tied down. It's doing, and I want to do it all with her. What fun is it if she's not there?"

The Emperor raised an eyebrow.

Jax tried to not smile. "Look," he said after a minute, "Oz can—and will—make her own decisions. She'll never ask my permission, but…I suspect that you're the man who would come to me and ask for her hand first."

Drew thought he might.

"When you both think the time is right—" he took a deep breath "—I give my consent. And my blessing. I know Aubrey will, too."

I jumped up on the table to head bonk Drew.

Me, too.

"And to the actual business at hand, which was not your intentions toward my daughter."

Drew twitched, and his face went a little bit pink.

"The intentions I meant were regarding Midlam. Do you truly not wish to be King?"

"I'd be a horrible leader, Mr. B. I've never been included in anything, not the way Oz has. The only reason I was named as the heir is because Carter threw a fit about it. He wants to play instead."

"That's not the only reason," Jax assured him. "Carter never had the temperament for it. He's always been impulsive and hot-headed. And you realize, as long as I'm alive and you want me to, I'll help. You won't have to navigate the particulars alone."

"Like you help my mother? I know you make most of the decisions for her."

The Emperor finally spoke. "Be honest about the scope of your involvement, Jax."

"It's not as much as you'd think. She's needed help throughout her reign," he told Drew. "Your father is a crucial part of that, as well. But the final decisions are always hers."

"Why?" Drew asked.

"I've known her my entire life, Drew. She wasn't prepared when your grandmother died, and she asked for guidance early on with the understanding that she might need it throughout her reign. I accepted the responsibility because Midlam's success is in Pacifica's best interests, and because she's my friend."

"You're a damn good friend, then."

"So is she. And right now she seems determined to abdicate. She's done. But if you truly don't want the crown—"

"You must think I'm a huge coward."

"No," Jax said firmly. "I think you're looking ahead and want what's best for Midlam. So do I."

"If she's going to quit, our constitution is pretty clear. She can't abdicate to you, so if she does, I have the job whether I want it or not. I agreed to it when I was sixteen. Formally and in public, even."

"Your plans with Oz still include someday unifying Pacifica with Midlam?" the Emperor asked.

"Someday."

"Midlam and Pacifica didn't unite in the beginning because of some strong political and ideological reasons," Jax said. "Have we overcome them enough to go there?"

Drew thought that if they hadn't, by the time he and Oz were staring down the thrones they could make it work. The countries were more alike than different, and the only reasons he could think of for the citizens to oppose the idea were all rooted in money. Pacifica has money, Midlam not so much.

"But we have agriculture, which I think is just as good."

"We would not fare as well without being able to purchase a great deal of our food from Midlam," the King agreed.

"If peace can be negotiated, do you think my mother will stay?"

"I'm going to try to make it happen, but you have to know, the First Minister has tunnel vision and doesn't particularly care about doing the right thing. If we can't figure out what it is he really wants and appease him, there's a good chance that Midlam will fall under heavy fire, worse than the attack on Chicago."

"And if I don't take the throne, my mother will fold. She'll surrender to him."

There was a beat of quiet that told Drew all he needed to know.

"Let's get through negotiations first. Stand in as if you have every intention of becoming Midlam's King someday. Minister Munson won't talk to your mother, but he will talk to you. Just follow my lead, don't let him rattle you, and you'll get a good foothold."

Drew looked to the Emperor. "You said before that we shouldn't let him get to us or act surprised. How big a jackass is this guy?"

"The comparison is an insult to jackasses."

"He's a hard man," the King said.

The Emperor got up to get a drink from the fridge. "Oz told me not too long ago that you were once sure that I dined on the brains and bones of small children." He sat down, popped the top off the bottle and then said, "Levi Munson? I wouldn't put it past him."

5

Drew was supposed to leave me at home; the King expressed a keen desire to not have everyone covered in cat hair and wanted them to all look their best, but after he left, Drew clipped a leash to my collar and told me as long as I behaved and didn't jump on anyone, it would be fine.

I liked the idea of people-watching and figuring out which one of them was most likely to stab someone else in the back and I wanted to be there if Jax really did wear the crown, but I didn't relish the idea of an evening spent on a crowded floor, staring up at people. The upside was that there was always a chance I could find an unused table to sit on, which might lead to food being snuck to me. Receptions meant food, and official receptions meant beefy goodness and bites of cheese. If I was lucky, it might also mean shrimp.

We rode the mile or so in one of the official cars; it was just an air car but had a shiny paint job with Pacifica's royal colors on the outside and smelled like feet on the inside. The King left ahead of us by nearly an hour, and the Queen did not go with him; Drew and Zed wanted to know why, but Oz decided it was a scab they did not want to pick at.

"They've never wanted to deal with the First Minister," she said. "So now we know she *really* doesn't want to deal with him. I think he'll be the first major dignitary she's ever snubbed."

The reception was held on one of the top floors of the Hyatt; it had once been the ballroom of the royal family house and had a view of the bay and the Bay Bridge that was, even to me, on the happy side of spectacular. The last time I'd been in the room the carpet was old, dusty, and worn, and a sour smell lingered in the air from being closed off for so long. Now it was fresh and smelled like spring time, and the new carpet was a deep red plush pad that felt like pillows against my paws.

If not for the circumstances, I would have rolled around on it, making my way from the door all the way to the other side, wiggling and squirming on my back. It felt like nap time should happen, if not for the hundreds of human feet I'd be trying to avoid.

Across the room from the windows were a dozen guards in dress uniforms; there were a lot of shiny medals hanging from chests, and rank bars on shoulders sparkled under the lights. They wore the formal uniform of the military, dark blue slacks with a wide red stripe, ironed with sharp, crisp creases, and matching dress jackets with bright white gloves. Even I understood the message: this reception was under heavy security, and those watching were the elite of the royal guard. Near them and in corners around the room were people wielding large cameras; the evening would be broadcast in every country on the North American continent, and would probably be available around the world.

Across the room from the double-door entrance, the King and Queen's ceremonial thrones had been set up. I'd never seen them before—they were usually at City Hall, a place to which I was never invited—and I had to fight the urge to run across the room to investigate. They weren't as ornate as I'd expected, but they were trimmed in gold—probably not real because real gold is spendy and that's just not like Jax and Aubrey—and the seats and backs were covered in a deep, rich purple that looked as soft as the new carpet. They had been placed on a raised platform that had two steps on the front, probably so Jax wouldn't have to jump to get into his seat.

I wanted to see that, actually.

Tucked into the corner just to the left of the thrones there was an orchestral quartet tuning up; they kept glancing at the guards and cameras, and I wondered if they were the understudies to the musicians who usually played for royal functions. The King glanced at them and the woman with the giant leg guitar suddenly looked like she was going to pass out. Her hand slid down the strings and made an awful sound, like a constipated cat in heat, and then she turned bright pink, which just made her feel even worse.

He pretended not to notice.

Zed snickered, but not loud enough for her to hear.

While the King was giving instructions to a guard with more shiny things on his chest than any of the others, he looked over and saw me on the floor hiding behind Drew's legs and he scowled, but he didn't tell me to leave and he didn't tell Drew to hide me somewhere. Oz deflected his attention away from me, stepping between Drew and the King so that she could kiss him on his cheek.

"Why are you already here?" she asked. "Shouldn't you make an entrance?"

"I'm making a point instead. And I know the Emperor has warned you already, but I need to remind you. Roll with the punches. I guarantee the First Minister will say things in a deliberate effort to surprise and offend you, but you can't let him get to you."

"The Emperor already told me I couldn't throat punch him," Oz said.

"You might want to by the end of the evening."

"I might want to the moment he steps through the door. I have a visceral reaction to even seeing his face on the news." She smiled then, and gestured to the formal outfit he'd chosen for her. "Thank you for not forcing me into a dress. This is amazing."

She was wearing a suit much like Drew and Zed, but hers was blue and not black, and the slacks flowed around her legs. It was more girly than she would have chosen for herself, but she was still happy with it. Zed and Drew wore white shirts with black bow ties, and her shirt was a pale blue with the bonus that she didn't have to wear the tie. By the end of the night, I expected Zed to be tugging at his, and Drew to be whining about it.

"You look incredible," Drew said.

"And you boys clean up well," the King said. "Oz, there's a reason for what I chose for you beyond knowing your tastes. I want Minister Munson to see you in a different light. He'll be unreasonably offended. To him, women should be appropriately and modestly dressed, and then seen and not heard."

Zed snorted. "Like that will happen."

The King looked past Oz to Drew. He was right behind her, his hand on her shoulder. "Andrew, did you bring Oz up to date on what we discussed?"

He nodded.

"Are you all right with this?" Jax asked her. "This intrudes on your relationship in a way I am very uncomfortable with. There's a method to my madness, but still. You can back out."

"I understand why, Dad. It's fine. Drew wants to barf all over himself, but I'm fine."

"You can throw up later," Jax said. He kissed them each on the cheek, even Drew, and then excused himself to talk to the sentry, who had just taken his spot near the door.

The sentry was a member of the royal guard, but his job on this night was to announce people as they arrived. He stood just inside the door, so stiff and straight that he could have had a metal pole stapled to his back, and he looked deadly serious. His jaw was clenched, eyes narrowed as he scanned the room, and his mouth was a tight line.

I think Jax just told him he couldn't have any cake tonight. Or beer. There'll probably be beer here.

Five minutes later the quartet began playing as the first dignitaries arrived. The Governor of Texas was first through the door, along with his wife and two kids, who had gotten a lot taller since I had last seen them. I heard the sentry announce people from Canada and New England, and even some from Japan, but I didn't know them.

Drew's parents were announced and they were greeted warmly by everyone as they worked their way across the room to speak to Jax. He muttered that she was in her element, working people while they were relaxed and happy, like a social butterfly with fangs. Oz thought that was kind of mean and was surprised he said it, but he hadn't meant it as an insult. "She knows how to make people respond to her, that's all. Sometimes she can nail a guy to the wall if she needs to, and she can do it with a look. If she had more confidence in herself, she wouldn't need half your dad's help."

"And we should go over there and all look like one big happy family," Oz said. "Maybe I'll get a good look at the fangs."

"She likes you," Drew said as he followed her over. "No fangs for you."

There were nearly sixty people in the room when the sentry bellowed out, "First Minister Levi Munson of Florida, and Second Minister Redmond Munson of Florida." The chatter in the room dulled and everyone turned to see what King Jackson would do.

He had moved from the center of the room and was standing closer to his throne, which was now bathed in bright light. He made the Minister come to him, and did not offer his hand; he only acknowledged the Minister with a curt nod of his head and an uttering of, "Levi."

Levi Munson nodded to him in return, and he acknowledged Richard, Drew, and Zed, but made a point of ignoring Oz and Queen Shazia.

He ignored me, too, but to be fair I was mostly behind Drew's legs, peeking around to see what was going on. I didn't want to make myself too visible, because he seemed like the kind of guy who would kick puppies and rip the fur off kittens. His entire disposition was sour; his mouth turned down in a perpetual frown, his giant hairy eyebrows knotted together over squinty eyes. Even his hair was trying to escape, and about ninety per cent of it had succeeded.

Levi Munson was old, and looked a lot older than his nearly eighty years.

Maybe that's why he was so angry. If he'd been born in Pacifica, he could count on living to around a hundred and it wasn't unheard of to make it to one-thirty. When Oz and Drew were reading up on people who would be at the reception, she found an article about life and death in Florida, and the average life expectancy for Munson was eighty-one.

I'd be upset, too, if I knew I only had a year or two left.

While the First Minister was turned toward Richard, the Second Minister smiled at Oz and mouthed, "Hello." She smiled back, but I wasn't sure if she was being polite or if she thought he might not have as massive a stick up his asterisk as his father. He seemed a lot more congenial to me; his eyes smiled even when his mouth didn't, and when he spotted me behind Drew he wiggled his fingers at me. As soon as the First Minister had turned back to look at Jax, though, he stopped.

No getting caught being nice to the cat. I got it.

While they endured the awkwardness—Jax had not said another word to either of them and they clearly expected to be addressed—the Emperor slipped into the room and gestured to the sentry to not announce him. He was dressed all in black; the lapels of his jacket were trimmed in black satin, his shirt was black with a black satin tie, and he wore thin black gloves. He'd gotten his hair cut and trimmed his beard into the goatee and mustache he'd had as a teenager, and he looked every bit as sinister as I know he intended.

He took the sentry's position, and when he spoke, his voice was like the crack of a whip. "Queen Aubrey of Pacifica."

She stepped in and accepted the hand the Emperor offered to her. Drew muttered *Dang!* under his breath, and the King inhaled sharply as his hand went to his chest. Her dress was a brilliant red that glittered under the lights, and it fit like another skin. She moved across the floor slowly, her fingers clutching the Emperor's slightly raised hand as she allowed the King to enjoy every moment of it, and the mass of people parted to allow her through. Their whispers turned to a loud buzz and their initial confusion—*where was the Queen?*—became smiles of admiration.

Jax could barely contain himself. His eyes sparkled as he waited for her, and his surprise that she had come at all transformed into a bright grin that poured out of every inch of him. I could almost hear the thought spinning in his head: *how did I get so lucky?*

The Emperor let go of her hand when they were close to the King and Jax reached for her, and then he pointedly bowed to her. He did not bow to the King—I'd never seen him bow before anyone when it wasn't a joke—but executed a perfect royal bow to her and then stepped off to the side where Oz and Drew and Zed waited.

Jax kissed her hand, and then her cheek, and for a moment I think they were the only two in the room.

The First Minister made a point of turning away as he moved across the room to mingle, but Redmond Munson stayed nearby, and he smiled softly when Aubrey kissed Jax on the lips.

That was the kind of kiss I liked to see. No one was sad and no one was going to start groping anyone else. That was her *I'm so happy to see* you kiss, and it was reserved for him.

The music went up a notch in volume and it looked as if they were about to follow his lead and mingle with the friends and other dignitaries, when the Emperor gave a slight nod to Drew.

Drew was pale and little beads of sweat popped out on his upper lip, and he looked even more like he wanted to throw up than he had half an hour earlier. He sucked it up and took a few steps forward to ask Jax, in a voice louder than normal, if he would be allowed to make a formal request of Pacifica's King and Queen.

The music faded and the buzz of voices dulled. Richard and Shazia glanced at each other; his eyebrows knotted together and she started to step toward Drew—*what the hell are you doing, Andrew?* painted across her face—but Richard's hand went to her arm and he stopped her. He was curious, but knew better than to interfere. Jax nodded and announced to the room, "Thank you all for coming. And please, give us a few minutes. The Crown Prince of Midlam has requested a moment."

The cameras were all turned to the King. Still holding Aubrey's hand, he guided her up the steps and waited as she sat, and then took his own throne.

He's trying to not smile.

The Emperor shushed me.

Well, I'm not wrong.

When Jax and Aubrey were seated, Drew sucked in a deep breath, stood before them, and then bowed.

A surprised series of murmurs floated through the room; Drew was not a subject of the King and Queen of Pacifica. He was a royal in his own right and had no reason to bow to them.

It was so quiet in the room that not only could you hear a pin drop, I think a feather landing on the floor would have produced a resounding splat.

Drew took several breaths, but then found his voice. "I apologize for disrupting the reception, but I need to ask you something, and if I have to wait any longer I'm pretty sure I'll wind up yelling it across the room."

"Go on," Jax said.

"Okay. Here's the thing. I've known you my entire life. I've spent more summers here than at home and I love you all, but more than that—" he glanced down at his hands, still nervous "—I've loved Oz since I was a little boy. She's been my best friend and confident for all of my memory, and every day that ticks off, I love her more, and I can't imagine getting through any more of my days without her."

He stood a little straighter and clasped his hands behind his back. "I am asking for your permission to propose marriage to your daughter. I know she loves me, too, and I don't think either of us wants to plan a future that doesn't include us being together."

Aubrey stood and walked down the steps to him. She kissed him on the cheek and gave him a hug, and then went to sit by Jax again.

The King looked surprised; he wasn't, not in the least, but everyone else watching had to think he was not expecting this.

"Andrew," he started, as if he was considering the request. "Oz is very much her own person. And while I appreciate your consideration, she does not need our consent. Your future together is yours to plan, whether I approve or not."

Drew glanced at Oz; she was hiding a smile behind her hand, clearly amused at his discomfort.

"Still, I know my daughter loves you. If it matters—and I hope it does—you've always had my approval and you certainly have my blessing." He turned to look at Aubrey. "I don't presume to speak for you, my love."

My love. I'm going to hurl before Drew does. What's next? Smoochie Pie?

"Wick," the Emperor hissed.

Aubrey's warm smile was genuine. "I already love you like a son, sweetheart. Of course you have my blessing."

Drew glanced at Oz again, and the King said, "Not now, Andrew. I wouldn't take that private moment from the two of you for anything. And when you do ask her, and she surely accepts, it will be reason for both Pacifica and Midlam to celebrate."

"Thank you," Drew managed. He bowed again—there were no surprised gasps this time—and went back to Oz. She threw her arms around him, but I was pretty sure that was because he hadn't hurled, and it wasn't part of the show. It didn't matter that Jax had asked for this performance; it was real to Drew and to Oz. He wanted the world to know his intentions, and she wanted them to see how much she loved him.

I just wanted to get to the part of the evening where the food presented itself.

The King stood and offered his hand to the Queen, and then addressed the room. "Thank you for your patience. Andrew has looked a little bit nauseated all day, and now we know why."

There was polite laughter, but the First Minister was slightly red-faced and not at all happy.

"There are hover carts circulating throughout the room now, with food and drink. If there's something you would like, just tell the cart and it will remember where you are, and then bring it to you."

From the back of the room, "What? What is this sorcery?"

More laughter.

"I employ the world's finest wizards," the King said. "Oh, and please be aware that our cat, Mister Wick, is somewhere in this room. He will use every bit of cute that he knows in order to persuade you to feed him. Don't feel obligated, but if you do, please don't give him anything with onions or garlic. Or alcohol."

The Queen added, "That last one goes to the kids, as well. I don't care if they're old enough to get married, they are not drinking on my watch."

People surrounded the King and Queen as they stepped down, and I thought that was the last we would see of them for the night, but as others were congratulating them they made their way to where we were waiting. The Emperor stood near us as if he was our personal guard, and did not engage either of them, which I found a bit odd.

They only wanted a moment with their kids before disappearing into the reception. Aubrey tried to apologize for her entrance—no, Jax had not expected her to be there and she was, indeed, caught off guard by Drew's request but was very happy for them—and asked that they bear with her; as the evening wore on she might not remain as happy as she was in that moment.

She'd barely been able to tell them that, when the First Minister elbowed his way over.

"I came for negotiations, Jackson," he grumbled. "Not a party."

"Come on, let everyone relax a bit first. Have a drink and enjoy the food. Play nice with the other guests. Most of them came to see you."

Like a zoo exhibit.

They expect you to fling poop.

When Shazia and Richard came up behind him, he turned to Richard. "You will be negotiating on Midlam's behalf?"

Drew started to say something, but stopped at the Emperor's warning glance.

Richard was not the least bit bothered by the Minister's tone. "You know as well as I do that I'm just the Queen's boy toy, Levi."

"You are her Consort," he said. If he could have hissed, I think he would have.

Aubrey slipped her arm around Jax's waist. "Are you still afraid of women, Minister?"

Death glare. That's the only way to describe the way he looked at her. He wanted her to spontaneously combust, right there in the ballroom in front of her family and half of the important people of the world. All he wanted to see was a tiny pile of her smoldering ashes.

"Keep your women in line," he snapped at Jax. "I'm not here to play games."

Icily, Aubrey said, "Neither are we. Might I remind you that you are in Pacifica, and will abide by our rules, not yours."

His eyes narrowed and red splashed across his cheeks. "I should have made your mother swallow you."

The Emperor was very slightly shaking his head the way he did when he wanted the kids to stop; they all twitched, but they didn't show the surprise that had just slapped them all right in the face.

"Ah, but by your own tenets, that would have been a mortal sin, Minister. And how is my mother?"

I was grateful for the quartet; they played at a volume that kept most of the people in the room from hearing, and if Aubrey had a meltdown, few would notice.

"My wife knows her place," he spat.

"As does mine," Jax said. "It is next to me, always. *Never* behind. And I caution you, Minister. I will not tolerate any disrespect toward my wife."

The First Minister moved closer and seethed, "Aubrey is my daughter."

The Emperor quietly stepped forward and placed his hand on the Minister's chest; Levi Munson looked suddenly and terribly pained, as if the Emperor's fingertips had tiny blades that had sunk into his chest and twisted.

"I stopped being your daughter when I was fourteen," Aubrey said, "when you wanted to marry me off to that poor, sweet boy who was clearly not compatible with me in any way."

The Minister's nostril's flared as his eyebrows tried to knot together; he stepped back and the Emperor's hand dropped away.

"Aubrey doesn't back down easily," Jax said. "And she is certainly not the girl you abused and intimidated as a child. Perhaps it's time you mingled and left her alone. Negotiations will begin tomorrow morning."

He was grinding his teeth together, still glaring at Aubrey.

Jax went on. "I'll chair the negotiations in good faith, Levi, but I remind you, this is Pacifica and my Queen will be protected at all costs. She's not your daughter anymore. Let it go, and leave her be, because if you don't? The wrath of God will be nothing compared to the hell I will bring down on Florida."

"You know nothing of God."

"Perhaps not, but I do understand a warning, and this is the last one I'll give on this matter."

The Second Minister took his father's arm and led him away, but he looked back once and seemed more sad than angry.

"I'll explain later, I promise," the Queen said to the kids. "When the reception is over, we'll go home and sit down, and we'll tell you what we can." She kissed them each on the cheek and when she got to Drew she said, "That means you, too. I know you haven't asked her yet, but you're my family, even so."

Jax reached for her hand and as they began to walk away he said, "Try to have some fun. Sophia and Marco Lopez are across the room, and they look like they could use some friendly faces."

Zed grabbed one of the hover carts as it passed. "Yeah, so friendly that Sophia might kick me in the balls," he muttered as he fumbled for the access panel on the underside. "Marco doesn't like me any more than his sister."

"That was a long time ago," Oz said. "And what are you doing?"

"Dad said to have fun. I'm having fun." He pulled a remote from the panel, and then detached a few wires from the circuit board. "I'm taking the cart offline, so that it doesn't head for the kitchen."

"Why?" Drew asked.

"Because—" he put the wires back, in a different order "—Wick shouldn't have to spend the night on the floor dodging feet. He should be up where he can see everyone." He reached down for me, and unclipped the leash from my collar before setting me on the cart. "All right, Wick. To go right just lean your head a tiny bit in that direction."

I tilted my head, just a bit, and the cart started to slowly turn.

"All right, that's mostly what you need to know. Whatever direction you lean, the cart will go. It doesn't have to be much at all, just enough to move the altimeter inside the cart. Lean forward a bit."

I did, and the cart floated right to him.

Spiffy.

"You can stay right here if you want, but if you want to ride around a little you can. Just don't go anywhere near the door, all right? You have to stay inside."

I'll stay here for a bit and get my balance.

"Man, we should have tried this a long time ago," Drew said. "How long does the power last?"

"Five or six hours. But I could easily fit a solar recharger onto it. We could literally take Wick anywhere we wanted."

They started talking about fitting it with a protective cage to keep me safe, trying to decide if the weight would throw it off kilter or if I would throw a fit being locked away in it. Oz was bored and scanning the crowd, when she caught Sophia Lopez's attention, and waved to her.

Sophia grinned and dragged her brother across the floor. She was a year or two older than Zed, and Marco was somewhere around the same age, but they both seemed a lot older than the last time I'd seem them. When Zed realized she was coming over, he froze for a moment, then said a word or two off the Bad Word List before standing up straight to greet her.

She went straight for him. "Zed! What do I smell like tonight?"

"Sophia, I am so sorry for that. I was a little jerk."

"You don't get off that easy. Come on. Tell me what I smell like."

He sighed and leaned in. "You smell…happy." He looked surprised. "Very happy."

"Yo, and me?" Marco said.

"Like…pizza. Come on, man, if there's pizza here, you better tell me where."

"Just ask the cart. It really will go get you what you want. You ask for pizza and it brings you these little rolled up things that have sauce and cheese inside."

"Uh, yeah. Those would be pizza rolls," Zed said. "Those are all right, but I'd almost kill for a couple slices of the real thing right now."

"No sneaking out," Oz warned him. "Stay for Mom's sake if nothing else."

"And you!" Sophia gushed. "You're getting married!"

"Eventually," Oz said.

Drew grinned. "I just wanted to make sure Mr. B wasn't going to hunt me down and then hang me from the flagpole in Union Square after I asked her."

"Surprised your parents, too, it seemed," Sophia said. She noticed me waiting on the cart, hovering near Zed. "Mister Wick! You're still here!"

I leaned the way Zed had told me to, and glided the cart until I was in the middle of the little circle they'd formed. She tickled me under my chin and said, "I am so happy to see you."

"You seem happy in general," Oz pointed out.

Sophia shrugged lightly. "Life has been a lot calmer since my dad remarried. We didn't exactly get along with his second wife."

"Maria is *really* nice," Marco said. "If he blows this one, we're leaving with her."

"Well, now I feel bad for telling you what you smelled like before," Zed said.

She forgave him, reasoning that he was a little boy then and obviously wasn't anymore. She then complained about how boring all the adults were being, and suggested they ask the orchestra to play something a little more upbeat. "Something we can dance to."

"It's not a party," Marco said.

"No, but we can turn it into one." She grabbed Zed's hand and pulled him over to the quartet, and didn't let go as she whispered into the ear of the violinist.

Marco grumbled about being left on the floor alone, as usual, but Drew pointed out the Japanese consulate's daughter. She was about his age, and standing by herself on the far side of the room. "Her name is Yuki," Drew told him. "No worries, she speaks perfect English, and is really nice. Ask her to join us. Sophia's right, the adults can be dull, but there's no reason we can't have a really good time tonight."

What about me?

"Wick, you can come dance with us, too," Drew said. "But you don't have to. You can ride around the room and sucker people into giving you snacks if you want. Just don't leave the room, okay? If you need something, come get me and I'll figure it out. I don't think you should bother the Emperor tonight."

I watched as they created a space for themselves near the thrones; some of the onlookers were taken aback, but the King and Queen seemed happy that the kids were doing something to have fun, and everyone else eventually took their cue from them.

I leaned forward a bit, testing the cart out, and slowly made my way to where everyone was mingling and talking. Most people were amused and pet me, and a few snuck bits of cheese and beef to me, but when I stopped near the First Minister and the Governor of Texas, only the Governor paid attention to me.

I hung there for a minute, looking around the room to see with whom I had the best chance to score more food. They were speaking quietly, but not whispering, so I listened.

"I'll leave Texas alone," Minister Munson said. "But I'm taking Kansas, and after that I'm going after the rest of Midlam. No mercy. That land should have been ours from the outset."

"Midlam has Pacifica's backing," the Governor reminded him.

"Jackson won't risk his family for a nation of misfits and low wage earners. He's soft. He'll put those kids before his country, and that will be his fatal mistake."

"He's shrewd, Minister. And he has a backbone."

"He's married to my daughter. I have a notion of his weaknesses. I don't have a problem with exploiting them."

I considered that Zed was right; the man really was a douche. He wasn't worth the effort it took to hold still, so I moved on, floating around people and hearing snippets of their conversations.

Canada supported Pacifica, but was lukewarm on Midlam. They wanted to take a wait and see position, but had no objection to the First Minister being removed from earth. After all, he had brought his bombers into their country under the ruse of displaying them in an air show in Winnipeg. He deserved whatever came to him for that alone.

New England was mostly concerned that they were next; knowing the First Minister's ego, he wouldn't stop at acquiring Midlam.

Mexico wanted to know how Florida managed to get all that ancient hardware flying in the first place, and what other weapons were they possibly hiding? Japan agreed, and feared there might be very old nuclear bombs hiding somewhere on the eastern seaboard.

I floated over to where the King and Queen were talking to Maria Lopez; that was a discussion I didn't mind hearing. She gushed about how wonderful her step-children were, and how adorable Sophia looked dancing with Zed. She laughed hard when Aubrey told her about the last time they had seen each other, and admitted that Sophia did look quite a bit happier now.

"So does Zed," Jax said.

The Emperor was still where we'd left him. He stood with his hands clasped behind his back, and he was scanning the room the way the King's personal guard was doing from his spot near the door. I went over to him, though I didn't stop in time and bumped right into his stomach. He didn't flinch, and didn't take his eyes off the room.

I need to tell you things tonight.

"All right."

And you'll need to tell them to the King.

"Does he need to hear them now?"

No, but soon.

"This will be over in a bit. Another hour, perhaps two."

It can wait that long. Can I go over and spray the Minister? Just a little.

The corner of his mouth lifted a tiny bit. "Go hover around Oz and Drew. I think they'll be leaving soon, and he'll take you home."

I wasn't too sure; they were having a lot of fun and I suspected they might be among the last to leave, but I'd be happier with them than moving around between all the somber people.

Besides, from there I had a good look at the First Minister, no matter where he went in the room. I could see whom he spoke to and how their faces looked as they reacted to the things he was saying, and across the board they all looked very, very unhappy.

6

Two hours later, right around the time the Emperor had supposed, we were back home. Oz and Drew changed out of their suits and waited together in the living room, and Zed went to the balcony to shout at his phone. It sounded like he was trying to explain why he was not asking to borrow the Emperor's car that night or maybe any other night, either, but I don't think the person he was talking to was very happy about it. I watched him argue for a minute and then went to see if Drew had food that I could share, because snacks always trump annoyed people.

They were on the sofa, looking at something on Oz's tablet, but there was no cheese, no salami, not even things I wasn't allowed to have. It felt like a wasted effort on my part, and I said so.

You're not doing a very good job of catering to my whims.

"I saw how much junk people gave you tonight," Drew muttered, not looking up. "You're not starving."

That's not the point.

Before I could make my case for fresh gooshy food, the elevator opened and Jax and Aubrey stepped out, with Drew's parents right behind them. I was sure I could get something then, because guests meant food, and the two of them together equaled guests. Aubrey would head right for the kitchen to get meaty edible things, and everyone would sit around sharing with me while they also imbibed red stupid drinks. Or blue stupid drinks. Anything to reduce the collective IQ by 16 points and turn everything funny.

It took exactly three seconds for my anticipation to come crashing down around me.

Richard and Shazia weren't staying; they only came in to say good night to everyone and to tell Drew that they were moving their things into the guest suite, so he had his apartment and his privacy back. He didn't even try to tell them it was fine, and he didn't mind if they stayed; instead, he was quick to offer to help them gather everything up and take it upstairs.

My gut said Aubrey finally told them to just move already. That many people in that tiny apartment was probably a fire hazard.

"You sit tight," Jax said. "I think they can manage a couple of suitcases and they have at least a hundred people on staff to help them."

"Seems like that," Richard grumbled.

I jumped on the coffee table to stare at Oz and Drew while Jax and Aubrey went to change. Zed was still on the balcony arguing with his phone, but the Emperor came up the stairs and he'd switched from the all black intimidation tux to jeans and a baby blue t-shirt. In a matter of minutes, he went from menacing to a fluffy marshmallow; he flopped into Jax's favorite chair and let out a tired sigh, then asked Oz and Drew if they'd actually had fun or if they were only being polite to the Lopez spawn.

"Genuine good time with them," Oz said. "And I think Zed offered to take Sophia out for lunch tomorrow, if he can weasel out of the negotiations for a while. They hit it off really well."

"His presence is not a requirement. As long as he clears it with your father before he leaves, it should be fine."

From down the hall Jax asked, "What's fine and who needs to clear what?"

"Zed," Oz answered. "He wants to take Sophia Lopez out for lunch tomorrow."

Jax scowled at the Emperor and told him to get the hell out of his chair. "I don't see why not. We'll break for lunch around noon, he can skip out then. Where is he, anyway?"

"On the balcony, telling the school skank that he's not banging her anymore."

"Excuse me?"

Oz didn't try to be any nicer about it. "For the last three or four weeks he's been seeing this fairly horrible girl who'll do just about anyone on a whim. Tonight he decided he should keep it in his pants because he realized he doesn't want to be that guy."

I could hear Jax's teeth grind together, and the little muscles at his temples were twitching. His whole body twitched a little, too, and if Aubrey had not come out of the bedroom he would have gone outside to interrupt Zed's argument. He twitched in the other direction when she told everyone to sit at the table. She'd made brownies earlier and thought they all needed a good snack.

"Don't argue," Jax said as he got up.

The Emperor was already on his feet—he always got up when she came into the room—and he went to get Zed.

Oz offered to help her, but was brushed off. "Just sit down, it will only take me a minute."

"You can do the dishes later, though," Jax said.

"Dishes!" Aubrey brought a plate loaded with brownies and chocolate chip cookies to the table and set them in the center. "Oh. I made cookies, too. I forgot to ask, who did the dishes the other night? I appreciated it very much."

"Oz and I did," Zed said as he sat down. "She figured you had to be super tired if you left them, so…yeah, she made me help. I whined about it the whole time, but I helped."

"He only whined because he realized he'd missed out on macaroni and cheese."

"I'll make some tomorrow," Aubrey said, kissing the top of his head. "And yes, I'm avoiding the elephant in the room. I'm sorry."

"You don't owe us an explanation right this minute, Mom," Oz said. "We get it. I don't think any of us would have wanted anyone to know if that bloviated, rancid cheese curdle was our father, either."

Jax pulled out her chair for her, and told her he would grab glasses and milk. She just needed to sit down, and take her own time in telling them. "And don't push her," he told the kids. "If you have questions, be careful with them."

"I don't even know where to begin," she said.

"Levi Munson wields his genitals as a weapon," the Emperor said. "He believes that women are possessions to do with as he pleases, and truly does not think that they are people. He is the bacteria that feeds off the world's largest pile of...manure. That's where you begin."

That's certainly the image everyone wants in their head while staring down a plate full of brownies.

No one reached for one.

Aubrey didn't refute his description. "My father considers any female to be about on par with the family dog, though he honestly would treat the dog better. William is right. To him we are property that he never wanted, and he was frankly disgusted that his wife bore him anything other than sons. My sisters and I were nothing more than God's punishment for whatever sins he had committed, and my mother was nothing more than a brood mare and housekeeper. I realize that sounds like an exaggeration, but honestly...I'm being kind."

Aubrey was the second of seven children that she knew about; she assumed there were more she'd never met. She had an older brother, Redmond, who was now the Second Minister, and he was four years older. There had been a child born between them that hadn't survived long after birth; Munson did not mourn her loss and forbade her mother from discussing the child around him. A new baby was born roughly every two years, and the more children she had, the better Levi thought he looked.

He accepted the necessity of girls being born and he fed and clothed his daughters well, but only because he knew it was what God expected of him. But, he did no more than what he believed those expectations required, and held a deep belief that anything more was a waste of time and energy that should be given to his sons, who were, after all, made in God's image.

Aubrey thought it was simply a neatly packaged excuse for misogyny. Not all men in Florida were like him, but those who favored their daughters tended to be left out of the inner workings of the church.

By law he was required to send all his children to school until they either reached the age of fourteen or finished their eighth year of education, whichever came first. After that, it was a parental decision and most kept their daughters home. The strong-held belief of the Church of Florida was that education for girls was only necessary so that they would someday be able to help their sons learn.

School was the one place Aubrey felt safe, and when she turned fourteen and he refused to let her go further, her heart was broken.

"He had made arrangements with our congregation's pastor," she said, staring at the brownies that no one touched. "I was to begin getting acquainted with the pastor's seventeen-year-old son, and when he turned eighteen we were going to—no choice in the matter—get married."

"Jesus, Mom," Zed muttered.

"He was such a sweet boy, but was no more interested in me than I was in him. Less, to be honest. We had fully supervised meetings three times a week at church, and the few times we were able to actually speak without someone else present…oh, that poor boy. I knew his spirit was being crushed, and if we followed through with our fathers' plans, we were going to spend a miserable and completely chaste life together. We agreed to tell our fathers that it was not going to work out, but…"

Her eyes filled with tears, but she didn't cry. "Simon—his name was Simon—tried to explain to his father that it was a bad match, and was beaten to a bloody pulp until he agreed that our fathers knew best because they relied on the Lord to lead them. I tried to tell mine—" she looked to Jax for help, unable to get the words out.

"Levi Munson's notion that women and girls are for personal use extended to some unsavory depravities and punishments," he said.

His voice caught and he couldn't say anything more, either.

The Emperor could. "The son of a bitch raped her. Repeatedly. From the time she was a little girl until she left."

"Mom," Oz cried.

Jax shook his head. "Not now. Just accept that punishments in the First Minister's household did, and likely still do, involve an incredible amount of violent sexual abuse. He excused it to her as an education for her future as a wife, and it was always brutal."

She reached across the table for his hand.

When she could speak again, she said, "We couldn't stay. If we had, it would have never ended, and I couldn't take it anymore. So one night we both snuck out of our homes and ran. Because of my father's inability to shut up at home, I knew where we could get through the wall without being seen, and we took off. We had enough money between us to get as far as Illinois, but by then?"

She started playing with Jax's fingers, rubbing the hairs on one of his thumbs, and tracing over his thumbnail. He carefully turned his hand over so that she could trace the lines across his palm, a move so practiced that only the Emperor realized what he was doing.

"You don't leave Florida without permission. There are repercussions. My father sent my older brother after us. He had no idea that Red had given me money in the first place, and when he caught up to us in southern Illinois, he put us in the car and kept driving until he ran out of gas, and then rented an air car to get us to Pacifica. Simon got out near L.A. and Red brought me to San Francisco, hoping I'd have better odds at surviving here. He gave me enough money to live on for over a year, kissed me on the cheek, and said he hoped someday he'd see me again, and that I'd be happy. But he wasn't taking me home to live through my father's revenge against the insult he would have seen my running away as being. Truthfully, I think Red was terrified that I'd be made an example of, and examples of apostasy are generally executed."

She had no idea what the fallout was, but felt guilty because she had two younger sisters who were left to suffer under his roof. "I couldn't dwell on it. I was fourteen years old and had to convince the world that I was here with at least a guardian, and I had to figure out how to find a place to live and to get enrolled in school. For the next few months I didn't have the luxury of worrying about anything going on back home, because I was just trying to survive. I was afraid to rely on social services because I thought that they would send me back, but somehow I managed to get a place to live, and then a job, and after that the pieces started falling into place. I was able to finish school and then college, and along the way I met this strangely dark young man who seemed terribly excited for me to meet his best friend."

I jumped from the counter to the table. There was a better than fifty-fifty chance that the King would make me get down, but I decided it was worth the risk. Aubrey needed a good head bonk and no one else was leaning over to give it to her. She scooped me up with her free hand—she was still clinging to Jax with her other hand—and pulled me close. I pressed up against her, and the King didn't say a thing about it.

"When I told your father about mine, when we were dating and it was getting serious enough that I felt like I had to, he promised me that my father would never step foot in a house of ours. I think my brain wanted that house to be all of Pacifica, so when he told me about hosting the negotiations…"

"I might as well have just slapped her," he said. "The betrayal was the same."

"No, Jax," she argued. "It was never a betrayal. I know you don't want this and don't want him anywhere near our children."

Jax said to Oz and Zed, "You are never to be alone with him."

Oz closed her eyes briefly and then sighed. "Are you sure I can't throat punch him?"

That made Aubrey smile. "Sweetheart. If it meant winding up with your father and the two of you, I would do it all over again. But now you know. I never talk about my childhood, because of him. I'm not likely to want to talk about much of it, but please don't let that stop you from asking questions if you have them."

Drew set his elbows on the table and rested his forehead on his hands, which were clenched in tight fists. He inhaled slowly, deliberately, and I could hear his sinuses gurgle a little.

"Mom." Zed sounded small, and his voice cracked. "How did you even—I mean, you and Dad. You…"

Oz touched his arm when the words got stuck. "We never would have guessed. You two are all over each other all the time and I'm not sure I'd ever get over something like that enough to be that physical with anyone."

"I never got over it," Aubrey said gently. "I never will. But I met a boy who was very kind and patient, and he loved me without expecting anything. He promised he would never use me, and he's kept that promise even in moments when I wouldn't expect him to.

When I thought I was ready…" She pulled his hand to her lips, and kissed his fingers. "There were a lot of false starts but he never once made me feel bad about that."

"She got professional help, too," Jax murmured.

"I don't think that's what they want to know about, sweetheart. They want to know how we got from there to here. I want my children to understand that their father is the one who taught me to trust and that he earns it every day. You loved me then just for being me, and all those times…"

Softly, "And that's enough." He got up, and then bent over to kiss her. "Wick apparently overheard some things tonight that he wants the Emperor to pass along. If you want to get away from all of this for a while, I'll debrief the cat and then join you."

But I'm not wearing briefs.

Aubrey got up but before she left she went to the Emperor; the whites of his eyes were stained red and hinted at the anger that was simmering just under the surface. She kissed his cheek again. "William. Thank you for your help tonight. I didn't think I would, but I loved seeing the strangled look on his face when you brought me into the reception. And thank you for watching over my children tonight."

He started to get up, but she patted his shoulder and told him to stay where he was. The King was amused, I think. He knew that being touched made the Emperor uncomfortable, but he never did anything to discourage it, not when it was her. When Aubrey was all the way down the hall, Jax sat back down, and pointed at me.

"If you didn't have something important, I swear I'd get a squirt bottle and make you want to get off the table."

"It's a losing battle, Dad," Oz said. "Just surrender already."

He wasn't about to do that. He didn't want me on the table but he listened as I told the Emperor everything I'd heard; he didn't seem surprised to hear that the First Minister wanted all of Midlam, but he was taken aback by the idea that he was so openly talking about it.

He glanced at his watch and told Oz and Drew that they needed to be ready to leave in the morning by eight o'clock, and told Zed to stay put because he wanted to talk to him about whoever it was that he'd been apparently dating. Zed glared at Oz, who shrugged.

"Is it all right if we go out for a walk?" Oz asked as she picked me up. "We won't try to lose the guards, I promise. And we won't stay out too long."

"Stick close," he said. "No further than Market, and stay where it's well lit."

She handed me to Drew, who put me on his shoulder with the promise that he would stop and get his sweatshirt before we went outside, and led the way across the living room. Before we got to the stairs, Zed called after her, "I really hate you, Oz!"

I don't think the idea bothered her much, because she laughed and yelled back, "Love you, too, mouth breather!"

*

It was cold outside. Not just the kind of cold that made the tips of my ears chilly, but the kind that reached down under my fur and made me shiver and made my nose run. Drew didn't seem to mind being outside without sleeves on his sweatshirt, but Oz made him walk faster than usual so she could warm up. I snuggled down into the pouch on his shirt and only poked my head out so that I could see where we were going. I had to watch, because if I didn't, he would probably trip or walk right into a wall.

He kept one hand under me to keep me from bouncing around and had his other arm around Oz's shoulders to keep her warm. I was used to them holding hands, it happened every day now—like not holding hands was going to make one of them stop breathing or just internally combust into a pile of horny little ashes—but this was new and a little bit awkward for me. It changed how he moved, and his hand did nothing to stop me for moving side to side.

I think he sensed my discomfort. "Zed and I really will get you a hover cart," he said when I shifted my weight for the twentieth time. "You'll be the coolest cat in San Francisco."

I already am. And I hope you put a heater on it. Face it, if I hadn't already been neutered, they'd be freezing off right now.

We lapped Union Square three times, picking up speed with each turn. Oz was laughing because she could hear one of the guards nearby swearing under his breath, and the only things keeping them from breaking out into a run were me and the promise to the King that she wouldn't dodge any of them.

I don't think Drew was exactly happy about it, either. He was breathing hard and trying to not show it, because Oz was not breathing hard at all.

She exercises, dude. You should try it sometime.

After the third lap around the Square they crossed the street and headed down Powell toward Market, walking right down the center of the street since the cable cars didn't run at night. Just before we reached the intersection I heard the closest guard grunt "dammit," immediately followed by the sound of squishy people skin hitting the pavement, but neither Oz nor Drew reacted.

Guard down at six o'clock.

He went 'splat.'

"Are you cold, Wick?" Oz asked. She reached over to feel the tips of my ears. "He's cold. We shouldn't stay out much longer."

"We're almost to Market. We kinda have to turn around there, anyway."

We could turn around now.

Yeah, I vote we turn around.

The mall was across Market Street, and there was a cluster of men loitering near the entrance. They were all dressed in suits and looked perfectly non-threatening, but even Oz knew better.

Suits don't mean nice.

Sometimes suits are just covers for creepy people.

Really, let's go back.

One of them, a not-too-tall guy with hair that was blond but not blond like Drew's, noticed us and stepped away from his friends, crossing the street in our direction. Drew flinched, taking a step back, until Oz told him to hold still.

"I saw him at the reception. He's definitely from Florida and I don't trust him, but running might make the guards think we're in trouble and they'd start something."

"Oz, I think we *are* in trouble."

She dropped her arm from around his waist and grabbed onto his hand; everything started to shift, and I could feel it, too. The world slid to the right, and my brain went with it.

"Where is he?" Oz said through clenched teeth.

Drew didn't have to ask. He glanced over his shoulder, and told her he was coming. When everything uprighted itself, Oz looked to see where he was; I could hear his footsteps, slapping against the pavement in fast, hard strokes, and when he was close he yelled at them to move.

They moved.

He was in the air before I could get a good sightline to him. I thought he was going to kick—he had a wickedly awesome flying sidekick—but he was headed for the guy in the suit head-first and he twisted his body mid-air. As he zipped past, the Emperor grabbed his wrist and snapped it, and then his knee went into the side of the blond guy's head.

He should have fallen; the crack of the Emperor's knee against his skull should have dropped him on the spot, but he staggered, bellowing in pain. The Emperor landed on his feet and took a heartbeat or two to assess: was he going to drop or not?

Blond dude had a knife in his uninjured hand, and before he could blink and see straight, he went straight for Drew.

I ducked into Drew's sweatshirt. I didn't want to see it, and since I was right there, I didn't want to know if I'd just used up my last life.

Instead, I heard another thud and then the sound of wetness. I peeked out; the Emperor was kneeling next to the blond guy's body, his hand around the knife that was sticking out of the dead man's throat.

Oz scrambled to him, while the men across the street ran toward us.

"I've seen this, Emperor," she said. "Run."

He looked up at her.

"Emperor. The portal. *Run!*"

She didn't have to tell him again. He jumped up and sprinted, and was through the portal before the others reached us.

Oz tensed, her hands clenched into fists, ready to fight.

The first one to reach us was Redmond Munson, Florida's Second Minister. He was with four others and I know Oz was calculating the odds, but Redmond held up a hand and told his men to stand back. His order was gentle yet firm, and all stopped behind him. He knelt on the street, sighing "Isaac," before closing his eyes and mumbling something even I could not hear.

"We all saw Brother Isaac draw his knife." He remained on his knees, his hand on the dead man's chest. "He attacked. This was done in defense of the royal family, nothing more."

One of them started to argue, but he snapped, "Our feelings don't change the truth, Brother Eli. And we will *not* lie to protect him." To Oz he said, "I am so sorry. If I'd had any idea, I would never have let him cross the street."

Oz was not relaxing. Her weight shifted onto her back leg, ready to kick.

"Was that your Emperor?"

She unclenched her fists, but her fingers twitched, still ready for a fight. "No idea who that was. Could have been anyone."

"Ah." He nodded knowingly. "Your people protect you."

There were more footsteps behind us, Oz's personal guard and two of his backups. Her guard had bloody arms and a split chin, and began making excuses—he tripped over the cable track, and the others were too far away—but she wasn't having any of it.

"You are *so* done," she growled.

Redmond Munson shoved his hands into his pockets and said unhappily, "And quite likely very dead."

The guard flinched, but Oz did not. "We don't execute people for being sloppy and stupid. He's fired, that's all. One dead man is enough for tonight."

Drew didn't seem as certain, and the guard, blood dripping from his chin, was definitely not sure. The other two guards stood next to him, grasping his arms in case he bolted, and we waited in the cold, listening for the sirens that were speeding toward us.

7

The conference room at the old Hyatt was on the first floor, so the view wasn't as spectacular as the one for the reception, but there was a giant window that looked out onto Herman Plaza and the view was pleasant enough. The fountain often wasn't running during fall and winter, but it had been turned on just for this, to give everyone something different to look at when they were sick of looking at each other. They also had a nice view of the tourists who stopped to take pictures in front of it, which at some point during the day would probably include a toddler trying to walk along the cement well-wall and then falling into the water, and three or four people fishing out their dropped phones.

It was good entertainment if you didn't stop to feel sorry for anyone.

Okay, also if no sticky people were hurt. The worst thing I ever saw was a two-year-old face-planting into the fountain pool, but it wasn't very deep and instead of crying he got up and started running through the water, first from his mom and then from a cop, who wound up having to wade in after him. He plucked the kid out and wagged his pointy finger at him, but the kid just laughed and ran, leaving wet footprints across the Plaza as his mom chased after him.

People pointed and laughed, because it was three or four kinds of funny to see their Queen chasing after tiny, wet, spirited Prince

Jackson, yelling at him to stop while his maniacal high-pitched laughter streaked right behind him.

If he repeated the performance, it would go a long way in making people happy during the negotiations.

No one looked terribly happy as they prepared to leave the house. Everyone but Zed had been up until after two in the morning, dealing with the aftermath of the attack and all the questions that Oz and Drew had to field from the police and from Florida's security delegate. They had to repeat their answers several times, and it took so long to detail the walk they'd taken that they could have taken it three more times.

At two o'clock, the King inserted himself into the questioning and ended it, ordering the officer in charge to let the kids go home. The police knew where to find them, and anything else could wait. He drove us home himself—a message to Oz's guards, I think—and when we got there the Emperor was waiting at the kitchen table. His shirt had a bloody handprint on the chest, and while he had washed his hands, there were still tiny flecks of blood on his neck.

As soon as Oz was close enough, he asked, "How did you know to tell me to run?"

She sat across from him at the table. "A couple of months ago Drew and I were walking down Market, and you were right outside the portal, trying to catch your breath. It just clicked with me tonight. You were wearing a baby blue shirt with a bloody handprint, and told us not to worry because it wasn't your blood."

"Ah. All right, so now I know that was you in the past and not in the future. I bolted through without considering where I was headed. I'm lucky I didn't wind up tripping through it without going anywhere at all."

"Take that shirt off," Aubrey told him. "I'll get you a clean one."

"It's probably evidence," he reminded her.

"Yes, and I'll burn it if I have to. Oz told the police that she didn't know who had defended them. And Redmond didn't push it. He only wanted to know why Isaac Young was apparently attacking Andrew."

She headed down the hall, but he left his shirt on.

"For certain he was going after Drew?" Jax asked. He reached into the refrigerator and grabbed a beer bottle, handing it to the Emperor before he sat down. "Yeah, you look like you need this. No chance he was after Oz?"

Drew didn't think so. "After the Emperor nailed him in the head, he headed right for me. It was like he didn't even see Oz. And now we know who tried to kill me when I was twelve, I guess."

The King's eyebrows knotted together and he uttered, "What?" as the Emperor closed his eyes and sighed hard.

I don't think you were supposed to tell, dude.

"There was an incident when he was a boy," the Emperor said. "A former guard of his made an attempt on his life, but I handled it."

"And I'm just hearing about this *now*? Nearly eight years later?"

"I made a judgment call, Jax. And I ask that you respect it."

I'd never heard the Emperor take that tone with the King, and it surprised him as much as it did Oz and Drew. Jax flinched a little; a flash of anger crossed his face, but it left as quickly as it came, and he leaned back in his chair. "All right." Turning to Oz, he asked, "Why tell him to run?"

"Gut feeling. If he'd stayed, they would have all fought back, I think. The numbers were good, pretty evenly matched, but all it would have taken is one wrong blink and one of them could have gotten to Drew." She shrugged. "Or fired a weapon. Men in suits, no telling what they're hiding."

"It was the right call," the Emperor said. "One more dead man on either side wasn't necessary." He left before Aubrey came back with the fresh t-shirt, saying that he would see them in the morning. Drew, sensing that he might be asked questions the Emperor didn't want answered, excused himself right after that, leaving Oz alone with her father. And Jax knew she wasn't going to say anything.

The next morning felt like the King's last hangover. Other than when he told Oz to bring me, without saying why, the total number of words spoken between breakfast and getting onto the elevator didn't even add up to thirty. I rode in the front seat of the car, sitting on a towel to avoid getting fur on anyone. We went all of five or six blocks, from the royal house to the old Hyatt, and when the car stopped Jax told Drew to put me on a leash and to keep an eye on me.

Maybe he wants me to bite someone.

I'm not a huge fan of biting. People don't taste very good.

The conference room was half filled, but there was no sentry to announce the King. He went straight in and headed for his spot at the giant table in the center of the room, dropping his briefcase onto it with a loud thud.

Drew entered just behind Zed and Oz, and stopped a few steps inside the door. His hand went to his shirt collar, and he groaned. "I didn't wear a tie. No one told me I needed a tie."

"You look fine," Oz said. Every man in the room was wearing a white dress shirt and dark slacks—except for the Emperor, who was again in all black—but Drew was the only one without a tie. "No one will notice."

The Emperor entered right behind Drew, and he dropped his bag to the floor and then knelt down to unzip it. "Red or black?" he asked.

When Drew didn't answer, Oz looked at his shoes and belt and said, "Black."

He opened a side pocket and pulled out a black satin tie wrapped in tissue paper.

"Thank you," Drew said. "And really, for a guy who lives in jeans, I never would have expected you to carry around dress clothes."

"This isn't my first rodeo, Andrew. I have been to many, though usually my job is to scoop up whatever the jackasses leave behind."

"There's going to be a lot of that today, I think," Oz said.

"And Florida can handle its own mess. I'm only here to keep an eye on you, Drew, and Zed."

Zed was halfway across the room, looking out at the fountain.

"He's not talking to me," Oz said. "I told my dad about the skank he's been seeing."

The Emperor scowled. "Oz."

"Well, she is. He can do better."

"Perhaps. Has it occurred to you that he has not once criticized your relationship? He's not entirely comfortable with it, yet he reserves his opinion because you care about Drew."

"What, he has a problem with me?" Drew asked.

"Not with you. With the two of you together. He thinks of you as a brother, Andrew. It's taking him some time to reconcile that with the idea that you may very well one day marry his sister." To Oz he said, "Allow him his mistakes, if she truly is one."

Oz had a lot more to say, but the Emperor picked up his bag and gestured to the table. "Drew, you'll be seated on the corner to the right of the King, next to your mother and father. Be sure to take the chair closest to him, and keep your mother in between you and your father. Keep anything she can use as a weapon out of her reach—her visceral reaction to last night was to geld the First Minister on the conference table, san anesthesia."

"Maybe we should let her," Oz said.

"Richard offered to hold him down. Nevertheless, it wouldn't take much to set her off again. The only thing preventing bloodshed is Jax's determination to end this soon."

Drew was a little surprised. "I didn't think my mom had that in her."

"She has it in her. Oz, you'll sit to the left of your mother, in the first chair. Supplies will be at that corner of the table, and if anyone needs something, hand it to me first. Whatever you do, don't let Drew's mother grab any of the pens, paperclips, and especially not the stapler. Zed will be seated next to you."

"Is Mom up to this?" Oz asked.

He grinned, and it was his evil, this-will-be-so-much-fun grin. "If given the chance, she will chew him up and spit him out. Don't worry about her. I'll be standing just behind her, to her left. You'll be able to see me in your peripheral vision." He reached into his pocket and pulled out his thin, black gloves and began to slide one over his right hand. "Just in case," he said when Oz looked puzzled. "Also as a courtesy to your mother. If I need to touch her—"

"Yeah, she touches you all the time now."

"Indeed. Privately. This is for propriety. I am a non-related male, and I should not make skin contact with her in public. When you marry Drew, I'll do the same for you."

"Not bloody likely," Oz said. "And as far as the world is concerned now, we *are* related. You're legally a member of this house, and Dad has formally announced you as his brother. You're my uncle, and you can touch me."

"All right," he conceded. "But I am still not considered to be a blood relative of the Queen, and I will not break protocol to make a point today. I want the First Minister and his son to see me as the wall between the Queen and themselves, and undue familiarity—"

"God, I hate it when you start talking like a history teacher."

"Fine," he sighed. "It's habit."

"The babbling is just distraction from the jerkoffs we have to play nice with today," Drew said. He reached for her hand, and they went over to the table. I followed because he still had one end of the leash and hadn't unclipped it from my collar.

The table was perfectly square, so that there was no discernable head, but the King had staked out his spot, which was in front of the gallery of witnesses—they'd put a bunch of theater seats on a pedestal that had levels, and it was for the heads of state from other countries—which effectively and intentionally put him at the head.

Levi Munson realized this, too, and grumbled though he didn't complain.

When everyone was there and Shazia Van Hoff had mentally incinerated the First Minister with her best death glare, the King bent over and unclipped my leash, and then set me on the table.

Oz's eyes went wide, but she didn't say anything, and no one was more surprised than I.

I suspected he wanted me there so that the Queen could reach out and pet me if she got stressed, even though she seemed fine, and Drew's mother couldn't resist leaning over the table to scratch behind me ears, squealing, "Mister Wick!" when she did.

Minister Munson was not amused.

I get it. I'm here to piss people off.

Before everyone sat—they stood by their chairs, waiting for the King—Redmond Munson cleared his throat. "Before we begin, Father, if I may?"

Munson scowled, but nodded consent.

"Jackson, I don't fully understand why Isaac Young attacked your children last night, but I was witness to it and they did nothing to provoke him. All they were doing was walking down the street. If

I had known he was armed, I would have stopped him from crossing toward them in the first place, and I'm sorry I wasn't paying close enough attention. I hope his actions won't adversely affect the negotiations."

Pointedly, Jax asked, "Are you here to negotiate in good faith?"

The First Minister remained irritated. "I'm here."

Redmond was more congenial. "We are. And please, accept my personal apology."

Jax nodded. "I offer my condolences." He gestured to the table, and sat down without offering an apology for their loss. Then without any opening, he looked at the First Minister and said bluntly, "What is it you want, Levi?"

His eyes flicked toward the Queen. "Kansas."

Shazia leaned forward to look past her husband. "No. Absolutely not."

When he ignored her, Jax said, "I remind you, Minister, that she is the Queen of Midlam and you must deal with her."

"I'll deal with her Consort. Or the boy."

Richard put his hands up and said, "Hey, I'm just here for support."

Drew opened his mouth, but Oz shook her head the way the Emperor did, very slightly, just enough to get her point across.

"Why Kansas?" Jax asked. "What possible reason could you have for wanting a piece of land in the heart of another country?"

"We want it, plain and simple."

Aubrey touched Jax's hand. "The Church of Florida believes that Kansas is where the Garden of Eden existed. It's a holy place to the faithful, and they also consider it to be a new Jerusalem, a place to which an official pilgrimage would eventually be made by the church's apostles and its elite. It's been a long-held belief that if a temple is built there, it will usher in the end of times."

Shazia jumped to her feet. "Are you insane? You laid waste to Chicago and killed thousands of people, and it never occurred to you to *ask* if you could build a temple in Kansas? That perhaps we would have been open to the idea because we accept *all* religions? Others have built temples in Midlam, yet your first move was to declare war?" She leaned over the table and reached for the stapler that was between Oz and the Queen; Oz snatched it up and pulled it back, but she was clearly trying to not grin when Shazia sputtered, "Just let me have it and I swear to God I will staple that bastard's eyelids to his eyeballs."

The Minister was clearly taken aback and heard every word, but he fixed his gaze on Jax and repeated, "We want Kansas."

"That's logistical idiocy, Levi. The closest border in common with Midlam is Kentucky southward to Arkansas."

He simply shrugged.

"Consider an outright purchase of the land on which you want to build the temple. Your needs can easily be met without Midlam giving up their land, and without inciting further violence."

Redmond Munson was clearly uncomfortable, staring at me instead of looking at anyone else. His finger began to tap softly on the table top, an invitation, and since no one else had a hand on me, I got up and went to his end of the table. The First Minister was annoyed, but Redmond was happy and asked me if it was all right to pet my head.

There was no chance he was going to do anything to me with so many guards in the room, so I stuck my head under his hand, and let him scratch behind my ears.

I barely listened to the others, because it was nothing but arguing; Florida wanted Kansas, Midlam wasn't giving it up. Florida refused to consider a land purchase, Jax refused to consider any other option. Shazia still wanted the damned stapler but Oz pointedly handed it to the Emperor, who set it far out of her reach. Drew proposed an embassy of sorts with enough land to accommodate all those already in Kansas, but the Minister wanted none of it.

He wanted the entire state. The value it held for his church outweighed any needs Midlam had; it was too important to give up any part of, and he was not going to cave in. He wanted it all, and in exchange for that, he would pull every member of his military out of Midlam. But that was all he was willing to do.

I was about to go back to the happy end of the table when his phone beeped. He looked at it and excused himself, saying he had to take it, and when Levi was out of earshot, Redmond Munson leaned forward and began whispering to me, talking as fast as he could.

"I know you're bugged somehow, otherwise you wouldn't be here, so whoever is listening...I learned early this morning that Isaac was meant to kill Prince Andrew, and someone else will try again. There's a bounty on him. My father doesn't just want Kansas, he wants all of Midlam, and he sees the loss of Andrew as his gateway in. He'll kill Oz to get to him, and he doesn't care that she's his granddaughter. I wouldn't be at all surprised if he's planning to attack them again by the end of the day, and it's likely to be attempted with firearms. Long range sniper is my best guess. Isaac had been trying to secure a laser rifle and someone else may have been successful. If you're not certain about my honesty, ask my sister. She'll know I'm telling the truth."

He sat up then, and realized she was looking right at him.

I went back to her, just in case.

"How is she?" Aubrey asked him.

"Same. Well enough, I suppose, but very tired."

"And you? Married? Kids?"

He nodded. "Four girls. And I promise you, it hasn't been the same for them. He's never alone with them. He barely acknowledges them."

She glanced up to see if the First Minister was done. "Have you been anointed?"

"Several years ago. When he's gone, I'll head the church. There will be changes. Freedom. As much equality as I can manage, but the will of the apostles will be difficult to bend."

She smiled softly, and reached out to pet me. I know she wanted to talk to him longer, but the First Minister had ended his call and was heading back to the table.

"We need to break," he said. "Isaac's body has been released from your morgue, and we need to pray over it before sending him home. You understand."

Jax stood up. "Yes, I do. We'll meet again tomorrow, same time. And please consider Midlam's offer, Minister. I don't think it will improve."

As Levi and Redmond Munson left, the witnesses in the gallery began talking amongst themselves, some filing out, others filtering over to the window to look at the fountain and discuss the too-brief meeting. The Emperor knelt next to the table; if anyone was watching, it looked as if he were being briefed by the King, though it was me he listened to.

I told him everything Redmond had said, as quickly as I could.

Before I was completely done, he stood sharply and said to Jax, "A word with you and the Queen. Now." They went to the far side of the room, away from everyone, and she kept glancing back at us. After a moment, I saw her mouth the words, "Yes. He's the brother who saved me."

Without waiting to see if they followed, the Emperor stomped back to the table, signaling everyone to get up. He ordered the guards to surround us—Oz, Drew, Zed, and me—and escort us to the car waiting out front. They were to stop for no one, and were to make sure that we got into the family's building and then upstairs. We could wait in the living room, but there had to be a guard with us at all times.

"One on the balcony, one at the head of the stairs on each floor, one at the elevator on each floor. I want guards posted at every entry to the building, including the roof. No one gets near them other than myself or their parents."

He didn't need to tell them what would happen if someone did get to them. Last night's guard was forced to resign, but if it happened again, the repercussions would be severe.

Oz held me close the entire ride home and didn't let go until we were safely in the living room. They did as they were told, and sat on the sofa to wait; I ran to the litterbox because I had a nasty feeling it might be my last chance for a while, and wanted to suggest they do the same, but even if they could understand, they were too worried to hear.

Zed grumbled that he suspected his lunch date was off, but that was the only thing anyone said until their parents came out of the elevator fifteen minutes later. The Emperor ran up the stairs; he had changed into jeans and a sweatshirt and was almost out of breath.

"Do you have a grab bag prepared?" he asked Drew.

"Always."

"Get it, change your clothes—jeans, t-shirt, and sweatshirt—and wait for us in your apartment." When his parents flinched, he said, "Go with him, help him grab anything extra, underwear, socks, and things that are light and fit in his bag, and take a few minutes to say goodbye."

Drew did what he said without question, but Oz jumped to her feet. "What?"

Jax stopped her from going after him. "Both of you, change quickly, and grab your bags, too. Take your computers and extra clothing. Just do it."

They ran toward their rooms, Aubrey right behind, muttering that she would make sure they took what they needed.

The King and the Emperor stood alone in the living room, and after a tense moment the Emperor said, "With my life, Jax."

He nodded, and then went to the hall closet to get another bag. It was mine, filled with cans of food and treats, and he said, "You know you have to take him. There's no telling how long you'll be gone and you've never been able to handle more than two weeks away from him without feeling ill."

The Emperor took the bag.

"Go get your things," Jax said. "We'll meet outside your apartment in five minutes."

*

We rode the elevator down to the pool level; I only knew of one other room near it, and that was the restroom. The King guided us toward the far side of the pool, where he flipped open an electrical panel, then pulled on the metal part where all the wires hung, exposing a keypad. He punched a bunch of numbers in, and a piece of the wall to the right of the panel slid open and revealed another elevator. We rode that down for what felt like a good six floors but could have been more, and when the door opened we stepped out into a loud, massive room that had at least thirty video monitors on the far wall, and as many tables with computers stretched out in front of us.

General Myers was there in uniform, and every other person in the room was wearing the same thing. Dark blue pants with a wide red stripe. Crisp, white dress shirts. Shiny things pinned to chests and shoulders. Few even bothered to glance up, and no one reacted to the presence of the King. He was not a big deal, not in there.

"War room," Jax said, leading the kids across the ugly green carpet. He took them along the back wall, trying to shield them from the images on the monitors, but there was no mistaking what we saw: Chicago in ruins, overrun with military, and the muted sound of gunfire.

I wanted to know if that was old footage or a live feed, but the Emperor was too far ahead and I couldn't ask him.

He took us into a transportation bay, where there was a car waiting that was different than any other I'd been in before. It wasn't an air car and it looked quite a bit like a hover car, but there was more space inside and its seats were lined up against the walls. The Emperor stood near the open door, tossing the bags to a guard inside who strapped everything down and then left, and while the King and Queen were telling the kids goodbye he buckled me into a clear plastic box near the center, where I could see right out the door.

Aubrey hugged each of them and kissed them over and over, telling them she loved them—even Drew, who seemed like he didn't want to let go. After a minute, Jax told her they had to leave, and he held her hand as the kids buckled into their seats. The Emperor didn't even look back, he just jumped into the driver's seat and started flipping switches on the dashboard.

As the door slid shut, I saw Aubrey reach for him. My King was crying, and I couldn't stay there to purr for him.

8

The engine sent a buzz underneath us, and both Drew and Zed scrambled to tighten the straps that held them down into the seat. I hated the noise that filled the air; it hurt my ears and I had no way to bury my head against someone to soften the sound. I wanted the door to slide back open, and I wanted to go to Jax to let him know everything would be all right.

I didn't get to promise him I would take care of everyone.

"He knows, Wick," the Emperor said.

A voice crackled through the speaker near his head, someone asking about our destination. He answered, "Denver Sands Hotel, Las Vegas," flipped another switch, and the car began moving. It picked up speed as it moved through the underground tube, until it was going so fast that the LEDs in the tunnel looked like twinkling Christmas lights. When we were going so fast that I thought we might wind up in Canada, he pushed a lever near his seat and we shot up and out into the sky, faster than I thought was possible in a hover car.

Slow down, dude. Lipstick tubes are not supposed to fly.

"You're fine, Wick," he said. "I know how to pilot a shuttle. I've been doing it since I was a little boy."

All right, so that solved one question. It was a shuttle. I'd never seen one and I'd never heard him talk about flying one before, so I wasn't as confident in his skills as he wanted me to be. I don't think

Zed or Drew were all that certain, either, since they both looked like they wanted to throw up. On the other hand, Oz leaned forward to watch clouds zip past the windshield, and wasn't at all bothered by the speed or how high up in the air we were.

When he flicked off the overhead speaker, she asked, "Where are we really going?"

"There's a safe house not too far from Denver. I'll keep you there until the negotiations are over and the First Minister is back in Florida."

"And at some point do we get to know what's going on?"

He glanced over his shoulder. "You can get up and move around if you like," he said. "We'll be there in about forty-five minutes."

"Emperor."

He explained what the Second Minister had told me; Drew was not the only one at risk, and the best course of action was to remove them all and take them someplace the First Minister couldn't get to. "This house is not known outside of the family and a few key members of the military and royal guard. Once the negotiations are over and the King gives me an all-clear, I'll take you home."

"Why me?" Zed asked. "I mean, I don't want anything to happen to them, but no one's after me."

"Levi Munson would have no issue with cutting out his own daughter's heart."

"He'd kill you to hurt Mom," Oz said.

"All right," Zed said. "But why Drew in the first place? There's nothing to gain by killing him."

"For essentially the same reasons," he answered. "Kill Drew, destroy his mother. Shazia is known to be somewhat mawkish and would crumble under the loss of her son. If she was given the chance to abdicate, Drew would be a much stronger leader, and the Minister would have no choice but to deal with him. Remove Drew from the equation, and she might surrender."

"If I'm dead, Carter—" He stopped, considering the possibilities. "They'd go after Carter."

Zed unbuckled his straps, and stretched a bit. "For a religious guy, Munson has no morals. Gotta wonder how Mom turned out so well."

"Presumably, her mother's influence," the Emperor said. "The First Minister couldn't be bothered to lower himself to dealing with a little girl."

"Unless it was to abuse her," Oz grumbled.

"How has Dad not taken the guy out?" Zed wanted to know.

"Your mother asked him not to."

They let that sink in. He wasn't saying so, but at some point that's exactly what Jax wanted to do: assassinate the First Minister of Florida.

"And you?" Oz prompted.

"She has requested that of me, as well. On multiple occasions."

Drew unbuckled, too. "I imagine in her mind that would relegate you to some level of Hell. She'd rather he lived than ask that of you."

"If Hell exists, I'm already headed there, Drew. His would not be the first life I've taken, and I expect it would not be the last."

"What?" Zed was surprised. "Seriously?"

"The man who attacked your mother in the plaza. He did not survive."

"Damn. You were only like sixteen or seventeen then, weren't you?"

"Eighteen. I had not intended to kick him as hard as I did, but…I had somewhat of an understanding of what Aubrey had been through, and even the suggestion that she would go through anything remotely like it again? The blow delivered was overkill, quite literally."

"Surely no one blamed you," Drew said.

"There was no blame. Considerable guilt, though." He put the shuttle on auto pilot, and spun his seat around. "Understand, from the time I could walk, the focus of my life was mostly about developing control. In that moment, I lacked any. He did not need to die, he only needed to be stopped. I allowed my feelings for her to get the better of me."

"What, you had a crush on Mom?" Zed asked, amused.

"No. But she was as close a friend to me as Jax."

Zed got up and leaned against the bulkhead, taking a quick look out the windshield. "Yeah, but…you met her first. Ever have the thought that maybe you wanted to ask her out? Beat your best friend to it?"

"Zed, he introduced Mom and Dad," Oz said.

"Indeed. And no, the thought honestly never entered my head. I met her, and knew she was perfect for Jax. Clearly, I was right."

"Yeah, but—"

"Celibacy is not something new to me," the Emperor told Zed. "Even if I had wanted to pursue her, it was not an option. But I honestly never considered it. I was firmly invested in getting her to meet my best friend."

"And this is where you leave it alone," Oz told her brother.

"All right. Yeah, I'm sorry. I wasn't thinking."

"You're allowed to ask questions of me," the Emperor said. "The things that were inappropriate when you were children are no longer off limits. If you delve into something too personal, I'll tell you."

Drew grabbed onto a sway bar overhead so that he could get closer to Oz. "All right, can I ask you something that isn't even about you?"

"You can ask. I won't necessarily answer."

"About my mom. Half of my brain has been occupied with why Florida bombed Chicago. Something you hinted at a few minutes ago—my mother can be a weak leader at times. Yet, she's very kind and I can't think of a single instance where a world leader other than the Minister has treated her as being less than what she is. She's sentimental, but she doesn't back down where someone else might, and she'll shout you down if she has a reason. I don't doubt that she would have used the stapler on his eyelids. She's tougher than I usually give her credit for."

The Emperor waited, letting Drew think out loud.

"Flip that over…she relies on Mr. B a lot, but doesn't always do what he suggests, and my dad helps her out all the time. I mean, just about every night, even if he's worked a fourteen-hour day, he sits down and reads the days' notes to her while she paces back and forth and repeats them, so that she can memorize every important detail. She can tell you every aspect of every contract, right down to the fine print, because she takes that time—"

He sat down, hard. The picture was forming in his head. "When I was little, the one thing I could count on was a bedtime story, every night. I couldn't count on anything else because of their schedules, but I knew that no matter what, one of them would tuck me in and tell me a story. My dad always let me pick a book and he read it to me a chapter at a time, but my mom…she always made up stories. She did it on the fly, too, and it was usually a great story, but she *never* read to me. I can't remember a single time. One time, Carter got really pissed off because he wanted her to read a chapter out of a book he got at school, and she wouldn't do it. Told him he needed to read that for himself. I didn't understand, because Dad did it all the time, even if it was for school. Her feelings were a little bit hurt, and I remember running across the hall to get her, to tell her that I wanted to hear her story even if he didn't. Carter was just a jerk."

"Well, yeah…" Zed muttered.

Drew looked up at the Emperor. "She can't read, can she? That's why she ran to Pacifica, and never answered my dad's texts. He never expected her to. He intended for her to just go and knew Mr. B would take her phone and then tell her where he was. That was the plan, wasn't it?"

"More or less," the Emperor told him. "Richard should have called her, or called Jax, but these were not expected circumstances."

"Why would she keep that a secret?" Zed asked.

"If you were the head of your country, would you want the masses to know that you're illiterate?" Oz said.

The Emperor held up a finger. "No. She is *not* illiterate. Drew, she's dyslexic and none of the usual treatments have worked. Reading is a chore that she can manage, but it takes tremendous effort to get through a simple paragraph. She's highly intelligent and can memorize things if she hears them. It is not a personal failing."

"But I would have helped her," he said. "If she'd let me know, I could have helped."

"And that is not a childhood she wished for you. Your father has always been there when she needed help the most. Your involvement wasn't necessary, though I suspect she would have told you sooner or later."

"Is it why Mr. B has had the bigger hand in Midlam's governing?"

"He is her most trusted advisor, but she makes the final decisions. Understand, they've known each other since they were infants. She knew she could trust him, even when they were children. He's known most of her secrets since they were old enough to talk."

"So, kinda like Oz and Drew," Zed said.

"Without the mutual attraction."

Zed snorted. "I wonder if Dad threw things at her the way Drew did Oz."

"Come on. I didn't just throw things at Oz. I threw things at everyone."

The Emperor turned his seat around and resumed control of the shuttle. "He did tell me they had an actual fight once. There was kicking and punching, and it ended when she bit him. He still has the scar on his shoulder. So all things considered, Drew's penchant for throwing water balloons and rubber balls seems rather tame."

He was looking out the windshield, peering so carefully that Zed leaned over to look, too.

"We're going to hit some rough weather in about a minute," he said. "We'll land in three minutes…strap in."

Zed stood up as the shuttle shifted, and he steadied himself by grabbing onto the sway bar Drew had been holding only a few minutes earlier. He was reaching for the shoulder strap on his seat when the shuttle took a hard push, and the air cracked around us, blinding-white light blanketing the windshield.

He crumbled, reaching out for something to grab onto as he fell, and his hand brushed the back of the Emperor's neck just before he lost consciousness and hit the floor.

"Stay put," the Emperor snapped when Oz started to unbuckle. "We were hit by lightning. Is he breathing?"

"I think so," she said.

"Then he's fine. Strap in, Andrew."

The nose of the shuttle dove sharply and seemed to pick up speed; the sky was suddenly gone from view and he was moving between trees, zipping back and forth, flying just above the ground. Drew closed his eyes, whispering a wish to not crash, and Oz was staring at Zed, counting each breath he took.

A minute later we came to a screaming halt inside a giant red barn, and Oz unbuckled and knelt next to Zed. The Emperor told her to hang on because we weren't done moving, and as the barn door slid closed behind us, the shuttle began to sink into the floor, lowering until we were at least twenty feet underground. When the shuttle stopped, there was a soft groan overhead as the barn floor closed back up.

Zed's eyes were open, but I don't think he was seeing anything yet.

He moaned and reached a hand up, flapping it around as he looked for something to hold onto. Oz grabbed it and told him to stay still; in a minute or so he would be all right.

"I'm fine," he muttered, though when he tried to sit up, he couldn't.

Drew helped him up, and when Zed couldn't bear his own weight, he picked Zed up, hoisting him over his shoulder. He was floppy weight that Drew struggled to stand with, and it didn't help when Zed started slapping the back of Drew's legs, begging to be put down. "Hit my ass, and I'm dropping you on your head," he grumbled when Zed slapped a third time.

Zed's head bounced off Drew's back as he walked across the garage. The Emperor punched numbers into a keypad on the garage wall to open the door into the underground bunker, and he told Drew to sit Zed upright on the sofa. He would be there as soon as he got me.

He pulled me out of the plastic carrier and told me to run before the door closed on my tail, and I told him he was a giant asterisk because he'd never really let that happen. Once he was inside, the door slid closed, and I couldn't tell there had even been an opening there.

It was massive; the room was a huge circle with brushed metal walls, and it was at least as big as the family apartment three times over. The Emperor described it like an old-style round clock; twelve o'clock was the kitchen; three o'clock was the living space; six o'clock was the garage, and nine o'clock was the communications and security system. The living area had a sofa and several floppy-looking comfy chairs, and there was a fake fireplace with a video monitor mounted over it. Next to that there was a kitchen and dining table, though it was sparse compared to the Queen's kitchen and it had cold metal countertops, and was not big at all. Across the giant circle from the living area there were several video monitors, and after he checked on Zed the Emperor went over and turned them all on, flipping switch after switch, until the panel of controls under them hummed to life with dozens of blinking lights. He checked each monitor and muttered to himself about needing to go outside to clean the camera lenses off, and then went back to check on Zed again.

I followed, not sure if I wanted to get too far from him. This place looked shiny but it smelled stale, and I wasn't sure something wouldn't pop up and eat me.

Zed was sitting upright, and swore he was fine. "Headache, maybe, but it's not too bad."

When he could stand, the Emperor showed them around. Just off the living area there was a community bedroom with a dozen bunkbeds, and there were three separate bathrooms. On the other side of the fireplace, between one and two o'clock, there was a gym; it had six treadmills, a boat that rowed to nowhere, and machines with weights that looked like they'd bite. There was also a large, empty floor space and in the corner a canvas bag hung from the ceiling; Oz lit up when she saw it.

After that, the Emperor took them over to the wall with the video monitors, and pulled up a picture of the place they were staying. Off the giant circle, which was in the center of the screen, there were long tunnels hidden behind the wall. He pointed to where each of them were, and told them how to access each one.

"The house is fully stocked and we have enough supplies that we could theoretically survive here for more than a year."

Drew groaned.

"No one expects that. But supplies are in this tunnel—" he pointed to a spot on the wall to the left of the monitor, at seven o'clock "—and I will periodically check to see what needs to be brought in. There are access tunnels at ten and eleven o'clock. And the one by which we entered leads up to the barn."

Oz was squinting at the picture. "How freaking long are those tunnels?"

"Several miles," he said. "They're intended as escape routes, but we can also use them for exercise. If you want to run in one, I can turn the lighting system on."

"How far under are we?" Drew asked.

"Deep enough to withstand nuclear impact. But not so deep that getting topside will be a chore. And we will be able to go up and outside. You're not stuck down here for the duration."

I have to pee.

Seriously. Like five minutes ago.

"Don't panic, Wick." He led me over to a spot just past the monitors; there was a little alcove, and behind the wall was a large, clean litterbox. "The litter might be a little stale, but it's self-cleaning. Use it, and five minutes later it turns itself on to scoop and your waste goes into the sewer system. I'll get fresh litter from the supplies in a little while."

I didn't care if it was fresh or not. I wasn't planning on sniffing or licking it. I was planning on drenching it.

When I was done, he was explaining the supply rotation. All food, even non-expired items, was replaced every six months. It might not taste great, but it was edible. He looked right at me and said, "You don't need to worry about food, Wick. If I run out of the cans that I brought, the types you like are also kept stocked here, and in an emergency, there are sealed foil pouches with generic cat food."

Nice to know you planned for me.

He pushed a button on the panel, and the door we'd come through re-opened. "Get your gear and stow it in the bedroom. When you're done, we'll contact your parents so that they know we made it here. They'll want to see you."

"You up to being seen, Zed?" Oz asked. "We can tell them you're in the bathroom horking up your toenails. Mom would believe that."

"Shut up," he said, poking at her arm. "But you can get my bag for me. I feel delicate right now."

He did look a little off, pale with little beads of sweat on his upper lip, but he held it together while talking to the King and Queen, and didn't need to sit down until after they had all promised to call again in the morning. As soon as the screen went dark, he stumbled to the sofa and sat back down.

"Nauseated?" the Emperor asked.

"Just the headache. It's not even all that bad."

The Emperor told Drew to open the first aid kit in the bathroom and find the pain meds. "You'll tell me if you feel worse," he said to Zed. "Anything. If the headache gets worse, or you feel like you want to throw up, I need to know."

"I only got hit by lightning, Emperor. No big deal."

Oz followed him to the kitchen when he went to get water for Zed. "His hand landed on you," she said in a near-whisper. "Is he really all right?"

He thought so. "He was too busy feeling all the electricity going through him to bother hearing anything rolling around in my head. Which, to be honest, was nothing but a lot of swearing at that point."

He watched to make sure Zed took the pills Drew handed him, and then headed back to the kitchen. He opened all the cupboards and pantry, checked the refrigerator, and then went into the supply tunnel. When he returned, he was carrying bags filled with white and black boxes, and announced that this was the food. Enjoy the beauty of generic and dehydrated meals.

Oz poked through the bags and began putting things away. "Are there staples?" she asked. "Like flour and sugar and stuff? I can make real bread if we have them."

"We do, and it would be appreciated. The bread-like product we have tastes more like stale pita shells and looks like a regurgitated graham cracker."

They wanted to know how he knew so much about the safe house and the food. While they fixed a late lunch together, he told them about his first full summer in this When, the year before he stayed forever. He was barely sixteen, and the old King decided that Jax not only needed to get to know the Emperor better, he needed to spend some time getting to know himself.

"So he sent us here, alone. We spent most of our time topside, but we explored every inch of this place. When things broke, we fixed them. When we were bored, we found new things to do. And when we discovered a cache of broken motorcycle parts in the barn...there are four working motorcycles stored in the barn. We rebuilt and repaired them, and I taught him to ride."

He'd come back a few times at the request of both the old King and Jax, so that someone remained familiar with all of the systems. Everything was maintained by the military, but in an emergency, someone needed to be able to operate it all.

"Well, that explains something I wondered about," Drew said while they were eating. "I was trying to figure out, like, why you? Why not send one of our mothers, or even my dad? I don't imagine any of them know this place inside out."

There was more to it; Aubrey was a necessary distraction in the negotiations, and there was no way to remove Shazia from them. She needed Richard's help, so he had to stay. "And there's the matter of my fealty. I am sworn to protect you all. Even you, Andrew, though I would do that regardless. Despite your childhood fears, I've never disliked you. You were simply fun to annoy."

"You *growled* at me, Emperor."

He thought for a moment and then said, "Will. Or William. All of you."

Drew shook his head. "I don't think I can. I'm not your equal, not yet."

Oz said, "I'm still planning on calling you Uncle Willie."

His Scottish spilled out as he sputtered, "You will not."

Zed laughed, but Oz leaned forward and said seriously, "But you are my uncle."

Softly, he agreed, "I am."

Holy hell, I'm gonna go barf in my box and then watch it clean itself.

She went on. "The title of Emperor is kind of like calling you 'Uncle' now, I think. I could easily call you Uncle Will, and I may someday, but there's something more about you being my Emperor."

Really, I will.

"Call me what you like," he said. "But there may come a time soon when it will be in my best interests to use my name. It might help to get used to it sooner rather than later."

"Can I ask something personal?" Drew asked. "Why does Finn call you Dash?"

"Because when he was a young man, an old Emperor told him that the dash etched into a tombstone was what mattered, not the years capped on either side of it. The dash was your life and everything in it, and the most important thing you would ever do. He remembered that and began calling me Dash when I was a baby, long before he knew who I would become."

"You're not old," Oz said. "You're closer to us in terms of life span than you are to our parents."

He jabbed his pointy finger at her. "If you tell me again that I'm a teenager."

She jabbed hers back. "You and Drew are both roughly at the twenty per cent mark in terms of years lived versus years expected. So…"

"Damn, Emperor, you'll probably outlive us all," Zed said.

That didn't make him happy. "That is not something I aspire to. Truly. I don't want to live longer than any of you. I already hate that I will likely outlive your parents. Don't make me consider losing you, too."

He looked sad, until Oz got up and took his empty plate from him. "I intend to have kids, and I want those kids to know their Uncle Will. And if I'm too old or feeble to get down on the floor and play with my grandkids, I want him to do it for me. We're not the end of the line, and there's a lot to look forward to."

"Wait. How many kids are we talking?" Drew blurted out, ignoring the Emperor's slight smile at the idea he would be around to see Oz's grandchildren. "I mean, I was getting used to the idea of them, but really. If we're having, like, a dozen, I need time to mentally prepare for that."

"Start with one," the Emperor said. "After that? Your second one might be a total surprise."

Like Zed? Wasn't he Aubrey's happy little accident?

Zed signed hard, looked at me, and said, "I'm pretty sure I was just dissed by the cat."

Oz started taking up all the empty plates from the table, and assured him that I had, in fact, dissed him. She was going to do all the dishes, until Drew got up to help her and said that they needed to come up with a chart or something, to divide up the chores. It all sounded a little too domestic, so I went to the living area and curled up on the sofa to take a nap, and fell asleep to the sound of them all laughing, and was glad that for now, at least, they were all safe.

9

On the first night, the Emperor warned them that staying at the safe house would feel a lot like punishment and perhaps at times like prison. He allowed them glimpses of above ground on the video monitors while he checked each camera, and promised that in a few days he would take them up top and let them explore, but he didn't want anyone leaving the safety of the underground bunker until he was sure that there was no one wandering around the cabin that sat directly on top of them.

They were allowed Internet access, although he told them to refrain from contacting their friends, and they were allowed to watch pre-recorded videos and entertainment broadcasts; he promised unfettered access to everything soon, including email with friends, when he was convinced the lines were as secure as they were supposed to be.

Drew wanted to know how that could be done; he could generally pinpoint someone's location online using only his phone, and given a computer with minimum hardware, he could even turn on their system cameras. "I once outed my parents. They were supposed to be at this retirement thing for a guy my dad worked with, but I located them at the Hilton halfway across town. Bridal suite, even. Mom's still embarrassed because I turned her phone on and started making these really loud kissing sounds."

"How old were you?" Oz asked.

"Thirteen? It seemed really funny then. Not that I wouldn't do it now, but at least I'd apologize after."

"Trust, me," the Emperor said. "Your father was amused. In any case, the lines run through the tunnels and data is pinged off a thousand different relays and proxy servers. If someone does try to find you through your Internet presence, everything will point to Las Vegas."

Zed snorted. "The mythological Denver Sands Hotel?"

"The hotel is real," Oz told him. "It's off the beaten path, though. We all stayed there for a couple of weeks when we were little—you were too young to remember it, but Drew dumped a glass of milk down my shirt during dinner on our last night there and his dad dragged him out of the restaurant screaming his head off. I still don't know why he did it."

Drew shrugged. "Boobs. Milk. It made sense to me then but I was only, like, six."

"So what?" Zed asked. "You were trying to inflate them for her?"

"I was trying to help."

"Big help there," Oz said. "Anyway, I think the only ones who can use it are family and guests."

"Any head of state can stay there," the Emperor said. "It's meant to be a refuge of sorts, where world leaders can send their families for media-free vacations. Technically, even Levi Munson would be welcome, although the moral aspect of Las Vegas has kept anyone from Florida from visiting."

Zed snorted again. "How is a hotel in the desert amoral?"

"Gambling. Alcohol."

"Hookers," Drew added.

"Wait, that's legal?" Zed asked. "Really? Can we go to Vegas?"

I wasn't sure if he was serious, and judging by the Emperor's half-raised eyebrow, he wasn't certain, either.

By the end of the fourth day, they'd fallen into a routine of sorts. Zed drew up a schedule of chores and they took turns cooking and cleaning up after meals. Drew learned to sort-of clean a bathroom—and felt bad because he'd never had to growing up, and now wondered who had kept his clean when he was staying in the guest room—because on the third day Oz declared that they were each responsible for a single bathroom; she was not using one after those two animals, so they each chose one to use and keep clean. She agreed to share one with the Emperor because he wasn't gross and disgusting and didn't leave behind evidence of his inappropriately long showers.

Yeah, he just cleans up after himself.

Mornings were spent in the gym, because the Emperor wanted them to stay in shape. Oz didn't mind because it was part of her routine anyway, and Drew liked playing with the weight machines that could bite, but Zed was not happy and spent his time walking slowly on the treadmill, grumbling about his long march to nowhere.

"I don't even have to take phys ed this year. This really isn't fair."

The Emperor told him that he wanted company in his misery, and they all needed to stay in shape.

"Round is a shape," Zed offered.

Afternoons—without any planning, it just seemed to happen—they spent studying. Zed accessed his school work online, and both Oz and Drew decided to follow his lead. They found free classes on the Internet and began doing the coursework. While they studied, the Emperor perused the security cameras or read books on his tablet.

They weren't bored yet, but I could feel it sneaking up on them. Only four days in Zed had a hard time focusing on his work, interrupting Oz and Drew as they tried to make sense of chemistry and classic literature, and disrupting the Emperor as he sunk into the history of cheese.

All right, I don't know if that's what he was reading. But it seemed like something he would read, just to have something to read, and I really wanted cheese.

After Zed's fifth interruption in half an hour—he wanted to know if there was any real world value to understanding Shakespeare's mistress-mocking poetry—the Emperor set his tablet aside and turned the news on. Cheese could wait until Zed was less bored. He flipped through channels until he found the San Francisco feed, which put any further studying at a grinding halt when the giant talking head started with a story about the negotiations.

It didn't look to me like things were going well. There was video footage of the First Minister leaving the building in a huff, stomping from the doorway to his car, and he was shouting at Redmond, who was scrambling behind him. The head reported that King Jackson and Queen Shazia had not left the building even hours later, while Queen Aubrey had left early in the afternoon but returned an hour later carrying a plain brown paper bag.

When the news anchor speculated that he thought that particular choice carried the Queen's stance against extravagance and indulgence a bit too far, the Emperor laughed.

"What the hell does that even mean?" Drew asked.

Oz was amused, too. "Mom and Dad have been pseudo-criticized for being really un-royal-like when it comes to spending the country's money on clothes and expensive accessories. It's tongue-in-cheek. There was a story in the Chronicle a few years ago swearing she would use a brown paper bag before she would spend the same five thousand on a purse that the Texas Governor's wife just had."

"And the people are fully aware that their King and Queen don't spend state funds on personal items," the Emperor added. "That was a jab at Texas and New England, possibly France as well."

"You know damn well Mom went home and made lunch for everyone, and that's what's in the bag," Zed said. "Order out? Why would we order out when there's perfectly good bologna and cheese in the refrigerator at home?"

Do we have bologna? I could go for some bologna.

"I would not be the least bit surprised if your mother fed bologna sandwiches to world dignitaries," the Emperor said. "She once horrified your grandmother by making grilled cheese and tomato soup for the German Chancellor and his family. They were thrilled. Finally, someone who understood that they were probably tired of being fed so-called authentic German food in other countries."

"I think I remember that," Oz said.

"You were fairly young. It was just before your grandfather retired. As I recall, he was just as happy because he hadn't had grilled cheese in years."

"The kids asked for more. I think she made like thirty grilled cheese and a gallon of soup that day."

"And she loved every minute of it," the Emperor said.

Drew's attention had turned back to the news. The reporters were speculating about what was going on in the old Hyatt if the First Minister was no longer there. Negotiations were effectively over, so what sort of contingency could they be working on?

"Do you have any idea?" he asked the Emperor.

"I have an educated guess. But don't worry—the King has a vested interest in both avoiding war and making sure you don't ascend the throne before you're ready."

"Or ever," Drew said.

The Emperor turned the monitor off. He leaned forward in his chair, and he considered what he wanted to say before he said it. "The plans you and Oz made included the idea that you would eventually become King of Midlam. Am I correct?"

"Yeah, but she would be in charge."

"You understand that there might be a great many years between your coronation and hers?"

That stumped him.

"I just assumed she would be first. I don't know why."

"And how exactly did you intend to merge Midlam and Pacifica?"

Drew had no idea.

"It requires an heir," Oz said. "We die or step down, our heir then takes both countries. I admit, it hasn't been a well thought out plan. We've just been trying to get to the part where we make a formal commitment to each other."

"You realize it could be a very long time before your parents either die or abdicate? You'll likely be married with kids for years before that happens."

"Unless my mom goes off the rails," Drew muttered.

Oz was more positive. "You mean we might get years together first? Time to have kids and get them mostly raised before we have to actually grow up? That sounds perfect to me."

"And you realize your father may not abdicate, ever? There is the possibility that he will hold onto the throne, and then outlive you."

"Well, hell," Drew muttered. "I mean, that would be great, if he lived to be like a hundred and thirty. But I don't think my mom will hang on any longer than she has to. If this war doesn't do it, when I turn twenty-five…yeah, she'll quit."

"We've never looked at the bigger picture," Oz admitted.

"So?" Zed shrugged it off. "You get married, his mom quits, and you become the ruler behind the King. Or co-rulers, whatever. As long as Dad is around, he'll make sure you don't bankrupt the country."

"Like he does my mom?" Drew asked.

"Don't get ahead of yourselves," the Emperor said. "Let's get through this first. I just want you to consider the direction you're going. Look at it from every angle, including the one where neither of you ever takes the crown."

"I could live with that," Oz said. "Become a teacher like Mom, never having to worry about leaving behind a job I love because I was born into one I might not? Huh. Why is it just now occurring to me that that's what I'd like to do?"

"Because now you have to think about it," Drew said. "But you're a step ahead of me because I don't really know. I don't even know how to get a regular job."

"Don't ask me," the Emperor said. "I basically get paid for babysitting the King."

"Any chance Carter would make a play for the crown?" Zed asked. "If he sees a weakness in your mom, will he try to exploit it?"

Drew didn't think so. "Unless I'm dead, he wouldn't even think about it. And if we have kids before then, it's not even an option. Carter has never wanted to be the heir. I always thought it was because he just wanted to play his life away, but I'm wondering now if it was because he realized when he was really young that the job sucks."

"Yeah, he's playing," Oz said. "All his talk of joining the military? When the bombs hit, he was off backpacking through Europe and didn't bother coming home."

"Consider that he might not have had a choice," the Emperor said.

"And I'm in hiding," Drew added. "So yeah, I'm not blaming him. Not one bit."

10

On the fifth day, the Emperor released a dozen mosquito drones. He programmed them to fly around the perimeter of the cabin and then several miles out, sending back video footage as they moved over and through the forest. He was looking for signs of other people and on the seventh day decided they were safe enough to explore a bit, and told the kids they could go up top.

"However, if I tell you to go back inside, you do it without question or hesitation. Drop whatever you're doing, and get below. Quickly."

He went to the control system and punched a half dozen letters on the keyboard, and from the wall between the video monitor array and the kitchen a long staircase slid out, unfolding as it was released, and a door opened at the top. He led them upstairs and into the cabin; it was rustic and old and smelled like stale potato chips and sweat, but it looked more like home than the bunker did and they were thrilled to be in it.

Compared to the bunker it sat over, the cabin was tiny. The staircase opened into the kitchen, which was only a line of counter space with a stove, and there was a small refrigerator next to a shelf with canned food so old that it was covered in a layer of dust. It butted onto the living room—one sofa in front of a stone-trimmed fireplace—and off of that there was a bedroom.

There were windows near the door that led outside, and all I could see, past the cleared patch of land, were trees. It was nothing but pine trees, reaching as far into the sky as I could see from the window, and as the Emperor opened the door I realized I had never been this close to nature.

There are things in nature that eat cats.

I'd like to stay inside.

Drew scooped me up anyway, and carried me with him.

Thirty feet from the door there was a three-foot-tall wall made of rock and stone, and it stretched around both sides of the cabin as far as I could see. There was dead, crunchy grass between the door and the wall, and for nearly ten feet beyond it.

Drew set me on the flat top of the wall, and sat beside me.

They were all marveling at how beautiful it was; I was looking for predators.

This is prettier from inside.

"You can roll around in the grass if you want," the Emperor said to me.

It might bite me. No thank you.

"The rules," he said. "You don't come out here without telling me. No one ventures into those woods alone, and never more than a hundred feet or so from the cabin. Stay in my sightline. If I'm not up here with you, I'll be keeping an eye on you from downstairs. Take the time to run. The terrain will be beneficial, more so than the treadmill. But never get far. I don't care if you just want to play tag with the trees—if you can't make it back to the front door in thirty seconds, you've gone too far."

"What's off limits?" Oz asked.

"It will take too long to get back if you go to the sides of the cabin," he said. "Stick to the front for now. At least until I'm comfortable." He looked to Oz. "You know, on pleasant days, forms practice and sparring would be quite a bit nicer out here than in the gym."

That surprised her. "Practicing forms I get, but you want to spar with me?"

His head tilted a little to the left as he considered it. "We don't have protective gear, but I promise light contact from my end. It's something we should engage in to keep your skills sharp. I may be rusty, but you need someone to fight with."

"Are you ready for that kind of touching?"

"With you, yes."

Drew chuckled. "Hell, I'll touch you if it will help."

"Perhaps," he said. "How well do you fight?"

He twitched. "Uh, no, I'll leave the fighting to Oz. My skills include not being able to kick my way out of a wet paper bag."

"You should know some basic self-defense techniques. Now is the time to learn."

"Like, right now?" Drew squeaked.

"Tomorrow, I think. Stretch your legs and explore a bit for the moment."

Big, brave Drew.

Drew and Zed took off, running into the forest, but Oz sat next to the Emperor on the top of the wall. "You know, not that long ago I had this odd dream about a boy in a dojo. He'd just mopped the floor with three other kids and then he cleaned his instructor's clock. That was you, wasn't it? I don't know how, but it was you."

She remembers. You have to be honest now.

She'd become curious about him, and went through portals to snoop in his past. She was trying to understand the Emperor, and he wanted to stop her. While she slept he'd touched her forehead, planting into her mind a few glimpses from his childhood, hoping she would understand and not feel as pressed to stalk his younger self.

He explained it to her, and then said, "So yes, I was the boy in the dojo. When my parents realized my life consisted mostly of torment at the hands of other children, they allowed me to begin training to defend myself. I studied three different art forms, from shortly after my fourth birthday until I left home."

"What rank were you when you left?"

"Rank is irrelevant. It's a stripe on a belt and has nothing to do with skill. Consider how many competitors you fought with in tournaments who had half the skills you did. In most of your matches, you might have both been black belts, but only one of you earned it."

"Come on. I saw a thirteen, maybe fourteen-year-old kid with four stripes, and that doesn't happen in any martial art that I know of."

He sighed, giving in. "Sixth in both Goju Ryu and Shorin Ryu, and fifth in Taekwondo. But realize, they were honorary ranks. I met neither the age nor time in training requirements. I simply passed the tests as I was encouraged to attempt them and was gifted the belts. There are no official rank certificates with my name on them. Truly, I am not a fan of the ranking system."

"Oh my God, you're going to destroy me."

"Oz. Your skills are formidable, and you can hold your own, but I want to push your abilities. I want you to be able to fight in real-world conditions, something the tournament floor does not give you."

"This is going to hurt," she groaned.

"Indeed. So for now, go explore with your brother and Drew. Just stay where I can see you."

She headed off, and he pulled me onto his lap. "How long can I protect them, Wick?"

Until your last breath, I imagine. No point in worrying about it.

"What should I worry about, then?"

Dinner. I don't suppose there's any shrimp here.

"Sorry, no."

Damn. We really are being punished, aren't we?

"Indeed."

*

When they woke up the next morning, first Oz and then Drew and Zed, the door at the top of the staircase was already open. Oz peeked into the gym, looking for the Emperor, and then they all went upstairs to find him.

I had nothing better to do. I followed, reasoning that I would probably be safe sitting on the wall, and if I ran fast enough from the door I could get over the grass before anything could rise up from the depths and take a bite out of me. There was always a chance that birds would notice me, but they weren't the city pigeons I sometimes chased, so I didn't think they had a grudge. There was no reason to worry that any of them would try to grab me and fly off.

The Emperor was outside, on the far side of the rock wall. He was wearing shorts and a sweat-soaked white t-shirt, and was flailing around like a swarm of bugs was trying to bite him in unpleasant areas of his body. Oz saw him through the window and said he was practicing a kata; I'd never heard pest avoidance described like that, but whatever.

The bugs were winning.

There was a note taped to the door: *breakfast is on the table. Eat first, and bring water with you.* On the table there was a platter with squished-up muffins, and Zed grumbled about the mutilated consistency of the reconstituted food they had to eat, but that didn't stop him from shoving four of them down his throat.

They watched the Emperor through the window as they ate, and when he jumped in the air and executed a round kick at his own head height, Drew groaned, "He's going to kick my ass."

"No worries," Oz said. "You'll get to sit there and watch while he kicks mine."

"And I'm fine with that."

"Me, too," Zed said around a wad of half-chewed muffin.

When Oz opened the door I bolted for the wall, making the jump before anything could bite. The Emperor stopped what he was doing in mid-punch; he was dripping with sweat even though the air was chilly, and his t-shirt was so wet his tattoos could be seen through it.

Oz was itching to get a good look at them, and she had her chance when he peeled it off and tossed it onto the top of the wall, but then he asked if she was ready to start.

"Not really, but let's do it anyway."

He instructed Zed and Drew to sit on the wall and observe, and to keep an eye on me. If I got too hot and was too stubborn to do anything about it myself, they were to take me back inside and shut the door.

Not gonna happen, but okay.

"Hit and kick as hard as you want," he said to Oz. "And leave your shoes on."

"Are you sure you don't want to put your shirt back on? If we wind up grappling, that's a lot of exposed skin."

"If you get that close, I deserve whatever you can do to me. And you'll have to deal with my skin being sweat-slick."

"Fine." She grabbed the tail of her shirt and pulled it over her head. "Two can play that game."

"Damn, Oz," Zed said. "You can't be out here in just your underwear."

"Sports bra, moron," she said. "Not a big deal."

If it were a big deal, the Emperor would have said so. Drew probably thought it was a big deal, but there was no way he was asking her to put her shirt back on. She looked at him with a "Well?" expression and he shrugged.

When Drew didn't object, she turned to the Emperor. "How do you want to start? Formally? I bow, you bow?"

He closed the distance between them and punched her in the face.

"Hold nothing back," he said. "As hard as you can." He popped her again. "No rules. All shots count."

She kicked at him, and he blocked it.

"Face, head, legs, all fair targets. Groin. I'm not wearing a cup. If you nail me, it's my own fault."

She had her target, and began fighting him in earnest. They moved furiously; she threw punch after punch, only to be pushed back. She kicked, but couldn't get inside the length of his legs. She dropped to the ground and tried to sweep him, but he jumped and caught her in the back of the head with his foot before he landed.

For twenty minutes they flew at each other, and the more they sweated the sicker the sounds of every bit of contact became. Every punch he landed on her came with a resounding splat, and sweat flew off them, pinging onto my furs. Drew muttered to Zed that it looked vicious, and Zed agreed, wondering why the Emperor wasn't giving her a chance. She hadn't landed a single punch, and the closest she came to getting him with a kick was when he blocked her with his leg.

She refused to back off and fought harder, until she suddenly called for a break and ran to the rock wall, bending over it as she vomited her breakfast onto the grass.

When she was done heaving, Drew offered her a water bottle, and asked if she was all right.

"I'll live," she said, sitting next to him.

"What did you learn?" the Emperor asked. He was barely breathing hard, but the sweat was pouring off of him.

"I'm telegraphing," she said. "I can feel myself doing it but I can't seem to stop. I drop my shoulder just before I punch, and you catch it every time. I twitch before I kick. And I can't do anything as fast as you can block."

"What do you intend to do?"

She swallowed a mouthful of water, and then got back up. "Fight until I fix it."

*

Nearly an hour later, after Drew moved me to the shade on the other side of the wall and made me drink water from his hand, the Emperor decided that Oz needed to stop. She argued that she was fine and could continue, but he wanted her to be able to move in the morning, and at the rate she was fighting, that was not likely. He told her to sit and rest while he showed Drew and Zed some basic techniques, and to watch them so that she would be able to help correct their mistakes.

"You know, this is going to make Drew afraid of you all over again."

He grinned. "There's always an upside."

As she passed him on her way to sit at the wall, she tried to backhand him in the stomach. He caught her wrist and put her in an arm lock. "Nice try."

She sat on the ground using the wall as a backrest, and I went over to sit with her. She was focused on what they were doing, watching until she realized they would learn a lot quicker if their mistakes could be corrected by repositioning their bodies, something the Emperor wasn't ready to do. After drinking most of a bottle of water, she got back up to help them.

Oz had already seen inside his head, and while she'd pushed all of his memories into the back of her mind, refusing to look at them, he didn't feel as if he had anything to hide from her. He was comfortable touching her and was learning to not look into her thoughts. He wasn't ready to try that with Zed or with Drew unless he had to.

Oz grabbed their legs to show them how to chamber their kicks, and she held their arms while they learned the proper way to punch. The Emperor decided what they would do and demonstrated; Oz made sure they did it correctly.

When the sun was directly overhead, the Emperor told them they'd done enough. They could go down below and shower, and he would make lunch.

Zed ran to the cabin, but Drew and Oz were slower to go in. As they got to the door, the Emperor called out, "And I meant separately."

You like to embarrass Drew, don't you?

"Little bit, yeah."

He probably wasn't even thinking about that until you said it.

"He probably was, a little bit."

Now that's all he'll think about.

"Then my job is done."

He picked his shirt up from the wall and slung it over his shoulder, and headed for the cabin.

What would you do if you actually caught them in there together?

He closed the door behind me. "Not a thing, Mister Wick."

The King wouldn't like that.

"Ah," he said, picking me up to carry me downstairs, "Jax would be uncomfortable, but I know his mind on this. I'm to leave them alone, to do whatever they will. As long as they're private about it, it's none of my business."

I wondered if he'd paid attention to the layout of the bunker.

If those two got busy, it was going to be everyone's business.

*

By the time she was done showering and had helped get lunch together, Oz already had bruises forming. Her right cheek was puffy and the left side of her chin was bright red. Her forearms were pocked with marks where the Emperor's punches had landed, and I imagined the rest of her body didn't look much different.

She moved like everything hurt, but she wasn't complaining about it.

The Emperor gave her pain pills with lunch, and told her to take them whether she wanted to or not. he said. "I know you can handle the discomfort. This is for the inflammation,"

Zed and Drew both looked like they wanted naps, but with Oz not complaining about being tired and the Emperor looking like he'd done nothing more than take a brisk walk, neither was willing to cave into the fatigue.

When they were done with lunch, Drew cleared the table and Oz sat back, looking at the Emperor. After a moment she said, "All right, I realize this is incredibly impolite of me, but I want to see the tattoos."

"I spend the morning shirtless," he pointed out.

"And I was too busy to get a good look. You have a couple of guys flying on your chest, and faces on your ribs, but I couldn't figure out what they were."

"All right." He peeled his shirt off, and stood up. Etched across his entire upper torso, were two men with wings, bare chested and wearing sheets for pants. On his right ribs there were two faces, and on his left, two crowns with tiny footprints underneath. "Icarus and Daedalus," he said, gesturing to the biggest tattoo. "And if you're unaware of the myth, look it up."

"I remember it," Oz said. "I paid attention in class."

"My mother told me the story often when I was young. I think she wanted me to understand the price of hubris, so that I would weigh my abilities against my ego. I got this as a way to still hear her voice, when I knew it would be decades before I heard it again."

He turned so she could see the portraits. "I didn't want to forget their faces," he said.

"And this is why we could never see you shirtless," Oz guessed. "You didn't want us to know what Finn looked like."

He nodded. "The only photograph I took with me was one they'd taken soon after they married. I knew he would look the same, and I considered waiting to get this, but…"

"Your mom and dad. I get it. What about the crowns?"

"My best friends. Other than my parents, the people I loved most. The feet represent their children."

Zed got out of his chair to look. "Are those our actual footprints?"

"Taken right after you were born."

Without asking, Oz ran a finger over the bottom outline of the crowns and over the edges of the footprints. "It forms a heart. Was that intentional?"

"How could it be?" Drew asked. "If he got the crowns first, he had no way of knowing if you'd ever be born."

"Really, Drew?" She tried to not laugh. "*He* hasn't even been born yet."

"Oh. Right."

Oz realized she was still touching him, and stepped back. "I'm sorry. How did you even manage this? Tattoos require touching."

"Several rubber gloves between my artist and myself. He's very understanding, though he has no idea why." He put his shirt back on and dropped into a chair in the living area. "I must admit, in spite of believing I would be nearly dead by now, I left my back open for future work. I had a glimmer of hope that there would be more of my story to tell."

"Any idea what?" Zed asked.

"I'm not sure. But I've always hoped your children would be a part of it."

Oz and Drew sat on the sofa, and Drew said, "Man, you really want us to spawn."

"Indeed."

"Almost like you have a personal stake in it."

He tried to not smile. "Indeed."

11

After a while, the days began to blur together. In the morning everyone went outside and either practiced kicking and punching, or they ran. The Emperor took them into the supply tunnel and made them pick out boots and then made them run in the woods wearing those instead of sneakers, which made Zed whine about blisters, and then whine about how badly Drew's feet smelled every afternoon when he took them off.

In the afternoon, after they had studied, he made them spend more time in the gym; he sparred with Oz, who still had trouble landing a punch on him but was determined more than ever to kick him onto his asterisk, and he taught all of them beginner forms from one of his martial arts. Oz learned right along with them, because they were kata she had never seen, and that was one of her favorite things to do.

Drew didn't understand the point of them at first, but he watched while she practiced the kata that she'd learned when she trained at home and appreciated how fluid she was. He recognized the strength and grace of her skills, and decided it didn't matter if he understood any of it, he just wanted to be able to do them half as well as she did. On an afternoon when Zed gave up and sat against the wall to just watch, Oz helped Drew with a sequence he was struggling with—a low forward stance with a punch, then a fast front kick followed by a round kick and then a sidekick, without putting his foot down—and she told him to visualize what he was doing as being one half of a fight. He started over and as he moved she provided the counter to each technique; after several minutes his eyes lit up as he grasped the point of them.

"So it's not enough to just learn the moves," he said. "You have to figure out both sides of it. Kinda like math."

"A bit like math," the Emperor agreed. "There's a balance to be found. And now, I want you to spar with her."

"Wait. What? I'm not hitting her."

The Emperor moved to the side of their makeshift ring, and folded his arms. "Oz. Go ahead."

Before Drew could react, she tossed him over her hip onto the floor and had one knee at his throat. "Get up and fight. If you land a punch, good for you."

Wide-eyed, he scrambled up, raising his fists like a boxer. She slapped his thigh with a round kick and warned, "Guard, or next time it'll be your groin."

His answer to that was to run. He circled the perimeter of the ring, backing away from her, until the Emperor shoved him back to the center. The shock of being touched by him made Drew drop his hands again, and Oz slid in to punch him in the face.

"Drew, hit back, or I swear I'll stop pulling punches."

He took a step back. "What? You're *not* hitting hard?"

Her answer was a sidekick to the chest that knocked him to the floor. The Emperor leaned over him and said, "She's barely hitting you. If she makes full contact, you will cry."

Struggling to get up, Drew grunted, "I might cry now."

They fought for ten more minutes, until Drew begged to stop. He was trying to catch his breath and could barely see for all the sweat that was running into his eyes. Oz didn't even ask the Emperor if they could stop; she kissed Drew on the tip of his sweat-shiny nose and told him to sit down for a bit to catch his breath, then to get on a treadmill.

She jumped onto one and turned it on, and within a couple of minutes was running at full speed.

I moved from my spot at the doorway and plopped down next to Drew as the Emperor left the gym. Whatever they were doing now, they didn't need him. Oz pounded away on the treadmill, and once he could breathe evenly, Drew told Zed, "I'll never be able to match her. I might be physically stronger, but she's faster and will always be a mile ahead."

"Yeah. I never realized how good she is. Sorry, man."

"Sorry, nothing. She can kick my ass. That's kind of hot."

Without missing a stride Oz called back, "I heard that."

"Stop listening," Drew said. "I have things to say about you."

She slapped the treadmill off to come sit next to me, and she leaned over to kiss him. "Keep practicing and paying attention, and one day you'll be as hot as I am."

"Yeah, but you'll just keep getting better, too, and you'll still be hotter."

"Oh my God," Zed groaned. "Stop it."

Dude, you haven't heard anything yet. Give them five minutes and you'll want to hurl.

"Fine, hot shot," Oz said. "What wonderful warm things do you say to Rhonda to get her going?"

He sighed, but then said, "Mostly just, hey, wanna do it?"

"Seriously?" Drew sputtered. "That works?" He looked at Oz. "That works?"

Zed muttered a couple things off the bad word list and got up, saying he didn't want to get in the middle of whatever weirdness they were about to start.

"I was just curious," Drew shouted after him.

"For the record," Oz said, "if we were anywhere other than here, it might work. Once. Maybe twice. I expect some effort on your part every now and then."

Offer her chocolate and a back rub. Sometimes that works for Jax.

"You know, the thought occurred to me that neither of us is actually in any danger. Your dad just wanted to torture us by throwing us together while having the Emperor supervise. Like, hey, you can be *this* close, but damned if you can really touch each other."

"I wouldn't put it past him. But we're alone now."

"Not exactly private. And sound carries. And we could get walked in on."

She leaned toward him, until their arms were touching. "I'm not suggesting we actually have sex here. But if you think about it, we've never really just made out. And we could get away with that."

"What if the Emperor walks in?"

"He'll do an about-face and walk right back out."

"So what are talking here? Just kissing? Second base?"

"Oh my God, Drew, are you negotiating this?"

"I just want to know upfront at what point you'll punch me in the nuts."

"Just kiss me, you moron. If my hand goes anywhere near your groin it won't be to punch you."

This is where I leave. You kids have fun.

I scrambled over Drew's legs before I wound up squished between them, and ran into the living room. The Emperor was stretched out on the sofa, reading, so I jumped to the back of the sofa and walked up near his head.

Don't go in there.

He peered over the top of his tablet. "The gym?"

Yeah. Touchy feely things are happening in there.

"Good for them."

They might miss dinner. Jax and Aubrey used to miss dinner all the time.

"I won't let them miss dinner, Wick. They'll smell it cooking before it's time to eat, and I'll call them in."

Zed came out of the bedroom with his computer and sat down in the chair near the sofa. When he opened the lid to turn it on, I warned him to stay out of the gym.

"What's he saying?" Zed asked.

"Telling you to stay out of the gym."

"Oh. Yeah. Dry humping in progress. No worries, Wick, I have no intention of going in there to witness him mauling my sister."

The Emperor had gone back to reading, but said, "Don't be so sure he's the one doing the mauling."

"Yeah, well, you'd think they could exercise a little self-control under the circumstances."

"I would argue that they're exhibiting an incredible amount of self-control. Let them have some time alone together. It doesn't hurt you at all."

"Sure. Like you wouldn't blow a gasket if you walked in there and Oz was straddling him, with her shirt thrown halfway across the room and his hands stuffed into her bra."

With a heavy sigh, the Emperor sat up and tossed his tablet onto the coffee table. "No, Zed, I would not. I would turn around and leave without a word. They have nowhere else to go, and I would never want to embarrass Oz."

"And Drew?"

"Oh, him I'll embarrass. I relish the opportunity."

Zed considered it, and said, "Fine. I'm cool with that."

He let it go, and began doing his school work; he asked the Emperor for help with alegbra, and was somewhat surprised when it was not anywhere near complex for him.

"My parents are physicists," he reminded Zed. "Math was practically a religion when I was growing up. Don't ask me to diagram a sentence, but this is easy enough for me."

Twenty minutes later, when he was done with the work for that class and sure that he had understood it, he told the Emperor that he should have been a teacher. He was better at explaining than any of the other teachers he'd ever had, and that included his best friend Jimmy's mother, Mrs. Okuda, who was now his algebra teacher. "Still not sure how she managed to have a dunce like Jimmy."

"He's your best friend, Zed."

"And I recognize that he's not especially bright. His mom is a terrific teacher, but I think you'd be better."

"In another life time, perhaps I would have been. I did envy your parents in their career choices."

"So why didn't you?"

"I dropped out of school in second grade. My mother home-schooled me after that, and it left me with without experience to confidently navigate the educational system. And later, I couldn't afford it."

"You couldn't do what Mom did? Work your way through college?"

"I would have liked to, but my employment choices were severely limited by order of the King. The opportunity passed me by."

"Wait. Grandad would have arranged for you to go to school."

He nodded. "Had he been aware, yes. If he'd known I wanted to further my education he would have paid for it, but I was not going to ask him to extend his generosity any further than he already had. He made sure I had a place to live and enough money to live on, and all he asked was that I keep your father from killing himself with his increasingly immature stunts. I made do. I availed myself of your father's text books and your mother shared hers with me, as well."

"Then when Dad became King—"

"My interest in a formal education had waned by then and I was otherwise occupied caring for you and Oz while your parents worked. When your sister was born and I had the chance to watch her during the day, I wanted nothing else. When you came along, I knew for certain that I was doing what I most desired. I was needed, and quite content in being with you every day."

"We're grown now, though."

"And my duties for your father have expanded considerably. I know it doesn't always seem like it, but I do have a lot on my plate."

"Vice-king."

"Not quite, but…similar. He keeps me in the loop, just in case."

"In case he dies," Zed guessed. "So Oz has someone to guide her."

He pretended not to notice when Oz slipped out of the gym and headed for the bedroom. "I prefer to not think of it that way, but yes."

"You should have had kids," Zed mused, looking back at his computer.

"That would have required a considerable amount of touching."

Instead of feeling sorry for him, Zed laughed and said, "A serious amount."

Drew didn't come out.

"I noticed, Wick."

Is he all right?

"I'm sure he is, which gives me reign to mess with him." He got up and stepped over to the gym, standing just outside the door. "Drew, if I come in there and your hand is shoved down into your pants—"

"God! I'm not…I just… I need a minute, all right?"

"Fine. But dinner will be ready in about three minutes. You have that long to finish up."

He came back to the sofa and sat back down; Zed was laughing hard enough that when Oz came back, she wanted to know what was so funny.

"Drew doesn't seem to want to come to dinner," the Emperor explained loudly.

"I'm coming. God!" Drew called out.

Zed snort-laughed so hard that it hurt, and he grabbed at his own face.

"That's a little mean," Oz told the Emperor. "Don't embarrass him."

With a shrug, he got up and went into the kitchen to stir the pot of stew he had simmering on the stove. Zed abandoned his homework to help Oz set the table, and when they sat down to eat, the Emperor looked at Drew and said, "Please tell me you washed your hands."

"I didn't—I hate you," he grumbled. "I hate you all."

*

He hated them less after dinner was over and they stopped picking on him. After the dishes were done and Oz was curled up next to him on the sofa, he didn't hate them at all. Instead, he was sleepy and fighting it; his eyelids looked heavy and he yawned a few times, but Oz had found a thirty-year-old magazine jammed between two books on a shelf between the kitchen and the gym, and they were poking through it together, mocking the things their parents had enjoyed when they were younger.

The Emperor was in one of the chairs nearby, his feet on the coffee table, and he was reading on his tablet. Zed had gone back to homework, and I was about to drift off in a warm spot right next to Oz when the Emperor's phone pinged. He read the message, and told Drew to turn the monitor on. The King was about to speak.

Oz gave voice to what we were all thinking: he looked exhausted. "I've never seen him so tired," she said. "Or old."

The Emperor's voice rode on his breath. "Indeed."

His hair over his ears is turning white.

The King was speaking from the ballroom in the old Hyatt. Behind him was the window with the view of the Bay Bridge, and it was already lit up for the night, the lines of white lights strung along the support wires twinkling against the black backdrop of night. Aubrey stood close by, to his right, and on his left Shazia and Richard waited. They all looked tired, but none as much as he did.

Is he all right?

Oz didn't understand me, but she scratched behind my ears anyway.

Jax did away with formalities and got to the point. He told the nation—and the world—that while the negotiations with Florida had reached an impasse, talks with Midlam progressed. The paramount issue agreed upon was that Florida could not be allowed to continue its march toward a bloody, long-term war. Midlam did not have the resources to mount a defense without considerable aid, and the preservation of Midlam was in Pacifica's best interests.

That did not mean that Pacifica was willing to blindly assume the majority of the costs of war, nor the risks to its own people. They agreed to look forward, to the inevitable unification of the two countries when their heirs wed.

The crux of talks between them centered of the idea that their merger was happening within the next fifty years, and by doing so now, with Pacifica acquiring Midlam as an asset, then assuming the risks and expenses of war—and ending it—were deemed acceptable.

"As of two p.m. today, I have reached an agreement with Queen Shazia for Pacifica to effectively acquire Midlam. This includes but is not limited to all land, mineral rights, contracts, debt, and assets owned and owed by Midlam. Payment for this acquisition will be divided among its three and a half million current citizens who have reached majority age on or before this date, in the amount of ten thousand dollars per person."

He went on to explain that as of the moment the pertinent documents had been signed by all concerned parties, every citizen of Midlam became a citizen of Pacifica, will all rights and privileges that afforded. Their Queen would continue to govern as Midlam's first Prime Minister, with a length of term to be determined.

"That's a hell of a lot of money and a metric ton of paperwork," Zed murmured. "It'll take years."

The King went on. "Because of our agreement with Midlam, as of today, Pacifica is, for all intents and purposes, at war with Florida, though I am extending an offer of renewed negotiations to the First Minister. However, he should make no mistake—we will defend our land and its people, from the Pacific Ocean to the farthest Midlam border and we will do so vigorously and without mercy."

Oz breathed out, "Holy hell."

"Indeed."

They were quiet, and when the King ended his speech the Emperor turned the monitor off. The tension in the room made me nervous, so I jumped to the coffee table in order to be able to see them better, trying to figure out who was the most upset.

It was Drew.

I wanted to jump onto his lap, but he leaned forward and put his elbows on his knees, and said softly, "I'm not the crown prince anymore. I'm...nothing."

12

Oz tried to convince Drew that he was anything but nothing. The Emperor set the remote aside and then quietly got out of his chair, gesturing for Zed to follow him into the bedroom. Drew didn't seem to want to talk, not until they heard water going through the pipes and knew that they weren't being eavesdropped upon. Even then, he didn't really want to, but it was rude to sit there and say nothing to her.

"I know this is a ploy to get Florida to back off and if I'd been there I not only would have agreed to it, I'd have been excited by it. I feel like I'm upset over nothing, but yeah…it bothers me. And it shouldn't."

"It would have been nice if you'd been given some warning."

"It would have been nice if we'd just been told it was an option. Like, right from the start of negotiations."

You kinda got what you wanted, you know.

It didn't matter if he knew or not. Oz was going to let him have his hurt feelings, and she slipped her hand into his and sat there with him until the light in the bedroom went off and the Emperor came out to find his tablet. He was only wearing shorts—that was new for him, at least around other people—and dropped into the chair near the sofa. Drew stewed for a few more minutes and then muttered that he was tired and just wanted to go to bed. Oz got up to follow him, only stopping when the Emperor muttered, "Separately."

"Squeaky bunk beds," she said, low enough that Drew couldn't hear. "Your sensibilities are safe."

"For now," he said to himself when she was in the bedroom. To me he said, "I doubt I'll sleep tonight, Wick. Feel free to take my bed."

The food's out here. If I stare at you long enough, you'll feed me.

He stretched to reach me, and tickled under my chin.

"Indeed."

*

He managed to sleep for a few hours, stretched out on the sofa. He dimmed the lights and intended to read quietly so that he didn't bother anyone else, but just after midnight he drifted off and his tablet slid to the floor. I curled up in a chair and slept, too, until I heard him in the kitchen at six. The light was still dim, but he'd turned one on over the stove so he could see while he made coffee, and it seemed to me that right then he was as tired as the King. He hadn't shaved since leaving home—none of them had—and his hair was now a bit shaggy and just starting to curl over his ears, and with fatigue coiled around him, he also looked sad.

I jumped over to the sofa so that he could have the chair when he was done making coffee, because it was the chair he seemed to like the most. He shuffled back, his shorts barely hanging onto his hips, and when he sat down they billowed over his legs.

Now I know why you never have visitors. You sit around mostly naked, don't you?

"When was the last time you wore pants?"

I have fur. Never mind. I've actually seen you naked.

"I have no idea what that means, Wick. Are you hungry?"

Use of your thumbs would be welcome right now. Thank you.

He finished his coffee while I ate, and then went into the gym. Bored, I followed him and watched as he stretched, gently at first, until he had warmed up and was down on the floor in full splits, his head on his knee as he reached for his toes.

That's not natural.

"You're this flexible," he reminded me. "Perhaps a bit moreso."

He wasn't wrong. And while he was bendy, I was willing to bet no one yelled at him for demonstrating that ability in front of visiting dignitaries.

Or maybe he had been. I don't know. I wasn't invited to all the parties.

When he was done stretching he started kicking at the heavy bag. He began gently, barely making contact, going for speed over force. Half an hour after he started, Drew was up and lingering at the door, watching quietly, until the Emperor kicked the bag so hard that it went horizontal.

"Damn," he said under his breath.

The Emperor stopped and caught the bag. "I'm sorry. Did I wake you?"

Drew said he hadn't. "Can't hear it from the bedroom. I just couldn't sleep anymore. I've been lying there for over an hour and figured I might as well just get up."

"I can empathize." He patted the side of the bag. "Come on. Give it a try."

"My efforts would be embarrassing by comparison."

"Everyone starts somewhere. In the beginning, I couldn't move the bag at all."

Reluctantly, Drew stepped into the gym. "Yeah, but you were what, six years old?"

"Four. But the bag was of a commensurate size. I spent many afternoons literally bouncing off the bag and onto the floor. I took it personally. I even cried once, but fifty pushups convinced me to never do that in the dojo again."

He started Drew with round kicks, but stopped him after a few. "Chamber more. You're kicking from here—" he showed Drew where his leg was "—and impact will be stronger if you chamber it back to here first." He pulled his knee even further from his body and let the kick go. It landed on the bag with a snap, and Drew grinned.

"I can do that." He started over, kicking slower but in the right position, and he connected hard. "Sweet."

"Keep at it. Ten on your right leg, then switch to your left. Then start over." He held the bag to keep it from swinging, telling

Drew that he needed to work on technique more than his ego needed to move the bag, because it would move—possibly in his direction when he wasn't ready for it. When Drew had changed legs a few times and looked less stressed, the Emperor asked, "How are you doing with the King's announcement, really? Don't stop kicking."

"I don't know. It shouldn't bother me, but it does and I don't know why."

He snapped his foot into the bag and it moved an inch.

"You've been a prince your entire life, and heir to the throne for almost four years. You're allowed to be upset over a sudden change in your identity, especially given that it was done without your consent."

"It feels selfish."

"I promise you, it's not. Mourning the loss of something, even if expected and needed, is normal and arguably necessary."

"I didn't want to be King. I still don't. This gives Oz and me what we wanted, and if Mr. B never abdicates, then we get a life together without all the crap. Yet…" He stopped kicking. "Hey. If I'm not in line to inherit the crown, there's no point in killing me."

"Punch," the Emperor said. "Concentrate on connecting with your first two knuckles. It doesn't matter how hard." When Drew started hitting, he went on. "Keep in mind, Oz is still a prime target."

"And they would still kill me to get to her." He punched harder. "Screw them all."

"That's a possibility, but regardless, you should continue to train and work on your strength and speed so that you have the skills to help defend her if needed."

"Emperor, come on. She can take care of herself."

"I know she can. I've seen her fight many times, but always in a controlled situation. An attack comes with no rules, and often at the hands of more than one person. If you're together and there are several attackers…You need to be able to have her back. You don't have to do this for yourself. You need to do it in case you find yourself in a situation where you need to save her life."

Drew punched again, and knocked the Emperor back a foot.

13

I lost track of time. I was sure we'd been there for a long time, because when we went outside the days were not as bright and the air was colder. The Emperor's hair was almost as long as it had been when he was a teenager, and his beard had grown in. Drew's abnormally blond hair was all black because he'd let Zed use clippers to cut it until it was only half an inch long, and all the glowing-blond hairs fell to the floor in duo-colored clumps. When he was done and Drew still had his ears, Oz asked Zed to try trimming hers to get it off her ears and neck.

Five seconds in, his hand slipped and he shaved a stripe onto her head, but instead of getting mad she shrugged and told him to just clip it all off, too.

"It's hair," she told him when he balked. "It'll grow back. It's fine, just clip away."

When most of her hair was on the floor, Drew grinned and said, "Damn. You look seriously bad ass."

"I am bad ass. And now I'm covered in tiny hairs that bite." She kissed Zed on the cheek and thanked him, even though he was at least four kinds of upset that he'd screwed up, and then said she needed a shower.

"Same here," Drew said. "My neck and back are on fire."

They headed toward the bedroom, and the Emperor called out, "Separately."

That started as a running joke, but the more often he said it, the more I think he meant it. He didn't care, but Zed did and was getting grumpier every day, scowling almost every time he saw them touch.

"He feels excluded, Wick," the Emperor said when I asked why Zed was so grumpy. "He's also missing his friends, and just wants to go home."

We all did, but that didn't seem like it would be happening any time soon. Every time the Emperor put the news on there was something depressing about Florida attacking troops outside of Kansas, or Pacifica using swarms of mosquito drones as weapons, surrounding enemy troops with thousands of the miniature mechanical insects, forcing Florida to retreat behind their made-up boundary lines near Toledo.

He was deploying tiny drones of his own to scan the sky around the cabin, and every now and then he spotted shuttles recently departed from California streaking overhead on the way to Midlam. He analyzed data provided by General Myers, and while he was confident our location was still safe, he was plotting passage to other safe houses and spent time every day trying to repair the damage done to the shuttle when it was struck by lightning.

Every morning they went outside to run, and then came back to fight each other in the gym. The Emperor sparred with Oz, and she sparred with both Zed and Drew, and while there were fewer bruises, they always had something turning odd colors on their bodies. They no longer ran in shorts; when they went outside it was in jeans that no longer fit well and sweatshirts that were too baggy.

Laps were no longer squishy, and I didn't enjoy sitting on them as much.

On a cold, drab day that felt like it should be spent inside in front of a fire, the Emperor surveyed the outside cameras, and absently mentioned that it was raining. They scurried over to the monitor to see; the rain was coming down hard, and the rock wall was just a blur on the screen.

Before they could ask, he said, "Yes, you can go up top and go outside, but stick close to the cabin. I won't be able to see you if you get even as far as the wall."

They raced up the stairs and were outside before I could get across the room to jump into the Emperor's lap. I didn't understand it; they were just standing out in the rain, faces turned to the sky as if they didn't even care if they drowned. He watched for a minute or two and then got up, setting me on his chair, and he told me to keep an eye on them for a minute.

If something happened I had no idea what to do for them, but I could scream like someone stepped on my tail, so I watched them as he got towels to hang on the bannister.

It must have been cold, because Oz and Drew stopped looking up at the sky and started hugging.

That's like Aubrey and Jax on the balcony.

"Yes, people tend to do that."

They're not sad, though.

He didn't understand. In his mind, two people holding onto each other was just something they did. I remembered Aubrey's sadness, and how Jax held onto her, trying to heal her.

"Sometimes people hold onto each other just to be able to touch," he said. "You've seen that often enough. Aubrey often just hugs Jax for no apparent reason."

Aubrey heals with hugs.

"Hugs and kisses," he agreed. "But sometimes she wants a hug just to be close to someone for a moment. That's all Oz and Drew are doing."

In only a couple of minutes they were heading back inside and I was going to jump down so he could have his chair back, but a light on the panel turned yellow and blinked and then made a pinging noise. He flipped a switch and stepped back as the screen changed from showing us the gray blur of rain—Zed was already halfway down the stairs with Oz and Drew right behind him—to the King and Queen.

It had been weeks since we'd seen them. They still looked tired, but not as tired as they had been at the press conference. When she saw Zed behind the Emperor, sliding across the floor in wet socks as he yelled "That was freaking cold!" the Queen smiled.

"Just checking in," Jax said.

Zed stopped when he realized they were on the screen, and ran over. Oz and Drew followed, and they were all dripping water onto the floor.

Don't get that on my furs.

Before they could say hello, the Queen's face went from hopeful to worried. "Look at you. You're all so thin! And Oz, what happened? Your face is bruised. And your *hair!*"

"The Emperor punched me," she said. She ignored the look he gave her. "It's fine. We've been sparring and I don't duck fast enough. And I asked Zed to cut my hair because it was getting to be a pain. It'll grow back."

Before the Queen could protest, the Emperor added, "I have been feeding them, Aubrey. I promise, they're eating and are all healthy."

"He's also been torturing us," Zed said. "Running. In *boots*." He lifted his shirt a little and patted his stomach. "I am getting a baby six pack, though."

"Mom, don't worry," Oz said. "The Emperor is keeping us on a tight gym schedule, that's all. A lot of running and sparring, and he's been teaching me some new techniques."

She still looked worried, but the King was amused. "Have you landed a shot on him yet, Ozzie?"

"No, but he sleeps sometimes, so I still have a chance."

"Sounds fair," he said. "Andrew, your parents are still in San Francisco and will probably stay here for the duration. They're doing well and want to know how you're holding up."

"Tell them I've come to terms with it," he said.

Jax didn't have to ask about what.

"Any word on my brother?"

"I'm sorry, but no."

"Yeah, I figured as much."

"When can we come home?" Zed asked. "I'm really tired of looking at these freaks all the time. And I miss you."

Aubrey's eyes filled with tears, and I could see Jax move his arm behind her, slipping it around her waist.

"Not for a while, champ," Jax said. "But I am sending a data packet and there are some things in it for you. It might take a little sting out of missing home." He looked to the Emperor. "There are several packets for you, as well. Information that you can update the kids with. Is there anything you need?"

There was. "I sent a supply request through channels last week but it seems to have stalled."

"I'll make sure it gets filled."

"I suspect it's being held up because of the contents. These kids need real food, Jax. I requested a tunnel drop with a significant amount of fresh meat and vegetables, none of which are on the standard supply list. I'm leery of keeping them on reconstituted food too long, not given as active as they are. The basic food stock is meant for a fairly sedentary lifestyle, and they've become anything but that."

Aubrey blinked away the tears, her sadness consumed by a surge of anger. "Oh, they will *not* ignore you, William. You send *me* that list and you'll have it all by tonight."

Oh, she's royally ticked off.

Ha. The Queen is not amused.

"I'll send it soon." He turned to the kids and said, "I need to speak with them privately for a moment, so now would be a good time to get out of those wet clothes and into a hot shower."

They said their goodbyes, told Jax and Aubrey they loved them, and as they headed for the bedroom the Emperor yelled out, "Separately."

Aubrey laughed, but Jax was horrified. "Please don't tell me that's a problem."

"No, it's not. Oz and Drew have been very respectful of the situation. Even if I presented them with the opportunity I don't think they would take it."

"Huh." Jax seemed surprised. "I would have."

"The bunker lacks the ambience I suspect Drew wants. And he's why I wanted to talk to you without them. I need your help with something."

*

Fifteen minutes later he had collected the data packets and forwarded them to each of the kids' email and had sent his supply list to the Queen—who was surely on the phone within ten seconds, elegantly berating whomever was supposed to pay attention to what we needed—and Drew was coming out of the bedroom in dry clothes.

He went back to the reading he'd abandoned when the rain started, but it wasn't making him happy. His eyebrows knotted together and he mumbled something not nice about someone named Avogadro and where he could shove his special little number.

The Emperor loaded the data he needed to assess onto his tablet, and as he headed for the living room said, "Don't worry, Wick, I didn't forget you. I asked for some shrimp and fresh packets of crunchy treats. If Aubrey secures nothing else, she'll make sure you get that."

She loves me.

"Indeed, she does. I expect that the shrimp will come parceled out and already chopped up for you. Somewhere in Denver there's an airman in a supply kitchen, wondering why anyone needs shrimp cut up into pieces smaller than a fingernail."

He's probably saying things from the bad word list.

"One would assume."

They all fell into their reading while I stretched out on the coffee table to remind the Emperor what real flexibility looked like. He looked agitated anyway and I don't think he liked the data the King sent him, so I figured why not? He'd either be grossed out or would think it was funny.

Turned out, he didn't think either.

You're supposed to be jealous. You're bendy but you can't do this. Or can you? I don't think I've ever seen you try.

Without looking up he said, "Wick. Really."

His phone pinged a couple of hours later and after he checked it he told them to all get their boots on and wear a sweatshirt, because he was taking them into one of the tunnels and it would be chilly. He hadn't taken them into anything except the supply tunnel because they just weren't interested, and he'd only made them go into it so that they could find boots that fit and sweatshirts that were warm enough. This time he was taking them into a long access tunnel, where they would meet an unmanned cart.

Without asking him for permission, Drew scooped me up and slid me into the pouch of his shirt, and I ducked down just in case the Emperor didn't want me to go.

"The supplies are dropped off at an access port roughly four miles down the tunnel," he said as he opened the door. "Normally

I would let the cart ride all the way in, but I want to check it before letting it get close."

"So we're not hauling stuff?" Drew asked.

"I want you to get used to the tunnel. Pay attention to where all the lights are, get used to the way sound carries, and listen."

Oz stated the obvious. "Because it's also an escape route."

"Every tunnel will take you from three to five miles out, and each has a minimum of four escape hatches. But I have an alternative use for them, and you need to adapt to the light and sound."

"What, we're really going to run down here?" Zed asked.

"That's a consideration. Certainly an option, if you would prefer to run inside once in a while." He flipped a light switch near the door and pointed to a rack along the right side of the tunnel. It was filled with rifles and hand guns, and next to it were targets painted onto thick foamy boards that were nailed onto a wheeled frame. "You're going to learn to shoot."

"No freaking way," Zed said.

The Emperor pointed down the tunnel. "First we get the supplies. Later we shoot."

It was cold, and the further out we walked the colder it was. He had them going at a half-jog and Drew kept a hand under me to keep me from bouncing, but I was beginning to wish I had stayed behind, even if that meant being alone.

They were capable of dragging groceries in without my supervision.

Slow down, slow down, slow down.

The Emperor slowed down. "Sorry, Wick. I wanted to reach the first hatch before the cart."

It was only a hundred feet or so ahead and there was no sign of the cart, so they slowed to walk at a normal people pace. Oz wanted to know if there was any new information in the materials the King had sent, anything he could tell them.

"Minister Munson is reportedly back in Florida," he said. "The Second Minister is in Kansas, allegedly leading their people in matters of faith and prayer."

"But?" Oz prompted.

"Your father suspects that the First Minister is counting on him to unleash hell on Kansas, to destroy the one thing he claims to want."

"Yet we know he wants all of Midlam."

"He'll play the hand he has until he gets new cards. Your mother believes that her father is aware that Redmond does not share his vision for Florida and no longer wants him as his heir."

"So?" Zed said. "Pick a new one."

"It's not that simple. Because of the structure of their government and the language of their constitution, which is based upon the belief that its leaders are brought to their stations by a calling from God, the only way to elevate someone else to the position is if Redmond Munson dies."

"So he wants Mr. B to do his dirty work," Drew said.

We reached the place the Emperor wanted to and stopped. There were a hundred things the King had informed him of, but there were few he could share with them. He leaned against the shiny metal wall, folding his arms together, thinking. "Intelligence suggests that the Second Minister is reasonably well protected by the citizens who are with him in Kansas, and they are likely unaware of the scope of the fight Florida has launched. They believe that few lives were lost in the attack on Chicago, and that God will end the war with minimal bloodshed. When it's over, they'll begin building the temple promised to them, and they don't know that Munson is willing for them to become collateral damage."

The King was not yet willing to destroy any part of Kansas and its infrastructure or its people, but he had built a strong defense around it. There were offensive strikes —mostly drone swarms meant to confuse ill-trained citizen soldiers, and laser fire intended to incite fear and serve as a warning—and the skies were heavily patrolled to prevent another major attack from Florida, but he was trying to avoid an aggressive confrontation that would cost thousands of lives.

"Make no mistake, people have died," the Emperor said. "There have been too many casualties on both sides and there's somewhat of a ground swell to push Florida into one central location within Kansas, but the goal is to get them to recognize Pacifica's legal claim to Midlam, and to back off."

"If the Minister doesn't?" Oz asked.

"Eventually Pacifica will take the fight to Florida."

"And destroy it," she muttered.

"Does he have any idea how bad that will be?" Drew asked. "Munson, I mean. One large scale attack, and their entire country could be pretty much wiped off the map."

"And why not just do it?" Zed asked.

"Because there are a few million innocent people in Florida," Oz pointed out. "They don't want a war. They only want lives of peace and of service. Chances are they have no idea that the head of their church and state is a megalomaniacal, perverted freak."

"And this is why we're learning to shoot?" Drew asked. "In case we have to fight here?"

The sound of an engine whining came from the dark end of the tunnel. "Nah," the Emperor said as he prepared to inspect it. "That's just for fun. I didn't bring it up before because I didn't have permission. Now I do."

When he was sure the cart was safe, he took me from Drew and set me on top of the box closest to the front, and told them to run back, then head to the gym to work out before dinner. Drew offered to help him unload, but he said no; he had a particular method of unloading and storing that would be confusing for two people, and sent him on his way.

You don't want any of them to see the supplies, do you?

"Indeed."

But there are real live fresh dead things?

"Enough meat to feed three hollow teenagers for a month or more, and plenty of shrimp for you."

Snacks for me. Snacks for you, too? Wait, you don't really snack. You don't even like sweet things very often. The kids do, though.

"I asked for teenager-friendly snacks. Don't worry about them. They've done fine on the food they've had but I'll feel better when they're eating fresh things. And a few cookies now and then won't hurt."

I won't tell and ruin the surprise.

"I knew I could count on you, Mister Wick."

*

It took two days for them to get used to the better diet, much of it spent in a food coma, and on the third day the Emperor made them get up early in the morning to run outside where it was bitter cold and there was frost on the ground. I watched from inside the cabin, sitting on the window sill where I could feel the cold bite at my nose and ears, but where I still had plenty of warm behind me.

Oz and Drew sprinted, but Zed barely jogged. The Emperor was prodding him to speed up, but when he moved ahead, Zed flipped him off behind his back.

I wasn't sure if that was something I should tell the Emperor about or not.

He made them dart between trees, like a game of tag with no winner at the end, and they were running their feet up the tree trunks, reaching to grab branches before swinging down. I wasn't sure what the point was, until he let them stop. He ran straight at a tree, scrambled partway up, and flipped off of it. He arched his back and threw his legs upward, until he'd made a perfect circle in the air and then landed on his feet.

Acrobatic evasion. I'll be impressed when you can do it inside, all the way to the ceiling.

Oz could do it, though she was a little bit off balance and had to take a few steps backward when she landed to keep from falling. Drew came close, landing on his feet before falling onto his backside. Zed could run two or three steps up the trunk, but landed on his back with a loud *oof* that I could hear through the closed window.

Half a minute later he was back on his feet, and they all tried it again, and then again, until the Emperor pointed to the rock wall. He made them vault over it, side to side, using their hands to push off the top of the wall, until Zed sat down and refused to move any further. Steam was rising off their heads and sweat poured down their faces; even Oz and Drew wanted to stop, so he relented and let them go inside.

He was doing everything with them, every jump and leap, but wasn't sweating half as much as they were.

After they had cooled down and didn't have sweat streaming off their faces, he pointed to the 10 o'clock tunnel and told them to go have some fun. They could go shoot at the target, but reminded them to carefully inspect each pistol before firing. They fired light rays instead of lasers, so he felt comfortable allowing them to shoot without his direct supervision. "Shoot at the targets, not at each other," he said, "and make sure you follow every rule I laid out."

"But we can't hurt each other if something goes wrong?" Drew asked.

"You can destroy your vision if the light ray hits your eye, so be careful."

When they disappeared into the tunnel, he picked me up and set me on the kitchen table. "Keep an eye on the door, Wick," he said. "Tell me if any of them are coming back inside."

All right. But I'm surprised you want your personal time right here in the kitchen. The bathroom doors have locks.

"Wick."

Hey. I know what you're all doing. Oz comes out of the shower in fifteen minutes, you guys take like half an hour and you're not any cleaner than she is.

"Just watch the door."

So I watched the door. He banged around in the kitchen, making enough noise that I was surprised no one else came to see what he was doing. By the time he was done, there was flour all over the counter tops and the air smelled like I wanted to eat it. I kept watching the door while he cleaned up, because he hadn't told me I could do anything else. I was still watching an hour and a half later when he scooped me up and took me to the tunnel to check on them.

They were clustered around a target thirty feet down, and didn't hear as he came up behind them. I meowed—it wasn't fair to sneak—and all three jumped.

"I told you to listen while in the tunnels," he said. "You're lucky it was Wick."

Contrite, they showed him the target. There were a few spots on the outer edge, but most of the light sensors near the center had been activated.

"Who shot?" he asked.

"All of us," Oz said. "We all had a couple hits to the outside, but either we nailed it or there's something wrong with the guns or the target. We've reset it at least twenty times, too."

He had them move back and handed me to Zed, then picked a gun from the rack, checked it over, and aimed.

He intentionally pulled a shot, and the outside of the target lit up.

He aimed carefully, and the bullseye turned on.

"Nothing wrong with either," he said. "You're just capable."

"Notice he didn't say we were any good," Drew pointed out.

"When every shot is in the center, then you're good."

He fired off a few more rounds, and all but one hit the bullseye. "I'm passable," he said. "Not good." He slipped the safety on and re-racked the gun. "Put everything away for right now. Lunch is almost ready."

"It was my turn to make lunch," Zed called out as he ran to get the target. "I was going to wow you all with cheese sandwiches."

"Grilled?" Drew asked. "Because I'd eat that."

"Phfft. No. Cold. I don't cook."

"We've noticed," Oz said.

"I'm being nice to you, you know. I'm just not any good at it."

They slid the target back into place and Oz locked the gun rack, then followed the Emperor back into the bunker. They each paused when they got inside, sniffing at the edible air.

"Damn, what smells so good?" Drew asked.

"Lunch. And dessert. Now go wash up."

He closed the tunnel door and set me on the floor, then went into the kitchen. Oz was the first to come back, and grinned when she saw what he'd done. By the time Zed and Drew came back, the Emperor had two large pizzas on the table, and in the center was a cake with chocolate frosting—I wouldn't get any of that—and he was lighting candles on it.

Halfway to the table, Drew stopped.

"Happy birthday," the Emperor said. "Welcome to the start of your third decade."

He still didn't move, so Oz ran to him and threw her arms around him, and gave him a kiss.

"Seriously?" Drew said. "I lost track. It's actually my birthday?"

"Happy twentieth," Oz said, pulling him toward the table.

"Emperor, you did all this?"

"I'm not a stellar cook, and the cake came from a boxed mix, but...I hope you enjoy."

"Damn. Thank you. Seriously." He nudged Oz. "Kiss him for me, will you?"

The Emperor allowed her to kiss him on the cheek, and while they ate he told them that the rest of the day was theirs. "Stay out of the gym. Forget homework. Watch videos or play games. Or both. Just try to have some fun today."

When they were cleaning up, he whispered to Oz and Zed, and they slipped into the bedroom while Drew was sticking leftovers into the fridge. The Emperor went over to the control center and then called him over while he pushed keys on the panel.

"Call your mother," he told Drew. "She misses you." He only had to put the last number in, and it would connect. While Drew did that, the Emperor picked me up and carried me into the bedroom to wait with Oz and Zed.

Oz bounced off the bed, and before he could protest, she hugged him. "Thank you for remembering. But seriously, he's never going to be afraid of you again."

"I can change that."

He set me down, letting me choose where I wanted to wait. I jumped onto his bed and plopped down on his pillow, waiting for him to tell me to stop getting my fur all over where his face would be later.

Zed slid off his bed. "Look, I know you're not ready, but...I don't care if you see inside my head. I want to hug you, too."

"I won't listen," the Emperor said. He held his arms out to Zed, and then held him close for a long time, only letting go when Zed did. For that minute, though, when Oz hugged him and when Zed didn't seem to want to let go, the Emperor was as happy as I'd ever seen him. He'd managed more than a fleeting moment of contact, and no one heard a whisper from his mind.

14

A week after Drew's birthday there was snow on the ground, but the Emperor still made them get up early every morning to run outside. They ran in tight patterns around the trees, often slipping on snow-slick patches of dirt, and Oz raced against Drew to finish the circuit first; the winner was the one who didn't fall, with bonus points for not bleeding if they both wound up on the ground, especially if it involved faceplanting into a tree trunk. Zed trotted along behind with his hands jammed into his pockets and refused to play; he was only moving because the alternative was listening to the Emperor urge him to run, or to Oz telling him he was being a pain in the asterisk.

Only she didn't say asterisk.

After they ran for an hour, trading bloodless victories, he made them walk on the narrow top of the rock wall. It was slick with frost and Zed complained that it was too slippery and someone was going to fall off, but the Emperor informed him that was the objective: find your footing and your center, and walk it until you can do it without wobbling. "If you fall," he said, "try not to break anything."

"What's the point?" Zed grumbled. "Staying in shape, yeah, fine, but I swear half the stuff you make us do is just to make us do stuff."

"That I expect you to should be reason enough."

I was tucked into the Emperor's sweatshirt because he didn't want me riding with anyone else, in case they did slip from the wall. He knew how to land and could guarantee it would not be on me, but he wasn't as sure about Drew. Oz would be able to land without turning me into a furry little pancake, but she didn't have the right sweatshirt to carry me in.

The Emperor followed them along the top of the wall, walking with ease where they were faltering, as it circled around the cabin and the barn. He intended to take them all the way, allowing them to venture further than they had before, risking the amount of time it would take to run back if they needed to.

Near the backside of the cabin, off to the left, there was a clearing with tall brown grass, the blades heavy and white-tipped with snow. It was an odd meadow in the middle of a forest, which made me think that the old King, or maybe even the King before him, had cleared it of trees and then planted grass and flowers, perhaps to make it nice for the Queen.

Or maybe Jax had done that. It was something he would do, just for Aubrey, even if she only saw it once.

Without asking if he could stop, Zed jumped down on the field side of the wall and headed into it. He got fewer than five feet when the Emperor barked at him to come back; no one was exploring that field, not today. Zed spun on his heels, turning back toward us, but he did not move and he was angry.

"It's just grass," he spat. "It's not a damned minefield."

"You don't know that."

"I'm not a freaking moron, Emperor. You wouldn't have taken us someplace where we could get blown up."

"Zed, just come back," Oz said.

"Not until he gives me a damned good reason."

Oh, I don't like this.

The Emperor stepped down off the wall, handed me to Drew, and then went to Zed. Before Zed could scramble, the Emperor picked him up and threw him over his shoulder, slipped back over the wall, and marched to the front of the cabin.

"What the actual freak!" Zed yelled, squirming against the tight hold the Emperor had on him.

Only he didn't say freak.

This is a first.

"Well, then," Drew said. "I guess we're going inside."

"Not sure I want to, but yeah. And it looks like Zed just learned that when the Emperor is fully covered, he'll haul someone's ass as far as he needs to."

Oz jumped down first and held out a hand to help Drew so that he wouldn't drop me, and they walked slowly back to the front door. I couldn't blame them—I didn't want to go inside, either. Staying outside snuggled in Drew's shirt seemed like a far better idea than going in and seeing what the Emperor was doing to Zed.

We could stay upstairs in the cabin.

You guys could cuddle on the couch and I could pretend to be keeping an eye on you.

They were already downstairs by the time Oz shut and locked the front door, and when we got to the head of the stairs Zed was standing in the middle of the giant bunker circle; the Emperor was pulling his sweatshirt off, and right when I thought that maybe it wasn't so bad, Zed cut loose with things off the bad word list, and ended with, "What the hell are you going to do? Ground me?"

The Emperor sat at the kitchen table and pulled his boots off.

"At least *say* something! If you're going to treat me like a damned child, tell me why."

"Because," the Emperor said, picking his boots up as he headed to the bedroom, "you're acting like one."

Drew set me down, and without saying anything to Zed he and Oz both went to put their things away. Zed stood there, snow melting off his boots, refusing to move.

No one else was coming out to make him feel better, so I stood up on my back paws and patted at his legs, hoping he wasn't mad at me, too. It took him a moment, but he sat down and pulled me into his lap, held me close, and fought like hell to not cry.

*

The Emperor waited, irritated, in the living room the next morning. He sat on the sofa with one leg crossed over the other, his foot bouncing up and down, waiting for them to wake up. He had already packed four large backpacks and set them at the foot of the stairs, and had pulled the plastic carrier from the shuttle, clipping straps onto it.

Drew was up first, and when he saw how aggravated the Emperor was, he turned back to wake Oz and Zed.

"I accept that you feel boxed in," he said before they could ask. "And I accept that you're angry for having to be here and for everything it feels like you're missing from home. But I will not tolerate outright disrespect and I expect that you're all mature enough to understand that I am not pushing you simply to torment you."

"No one thinks that," Oz said.

He ordered them all to sit, and singled Zed out once he was in his chair. "You've had time to think about it. Why didn't I want you to wander into that field?"

"Do you want an honest answer or the one I think you want?"

"Honest."

"I think you pulled me back because lately, you've been kind of a dick."

The Emperor got up and went into the kitchen without saying another word.

"What the hell, Zed?" Oz said.

"Oz, I'm tired and I want to go home, and there's no good reason for half the things he makes us do. It was a damned empty field. Exploring it wouldn't have hurt anyone."

Oh, you're about to get schooled, Zed.

"It wouldn't have hurt until you got too far from the cabin to get back in time if something happened," Drew said. "You would have been completely exposed out there, and exposed all of us while you were at it."

"We're exposed every time we go out."

"But we don't go far and can get back in less than a minute if we have to. We're also protected from an overhead view by the canopy of all the trees. There's a measure of safety in the woods that you wouldn't have had out in that field. Even on the wall toward the back of the cabin, we could have made it to the barn and dropped down the access ladder if we'd had to. Out in the field? You're a viable target."

"Cripes, you sound like him."

The Emperor came out of the kitchen, put plates of scrambled eggs and muffins on the table, grunted, "Breakfast," and then headed into the bedroom.

No one moved until he called out, "Everyone get over there and eat. It'll be the last hot food you have until tomorrow night."

They got up, but Oz turned to Zed and said, "You owe him an apology. And it better be a damned good one."

*

There was no apology.

After they finished eating, the Emperor gave them ten minutes to get ready: boots, warm clothes, jackets, gloves, and if they were smart, an extra sweatshirt. Oz and Drew went to get their things without asking why, but Zed hesitated a moment, staring at him defiantly before he thought better of it.

He offered no explanation until the bunker was locked up, the front door to the cabin secured, and they were fifteen minutes into hiking out. I rode in his sweatshirt, but he had the plastic box clipped to the back of his backpack, and I realized that at some point, I was probably going to be in that thing.

The plastic tomb.

He took them further from the cabin than they had been yet, and a mile into it he said, "Twenty miles. You can do it."

Drew grunted but Zed blurted, "Are you insane? You expect us to walk ten miles out and then all the way back?"

"No. I expect you to walk twenty miles today, camp out, and then walk twenty miles back tomorrow."

"Just do it," Oz snapped at her brother.

This is going to be fun.

"That's an understatement," the Emperor said under his breath.

Oz and Drew marched on, staying a few feet ahead of the Emperor, frequently checking to make sure they were headed in the direction he wanted them to go. Zed lagged a bit but was keeping up, even when he grumbled complaints to himself. When he muttered an expletive and said this was the definition of insanity, the Emperor called back, "So is talking to oneself."

An hour later Zed was still behind, but he had picked up his pace enough that no one had to slow down for him. Oz and Drew were walking alongside the Emperor, and after hearing Zed grumble for the tenth time she asked, "What is his problem?"

The Emperor snorted. "He's sixteen. That's his problem."

"I was not that big of a jerk two years ago."

"No," he agreed. "You got it out of the way early. If we'd made this hike when you were thirteen, you'd have started crying half a mile in, picked a place to sit down, and then would have refused to move, whining 'why are you so mean?'"

"I would not have."

"Yeah," Drew laughed, "you would. And five years ago? Zed is essentially me at fourteen and fifteen. Cut him a break. He usually has to be super mature because of his job…he's finally getting to let it out and deep down he knows we won't hold it against him. At least not for long."

"Fine," she said. "But if he calls you a dick again, I'm kicking him in the balls."

"I can handle his mood," the Emperor said. "And we're about to increase elevation, so don't be surprised if he becomes far surlier. He hasn't worked as hard as I hoped, and this will not be easy for him."

"Is that why we're doing this?" Drew asked. "To show him he has to work harder?"

"No. To show him that he *can*. Once he sees for himself that he's capable of more than he imagined, I'm hoping he feels better about himself. He needs to be able to do this."

So everyone gets tortured to teach Zed a lesson. Wonderful.

"I'm not torturing them, Wick. We all need to know we can do this."

"Have you ever made this hike before, Emperor?" Oz asked.

"Many years ago, with your father. And trust me, Zed's whining has nothing on Jax at eighteen. He'd only recently become serious with your mother, and I'm certain he thought the time apart was going to kill him and he was beyond being remotely reasonable in his anger that he wasn't allowed to bring her."

"Obviously, he survived."

"Yes, but by the time we were at the halfway point, part of me wanted to accommodate that surly prediction. It was the first time I wondered if I had made a mistake staying in this When."

"Man, lately Zed's uncomfortable with us just holding hands," Drew said. "I can't imagine how awkward it would have been for you with Mr. and Mrs. B locked up in the bunker."

"No more than Zed is. Their relationship was serious but had not yet progressed that far."

"Huh," Oz grunted. "I thought they kind of jumped right to that. I mean, that night we were looking through pictures you kind of outed him losing his virginity at eighteen."

"No. I hinted that he was having sex with *her* at eighteen. But that had not happened yet. The possibility was half of why he was angry we were here, I think. He'd been helping her work through the process of ridding herself of the demons that she carried, and—" he shrugged "—they were close."

Demons? Is that what we're calling the freakwad?

Only I didn't say freak.

My apologies to the Queen.

"All right. I admit, I'm surprised. I just assumed she was the only one, I guess. And I also assumed it was like…they met and were doing it the next day. We saw the picture you took of them on the day they met. There was no hiding it, they really dug each other."

"Oz…" he hesitated, unsure he should go on. "He loved her from almost the moment he met her, and those feelings were definitely mutual, but she had baggage."

"I know. Daddy Dirtbag."

"Jax was perhaps not as mature as one would hope at that age, but with her…when she told him, he didn't run. When she asked him for patience, he told her he would wait as long as it took." He looked to Drew. "He respects your willingness to wait, Andrew. He understands it on a fundamental level that many would not."

"Wait," Oz said. "What? You talked to my *dad* about us having sex? *We* haven't even really talked about it."

"And with that," the Emperor said, gesturing ahead, "I'll fall back and walk with Zed, and you have the discussion you should have had weeks ago."

Drew wants to do bad things to you now.

"I know."

So two out of three of them are not happy with you today. Maybe all three.

"I know."

And you're okay with that.

"I am."

He slowed down until Zed caught up to him, and suggested they leave Oz and Drew alone for a while, because Drew was likely inventing new ways inside his head to drop him onto his asterisk. "You'll have help smothering me in my sleep tonight."

Zed snorted. "I know I'm a pain in the ass, Emperor. I just want to go home, that's all."

"As do we all."

"Yeah, but I honestly don't get why I even have to be here. I know why you have to protect Oz. She's the next in line. Drew has to be here because he was the first target. But no one's coming after me. Mom's heart would be broken enough just losing one of them. I'm only here to stay out of their way."

He considered it for a moment. "Zed, do you understand why you were born? Aside from the obvious biological gymnastics."

"The condom broke, I presume. I was an unplanned mistake."

"No, you were not. And never think that. If anything, you were a happy surprise. Your parents planned on a second child and when your mother realized that you were coming a year earlier than they'd considered, there was no one in that house who was not completely thrilled, except perhaps for Oz and she was too young to really understand."

"So? Why then?"

"The social norm in Pacifica is for couples to bear one child."

"I know. Not a rule, but just kinda the way it is."

"Royal families, on the other hand, are expected to have at least one more. Crudely expressed as 'an heir and a spare.' Although, your father loathes the notion of a spare and he was absurdly happy when he found out your mother was pregnant again. I don't think anything other than your mother has made him as happy as being a father."

"You don't have to explain, Emperor. I know I'm wanted and I know they love me. Telling everyone I was an accident is just a joke."

"Good. But you also know that if something happens to Oz, you're next in line. So yes, you need to be every bit as protected as she is. And you need to pay as much attention as she does, in the event that you do become King one day."

"Ugh, no thanks. They should have had an extra spare. Kind of surprised they didn't. Hell, why didn't they? They both love kids."

"I am not privy to that information. But my best guess? Oz turned three and made them realize that toddlers can be awful little people."

"Dad calls that her threenager stage."

"I don't think she was quite that bad."

"Yes, she was."

Up ahead, Oz and Drew had stopped, and were so deep in discussion that they didn't notice when we passed them.

"Keep walking," the Emperor said to Zed. "They'll catch up."

"Are they fighting?"

"No," he said. "Simply talking. If they lag too far behind, I'll yell for them to start walking."

"Screw it." He picked up his pace. "Make them run."

*

Five hours after we left the cabin, we came upon the campsite the Emperor had been hiking toward. It was well-used, with six long logs forming a rough circle, and in the center of that there was a smaller circle made of stones. Before he let them rest, they had to clear the ground between the stones and the logs of pine needles, and then gather up wood for a fire.

While he placed me in the plastic tomb, Oz started pushing the needles to the other side of the logs using the edge of the sole of her boot, but asked him if that was a good idea. "Won't they provide insulation?"

"They could, but they're also very dry and I'm starting a fire soon. The sleeping bags will suffice. They're intended for cold, wet ground."

Zed and Drew collected several loads of wood, and when Drew dropped the last armload he said, "I hope you know how to start a fire. I don't have a clue."

"Not a problem." He dug into one of the front pockets of his backpack and pulled out a one-inch sized cube and placed it in the center of the circle, added some dry pine needles, and then smacked it with the palm of his hand. It popped and then sizzled, and after a second or two, flames shot up. He slowly added pieces of wood, until the fire was several inches tall and giving off heat.

"It's almost like you've done this before," Oz said.

"A few times. I have also set my pants on fire, so don't be impressed. Never set off one of the starter cubes with the bottom of your foot."

For the first time that day, Zed laughed. "You were a special little snowflake, weren't you?"

"I was a city kid from an entirely different time. But I learned."
I want out.

"In a minute, Wick." He added a little more wood, and told them they could sit down if they wanted. "Had things gone differently, Jax and I considered bringing you out here next summer. At some point, we had to."

"Still can," Oz said.

"Only if there's less torture," Zed grumbled.

"Holy hell, Zed. When we get back to the bunker, take a look in the mirror. You're mostly muscle now, and completely shredded. You're going to be flicking girls away like fleas. Boys, too."

"Fine. There's been some benefit."

"Granted, they'll be shallow and only after your body, but still."

"I'd like to keep it up when we go home," Drew said. "I don't care if it hurts. Make me work out, Oz. If I can't be a prince anymore, I want to be a stud."

"Why would I do that? I don't want other women fawning all over you."

"Oh, God," Zed sighed. "I'm going to go find a place to pee. Please be done with the foreplay by the time I get back."

Oz scowled. "Cripes, it's not like I was going to lean over and lick your face," she said to Drew. "At least not until you shave off that mop."

He scratched at his beard. "Don't like it?"

"It's like kissing a toothbrush."

"Get used to it," the Emperor said. "He doesn't look like himself right now. Very few people would recognize him. I want him to stay that way."

"You should talk. I'm not sure your own mother would recognize you right now."

"Were I younger, she would," he said. "This is not new. There were battles when I was a teenager. She wanted me clean cut and I wanted long hair and a beard. Quite possibly the only thing we ever actually fought over."

"What, you didn't have a Zed period?"

"I'm sure I would have under other circumstances. But I had karate as an outlet, and because of their schedules I had few opportunities to dig in and piss my parents off."

Oz looked at Drew. "Make note of the date. The Emperor said 'piss.'"

"I'm not even sure what the date is. If he hadn't remembered my birthday I wouldn't even know what month it is. Seriously losing track here."

Zed shuffled back to the camp site. "Track of what?"

"Days. How long we've been gone."

"Too long," Zed said. "But we've been gone for over two months. Thanksgiving is coming up. We'll probably miss that. And then we'll miss Mom's birthday."

"I'm sorry," the Emperor said quietly. "I do understand."

"How long did it take you to stop missing your parents so much?" Zed asked him. "You weren't much older than me when you stayed here for good. It got better at some point, didn't it?"

"I missed them until the day I saw them again. There wasn't a day that I didn't miss them. I still do."

"Even though you got them back?"

"I miss all the years we didn't have. You'll get home, Zed. This isn't forever."

"It feels like it."

I think the Emperor empathized with that, but there wasn't anything he could do about it, not unless the war suddenly ended, and that would come with a bloody price tag attached to it.

*

When it was dark out, after they'd eaten—complaining about the dry, chewy ration bars that made up their dinner—and had ventured out into the woods to take care of personal business, the Emperor pulled eight fist-sized balls from his backpack and placed them around the perimeter of the camp, on the far side of the logs. He used his phone to activate them, and a gentle hum lifted above us.

"A force field of sorts," he said. "It will keep animals out and Wick in, and will somewhat retain heat from the fire, but not a lot. And if it rains, we're getting wet."

"Wonderful," Zed muttered.

"If you need to get out, wake me up. And no one goes out alone."

Dude, what if I need to pee?

He pointed to a space between two of the logs that were the farthest from where they were going to sleep. "There's a little pile of pine needles you can use to bury things, if you want."

I went over to sniff the spot.

It'll do.

"And Wick. Don't get too close to the fire. If you get cold, climb into the sleeping bag with me. I won't roll over on you."

It didn't take long at all before I started feeling cold. The fire only kept one side of me warm, so I slid in with him and used his arm as a pillow. Oz was on the far side of the fire and she was shivering hard, even though Zed and Drew seemed comfortable.

Drew hadn't fallen asleep as easily as Zed and the Emperor had—which surprised me, because he still didn't sleep often—and he could hear her teeth chattering.

"Oz? You okay?" he whispered.

She was not as quiet. "No. This bag is made for someone three times my size and isn't holding my body heat. It's got to be twenty, maybe twenty-five degrees out. I'm going to be frozen solid by morning."

Drew unzipped his bag and told her to climb in with him. "No funny stuff, I swear. You have to keep warm and I have room."

She didn't argue; she scrambled to get in with him and zipped it closed as fast as she could. "Funny stuff is not off the table," she said.

"Yeah, with my luck the Emperor would wake up."

I crawled out of the bag to sniff at them.

I'm not asleep. I can tell him things.

"Get back in that bag with him, Wick," Oz whispered harshly. "You'll freeze."

Fine. But I can still hear you even if you're whispering.

She turned in the bag so that her back was to him and he could get his arms all the way around her. "Second base, right there, you know."

"Stop it." He was trying to not laugh. "And I'm apologizing now for the inevitable. I can't help it."

"Unless my parents are in the room, never apologize."

"The Emperor—"

"Is one of the parents. But he's asleep, so…no apologizing. No grinding, but no apologizing."

"Hey. If I fall asleep, I can't help that."

Kill me now. I know how Zed feels.

I felt the Emperor's breath skip over my ear furs, his voice barely a whisper. "Leave them be. They won't actually do anything."

Fine, but if Zed wakes up, he's gonna break Drew's fingers.

I could feel the Emperor laugh. His eyes were closed and he was on his side with his arm curled around me, but he wasn't sleeping. He kept his breathing shallow so that they wouldn't know, and for a minute I wondered why he didn't just go to sleep. I could feel how tired he was just by the way his hand kept falling away from my side, and I know he didn't want to eavesdrop on purpose.

Then I heard a howl in the distance, and understood.

He wasn't sleeping so that they could. Someone needed to stay awake to keep the animals at bay. Especially the two-legged kind.

Oz snorted. "You're not very good at baseball, are you?" There was some rustling and she added, "They're cold. Help me out here."

"Jesus, Oz."

"Oh, hello. There we are. No grinding."

He surrendered to the inevitable. "You know, when this all blows over and we get to go home…I don't see any point in waiting too long. I want to marry you."

"Is that a proposal?"

"I don't have a ring—"

"I don't need one."

He lifted his head so he could see her face. "Look, we've handled being stuck together in the bunker all this time and we've done pretty well with it. You've seen me first thing in the morning with raging bed head and haven't run screaming from my morning dragon breath. I'm still pretty determined to grow old with you and I just want to get started on that life. So yeah. I'm asking. Will you marry me?"

She turned, wiggling in the bag to face him. "If I say yes, will my totally hot boyfriend finally sleep with me? Because I get it now, why you really wanted to wait. But I'm not her, Drew, and you're not Carter. You are so much more than he is."

"If we ever get any real privacy? Oz, I swear, the day we get home…I will disappoint you all night long."

"Stop it. I'm not going to be disappointed. And I would've said yes even if you'd said no. Are you sure you want to give up all the stupid teenage stuff first? We never even got that first date."

"I know. And if you wanted, we could date our freaking faces off first but I'm pretty sure I've been the only one holding out here. And I don't want to anymore."

"You know when we get home our parents aren't letting us out of their sights for a day or two."

"We'll get the Emperor to distract them. He weirdly seems to want us together."

"He understands the inevitable."

"What do you know that I don't, Oz? He knows our future."

She took a deep breath, and then kissed him. "I swore to him I put all of that into a box in the back of my head, and that I wouldn't look at it. Don't ask me to."

"I'm not. I'm just asking if you know something that's not in the box."

She was quiet for a long time. "Protect the Emperor," she finally said. "As hard as he protects us, protect him. Because if something ever happened to him, my heart would shatter."

*

The sky was still a little bit dark when the Emperor crawled out of the sleeping bag to add more wood to the fire. He tucked the bag so that there was no extra space around me and told me to stay put so that it would keep me warm. Remembering how hard Oz had shivered, I didn't argue.

Sometime during the night—I had a sleepy, vague memory of him getting up for a few minutes—he'd taken Oz's abandoned sleeping bag and covered Zed with it. Oz and Drew were still curled around each other, and they'd pulled the edge of the bag up over their heads, making them look like a giant blue forest slug.

Zed began to wake first, and the Emperor grabbed a sweatshirt out of his backpack and then knelt by him, whispering for him to stick it in the sleeping bag to warm it up first. He'd need it when he crawled out.

When he was more awake, he sat up and wiggled into it, and then crawled over to sit closer by the fire. He scowled when he saw Oz in Drew's sleeping bag and grumbled, "Aren't you going to do something about that?"

"No."

"You're supposed to protect her."

"From Drew? He makes her happy. Why would I protect her from that?"

Zed was not in a better mood than he'd been in the day before. "That's not what I meant and you know it."

The Emperor sat back on his log, and stared at him. I was almost uncomfortable enough to duck my head back into the sleeping bag, but I also didn't want to miss it if someone actually did kick Zed in the groin.

"I'm just saying," Zed griped.

"You're concerned about your sister's sex life? What about your own, Zed?"

"That's not the point."

"It is. You're being incredibly hypocritical."

Zed tried to argue that Oz was different; as the crown princess, her standards needed to be higher. Like it or not, there was a moral yardstick and she needed to measure up. The Emperor tossed another piece of wood onto the fire, a little more enthusiastically than he needed to, and sparks shot up. "She didn't have sex in the back of a car parked at Ocean Beach for no reason other than to have sex. You have no moral high ground here."

"Wait—"

"It's my car, Zed. Your parking tickets come to me. I use it every now and then, and you've also left behind enough undeniable evidence to nullify any stand you have on the topic. If they want to be together, I will not stop them, and you need to understand that it's no more of your business than it is mine. They're adults. And you… are not."

Oz was awake, and said, "Thank you." She was up on one elbow, looking not terribly happy. "I honestly appreciate that you want to look out for me, Zed, but you can't stop this and I don't want you to. Drew is the only other person who has a say."

Drew curled up into the bag more, and snorted loudly.

The Emperor laughed through his nose and said, "Yes, I can see how you're so anxious to be with that."

*

They made the return walk faster, anxious to get out of the bitter cold and into hot showers. Oz promised them she would make dinner, something hot and savory and loaded with gravy that even I could have. Even Zed moved faster, until he was nearly jogging with two miles left to go.

The Emperor told Oz and Drew to let him enjoy it, but to try to keep him in their sights. They walked quickly so that he could take his time—he was carrying the largest backpack, with the plastic tomb clipped on the back, as well as holding me—but none of them were ever really out of his sight.

I think he was enjoying the slower pace until Zed's voice cracked through the air, calling for him.

He ran.

I bounced against his body as he ran hard and I could hear him chanting under his breath, "Be all right, be all right, be all right."

He dumped the backpack and passed Oz and Drew, who were running at full speed but still not quite as fast as he was. He skittered to a stop a few feet from Zed, who was kneeling near the body of an older man. Before the Emperor could tell him to back up, he was reaching to check for a pulse.

As soon as his hand made contact, he yelped and scrambled back several feet. "He's not dead."

The Emperor bent down to check. The man on the ground was pale and not breathing. "I think he is, Zed."

"No way. He said something."

The Emperor took a chance and felt for a pulse, and then said, "No. He's gone."

Zed crept back to check for himself, and when he touched the body again, he sucked in a hard breath. "I can hear him." He rested his hand on the dead man's arm. "'Martin,'" Zed said. "'Smith. Hard tack? Red setter run.'" He let go. "This isn't possible. He's still thinking. I can hear him."

"Oz." The Emperor waved for her to come over. "Think of a single word, and hold it in your head."

"God, no. You don't think—?"

"Just do it. Zed, take Oz's hand. Tell me if you can hear anything."

He didn't want to. He knew exactly what the Emperor was afraid of, and didn't want to know. But he took Oz's hand and closed his eyes, listening carefully.

"Nothing," he said after a while. Then came the relief. "Nothing."

He sat in the dirt, shaking, and then reached out to touch the dead man again. "'Martin. Red setter run, red setter run, red setter run,'" he repeated. "How?"

The Emperor was on his knees. He set a hand on Zed's cheek and asked, "Can you hear me?"

They were quiet, until Zed swallowed hard and whispered, "Yeah. I love you, too."

"Come on. We need to get back." He touched the dead man one more time, too, but didn't hear anything, and then just wanted to get them back.

They moved quickly, backpacks bouncing, and didn't stop until the cabin door was locked behind them.

15

No one left the bunker for over a week. The Emperor spent most of his days and a good chunk of each night in front of the monitors, scrutinizing the outside through all of the security cameras. He sent up dozens of the bug-sized drones, searching in miles-wide circles, looking for signs of other people and then watching for long stretches when he spotted hikers and hunters; when he wasn't scanning the outdoors, Drew was. While Drew monitored things outside, the Emperor sparred with Oz, taking the risk of prolonged skin contact by grappling with her.

"I have nothing to hide from you," he reminded her when she balked at the idea. "Anything you might hear is already there somewhere in your head."

"Yeah, except for whatever perverted thoughts you've had in the last few months. I don't want to know what kind of porn you're watching."

"I'm not—"

"Give him a break, Oz," Drew said. "I'm sure he watches perfectly normal porn."

"I don't—"

Zed had been in the other room, and when he dropped into the chair near the sofa he asked what the Emperor was denying.

"His porn collection," Oz said.

"Oh." He looked at the Emperor. "Can I borrow your tablet?"

"There is no porn on this tablet. No, I do not watch porn. Why would I?"

"Just because?" Zed teased. "You know, so you have an idea what some things feel like…I suppose you can guess at others."

The Emperor sighed. "I know what an orgasm feels like, Zed. I'm not a eunuch, just celibate."

"Now, see," Oz said. "You're thinking about it, and that's what I would wind up hearing. I don't want to know what you're thinking about when you, you know."

"For God's sake. All of you. And you have nothing to worry about, Oz. That's certainly not something that would cross my mind when sparring with you."

She was sure she could keep closed the window she'd created in her mind; she also wanted him to know for sure whether he could be distracted and still not listen. He needed to try, and she decided they could both live with whatever thoughts he plucked from her brain. "But I don't apologize if anything embarrasses you. I'm pretty sure you've figured out where my brain is half the time these days."

Zed stopped complaining. He ran on the treadmill without being prompted, he pointedly asked Drew to spar with him, and he played with the weights. The only thing close to renewed whining came the morning after his first workout with heavy weights, when he had a hard time rolling out of bed.

There may have been a little more moaning when Drew wanted to spar with him after breakfast.

He still wouldn't apologize to the Emperor, but he made an effort to be pleasant.

On the fourth day, while Drew kept an eye on the monitors and Zed studied, Oz shouted "Victory!" in the gym. It was loud enough to startle us all, and we ran to see what had happened—and whatever had happened left the Emperor curled up on the floor, knees drawn toward his chest, and hands between his legs. He looked like he wanted to throw up or cry, or quite possibly both.

Instead of feeling bad for him, they both laughed.

"You said if she could do it, you deserved it," Drew reminded him.

When he could finally stand up—which took a lot longer than I would have supposed—Drew told him to open his mouth. Confused, the Emperor did; Drew peeked in and said, "Yep, there they are."

He backed out of the gym quickly, but I don't think the Emperor could have moved fast enough to get him. He placed his hands against the wall and stood there, trying to not throw up.

Zed leaned his back against the wall next to him and said, "Hurts, eh?"

"I had no idea."

"Seriously? That's the first time you've ever been racked?"

"Never. And she kicks—"

"Not sorry," Oz said.

"I know." He pushed off the wall. "I need to go throw up now."

On the fifth day back, the Emperor opened the door that led to the garage. He wanted to check the shuttle and its fuel levels, and he ran a new cable from the solar capture lines in the shuttle's shell to the roof of the garage. After inspecting the connections inside, he decided that in another day or two he would go up top and make sure the joint line in the barn was still functional.

Oz wanted to know if he was planning on leaving.

"It may be time to move to the next safe house," he told them. "General Myers has expressed that he is not opposed to relocation… which tells me he thinks we've been here long enough."

"Where to?" Drew asked.

The Emperor pulled up a map, showing them where in Colorado we were, and drew a line to the next safe house.

"There are several in Pacifica," he said, "but I think one in Midlam would be the least likely suspected location."

Oz exhaled sharply.

"Kansas."

*

He spoke to Jax in the middle of the night when everyone else was asleep. The body of the dead man had been recovered and was identified as Martin Smith of Miami, Florida, though he was believed to be a part of the exodus to Kansas. As Zed thought, he'd died of a heart attack, likely fewer than three hours before Zed stumbled upon him.

As a courtesy and a show of good faith, the body had not been cremated and was returned to his family. There was no mention of by whom he was found and exactly where, only that he was discovered by hikers in Colorado, who in turned called the authorities.

Jax wanted to know how Zed learned the man's name, but the Emperor was hesitant to tell him. He grappled for an easy way, and couldn't find it.

"Your son has been scent-intuitive all his life," he said. "It's possible that this is an extension of that ability."

"How?" Jax demanded. "There was no identification on the body."

He couldn't lie. "Zed touched the body before I could stop him, and he heard a voice. It was mostly gibberish, but he got the man's name."

"Son of a bitch. Will—" His voice broke, pleading.

"No," he said. "Don't even *think* that. He's since touched Oz and Drew, and heard nothing. He is not burdened by my mutation."

Jax didn't look like he believed it. He looked angry and sad and scared, and then he asked the Emperor to withhold the information from Aubrey. "For now," he said. "She's already stretched to the breaking point and I'm having a hard time keeping her from leaving here to stay with the kids. Until you understand more, just…don't."

There wasn't much to understand. The Emperor had no idea why he could hear into other peoples' heads. There was no explanation why Jax and Oz could see sound, why Aubrey was empathic, or why Zed could smell feelings. No fundamental reason why the Emperor could understand me.

If Zed could hear dead people, the Emperor didn't want to examine it too closely.

He hoped, down to the depths of his soul, that it was nothing more than that, that Zed would not eventually glimpse into others' thoughts through simple touch. He also couldn't shake the thought that Zed had touched him while being exposed to lightning, and he had no idea what that could have done.

"I'd give my life to guarantee that wouldn't happen to him," he whispered to me late at night.

He'll need you if it does. So maybe practice not hearing more. So you can teach him.

He was ready to risk some touching with Zed, but perhaps not as much as he risked with Oz. "When he's a little older, Wick. Right now…there are things I've done he wouldn't understand. And things that, perhaps, he could not yet forgive me for."

You need to forgive yourself first.

"Indeed."

16

"If at any point we become separated from each other, this is what you head for."

He printed out maps and pictures of the Kansas safe house, urging them to memorize every detail they could. It was located a few miles outside of Newton, which was roughly 600 miles away. If something happened, they only needed to reach Denver on foot— Zed finally understood the purpose of all the running—and from there they could access public transportation to Newton; after that they either had to find their way with an air bike, a bicycle, or on foot. He didn't want them renting or hiring a car or taxi, nothing that could be tracked or traced.

"Wick is not to be out of anyone's sight, even for a minute."

"He needs to stick with you," Oz said.

"But if it happens—whoever has him, keep him safe."

Zed studied the map closely, but muttered, "How about we just make sure we all stay together?"

The Emperor wanted to take the shuttle as far as the Colorado border and then assess the situation before crossing into Kansas, but he wanted it clear: if it happened, if any of them wound up on their own, the safe house was where he would look for them.

Their backpacks were kept packed and stowed under the stairs; he taught them how to use the fire-starters and portable force field, and placed enough of each into each bag for a week. They had ration bars for food, and several filtering canteens for water. There was cash.

"Parcel it out. Some on you always. Some in your bag. But under no circumstances do you use a credit or cash card. Carry no identification. Lie about who you are."

He drove that home; if they were separated, choose a new name, and if anyone suspected, deny.

"And this is where you have to get used to something you've already resisted. As of now, I am no longer the Emperor to you. Use my name, and get used to it."

Drew didn't think he could. "I still can't bring myself to call Mr. and Mrs. B by name, either. So…Mr—? What the hell is your last name?"

"Blackshear," Oz answered for him. "We adopted him, he's a Blackshear."

"All right, but that'll get confusing at holidays," Drew said. "Pass the gravy, Mr. B. No, not you, the other Mr. B. JB not WB. And God, if Finn is there I'll feel like he's another Mr. B."

The Emperor was amused, but firm. "Will. Or William. No one outside the family knows my name. So use it."

Drew pretended to consider it. "No. You had that whole evil, black from head to toe thing going on and it worked for you. You need a nickname. We'll call you Blackie."

"You will not."

"Fine," Oz said. "Uncle Willie. I knew I would win that one."

*

On the eighth day back, he wanted to go up top to check the line that ran from the shuttle, through the barn to the roof, to the solar filaments woven through the shingles. The battery gauge hadn't budged in two days, and while it was overcast, he still thought there should be more power stored in the shuttle.

It meant going on the roof with a tool bag, and he thought he might need a second pair of hands, so he took Drew with him. I ran along behind them, wanting to go outside and get some fresh air; the ground was cold but the barn door was open, so I had somewhere to go if I needed to warm up.

The Emperor didn't like it, but he didn't make me go back.

I sat on the ground and watched them climb the ladder; the Emperor went up first with the tool bag tied around his waist, and Drew followed. He was not at all happy about it, pausing every three or four rungs to comment about how high up they were going.

"I didn't know you were afraid of heights," the Emperor said.

"Yeah, neither did I."

It didn't look that high. And the rungs were nice and wide with black traction pads. Once Drew made it to the top without wetting himself, I decided it couldn't be too terribly bad, and climbed up after them.

They were near the bendy part at the top of the roof when the Emperor realized I was up there with them, and he let loose with a bunch of things from the bad word list. He ended with, "How the hell do you think you're going to get down, Wick?"

I suppose you'll have to carry me.

"Down a ladder."

I weigh less than the tools.

"I can carry him in my shirt, Emperor," Drew said.

No response.

"Really, he's like six pounds. I can tuck my shirt in and he can ride in it. I'll still be able to keep both hands on the ladder." He pointed at me. "You keep your claws to yourself."

The Emperor dug through the tool bag for a wrench and handed it to him. "Three feet to your left, there's a small black bolt with a thin black wire coming out of it. And three feet beyond that, another. Check to make sure the wires are connected to the bolt and that the bolts are tight. If not, tighten them."

Slowly, Drew eased his way over and checked the first one, tightened it to be sure, and went to the next.

"I think this one is stripped, Emperor."

No response.

"Emperor. Do you have another bolt?"

He looked up at Drew, but didn't say anything.

"What? I need a bolt. What's the problem?"

He dug into the tool bag and grabbed one, but held it up so that Drew could see it.

"Really, Emperor, what the—" He sighed hard. "Will."

"Get used to it."

"I'm still not sure I can. But at least answer and remind me instead of making me think I did something wrong."

"Fair enough." He stretched to hand Drew the bolt. "I'll save the torment for Zed, for the time being."

"So your goal is to make him afraid of you, instead of me?"

"No reason I can't have both."

"Hell, just tell him you're going to spar with him. He'll run and hide."

"Ah. I seem to recall you hiding in the closet when you were a little boy. All I had to do was look at you. I miss that."

Drew carefully scooted back to the first solar line. "One day I'll have kids, and you can torment them. I'll be sure to tell them how you used to dine on small children, using their tiny, delicate bones as toothpicks."

"You know, a few months ago, you weren't entirely sure you wanted children."

A few months ago, the Emperor laid down on the grass roof at home and listened while a confused Drew thought out loud, trying to figure out what Oz wanted from him.

"I don't know anything about little kids, but I imagine I won't screw one up too badly."

"You'll have help. Your parents, Oz's, mine. Me. I love little kids. I would not mind spending my afternoons caring for them again."

"Oz says you basically half-raised her."

"I babysat while Jax and Aubrey worked. They made the rules, and I broke most of them. I'd be happy to do the same for you. I even remember how to change a diaper. Potty training and being thrown up on does not flummox me. The terrible twos amused me."

Ask him about the threenager phase. Everyone was bothered by that.

Really. If your kid hits three and is like Oz, you won't have another.

"Stop, Wick. Three-year-old Oz was not *that* bad."

"Yes, she was," Drew said. "But, yeah, I'm sure I'll need help. And I'm not anywhere near certain what I'll do for work to pay for raising a family. My plans pretty much evaporated and if it were all happening right now, I'd be home with the kids, trying to not mess them up too badly and wondering if panhandling is my future."

"Oz thinks you should write."

That surprised Drew. "She told you that? I mean, she mentioned it to me once, but I'm not sure why. I read a lot but I've never written anything that I'm willing to show anyone."

"She knows you. She's also intelligent. You should listen to her."

Drew snorted, "Indeed."

They checked three more lines, then Drew tucked me into his shirt and began the climb down. He stopped halfway, when a whirring sound rode on the air in the distance, and he listened for a moment before shouting, "Did you hear that? Will? It sounds like an air car."

The Emperor was scrambling. "Move!" he shouted.

Drew lifted his feet and slid down, and was running before the Emperor was on the ground. They cut through the barn and dropped down the access hatch, sliding on the narrow ladder that went into the garage. Drew pulled me from his shirt as he ran from the garage into the bunker, and he slid on the soles of his shoes when he tried to stop.

Zed was on the floor near the staircase, flat on his back with his arms flung out from his sides; his eyes were closed and blood trickled from his nose, dripping into his ear. He was barefoot, wearing his gym shorts, one side bunched up near his groin, and both of his knees were bright red. There was a scrape along one of his shins, and his knuckles were bloody.

Two feet from him, a heavyset man whose neck was oddly bent lay in a lump on the floor, and as we made our way in there were more bodies strewn across the floor. Four others dead, all men, all with heads twisted unnaturally on their necks, broken bones protruding through pants legs, and blood pooling under them.

Drew was still holding me, clutching me to his chest, and I could feel his heart pound against my head. His fingers dug into my skin, and he didn't move, the only sound coming from him the increasing drum beat in his chest.

Every tunnel door was open, but the door leading into the cabin upstairs was closed, the lock still in place.

The Emperor ran through the bunker calling for Oz, then screaming her name. He darted into the bedroom and opened every bathroom door and closet, then skittered into the kitchen, checking the pantry and even the refrigerator. Met with silence, and nowhere else to run, he dropped onto his knees near Zed. And pleaded, "Please, Zed, please. Be all right."

Zed coughed and moaned, but didn't open his eyes.

Drew was frozen in place, not knowing what to do or say. There was only one obvious thing, and neither of them wanted to say it.

Oz was gone.

17

Zed came to in fits and starts. He coughed, his eyes fluttered open and then closed, and he moaned. The Emperor was on his knees next to him, trying to coax him to consciousness. It looked a lot like begging from where I was, still cupped in Drew's hands and squished up against his stomach. When he was finally awake, trying to sit up, the Emperor put a hand on his chest and told him to wait a minute; he wanted to look into Zed's eyes.

When he was certain Zed was mostly all right, he picked him up and carried him to the sofa the same way he had when Zed was a tiny, cranky toddler after falling asleep in the living room; he always let Zed try to wait up for Mom and Dad, and once he had drifted off he'd carefully lift and cradle him close, then carefully take him into his bedroom, tucking him in without waking him. He told him to sit up but whatever he felt like, absolutely do not go to sleep.

Zed held his head between his hands and said he would stay awake, but I had doubts.

Drew finally set me down, and he began wandering from spot to spot, walking along the length of the circular wall. He was obviously hoping to find Oz, perhaps hiding in a nook the Emperor had failed to notice, or even in the alcove with my litter box. His breathing came in tight hitches as he fought against the panic that was bubbling inside and I tried to follow him, willing him to be all right.

He was bleeding through his skin and from his breath without there being any actual blood, and he was choking on tears he didn't dare give into.

It's okay to freak out. I'm gonna freak out in a minute, too.

After getting Zed to the sofa and making sure he could stay upright, the Emperor went to the wall of monitors and pulled up video footage from the security cameras in the bunker. He fast-forwarded through breakfast and their movements around the bunker as they'd gone into the gym, stretched out on the sofa to read, and later when he and Drew headed into the garage, with me running to catch up to them.

When he reached the part he both did and did not want to see, Zed was up and standing behind him. He refused to sit down again until he'd seen the whole thing. He thought it was his fault; he'd tried to protect her but couldn't, and his brain could not make sense of the sea of black uniforms that had seemed to swallow them whole.

Every tunnel door opened with synchronized precision, and from them streamed man after man, all dressed in identical black uniforms: cargo pants, t-shirts, webbed belts, and holsters with black-gripped guns. The Emperor counted in fives, until he reached twenty-five and stopped, because counting didn't matter anymore and they were still coming. They swarmed toward Oz, who had been coming out of the bedroom with her shoes in hand, and she began to fight from almost the split second she realized what was happening. There was no sound but she was yelling, and it looked as if she shouted for Zed.

I thought she yelled for him to hide, but I couldn't be sure.

Zed bolted from the gym, a small medicine ball in one hand, and he threw it hard. It bounced off the side of the head of a man who stood at least four inches taller and was over a hundred pounds heavier, but the size difference didn't stop him. Zed went on the attack and fought clear across the room, landing more blows than he was taking. They moved in a line across the floor, his hands pounding into his attacker's chest and stomach, with a few palm heel strikes to his throat, until Zed reached the staircase. He took three steps up and jumped, wrapping his legs around his opponent's head, and then twisted his body until the man's neck snapped.

He was already looking for his next fight before his feet hit the floor, but then he bent over to check the man's pulse to make sure his first had actually ended. When he started to look up, someone came in from his left, slammed a knee into his head, and he went down. He fell where we found him, twitching once or twice before going out.

The Emperor switched camera views; Oz was near the center of the bunker, trying to stave off two and three men at a time. She was getting in blows that broke bones and made them double over, and in rapid succession she took down four of them. A kick to the groin, then a twist of a head. Palm heel to the gut, air knocked out, broken neck by virtue of clamping her leg around his head and stomping. Sweep to the floor, dropped to her knee to the center of his face. When she took the last man down by jumping at him and just grabbing his head, everyone stopped.

Oz was panting, trying to catch her breath.

One man stood between her and the tunnels; the others had backed away. Her eyes flicked toward Zed, and we could all see it: she was trying to calculate the odds of getting to him and dragging him off, over just running for it and hoping they would follow before hurting him.

The soldier unholstered a blunt-ended firearm and pointed it at her, and her decision was made. She was going to run for it.

She got six steps before he fired, sending four wired darts into her chest. She stopped abruptly, twitching and flailing, and dropped to the floor.

"Taser," the Emperor muttered.

After that, she was scooped up and carried off; they ran into the tunnels, and it was nearly five minutes before the video showed Drew running in.

"This was my fault," Zed croaked. "I never should have—"

The Emperor cut him off. "You couldn't have stopped this, Zed. We could have all been here, and not stopped it. There were too many of them."

Drew backed away from the monitors, and looked down at me. I was standing near his feet, trying to figure out what I could do next. What help I could possibly be.

He didn't see me. His eyes darted back and forth as his brain kicked into overdrive.

"Red setter run," he said, half under his breath. "Red setter run. Red set ter run. Red set ter run. Red. Set. Ter. Run. Redsetterrun. Redsetterrun, redsetterrun, redsetterrun." He looked up. "Red said to run. It was a damned *warning*."

The Emperor kicked at his chair, sending it rolling across the floor until it hit the legs of a dead man and then tumbled over the body. He was caving into the anger and fear, and while I'd never seen him lose total control, I was afraid he was about to punch his fist into one of the monitors. "This should not have happened," he muttered to himself. "It didn't happen. It didn't happen."

Oz. We have to go get Oz. Calm down. Think of her.

"Do you think you can you move easily?" he asked Zed. "Think clearly?"

Zed thought he could.

"Go get some clothes on. Warm clothes. Grab extra sweatshirts for all of us. Get Wick's sweatshirts." To Drew he said, "On the upper shelf of the pantry there are boxes with cat food in pouches. Grab them. We'll each stuff some into our packs."

While Zed and Drew ran to do as he'd directed, he dumped the contents of Oz's backpack onto the floor and picked through everything, parceling out as much of the food as he could and he divided the cash, shoving some into the side pockets of each of their bags. He grabbed her canteens and jammed them into Drew's and Zed's backpacks, and when Drew brought the cat food to him, he slid the pouches anywhere he could make them fit.

When he was done, he went over to the control panel and began jabbing at things on the keyboard. Drew watched for a moment, and when the Emperor paused he asked, "How the hell will you be able to tell Mr. B? This will kill him."

It's killing you, too, dude. You're one bad thought away from wetting yourself.

"I'm not. Not yet."

Zed had the sweatshirts balled up in his hands. "You have to tell Dad. He needs—"

"We leave first," the Emperor said firmly. He entered more information into the keyboard, and on the biggest monitor flashed a red screen. EMERGENCY EVACUATION. EMERGENCY EVACUATION. EMERGENCY EVACUATION.

He hit one more key and then said, "Get into the shuttle. He'll know something has gone wrong in about a minute."

18

The Emperor's plan was to skirt south of Denver and then land near the Colorado-Kansas border. He wanted to take time to assess the conditions there; the reports he'd most recently read suggested that there was fighting all the way around Kansas, and where there was no fighting there was heavy guard. He didn't want to try to fly in blind, because there was a good chance that the shuttle would be mistaken for an enemy vehicle by both sides, and would probably be shot down.

We should just go to Denver. Call someone from there.

"I'm not trusting anyone right now, Wick," he said as he buckled in.

Drew clipped the plastic tomb into place as the Emperor fired the shuttle up, and the engine was whining so if he said anything after that, I didn't hear. I flattened my ears against the noise, which sounded like angry bees looking for something sticky and delicious to devour, and looked around just in case there really were stinging things swarming around us. I was relatively safe in the plastic tomb, but warning them they were about to be stabbed to death by tiny little pricking things seemed like the polite thing to do.

As soon as Drew was buckled in we took off, and the shuttle whined and moaned as we lifted toward the sky. It didn't want to leave the bunker any more than I did and had about as much say in the matter. It mumbled *no, no, no, no* and on the shuttle ceiling, just behind the Emperor's head, it fought back with a spider web of tiny cracks.

"That doesn't sound good," Zed muttered after a couple of minutes.

"We were hit by lighting coming in," the Emperor reminded them. "There may be some structural damage that I hadn't found yet."

"Shouldn't we have checked for that when we landed back then?"

The creaking sound coming from the left side of the shuttle wall answered for the Emperor. He banked right, going south of Denver, and the ship wasn't a fan of the maneuver, shuddering in a violent ripple that had Drew and Zed clutching at their chest harnesses. It continued to make shrill, obnoxious sounds, until the Emperor started turning in the other direction.

It yelled.

Loudly.

It belched until it cracked, sunlight streaming in through a split seam in the roof just behind the Emperor's seat.

"Brace!" he shouted over the sound. He was frantically slapping at controls and Drew looked at Zed like, "Brace against what?" when the shuttle started falling.

I pushed myself against the back of the plastic tomb, for all the good I thought it would do me. I had several un-cushioned inches all the way around myself, plenty of space to bounce around and break things.

He aimed for the very tips of tree tops, and then pushed down between them, trying to cushion the fall. The air screamed around us as needle-tipped branches slapped against the shuttle's hull, cracking as they splintered, until the slice of daylight that streamed through the seam where the panels once met together became a spotlight.

The shuttle landed with a thud, wedged between two massive pine trees, inches off the ground. The Emperor made them wait before they unbuckled, until the weight of the shuttle forced it to settle. Only then did he completely exhale and ask if everyone was all right.

"Physically fine," Drew said.

"Same," Zed said.

"Wick?" he asked.

I think I peed a little.

"You can unbuckle, but don't get up yet," he told them. He slid his phone from his pocket and pulled up a map, trying to pinpoint our location. We'd made it past Denver, but were over a hundred miles from the border.

"So do we walk back to Denver or push on?" Drew asked.

The Emperor unbuckled and moved very slowly as he got out of his seat. "Push on. It would take a day and a half to walk back, only to have to find transportation that would take us to the border. I'd rather not be seen." He stood in front of Zed, and made him open his eyes wide. "Just checking your pupils. And I need your promise. As we walk, if you feel off at all, nauseated or overly tired, speak up. Headache? Tell me."

As Zed unbuckled he said, "I took a hard knee to the head, Emperor. I have a headache. It's fine."

"Use my name," he reminded Zed. "And if it gets worse at all, let me know."

Drew was reaching for both his and Zed's backpacks as the Emperor opened the door. "Don't lie about it either, hotshot. The last thing we need is you dropping dead because you were too stubborn to say something when there was still time to get help."

He'd considered it, I could tell by the look in his eyes. "I won't lie," he promised. "I won't do that to you."

Before we set out, the Emperor gave him something for the headache he already had, and I could still see the angst dripping from him: *please be all right.*

It was his new mantra, hope riding on each breath he exhaled.

I rode on his shoulder; it wasn't terribly cold out and I liked the view from up there. I also liked the odds; he was a little over six feet tall, so that meant that anything wanting to eat me had to either jump—which gave him time to protect me—or come from the sky. Since we were in the woods, I was reasonably sure I was safe from the pigeon gangs.

The first thing he did was plot out where the main highway was, and turned us in that direction. Once we were close to it, we followed along its path but stayed deep enough into the woods to not be seen, and when we came upon water he told Zed and Drew to fill every canteen they had.

"Just in case," he said. "The river will head north of our direction eventually, but there's a man-made creek a mile or two inside the forest that runs along the old Interstate. It empties out into another river, but until I'm positive it's not dry, we refill often, all right?"

They moved quickly in spite of the weight of the backpack each carried, and the Emperor bore the additional heft of the plastic tomb and me, but the weeks of his forcing them to run in boots and work out in the gym made it a bit easier. If they'd had to abandon the bunker within a week or two, no one would be faring half as well as they were, just a few miles into the trek.

Oz could have pushed herself to keep going, but neither Zed nor Drew could have managed hiking for more than a couple of hours, and it would have been at a snail's pace.

This time Zed didn't complain about the hike; he gripped the straps on his backpack and marched forward, determined to get as far as he could before tapping out.

We walked until dusk, when Zed admitted to feeling too fatigued to go on much longer. He wanted to warn them ahead of time that he needed to stop soon, so that the Emperor could find a decent place to camp. He would not, I heard him mutter to Drew, be the thorn in the Emperor's side; he refused to be the reason they failed to get to Oz.

Only a few minutes after Zed warned he was going to have to stop, the Emperor found a spot that was surrounded by trees but left him enough space to start a fire and was also close to water. He made Zed sit down while Drew searched for wood, and he dug into the ground to create a place to have a fire that he could bury in the morning. Zed grumbled that he could help; he was tired, not sick.

"I'm not taking that chance and this will only take us a few minutes. And fair warning. We'll be waking you every couple of hours tonight, just in case you have a concussion."

"Fine," Zed agreed. "But I'm making dinner."

Zed dug into his bag for the dense, chewy, and—based on their facial expressions as they ate—generally unpleasant ration bars and handed one to Drew and then the Emperor. They were filling if you drank water with them, and were supposed to be nutritionally complete, but watching Zed swallow like he was eating dirt made me glad for the pouches of wet food they'd brought for me.

The chopped-up bits of unidentifiable meat weren't my favorite by any stretch of the imagination, but it at least went down without a fight.

It might have been chicken.

It might have been fish.

I doubt I'll ever know. I doubt I want to.

After he was done gagging his food down, Zed climbed into his bag and was asleep within minutes. The Emperor told Drew he would stay awake to keep watch and would wake Zed as needed, but Drew didn't think he could sleep.

"Not yet, anyway. Every nerve in my body is screaming at me to get up and go find her, that we're wasting time. And my stomach is twisted into knots worrying that we're too late. That we were too late ten minutes into this."

They sat near each other in the dirt, cross-legged; both stole glances at Zed and at the fire, but not at each other.

"You're deeply invested in finding her. Of course you're nervous."

"And I'm being selfish, I'm sorry. I know you're just as worried."

"Andrew." He took a deep breath and looked up. "If not for the limits of the human body, I would keep you both walking until we reached the safe house. We wouldn't take more than short breaks and we would push on every minute we could. We would march to Oz until our feet were bloody stumps. You're not being selfish."

We can all be selfish. It's okay.

Drew fought for control over his breathing—he was not going to cry, not now—and the Emperor waited. He pretended to not notice how many times Drew swallowed, nor how hard his jaw twitched as he clenched his teeth.

When he could speak, Drew said, "You love her as much as I do, I know that."

"I do. But I also love her differently. I appreciate the distinctions, and I think I understand how your heart hurts right now. Make no mistake—I would die a thousand times over for Oz, but I know she's the most critical part of your future. So I get it."

"Spoken like Bonus Dad," Drew said. There was no lightness in it, though. No teasing. "It's bothering me, Will. Not the worry, but knowing what I'll do to anyone standing in my way. I should care about those people, but I don't. I should think about why they're there, and accept that they're likely innocent, but the truth is that I just don't give a damn. If it's a hundred people versus one Oz... It's wrong, but to me they are so much less than she is. I think I'd kill them all."

"I know."

"And you don't think that's morbid? Wrong?"

"I think you're feeling what you're feeling, and it's what will keep you moving. I certainly won't try to talk you out of it. And I understand heartache. Yours won't heal until she's safe."

I could hear Drew swallow hard. "You know a little about heartache, don't you?"

"Doesn't everyone?"

"A while back you told me you'd never been in love. But you *had* loved. I just thought it meant, like, you loved Mr. and Mrs. B and Oz and Zed, but hadn't ever had a girlfriend or a boyfriend or anything. And yet, I think you understand us more than anyone, you and Mrs. B. There was someone, wasn't there? Someone you at least wanted the chance to fall in love with?"

Six months earlier, I don't think the Emperor would have answered him. He would have just left it at "no romantic relationships" and then walked away, because it wasn't anyone's business. Now, though, he took a minute to decide how much to say, and then decided to talk.

"There was a girl, once," he said. "Aisha Salazar. She was a student of Aubrey's while she worked as a TA during her graduate studies. If there had ever been any hope, it would have been her."

"I'm guessing there was at least some hope."

"There's always been a little bit, somewhere in the back of my head. But I certainly never intended to fall into a relationship, no matter how respectful she was about my quirks."

"Quirks." Drew managed a wan smile. "That's one way to put it."

He's being nice about himself.

"Before Aubrey introduced us, she warned Aisha that I did not touch anyone. Period. I don't think she entirely believed it until she'd known me for a while and realized the lengths I went in avoiding people...but she had no intention of becoming involved with anyone while she was in school, so it didn't matter. She was happy to be friends."

"And then you opened your mouth and she just couldn't help herself?"

He grinned a little. "I flirted, horribly, but really, we simply became good friends. We had a significant amount in common, from the books we loved to the music we enjoyed, so it was easy to spend time together. When Aisha and Jax studied together, Aubrey and I were usually there, either helping or getting in the way, but we eventually began spending time alone. The semester she had to take an art history class we went to museums frequently, and we spent most afternoons in coffee shops while she studied. Sometimes we just sat at a table in the parklet and talked until she needed to get home. We could spend hours together and not even have to talk often, really. She would study, I would read. We were just comfortable together."

"So you started falling and didn't have much to grab onto."

"I certainly had feelings for her. And I tried to tell myself that I only felt that way because Jax and Aubrey were planning a wedding, and then after they married...I wanted to believe we were just caught up in the wake of their excitement. I had even started playing this cruel little game of what-if with myself—what if we were headed in the same direction? What if my circumstances were different and a simple touch was not off the table? What if we just let go of the laundry list of plans she had and the ideals I hid behind and just let ourselves drift to the place where we wanted to be?"

"She didn't know why you don't touch anyone."

"She thought it was a religious issue, which was a reasonable notion that I did nothing to discourage. After all, I existed, which meant I had parents, so eventually people in my family had physical contact with each other. When we were first getting to know each other, I hadn't considered that this girl would begin to see me as anything other than a friend, and she would possibly hope that we were headed where our friends had gotten to."

"Until you started wanting the same thing."

"I was eighteen when we met. I percolated hormones in the worst way and had no real outlet nor any hope of one. I didn't know if I actually loved her or just wanted to be with her, but my brain certainly tried to convince me that I wanted a relationship. And I made the mistake of admitting that. I told her that if it was ever going to be anyone, it would be her."

"And she thought that just meant she needed to be patient."

He nodded. "She was, she was very patient. I was careful to never actually say the words, but she knew I loved her. And then the week before my twentieth birthday Aubrey told me that I didn't have to have a party or celebrate—Jax warned her I wouldn't—but I was damn well letting her bake a cake and then sitting nicely while they sang Happy Birthday to me, so I'd better start thinking what I'd wish for when I blew out the candles."

"And you knew you'd wish for what you couldn't have."

"Just a kiss," the Emperor said. "I knew there was no possible way I could do anything more than that, but I started believing I could close my mind off long enough for a kiss. And I almost made up my mind, not only would I wish for that, I'd be honest with her and tell her that's what I wanted. Just a simple, single kiss."

"Did you ever get it?"

"Three days before my birthday I met her at Union Square. I don't even remember what our plans had been. But, she got there first and while I walked across the square, looking at her as she waited for me, I realized that I would never be able to stop at a kiss. I loved her, and was coming dangerously close to being in love, and it wasn't fair. She should have a life that included the child that I knew she wanted and the passion she deserved, and I couldn't give her that. I couldn't give her any of the things that Jax and Aubrey had. Then before I could get my mouth open she started confessing her own feelings—I was wearing a hooded sweatshirt, and she began toying with the string on it, trying to sound amused, but…it felt somewhat sad when she said that she thought that if she couldn't actually touch me, that would do. But she hoped that we were heading towards a commitment, and she was fine waiting for that. Not even just a kiss, Andrew. She was willing to wait until marriage to simply hold my hand. And that's where she saw us winding up. Married, a child, careers, and happily ever after."

"Damn," Drew breathed out. "What'd you do?"

"I destroyed her. I told her I didn't feel that way, and I never would. I didn't understand how she could have misread me so badly…and that it would probably be a better idea if we didn't see each other at all anymore. I literally said 'I don't love you, I will never love you' and I pretended like her tears meant nothing to me. I snatched the stupid string out of her hand, and walked away. I knew she was sobbing and would hate me later, but I never looked back."

"Jesus, I'm sorry. I really am. That had to hurt like hell."

"I swore I would never put anyone in that position again. And now Oz has me wondering if there's even a slight chance that I can get to that place."

We all wonder, dude.

"She says you have really good control, Will."

"I can touch her for a few minutes at a time. But it's hardly the same thing, essentially no different than touching my mother. I've seen how completely stupid Jax gets when Aubrey just brushes a finger over his lips. I doubt he can control anything at that point."

"Well, to be fair, there's probably no blood in his brain so he's not thinking anyway."

That made him laugh. "All right, add that to the list of possible reasons why I someday might be able to survive something more than a friendship with a woman. But yes…there once was a girl that I loved. And yes, I have a notion of heartache. I don't want either of you to go through the pain of losing each other. So even if Oz wasn't the daughter of my heart, I would be here with you, just to spare you both that."

"I'm still wrestling with the idea that we're too late."

"They used a Taser," the Emperor reminded him. "It's very old and barbaric, but it means they wanted her alive."

Drew's elbows were on his knees and he stared down at his hands. "Would it have made a difference if we'd all been in the bunker? Could we have stopped them?"

"Andrew—"

"I have to know, Will."

"I lost count at thirty men. They were armed. They clearly intended to take her alive and Zed was not a threat to that, but had you and I been there…my gut says we would have been shot on sight. I doubt that when they saw Zed was alone with her there was any expectation that he would fight as hard or as well as he did. And he did fight well."

"I wish I had sent Zed up top with you," Drew said after a while. "I promised I would have her back, and I didn't."

"And I swore to protect her life with my own. We haven't failed yet, and I refuse to believe that we will. We'll find her."

Drew nearly crumbled under the weight of what might be. He wanted her to be alive; he understood who had taken her, and the things he had willingly done to his own daughter. Drew had no doubt he would do worse to Oz, simply out of spite.

"If something happens to her—"

"Don't go there."

"If something happens to her," he repeated, this time firmly, "if she *dies*…what happens to you?"

"After my heart renders in two and I give myself over to a slow and painful death?"

"No, I want to know how it works. If she dies, do you just vanish? Would it be in a blink or a slow fade? Would I even remember you? What?"

"I don't follow."

"How far down the line are you?" Drew pressed. "Oz's great-great-great grandson? Further?"

Tell him.

And don't look at Zed. I already did. He's really asleep.

Taking a deep breath, the Emperor said, "I am fairly certain that I would continue on, but would then never be born. It's complicated, Drew. There are issues with time being manipulated, and the When of Finn's existence compared to the When of his conception, which are not the same…"

Softly, Drew asked again, "How far down the line?"

"Before I tell you, remember that time travel exists right now. There are the portals, and soon we'll be able to step into the When of my father's middle-aged years, and then step back to that sliver of time when portals didn't exist. It did become quite complicated, with some people having lives that touched more than one When."

"Uncomplicate it for me."

Just tell him.

He'll just keep wondering and asking. He knows something even if he doesn't know that he knows.

The Emperor caved. "Finn is your grandson."

Drew got to his knees, and I thought he was going to try to run, possibly taking the force field with him, wrapped around his body like an invisible sheet, leaving us exposed. Instead, he reached out and grabbed the Emperor's face with both hands, squishing his cheeks. "I don't care what else you hear inside my head, but hear this. If you put everything else aside, even how I don't think I want to live in a world where she doesn't, I swore I would also protect you. And I don't lie to her."

He grabbed Drew's wrists, and I was sure he would push Drew away, hard. No touching. That was the rule. Drew knew that was the rule. Only Oz and the Queen could touch the Emperor without warning. If he didn't push Drew away, I was afraid he would break his wrists.

Instead, he held on.

"Oz comes first, Andrew. No matter what she says, no matter what she wants, her life comes before mine."

They let go of each other then, and Drew breathed out, "Always."

*

Hours later, when he was in his sleeping bag but still awake and the Emperor was adding wood to the fire, Drew sleepily said, "Man you must have been so proud."

"Of?"

"Terrorizing five-year-old me, knowing who I would eventually become."

"I wouldn't say proud, but the notion often amused me."

"I was really a jerk to Oz when we were little."

"Not really. You were never mean. And we never tell the other side of the stories, when she instigated most of it. She always tried hard to get your attention."

"She succeeded." He was quiet for a few minutes, and then drowsily said, "I'm apologizing now if I turn into an emotional wreck, Will."

The Emperor poked at the fire with a stick, causing sparks to lift. His expression turned soft, his face crinkling near his eyes. "You're allowed to cry, Andrew."

"I have."

He was staring at the fire, the stick still in his hand. "So have I. So we just accept that it will happen, and it's all right."

"I don't expect, like, hugs or anything."

He smiled at that. "It's all right if you do."

There was another long beat of quiet. Drew folded his hands under his head and breathed out, "Damn…the sky, Will. That can't be northern lights down this far."

There was a blanket of red and purple stretched over the trees, and the stars were crisp and bright, and they felt close enough to touch. I turned around to look between the trees and it was all around us, in the distance, as if we were surrounded by a forest trapped in a bubble in space.

"It's possible," he told Drew. "It doesn't happen often, but every now and then they can be seen this far south."

"And the stars…I've never seen them so bright."

"No city lights to obscure them."

"Oz would love this."

"Indeed. You'll have to bring her here."

"Yeah." His voice cracked a bit, and his breath hitched. "Maybe for my birthday next year."

"I'll make note of the coordinates so you can find it again. Now stop fighting it and go to sleep."

Drew drifted off after that, and I suspected the Emperor was going to be the one waking Zed off and on the rest of the night.

Zed can hug him.

"I can, too, Wick. Under the circumstances, I'll take the chance."

I can purr for him. Should I climb into his sleeping bag?

"Not right now, but if you think he needs you to at any point, go ahead."

I'll purr for you, too.

He pulled me into his lap. "I know you will. But Wick…let me know what I can do to make you feel better. I would guess you're at least a bit afraid, too."

Tickle my armpits. That always makes me feel better.

I rolled onto my back, my head on one of his thighs and back legs over the other. He looked down at me, one eyebrow arched. "You're a little bit of a freak, Mister Wick."

But you're going to do it. You know you are.

He sighed.

Of course he did.

*

When Drew woke Zed up at daylight, he put his hands over his face and groaned, "God, just let me sleep for more than an hour."

"We let you sleep for two, and waking you up is for your own good."

"Yeah, but the dreams you interrupted…let me get back to that."

The Emperor was opening a pouch of food for me and muttered, "Did they include cleaning up the empty condom wrappers and sticky tissues from the back of my car?"

"Jesus, Zed," Drew said, laughing.

Zed sat up. He sighed and then said, "Yeah, and they even included me paying you back for the parking tickets. I'm a jerk, I know, and I'm sorry. But Rhonda—"

"I don't need the horny details, Zed."

"Yeah. But when this is over, when we're home, remind me I probably owe her an apology, too. Oz was right."

Drew was impressed. "Are we experiencing personal growth right now?"

"I believe that was the issue in the back of my car," the Emperor said.

"All right." Zed crawled out of the sleeping bag. "Oz was right, twice. We're calling you Uncle Willie from now on. And you're too perverted for me to believe that you honestly have no porn on that tablet. You're a horny old man with maybe too much personal growth of your own."

"I truly do not have any porn. And I'm not old."

"Okay, so now we know for sure that you're a real live boy and you have hormones. Then what the hell do you *do*?" Zed wanted to know. "Because I think I would go about six levels of nuts if I were you. I hit fifteen and damn near lost my mind the first time a girl even hinted at what she wanted to do to me."

"Damn, Zed," Drew uttered. "I thought *I* had asked him too personal things before."

The Emperor was less troubled by the question than Drew. "Same thing you both do. I told you before, I'm celibate, but I'm still human and…things…occur to me. No one else needs to be involved."

Drew was rolling his sleeping bag, and started talking to himself. "Oh, sure, Oz, it was a perfectly normal hike to go find you. We walked and slept, and then discussed how the Emperor gets off."

"Will," the Emperor said. "Use my name."

19

The woods were starting to thin out by the time we camped the next night. The Emperor thought they'd covered a little over fifty miles since the shuttle crashed, and they would be walking out in the open in the morning. If they could cover enough ground, fifteen to eighteen miles, they would be back in the protective cover of the woods.

"So we haul ass tomorrow to get back to the forest," Zed said.

"Indeed."

Earlier in the afternoon, Drew noticed that there were more aircraft than typical; for an hour it was one shuttle after another, all on the same general flight path, and if he was any good at guessing, he thought they were headed from Denver to Chicago. And then he wondered if they should find a way to contact home, and get help.

"I weighed that option," the Emperor told him. "I balanced the certainty that Jax knows we abandoned the safe house and are headed for another against the idea of what he would do once told that something had happened to Oz. I realized that he could potentially unleash everything he has on both Kansas and Florida, and if that's where they've taken Oz—"

"But he'd think of that," Drew argued.

"Maybe not," Zed said. "If it were someone else, he might think that clearly. But for Oz—or even you or me—he would destroy anyone hurting her."

Aubrey would stop him, wouldn't she?

"Understand I am not entirely comfortable withholding this from him, but I believe it's in Oz's best interest. The alternative is sending the military after her, and the only way the safe house was breached is if someone trusted with the details, someone military, turned."

Hey, you're not running away…

"Dad will forgive you," Zed said.

The Emperor shrugged. "If not, I'll learn to live with it."

I hope you didn't just jinx yourself.

He ignored me, until Drew said, "Look, we know you understand him. You don't have to pretend you don't, even if it does still feel a little weird."

"Not everything he says merits an answer."

And you can kiss my furry asterisk.

"Such as that."

He fed me anyway, and let me curl up on his lap when I said I was cold. We both knew that I had heard something in the distance, a howling cry, and that I didn't trust that whatever it was wouldn't come and try to eat me. He made sure I saw him set up the force field, and he set the plastic tomb near the head of his sleeping bag.

"If anything comes near, climb in and scream. I'll wake up and slam the door shut, but you can be sure nothing will get past the force field."

Zed and Drew were both sleepy, but he wasn't letting them slip into their sleeping bags until they'd eaten every bit of their ration bars and had at least a half a canteen's worth of water. He didn't like the bars, either, but if they expected to have enough energy to walk as far as they hoped to the next day, they needed to eat.

They all ate the way Zed and Oz had when they were little and there were green things on their plates: tiny bites with lots of grimacing, and it took over an hour.

Zed crumpled the empty ration bar wrapper and shoved it into a pocket on his backpack. "When we get back, I swear I'm going to lick my Mom's toes in appreciation for all the cooking she does."

Drew's face pinched. "Jesus, Zed."

"That's your father's job," the Emperor said.

Zed grimaced. "And now I think I'm emotionally scarred for life. That's what I get for making the most stupid statement of the day. I meant, like, kiss her feet or something."

"We knew what you meant," the Emperor said.

Drew was not as generous. "Yeah, but we're not letting it go. Henceforth, you are Zed the Toe-licker."

"Prince Zealand Marcus Blackshear, Toe-licker." The Emperor laughed. "I feel like I should be a little bit drunk for having said that."

"I feel like I should be at least buzzed for having thought it," Zed said.

"I don't even drink but right now I don't think I'd mind the numbing effects," Drew said. "I wouldn't mind not feeling anything for a couple of hours."

Me, either. Someone should have brought along my good catnip.

"What's the deal with you and booze?" Zed asked. "Aside from your age. Even I've had a beer or two. The world doesn't end if you take a few sips before you're officially twenty-one."

"Do your parents know this?" the Emperor asked.

"I was with Dad. Really, only like half a bottle a couple of times. And then he tried to convince me that it would take twenty-four hours for the alcohol to work its way out of my system since I was an immature drinker, so I would have to stay home all that time. He was really disappointed when I didn't believe him."

"All right, I remember that," the Emperor said. "I'm fairly certain I'd had a beer or two, myself. You took one sip, coughed your damned head off, and while you were wheezing you tried to tell us it was great beer."

"Yeah, fine. I don't like it all that much. But I'm not opposed to the *idea* of beer. Unlike Twinkletoes over there."

"It's not my age," Drew said. "You can drink beer at sixteen in Midlam, harder alcohol at nineteen. It just doesn't interest me, not after seeing how completely stupid it made my friends. A lot of bad decisions are made after drinking."

"Which is why the drinking age in Pacifica is twenty-one. You're not an idiot, Drew. It's not like you'd suck down a beer and then take my bike down Market Street with the throttle cracked all the way open."

"Yeah, you'd think. But I watched Carter do pretty much that and more."

"Stop measuring yourself against him," Zed said. "He's compensating. Probably has an inverted dick."

Yeah, sure, try to not laugh at that, Emperor.

He tried not to.

He failed.

*

You're punch drunk, Emperor. You have to sleep tonight.

"Someone has to keep watch."

Zed is fine. The field thingy works. Go to sleep.

Zed and Drew were both deeply asleep and had been for an hour. He fought it, too afraid to let either of them out of his sight.

I can stay awake. If I see something, I'll scream like my tail was stomped on.

"Wick, you're a cat. You'll be asleep in ten minutes."

Maybe, but I wake up at the slightest sound. They need you rested, William. Their lives depend on it.

He added a little more wood to the fire and climbed into his sleeping bag, leaving a space for me. I made sure my head was sticking out so that I didn't get too warm, which would make me extra sleepy, and I started to purr for him.

"You're still my anchor," he said, planting a kiss on the top of my head.

Yeah, so go to sleep, before I sink and drown you.

"That's stretching a metaphor, but fine. Wake me even if you're not certain, all right?"

I swear to Bast, if anything happens, I'll scream in your ear so loud your eardrum will pop.

I meant it, too.

I'm awesome that way.

*

They only slept for a short time and each woke up several hours before dawn, and then quickly got ready to leave. The Emperor's concern that Drew and Zed needed more rest was softened by the collective desire to get moving and across as much of the open space as they could before daylight. They ate while they walked, and when he was done choking down the ration bar, I took chunks of my food off the Emperor's fingers. Just before we left the edge of the woods to head out into the open he set me down so that I could pee, and told them to each pick a tree and do what they could, because once we were exposed he didn't want to have to stop.

"Keep drinking, but if we can avoid it, I'd rather not stop."

Zed was pretty sure he could walk and pee at the same time. Drew was pretty sure he didn't want to see that.

I do. I want to see him dance, trying to not dribble on his boots.

By the time the sun was all the way up, they'd covered most of the twenty miles. The Emperor guessed they were walking at a five mile an hour pace—just shy of jogging—and he could see the next spread of trees ahead. "We get there, then slow down," he told them. "Find a place to rest for a bit, and refuel."

Drew groaned at the idea of another ration bar. "I've always despised hunting, but right now, if I thought I could handle it…"

"If you need fresh meat, I can—" the Emperor started.

"No. God, no." He grimaced at the thought. "I want food, but there's no way in hell I can stare down a bunny and then kill it. If I have to gut it? It would wind up being wasted food and I'd lose my appetite for days. I prefer to not really think about where the meat I eat comes from."

"If I ever hunt, my mom will disown me," Zed said. "She barely tolerated it when Dad went fishing with you."

"You both realize that the meat you consume comes from animals that were recently alive? Someone has to end the lives of those animals in order for you to have hamburgers and pizza toppings."

"I know," Drew said. "And when I die, if there is a life after this, I hope I can thank each and every one of them for what their sacrifice did for me, because I am grateful. But I won't kill one unless I have to and I sure as hell won't ever do it for fun."

"Seriously," Zed said. "You'd do that? Find a bunch of random cows and chickens and pigs and thank them?"

"I imagine I'll have an awful lot of time to do just that. And after choking down those bars, I have a new appreciation for food."

I am not food. We're clear on that, right?

"We're clear on that, Wick."

Good. There will be no kitty cacciatore on the menu.

"If we run out of food for Wick, I will certainly have to hunt," he told Drew. "You may have to adjust your thinking to allow for that."

Drew was sure he would be all right with the Emperor stabbing some poor bunny or chipmunk to death as long as it was to feed me. No one asked what I thought. I didn't like the idea, either. I didn't want to dwell on the source of my dead delicious things any more than Drew did.

I bit a mouse once. That was enough.

We reached the next cluster of woods by seven; we hadn't seen any air traffic, and there were no air cars on or hover cars over the main road. It cut through the forest, winding along the bank of the river; we could see if anyone passed on the road, but were far back enough that the Emperor felt comfortable taking a rest break.

"Two hundred years ago," the Emperor said to no one, really, "there was no forest here. It was wide-open space all the way to Kansas. We can thank a dedicated group of preservationists for demanding tree growth for the next sixty to eighty miles. There was an explosion of reforestation roughly a hundred eighty years ago—this is just a small part of the effort."

"Sixty more miles," Zed groaned. "Damn."

"We just did twenty," Drew pointed out. "You know, the distance you whined and pouted about not too long ago."

"Shuddup." And then, "Damn, that was less than two weeks ago. It feels like forever."

"Still mad I shared a sleeping bag with your sister?"

Zed sat on the ground, leaning against a tree. "At this point? If we can find her, you two can go do whatever the hell you want to each other. I'll even rent you a hotel room if you want. I don't even know why it mattered to me."

"Because you've felt left out," the Emperor said, sitting near Zed. "They had each other. You had no one. And I don't think I counted."

"Plus, you wanted your mom," Drew said.

"Thanks, make me sound like a piece of fluff."

"What? I wanted my mom, too. Hell, I wanted *your* mom. The whole time we've been gone, a huge part of me has wanted to turn into an eight-year-old, and I want to run to my mom so she can make me feel better. I just freaking want a hug from my mom."

"Fine, so we're both delicate little pieces of fluff."

Drew took a long drink from his canteen and then said, "I'm fine with that. Oz seems fine with that. Not really worried what other people think."

"You know, you two have morphed into one slobbering entity. It's never just, like, there's Oz and there's Drew. It's OzandDrew. We all do it, smash your names together like you're one person. Ozoo."

"Ozoo," Drew repeated. "God, if you tell her that…"

"Yeah, she'll run with it. So you *know* I'm telling her. Ozoo. Oz*ooo*. Oh, man, this needs to be official."

"Fine. It'll be my first tattoo. Big block letters, right on my forearm."

"I'm holding you to that."

Slower than he normally would have, the Emperor got up. "All right. Regrettable tattoos later. Refill the canteens, and let's go. We need to stop before dark tonight but I'd like to get as far as we can."

You need to sleep tonight, more than you did last night.

"I'm fine, Wick."

"What?" Drew asked as he got up. "Are you feeling like crap? Wick, is he all right?"

"He'll answer you," the Emperor said, "but that doesn't mean you'll understand."

"He's clever. Show me, Wick."

Fine.

I head butted the Emperor's leg, then laid down and curled up, closing my eyes. Drew guessed that he was tired, but they were all tired. He wanted more, so I did it again, keeping my eyes closed longer, until he understood.

"He needs to sleep."

Bingo.

"Wick," the Emperor argued, "I'm fine. I'm used to not sleeping."

"Being used to not sleeping and not needing sleep are two different things," Drew said. "You're taking a break tonight. Sleep. We can keep an eye on things."

"That's easier said than done."

"We'll take turns," Zed said. "You sleep, and Drew can sleep for a few hours while I keep watch, then we'll switch. But yeah, we're tucking you into your sleeping bag and if you don't sleep, you don't get dessert tomorrow. I'm preparing a delectable ration bar from a shiny silver wrapper, so you don't want to miss that."

"We'll see."

That was as far as he was willing to concede. He wanted to push on, and however much or little he slept later would be decided when we set up camp. Until then, we were walking between the river and the road, staying as out of sight as we could.

An hour later, he was throwing up whatever was left in his stomach from breakfast. He waved them both off, swearing he would be all right. After taking a swig from the canteen to rinse his mouth out, he started walking, leaving them to follow.

Within half an hour he began to slow down, and his pink skin went pale, but he kept moving forward, even when Drew pleaded with him to stop.

An hour after that, he was dry heaving.

Drew convinced him to sit for a while; if he wouldn't stop for the day, then at least rest. "Give me a chance to get a little closer to the road and see if it goes straight or turns off. If we have a better idea of the direction it goes, we won't waste any time later trying to recover ground if we stray."

With a slight nod, the Emperor gave his consent. While Drew headed to check out the road, Zed crept over rocks to wet a t-shirt in the river, something the Emperor could use as a cool rag. He took it and wiped the sweat from his face, and then draped it across the back of his neck. I sat at his feet, trying to get a better look at him; his eyes were closed and his breathing was shallow, and I was sure that if I touched him, he would be warm.

Just a few minutes after he left, Drew ran back, breathing hard from the exertion.

"Air van," he said. "It crashed at the tree line about a quarter mile ahead...no tags on it, either."

Whatever ailed the Emperor, he shoved it down deep and jumped up, grabbing his backpack while he barked at Zed to pick me up. They ran toward the van, which had veered off the road and between several trees, stopping when it hit front-first into a pine tree several feet into the woods. It was larger, somewhere in between a van and a shuttle, the kind I usually saw making deliveries around downtown San Francisco. When they were close, he held up his hand, signaling Zed and Drew to slow down. He wanted to be careful, to make sure that there were no surprises around the wreckage.

The doors were open, and he crouched down as he approached, first peeking into the back window, and he stayed down as he slid up the side to the open back door. He listened first, and then slowly peeked around to look inside.

He relaxed, and then waved them over.

There was a body in the front passenger seat, his chin and chest painted in blood, and on the roof above his head, there was a bloody footprint.

Drew crawled into the back; it was fairly open, with only one passenger seat in the back. Wrapped neatly around the security strap was a torn strip from the hem of a red t-shirt, and the arms of the seat were broken and bent.

"Oz was here," Drew said.

"Bread crumbs," the Emperor muttered.

Zed was looking at the dead man, and said, "Yeah, and this is her brutal calling card."

"Good," Drew said. "Good for her." Then under his breath he said, "Kill them all if you have to, Oz."

The Emperor sat down on the floor of the van, his legs hanging out. "She just needs to stay alive, Drew."

Zed wasn't paying much attention. He'd let me into the back of the van to sit near the Emperor, and without warning anyone that he was going to, he set a hand on the dead man's bare arm and listened.

The Emperor gestured for Drew to not say anything; he was still wary of Zed's new ability, but he was as curious as he was worried. They waited quietly while Zed listened, and it took a few minutes before Zed began to speak.

When he did, it was barely a whisper. "'I deserved this. This was wrong. Munson. God, he's the anti-Christ. Please forgive me. Please keep her safe.'" He listened quietly for a long time, his eyes closed, and then said, "His name is Tyler Bledsoe. He's twenty-eight and married with three kids. He's a reluctant conscript in Florida's military who hates the First Minister, but follows orders to protect his family. He didn't want any of this."

I don't think the Emperor cared at that moment. "Is there anything about where they're taking Oz?"

"No, I'm sorry. His last thoughts were only about his kids."

"She's fighting," he said. "And if she escapes, she'll head for Newton."

"She has nothing, though," Zed pointed out. "No money, no food, no maps."

"It's Oz," Drew said. "She'll manage."

*

Drew took charge. He made the Emperor lie down in the back of the van while he and Zed pulled the dead guy from the front seat and dragged him just far enough into the woods to not be easily seen, but not so far that he wouldn't be discovered. He had Zed go top off the canteens and while he was gone Drew worked at getting the lone back seat out; the Emperor was not keen on the idea, but we were spending the night in the van.

"You have to stop for the day, Will. You're worried about staying awake so you can keep an eye on things? Well, this gives us shelter, and someone would have to make a hell of a lot of noise to get in here. The doors will be locked, and I'll put the force field around the van before we're all ready to go to sleep."

"We're too visible from the road, Drew."

"So? We'll take that chance. I'm willing to bet this was just part of a convoy, and they're not coming back for it any time soon."

"Anyone could stumble upon it."

"Will. You're sick. We're staying."

Resigned, he climbed all the way in, and sat with his back against the wall. "I don't have the strength to argue. But we'll lose valuable distance."

"Look on the bright side. We know Oz was in this van. It's confirmation that we're heading in the right direction."

*

The Emperor slept.

Zed and Drew sat just outside the van until the sun began to set, giving him quiet. I stayed curled up by him in case he needed me, but I could hear their voices rumbling through the open door, even when they tried whispering.

Zed was worried what they would do if the Emperor was truly ill. Stay in place? Call for help? Sit on him to keep him from trying to walk in the morning if he still looked horrible?

Drew hoped it was just a matter of exhaustion. "He hasn't slept more than a couple hours a night, and that's an average. Most nights, he's awake, guarding us. If he can sleep straight through until morning, I'm hoping he'll feel better."

I wanted to touch my nose to his skin to see if he was hot or not, but my nose was cold and that might wake him up.

After they'd eaten and taken care of personal business, Drew set the field up around the van and they climbed in, making sure every door was locked. It was warm enough, more comfortable than we'd been since running from the safe house, and it didn't take long for everyone to fall asleep.

I snuggled up to the Emperor's head, hoping to peek into his dreams, but the warmth inside the van made me sleepy and I drifted off.

20

Drew woke up before sunrise and carefully slid the door open so that I could get out to pee. He told me to just go under the van because the force field was still up, and then to come back inside for breakfast. He tried to be quiet as he tore open one of the foil food pouches for me—whispering an apology because he was sure it tasted as bad as it smelled, even though it didn't—but Zed stirred and muttered, "Go away."

He must be dreaming about the skank.

All right, I know that wasn't nice of me. But if Oz doesn't like someone they have to be kind of not-nice themselves. Right?

It would be nice if you could freaking understand me. This is a bonding moment, you know.

There was no bowl for me to eat from; the Emperor had little silicon pads he could use in place of plates, but finding a way to clean those three or four times a day was time lost to forward movement, so they were carefully pulling the pouches apart until the food sat there like it was in a little foil dish. When I was thirsty, they poured water into their cupped hands and let me drink from them. After I finished eating the cat-food-like chunky paste, Drew cupped a handful of water, and when I finished it he told me to drink more if I could.

"You're not drinking enough, Wick," he said. He carefully pinched the skin on my back and pulled up. "Your skin isn't as elastic as it should be. Make sure we stop to get water for you more often. I'm not sure how long cats can go without getting enough, but we have it and it's okay to ask someone to get you a drink. I tell you what, if the Emperor is asleep or doesn't hear you, lick the palm of my hand, and I'll know you want water. Okay?"

You're gonna be a good dad someday.

Well, except for maybe diapers. And baby food.

Zed sat up and whispered, "How is he?"

Once I'd finished enough water to make him happy, Drew wiped his hands on his pants and crawled over to the Emperor, ignoring Zed's sharp intake of breath when he reached out to touch the Emperor's forehead.

"No fever," he said. "Just let him sleep."

"That was ballsy," Zed said as he crawled out of his sleeping bag. He scooted over to the door, stretching as he stood just outside. "He'd have probably broken your arm if he'd woken up."

"Maybe. Pee against a tire or right behind the van," Drew said. "I don't want to take the force field down until I have to."

"Fine, Dad."

"I didn't mean—"

"Come on, I'm just giving you crap," Zed said. "You're starting to sound like the Emperor, though."

"You mean *William*."

"Uncle Willie. I swear, if Oz doesn't really start calling him that…" He sat on the floor of the van, legs hanging out the open door. "Jesus, I hope she's okay. I spent half of last night worrying that we're taking too long or headed in the wrong direction."

"We know we're going the right way," Drew said. "But yeah. All I can think about is finding the fastest way to get to her."

"I really wish I hadn't been such a douche the last few weeks. What the hell. Would it have killed me to be nice to her?"

How about to all of us?

"Probably. But yeah, don't worry about it. I have my own regrets. I know she understands, Zed. Don't think anything different, other than about how you'll apologize to her later."

"And to him," Zed said, nodding toward the Emperor.

"Yeah." Drew started to crawl into the front seat. "I've heard what she's planning on doing if you call him a dick again."

Cross your legs, dude. You saw what she did to the Emperor.

"I just didn't get it. Still don't, not completely. It seemed to me like he was just trying to keep us busy. I can do that on my own."

Drew probably could have explained it to him, but he was busy poking through the storage compartment in the dashboard. Papers fluttered out and one stuck to a glob of congealed blood on the passenger seat, and a few more slipped to the floor. He pulled everything out, including a map of Kansas that was marked with cities where Florida had a strong presence, a technical manual, and a hand-held wide-band radio.

Zed thumbed through the manual while Drew crawled outside to turn the radio on. They sat in the dirt, heads close to the radio speaker as they strained to hear voices in between bursts of static. I sat on the van floor near the open door, trying to hear, too.

There was movement at the border; there were scouts from Florida trying to get into Colorado, heading for both Denver and Colorado Springs, but a convoy of unmarked trucks kept them inside Kansas and they weren't sure to whose military the trucks belonged. They would wait a few miles inside the border, until given the all clear to proceed.

It could be a day or two, they were warned. There were three armies playing on the same field, and if they came upon squadrons from Pacifica or Midlam, they wouldn't make it fifty feet over the border.

They kept listening, hoping for a hint about Oz, but it was mostly static and a repeated reminder that the area was crawling with Pacifica's military.

After going through the manual, Zed found tools under the passenger seat and set about removing side panels from the car. "There's storage behind them," he explained when Drew wanted to know why. "Air vans are manufactured with a few compartments for extra tools. Big wrenches make for good weapons."

"Yeah, but you also have to carry them. Big wrenches are heavy."

Zed thought it was worth a look, and he worked as quietly as he could. There was some creaking as he turned bolts, and a popping sound when the panel came loose, but the Emperor didn't stir.

"Drew! Holy hell, come here!"

I jumped out of the van to see what Zed was excited about. There was a rack behind the panel, and clipped into neatly lined up slots were several pistols. He carefully pulled one loose and pointed it away from himself, and asked Drew to take down the force field.

"In case it goes off. I'm not sure what kind of ricochet effect would happen."

Yeah, don't want to go boom.

He turned the gun over in his hand, looking closely before pulling on the hinge at the bottom of the grip. The ammunitions clip slid out easily, and he said, "It's a charge pack. These are laser pistols."

"Like the light guns we were firing at the bunker?"

"Almost identical, only these are live and pretty freaking deadly. More deadly than I'm comfortable with." He put it back, and then pulled from the underside of the rack a thin metal box. "Rechargers. At least ten of them. And there are twenty other boxes."

He put the box back but left the panel off; they both assumed they'd leave the van later fully armed, but weren't doing anything until the Emperor said to. With the panel off they could get to the guns quickly if needed, but Drew didn't see a reason to sit in the back of the van with a gun, and Zed was deferring to him.

Is this an age thing? If it is, I'm in charge.

Mid-morning, the Emperor woke with a soft groan; he was on his back and covered his eyes with his hands, taking a deep breath before trying to sit up.

"'Morning, sunshine," Zed said.

His hair was plastered to his head, except on one side where it stuck straight up, and he had deep bags under his eyes. He was still pale, but his cheeks were pinker than they'd been, so I jumped over Drew's legs to get a close-up view, just to make sure he was all right.

Dude, you need a shower.

"Yes, I know, Wick. We all do." Sleepily, he scooted backward until he had something to lean against. "How late is it?"

"Maybe ten or so," Drew answered.

Grumpily, "You should have woken me at dawn."

Drew shrugged. "Judgment call. I thought you needed sleep more than we needed a few extra miles under our feet."

The Emperor leaned his head back and closed his eyes. "This

feels like hangover hell," he muttered. "I almost feel bad for all the ones Jax has suffered at my hands. Almost."

"There you go. Another reason to not drink. Other than that, how do you feel?"

He took time to answer. "Better, I think. Once the headache lets up."

Zed dug into his bag for pain medication. "Yeah, that happens when you've slept for sixteen hours. You're probably dehydrated."

He wouldn't eat, but accepted the canteen Drew handed him. They outlined what they'd been doing, listening to the radio and pulling the panels off the van, discovering the laser pistols. He agreed that they would make use of the guns and take as many of the recharge packs as they could. "One in the gun, one in a pocket, the rest in your packs. And let me see the map."

Drew got it from the front seat, and as he handed it over said, "It's a basic map of the state, but someone has drawn red stars over several cities. I'm guessing it's where they either have a stronghold, or at least a decent sized contingency."

"How?" Zed asked. "It hasn't been all that long, really. How long would it take to get a firm foothold in a major city?"

"These aren't all major," the Emperor said as he looked at the map. "There are clusters of small towns and even farmland. But we can assume that Florida has been sending people into Midlam for years. Long before the exodus began."

"Is this worth keeping?'" Drew asked.

"Indeed. If Oz is not at the safe house, knowing where they have even small populations may be helpful."

Drew began to repack the backpacks, rolling the Emperor's sleeping bag as tight as it would go. "There was enough juice left in the van's battery to charge your tablet and phone, and no, I didn't let Zed peruse your porn."

"I don't—" He sighed and gave up. "Fine."

"Other than getting food into you, when you're ready, we can head out."

The Emperor started for the door, stretching when he was outside. "I can eat along the way. Fill the canteens, water a tree, and let's go."

You're turning into a classy Emperor, aren't you?

After they filled the canteens Drew made me drink more. When I finished, he told the Emperor they needed to make sure I was taking in more water and if I started licking palms, that meant I was thirsty. "I'm assuming he would just tell you, but who knows? But his skin doesn't snap back the way it should, and I'm afraid he's getting dehydrated."

He apologized for not noticing. When everyone had their backpack on and I was tucked safely into his sweatshirt, the Emperor told them he wanted to make up at least some of the distance they'd lost. "We'll walk past dark if we can."

Drew agreed but added a caveat. "If you start to look sick at all, we're stopping and I get to make that call."

"I'm fine, Drew."

"Look, I want to get there as much as you do, but we need you well. If everything goes south, you need to be able to fight. I need you to be able to fight. Oz especially needs you to be able to fight."

That was the battle cry.

For Oz.

The Emperor wasn't going to argue against that.

Ozoo.

*

A day and a half later, the river had narrowed until it was basically a creek, but the water was still moving, swirling around river rock, and the sediment was low enough that the canteens could still filter it. There were fish—big enough to be more than a two-bite snack—hiding between the rocks, so the Emperor decided it was a good time to take a break; he had some fine netting and he had patience, and declared there would be something fresh for dinner.

"We need protein. And I would like a break from the ration bars."

I like fish.

"I loathe fish," Drew said, "but if you can catch it and clean it, I'll eat it. Just don't make me look at the guts."

I like fish.

Zed dropped his pack to the ground and sat down hard,

just grateful for some extra time to sit. "My feet feel like size ten swamps," he grunted. "I can feel the sweat gushing between my toes."

"Take your boots off," the Emperor called back. He was spreading a fine net into the water, lying on his belly across a boulder. "Let them dry and then put clean socks on."

"I will in a minute. When they stop throbbing."

Half an hour later the Emperor was crawling off his rock and had seven decent sized fish in his net. Zed had barely moved but he'd taken his boots and socks off and propped his feet up on his backpack. His soles were raw and red, with giant blisters that spanned the balls of his feet. Drew looked and grimaced; the Emperor looked and sighed.

"Keep airing them out. I can cushion the blisters, but let me clean the fish first."

I don't know what bothered Drew more: Zed's feet and how badly they smelled, or the sight of fish guts being tossed back into the water. I watched, because that was food that I wanted and I didn't care about the blood or creepy looking insides. It smelled like dinner, and if he was too squeamish to eat any, I'd happily take his share.

Once the fish were clean, he told Drew to start a fire. He sat down by Zed and gently poked at the bottoms of his feet, and then asked when the last time he changed his socks was.

"I have no idea. It's not like we have a wardrobe to choose from."

"Socks and underwear," the Emperor said to both. "While I cook the fish, dig what you've used out of your bag and try to wash them in the creek. We can dry them over the fire." He turned and dug into his bag, pulling out a clean pair of socks and a first aid kit. After slathering an ointment on Zed's feet, he covered the blisters with a thick, spongy pink pad, and then covered that with wide white tape. "It'll sting, but you can still walk on them. Just leave the tape alone…you'll feel it if the blisters pop, but it'll be all right."

He tossed the socks to Zed and then added, "You owe me a pair when we get someplace we can actually do laundry."

Drew was already leaning over the side of the creek with his underwear. "I want a hot shower, too. I know I stink, and things are chafing."

"Seriously," Zed said. "My junk, my armpits, my nipples. My freaking *nipples*. I think one even bled yesterday."

"Wash up, and then cover them with bandages," the Emperor told him. "Your nipples, not…everything else."

While they cleaned up and rinsed out their underwear, the Emperor pulled short metal rods from a half dozen different places in his backpack, and snapped them together until he had a small rack. He cracked the fish all the way open and put them on the rack, and then shoved his knife into the fire to kill any germs before he used it to flip the fish over.

You've done this before.

"Jax and I have camped a few times, Wick. His father was keen on us learning some basic survival skills. He said it was in case of an emergency, but I suspect the real reason was that he was tempted to drop Jax off somewhere and let him go feral."

"Dad was that much of a handful?" Zed asked.

"He had his moments. But truthfully?" He poked at the fish while he considered what more he wanted to tell Zed. "I honestly think that if not for your mother, he wouldn't be alive now. That stunt with the bike on California Street was just the tip of a very frustrated adolescent iceberg. He had no sense of purpose…"

He shrugged.

"Until you dropped Mom right in front of him."

"It's very cliché, but yes. He wanted to be a better man for her."

Zed watched him flip the fish over. "Yeah, but he'd still be alive. He had you. Sooner or later you'd have taken him on a march through hell just like this one, right at the start of winter, and somehow straightened him up."

"Perhaps. But he vomited at the sight of the inside of a rabbit, so who knows? He might not have survived a week of twenty to thirty mile days stomping through the woods."

"Aw," Drew groaned. "You really did kill a bunny."

"We had to eat. While I'm fundamentally opposed to hunting for sport, when it comes to survival? I respect the food chain."

He didn't have any plates to put the cooked fish on, but he had the thin, flexible silicon pads, and when lunch was ready he speared them with the knife and dropped two fish onto each pad, then handed one to Drew and one to Zed.

"There's plenty, Wick," he said before I could point out that I would not mind a fish of my own. "Yours needs to cool down." He nodded to Drew's backpack and said, "Outside pocket, down deep. Tiny metal forks and knives."

"You were freaking prepared," Zed muttered as he dug his out.

"Military issue. All I did was grab the bags from the storage tunnel and add a few things."

Drew poked at his fish with the fork. "Guys, this is where I will seem incredibly entitled. I have never had fish with the bones still in it, and have no idea how to get rid of them. Do I eat them, or what?"

"Just pull the meat off with your fork and leave the bones behind," the Emperor said.

"And the skin?"

He shrugged. "Eat it if you like, but I don't think you'll like it."

I'll gnaw on it.

Drew picked a piece of fish from his plate and held it out to me. "You're being pretty patient there, Wick. You have to want this even more than we do."

"Don't let him sucker you. I saved a fish for him. He just needs to be patient a bit longer."

Don't listen to him, Drew. I'm saving you from tapeworms and other fishy cooties.

When it was cool enough, the Emperor broke up the fish he'd set aside for me and put it on his pad. He left a little extra from his own, and then Drew and Zed let me lick their pads clean. By the time they were washing up in the creek I was stuffed, and just wanted to curl up and sleep.

"Just a few miles further today," he said when I asked if we could take naps. "Once the clothes are dry, we'll go. But I promise, Wick, we won't walk more than a couple of hours."

An hour later we were near the border, and the road was crawling with trucks that Zed thought had been driven straight out of a museum. The Emperor said they appeared to be modeled after military Jeeps from the twentieth century and transport trucks from the early twenty-first, and then asked them to be quiet while he listened.

Zed and Drew, not the trucks.

The trucks were going to make whatever noises trucks make.

"None of them sound like they have internal combustion engines. I hear the whine of air jets and the clicks of magnets."

"So Florida has tech newer than we thought?" Drew asked. "They've just used older shells?"

"We know that they have access to air vehicles. But this is potentially much better than that," the Emperor said. "We have the capability to mass produce replicas of just about anything. With enough manpower, a significant portion of our transport fleet could be retrofitted to look very much like the vehicles Florida is using."

He wasn't going to swear to it—Florida had surprised everyone with the ability to get their airplanes flying, and then getting them into Canada in order to attack Chicago—but he thought we were most likely looking at Pacifica's army on its way to push into Kansas. "This illusion can get the troops inside the border without a fight."

"So do we wait, or what?"

"We wait."

It was a miles-long convoy and we sat there until almost dark, with the beams from truck headlights slicing through the trees. When we could see the end of it approaching, I thought we would be able to move on, but he told us to be especially quiet, because near the tail end there were soldiers on foot.

Any noise we had made before could be lost to the sound of traffic; any noise we made as they passed could likely be heard.

The footsteps fell hard and loud, metallic clicks and pops that pounded against the pavement, and even the Emperor looked confused until he dared to peek around the tree he was behind. Zed and Drew looked, too, and it took everything they had to not pop out with *What the hell?*

The soldiers made enough noise that the Emperor felt comfortable talking. "Those are definitely from Pacifica and Midlam."

"What are they wearing?" Drew asked. "They look like freaking black ghosts."

Each soldier was covered from head to toe in skin-tight, flexible armor that had a carbon fiber pattern and seemed to absorb the night. Light didn't reflect off them, but seemed to vanish as the soldiers walked through it. I couldn't make sense of them; I could see the soldiers were there, but brain couldn't admit they were there.

"Exoskeleton prototypes, based on mid-twenty-first century technology. This is largely what your father has worked on for the last twenty years, Drew. The suits are designed to function as armor, but also allow soldiers to run faster, jump higher, and fight stronger. They fit like a second skin, which alleviates some of the weight."

"I knew he worked on military applications some, but I had no idea…damn, I'm impressed."

"He has a dozen irons in the fire. The original use of these exoskeletons was to provide mobility for people disabled by spinal fractures or muscle atrophy, but he retooled the materials to be significantly lighter, and to withstand ballistic and energy strikes. Bullets, laser bursts, pulsar rays, they all tend to bounce off or warp around the suits. He also added robotic elements for increased strength and speed. I imagine this is the first major practical application test he's been able to run."

"I thought he was working with Finn," Zed said. "To build another gate."

"As I said, he's involved in many projects. He has ideas about how to improve the structure of the gate, which was admittedly put together hastily."

"Hey, it worked," Drew said. "You sent Finn home, back to Jo."

"Indeed."

Zed started counting on his fingers. "All right. If your birthday is when you say it is, based on when Finn shot through the gate… you sent him home to get laid. And then there was you."

"Really, Zed?" Drew said. "Is sex all you think about?"

"Pretty much."

The Emperor was fixated on watching the soldiers march past.

"Just because he went back when it was August for us, does not mean it was August on the other side of the gate. I sent him to a specific date and time."

"Yeah, but I bet it was August, and then nine, ten months later there was you, right?"

With a sigh, the Emperor conceded. "Yes, I was born a little over nine months later. But it means nothing. My mother's timeline was such that they had been together just two nights before we sent him home. It doesn't matter that he hadn't seen her for weeks. There's every chance I was conceived before he was lost in time. Don't think that hasn't occurred to me. I sat on the steps at Herman Plaza with her for hours, and I realized that they very well could have conceived me the night before. Or that morning, who knows. They were essentially newlyweds then."

"Kinda hope so," Drew muttered.

"Does it matter when?" Zed asked. "He's here."

"Time isn't static in my head anymore. If there's ever a loop of this When where Finn doesn't get home…I prefer to think that Will was born anyway."

"Fair enough."

The last of the foot soldiers passed, but we waited still, for them to fade from sight. After that, the Emperor wanted us to push on, to get into Kansas under cover of dark, because there wasn't much of the forest left to hide in. He said he would reassess once we were close to the point where the trees were not dense enough to provide the protection level he wanted.

The further we walked, the further from the road the trees were. The creek turned away from the direction we were walking, and while all the canteens had been refilled, I know the Emperor was worrying about where they would find more water. There was a small mining town ahead, but he also knew it was non-operational and he had no idea if there were still residents or if any of the utilities worked.

They walked without talking. I could almost feel the crunch of dry grass under the Emperor's feet, and could feel the subtle change in the air temperature on the tips of my ears. It wasn't as cold, and I could hang half out of the sweatshirt pouch without freezing. We stayed within the tree line, but the trees were becoming fewer, and in another hour, we would be past them.

He began looking for a good place to set up camp, even if it meant getting further away from the road. They could sleep unseen out in the open if they didn't start a fire, but late night was too cold for that, and he was working out the logistics, watching for a thicker grouping of trees, when Drew stopped and told him to look ahead.

A few hundred yards down the road there was an old white van parked on the shoulder. Its side doors were slid open and the driver and his passenger were in the front seat with windows down, heads leaned back. "Dead or sleeping?" he asked.

"Dead if they had Oz," Zed guessed.

They stood still, listening. "I hear music," the Emperor said.

"Scouts?" Drew asked. "We heard on the radio that they were waiting on the Kansas side for the convoy to pass."

"If that's them, we don't have much time," the Emperor said. "They'll head out soon."

"Then we need to get closer," Drew said. "They have a van, and we need one."

With a nod, the Emperor directed them to head for the road, and then walk along its shoulder. Drew was right; we needed a ride. Walking was taking too long, and Newton was still a couple hundred miles away.

"I really don't want to kill anyone," Zed said. "Not again."

"They took Oz," Drew reminded him. "I'll do whatever I have to."

"But it might not have actually been *them*."

The Emperor made the decision. "I'll handle it. Say nothing, and let me do the talking. We're just hikers, that's all. That's all they need to believe."

He led them along the road, walking as if he wasn't both afraid and angry. He made noise as he approached the car, and when he was close enough he called out, "Hey! Are you all right?"

Not a trace of his Scottish accent.

The driver startled and scrambled to open his door.

"We saw you from a ways back. Broken down?"

He'd obviously been asleep, and was trying to make sense

of the hairy and unwashed men standing by his van. "Uh, no," he finally said. "We're just waiting."

"Ah, well, there was a line of military vehicles a few miles back. Not sure where they're headed, but it looked like they meant business. If that's who you're waiting on, they've passed."

"Whose military?" he asked.

His passenger got out and came around to the other side of the van. "What'd they look like? Trucks or cars?"

The Emperor shrugged. "I've never seen trucks like these. Except maybe in books. But they were definitely military, had that look."

"Ours," the driver said to his companion. "Any idea how many?"

The Emperor set his backpack down and made a show of stretching. "It's dark, hard to tell. Took about fifteen, twenty minutes for them to pass. They headed that way."

He pointed down the road, to where we'd come from, and when they both looked away from him, he moved. His hands shot up, and he slapped their heads together; there was the grimace of sudden pain on both their faces, but nothing else as they fell to the ground.

He dug into their pockets for wallets and keys, and then searched them for guns, while telling Zed and Drew to throw the bags in the back of the van. When he'd taken their keys and phones, he jumped into the driver's seat, fired the engine up, and took off.

"They're not dead," he told Zed. "They'll want to be, but they're not dead."

Zed watched them from the side mirror, but I don't think he really cared. We had a van, we were off our feet, and speeding toward Newton and hopefully, toward Oz.

21

The van was slower than what the Emperor was used to. It was decades-old with a gas-powered engine, and the fastest he could get it to go was roughly half the speed of an air car. We felt every bump and dip in the road, and I learned a couple of new things for the Queen to put on her bad word list.

Drew learned that he was just tall enough that a big bump in the road meant he would hit his head on the ceiling of the van, and Zed learned that pot holes when combined with seat belts and a full bladder equals pain. The Emperor learned he still needed to work on patience.

He wanted to get to Newton in the same short time frame he could have in his own car; what he owned was not the speediest vehicle ever made, but it could sing at a hundred fifty miles an hour, and scream at a hundred ninety. In his car, we could get there in a little over an hour; in the van, it was going to take three, and that was presuming we didn't run out of gas.

If we ran out, we were walking.

We were done with walking.

Drew reminded him that if he slowed down a little, he'd get more mileage out of the gas that was still in the tank. "Better to drive a little slower and get all the way, than have it run dry ten miles out and have to walk."

He hated it, but knew Drew was right.

"How do you even know how to drive this?" Zed wanted to know.

"I can drive an air car. I can ride an old motorcycle. The skills can be extrapolated," he said, but I think he was just making it up as he went along. If he actually had those skills, we wouldn't hit every single bump in the road.

Zed's takeaway was the motorcycle. "I really want you to take me for a ride on that someday. Just don't tell Mom."

The Emperor chuckled. "I'll even teach you to pilot it when you're older. It's not much different than your bike. But no, don't tell your mother. Your father, on the other hand, would be happy to join us."

Secrets from the Queen. Shame on you.

The road we were on had once been part of the United States Interstate infrastructure; this one had cut through most of the country, a line from Utah to the east coast, several lanes of asphalt over which millions of cars had been driven. When transportation needs changed, it was dug up and had all the pieces and parts needed for air and magnetic vehicles to travel over it buried underneath, and was covered with a thin layer of pliable synthetic tar and gravel. It was less maintained than it needed to be for older vehicles that actually made contact with its surface, and over time the dust and dirt and tiny little pieces of wheat that were cultivated across Kansas covered the tar and stuck to it.

The once-black Interstate was now a yellowish thoroughfare, hundreds of miles of sticky chaff that hadn't been perfectly flat for a hundred years.

Ours was not the only ground vehicle that had been on it lately; there were tire tracks that stretched before us, from the front of the van to the horizon. I didn't want to think about who that might have been. It could have been cars or trucks or vans just getting from point A to point B, or it could have been the convoy that had Oz.

The closer to the city we got, the more traffic there was buzzing overhead; hover cars and shuttles cut through the sky, high enough above that we couldn't easily make out where they came from. The only thing we were certain about was that it unlikely that any of them were from Florida, which made the Emperor a little uneasy.

Our van clearly was from Florida; that made us a target.

I was in the plastic tomb and didn't have the best view, but if I stretched and pushed my face against the plastic I could see out the front window. We were driving through a stretch of boring nothingness, but in the distance, off to the sides of the road, there were cities. Tall buildings practically glowed for the sunlight bouncing off glass, and air traffic left speckled shadows around them.

That should have prepared me for the sight of Newton, but it didn't. I knew it wasn't huge, probably a little bigger than San Francisco but not by much, but its buildings stretched toward the clouds, all shiny and new and made of metal and glass, with no bricks or mortar, and there were cars everywhere, in the air and on the ground.

It had been a very long time since I had seen traffic like this, with cars zooming in the air and hovering between buildings.

I didn't like it.

There were also people everywhere, walking in little crowds that reminded me of the San Francisco of four hundred years ago. I didn't think I would enjoy being out in that crowd any more than I did the times the Emperor took me back to have shrimp on a bench outside the Ferry Building while he watched people and judged them for their lives of consumption and self-involvement.

Okay, I was guessing at that.

Newton looked like a video; I'd seen all of this on the monitor in the living room, but it never felt real.

It still didn't.

The safe house was just outside the city in a small sliver of suburbia. He parked the van at a shopping center half a mile down the road—it was still dark out and he wanted to get to the house before sunrise but also didn't want the van anywhere near it—and we walked the rest of the way.

"We look derelict," he said when Zed asked what the hurry was. "Certainly not like anyone who would be expected to walk into a house here. I'd like to get there before we're most likely to be seen."

They walked fast. No one even bothered to take me out of the plastic tomb; the Emperor had Drew clip it to his backpack and I rode in it, jostling back and forth, slamming into the sides of it just as much as I had every time he'd hit a bump in the road with the van.

It took less than ten minutes to get there, but after bouncing around for three hours in the van, I was ready to be let out.

The house was on a corner lot, and looked like every other dwelling on the street. They were all made from the same type of prefabricated fireproof and weatherproof sheets, painted with different colors and textures, and they were all formed into a similar square shape. Some were bigger than others, but the neighborhood had a generic quality to it.

It was the residential version of the reconstituted food they'd had to eat in the first safe house.

Zed had lived his entire life in a city where apartments were the norm—even the structures that looked like houses had three or more apartments inside—and the idea of each of these homes being for only one family struck him as being wasteful.

"You also think graves are a waste," the Emperor reminded him. "Perhaps the argument for that can be made, but those who want them don't feel the same way."

"Most areas of Midlam have more open land than San Francisco," Drew said. "We never really had to build up, except in the major cities. Building out has always been an option."

So was building under. Like the safe house in Denver, once we were inside we headed down a staircase that was hidden in the front closet, and found ourselves in a huge bunker. It lacked the tunnels of the Denver house, but it had everything else. Living room, kitchen, gym, and giant bedroom with bunk beds. Zed grumbled at the community showers—it was a giant tile-covered room with eight showerheads—and there were toilet stalls instead of private bathrooms, but he decided the health-club amenities weren't worth getting too upset over since they weren't planning on staying long.

There was also a similar setup of video monitors with a panel mounted to the wall, and built into it was a keyboard along with all kinds of switches and buttons. The Emperor carefully pulled his backpack off and let me out of the tomb, and then stared at the blank monitors for a long time.

He knew what he had to do.

He just didn't want to.

Drew and Zed waited just behind him; they didn't want to do it, either. Turning the system on meant notifying the King of their whereabouts and then telling him they were chasing Oz without a clear idea of where she was.

He'd had a glimmer of hope that she would be waiting for us in the house, but wasn't willing to voice the crushing disappointment when she wasn't.

"He'll understand," Zed said softly.

Dude. You have to.

"I know."

He reached down and flipped several switches, and when the monitors powered on he typed onto the keyboard, and then waited.

He won't be mad.

It's not your fault.

"It feels like it is."

The main monitor flickered, and without the usual Pacifica screen popping up first, Jax was there. Before the Emperor could even get his mouth open, the King held up his hand to stop him.

"I know they have Oz," he said. "We pulled the security footage from Denver. That was a no-win situation, Will, so don't even try to apologize." He looked past the Emperor to Zed. "Are you all right, Zed? I know you left on your own power, but…"

"No worries, Dad," he said. "They took good care of me. What about Mom?"

"Frantic," he said. He looked sad before, but after saying that he looked even worse. "Will, I'm splitting the screen so you can get a look at Florida's most recent news footage." He looked at Drew and Zed and added, "This is hard to look at. But she's alive and moving under her own power."

The screen split, and to the right of his face was a grainy recording of Oz being pushed into a room that looked a little too staged; there was a desk in the center but not much else, other than the Florida flag on a pole that listed to the left. She was shoved through the door by an old man in an ill-fitting military uniform; her hands were cuffed together, and her feet shackled with only inches between them for her to be able to move.

Oz's face was bruised, eyes blacked, chin scraped. Her bare arms were pocked with little bloody holes, and there were lines of scratch marks running from her wrists to her elbows. A cut near her ear ran into her hairline, and her lip was split near the corner of her mouth, leaving a faint trail of blood where it had dripped over her jaw.

Her shirt had dozens of bloody holes in it; the Emperor didn't need to tell us; they'd been using the Taser on her, probably to control her defensive moves.

The First Minister stepped toward the desk from off camera and sat with dramatic flourish, pausing for effect before he proclaimed Oz to be an enemy of the church. She had been arrested while fleeing from Florida's security task force and would be tried for her many crimes against the Church; she repeatedly denied that it was the One True Church, and refused to recognize the First Minister as God's prophet. She had committed offenses against nature by refusing to dress appropriately to her gender and by refusing to accept a blood-related male spokesman. This deliberate embrace of apostasy could not be dismissed.

And then as an afterthought, as if it mattered that much less, she was charged with the murders of seven of God's faithful servants.

There was no mention that she had killed them while defending her own life.

The screen cut back to just Jax. "The video bounced off over ten thousand proxy servers. We don't know where she is, but she's on her own two feet. The so-called trial is slated to begin next week and will be televised globally."

"What are they waiting for?" the Emperor asked.

Jax sighed audibly, sadly. "Holidays, supposedly. Munson wants something else, I can feel it. He would have killed her outright otherwise."

"Aubrey," the Emperor said. "He may have started this wanting Midlam, but once he saw her face to face it became far more personal. He's not done torturing her."

"The son of a bitch would trade mother for daughter," Jax said.

"That won't happen."

Drew stepped up. "What the hell is wrong with him? He wants

Kansas. He wants Midlam. He wants Mrs. B. What does he really want?"

The Emperor turned to him. "He wants it all, Andrew. Control and vengeance, and he has millions who will follow him because they believe he's God's voice on earth."

"Don't they grasp that God's not a prick?" Zed sniped.

"They know," the Emperor told him. "But they're also afraid. Munson has a history of executing people with thin justification, and the members of his church will believe and do what they need in order to survive. They've grown up with the absolute certainty that this man will lead them to their salvation, and they'll swallow the doubts because they don't want to face the idea that Hell might be waiting for them."

"That's *not* what Mom taught me," he said. "It's not supposed to be about fear."

"Because she doesn't want you to be a dick," Drew told him.

"Trust in what she taught you," Jax said. "We need to get to him, Will. There are a hundred places in Florida he could be, but we don't have anyone on the ground there. We've sent in swarms of drones and are utilizing satellite surveillance, but nothing has pointed our way to his location. Or Oz's. Florida is now technically savvy enough to point their proxy servers to data ports around the world and half of them point to Russia—"

The Emperor cut him off. "We start with the son. Redmond Munson tried to warn us, but we didn't understand the mutterings coming from a dead man's mind. We find him first, and hope that he can lead us to his father."

"We know where Redmond is," Jax said. "It's access to him that's problematic."

"How many more days until the trial? I've lost track of time."

"Six."

"Then we'll take today and tonight to rest. I don't think I can push them any harder than I already have."

Drew was not happy about that. "I'll leave right now if it means getting to Oz."

Jax tried to smile. His lips barely moved, though, and he had to swallow past the lump in his throat. "You look like hell, Drew. I want my daughter back, but…just do what Will says, all right? If he didn't think you needed some down time, he'd be half out the door already."

Drew could see the fatigue that was cutting through the Emperor, too. He nodded, accepting that we would stay one night, for no reason other than he didn't want to push the Emperor just yet.

"I know how badly you want to leave and I won't delay any longer than we need to," he said to Drew.

"They won't kill her," Jax said. "Remember that. They need her alive right now." He said that as if he was reminding himself, using it to push down the anger he did not want Zed or Drew to see.

He didn't believe it.

The Emperor could feel it, and with it the questions Jax refused to ask. *Where were you? My daughter fought alone. Where the hell were you?*

"Will, contact me in the morning before you leave. I'll have General Myers compile troop locations for you. And when you get to Redmond, warn him…I'll kill Munson myself if I have to, and I won't bother worrying about who's standing in front of him. If he protects his father—"

"I'll make sure he understands."

"Hell, Mr. B," Drew said. "I'll kill them both with my bare hands if I have to."

Jax nodded, but I saw the look he gave the Emperor.

You won't let that happen, will you?

When the screen went dark, he picked me up and carried me to the kitchen for food, but whispered to me, "I'm not sure I can stop him, Wick."

Maybe I can.

"You have my permission to jump on his face and dig in with claws if you have to. But stay out of harm's way. I need you alive and well."

I agreed, but wondered if his need for me was as great as it had been even a few months ago.

Maybe he didn't need an anchor anymore.

Maybe he needed something to lift him up instead of holding him down.

22

I wanted to make fun of how long they were each in the shower, but then Zed said it hurt at first, the hot water pinging off his chafed parts, which sucked the fun out of it. They also smelled significantly better when they were done, and their hairs no longer looked weighed down by bacon grease and salt.

I wanted bacon.

There was no bacon.

Drew wanted to shave when he showered, probably so that his face was kissably soft when they found Oz, but he couldn't find a razor. The Emperor thought there was probably a box somewhere in the house with shaving supplies but he didn't want to go look for it. He just wanted to eat food that wasn't compressed into a dense bar that tasted like defeat wrapped in foil, and then he wanted to sit back to do nothing for a while. Drew agreed that sounded fine, and while the Emperor showered he dug through the kitchen and found enough unexpired cardboard food to make a passable lunch for everyone.

Zed did laundry, cringing as he pulled everyone's dirty, sweat-soaked clothing out of the backpacks. Washing things in the creek hadn't helped much, and most of it was so stiff it could stand up on its own.

By the time they had all showered, eaten, repacked their bags, and eaten again, it was late enough to go to bed. Zed and Drew headed into the bedroom, but the Emperor had downloaded the things Jax sent and he wanted to go over them. I thought he needed to sleep more than he needed to read, but he wasn't listening.

"I wish I could keep them here for a week, not just a night. They need sleep and food, not more stress. They certainly don't need the risks that will come with trying to get through to Redmond's compound."

You need that, too. Lots of rest. So maybe next week, after you get Oz, we will. We'll either go home or find a new hiding place, and everyone can rest.

"I wish I could have left you at home, too. If I'd had any real idea…"

I'm fine. I'll never want to leave home again, but I'm fine.

He set the tablet aside and leaned his head on the back of the chair. "What am I going to do, Wick?"

Go to where Redmond is. That's the first thing.

"He's hidden away in a compound, surrounded by his faithful. Surrounding the compound are Munson's minions. Surrounding *them* are Pacifica's and Midlam's troops. Oz won't be there, and yet I still feel like I have to risk Drew's and Zed's safety to get through all three layers, and that's just to *talk* to Redmond. I really have no idea what I'm going to do."

Drew's voice cut through his self-contemplation. "You're going to go to bed." He was lingering at the doorway, leaning against the wall. "You need it every bit as much as we do."

"I won't sleep."

"Can't force that, but you can at least rest. Lay in the dark and let your mind wander, maybe something will come to you."

I'll lie across your face if it will help.

"Big help, there, Wick," he said. But he got up, and headed for the bedroom. Whether he could sleep or not, he was going to do what Drew told him to.

*

He went out like a light.

Less than a minute after his head hit the pillow, the Emperor was asleep, and that honestly worried me. Sleeping was not something he did much of, but lately he'd slept a lot. Falling asleep even when he was tired enough to manage it generally took over half an hour, so this being completely gone before I could even get curled up near his head was bothersome.

Months earlier, he'd worried that his time was coming to an end, but Oz was positive that by having changed the timeline— sparing me from being swallowed forever by a half-closed portal— he would live. The history books of his youth noted that the Emperor of San Francisco had slept less and less, until he finally could not, and he then stared at his own death approaching until he embraced it, simply for the relief.

I worried that by flipping the switch, he was sending himself in the opposite direction, sleeping until he couldn't wake up.

That felt unfair. He'd lived for the sake of others his entire life, and he should have a chance to live for himself. I wanted him to find Oz, go home, and live happily ever after. I wanted that for them all, even if it meant I had to suffer through more groping and drooling and the inevitable bouncy things that Oz and Drew were contemplating.

No matter what, the Emperor didn't feel well. I knew Drew could see it, and I think Zed would have if his brain wasn't half filled with the girl he wanted to apologize to, the girl he wanted to take to lunch, and the rage he felt at his sister being gone. I'd seen the Emperor sick only a handful of times, but there was always the feeling that he would be fine. He'd cough for a few days, complain about the volume of gunk floating in his sinuses, and then it would stop. Or he'd throw up a lot, complain about the things the Queen forced him to drink and the hot soup she expected him to at least try, and within a few days he was better.

He didn't slowly slide into illness.

This felt like sliding.

I wanted to curl up on his pillow until it was safe to touch him and then peek into his dreams, but if he really was sick I didn't want to chance waking him up. There might be things in his dreams that would tell me what he needed: pain pills, something to calm a touchy stomach, or different food, but even if I could figure it out I had no way to tell Drew or Zed, and the Emperor would ignore anything I suggested. He would appease me, but he wasn't going to take care of himself until Oz was safe.

I slept near his head, half listening in case he woke up, but he laid still for hours. He was flat on his back and the only movement was the soft rise and fall of his chest.

Before dawn, Drew carefully crawled out of bed and went into the living room. I knew he hadn't slept well; he tossed and turned, kicking off his blanket and hugging his pillow to his face. Every now and then I could hear his breath catch and nose gurgle, but he didn't seem sick so I didn't think he was catching a cold.

I hated it all. I couldn't make any of them feel better.

Purring wasn't even making me feel better.

When I heard the monitor in the living room click on, I jumped down from the Emperor's bed and went to see what Drew was watching. He'd found a local newscast, and was watching footage of a small band of Florida's military attacking a lone cargo truck from Pacifica. There were more reports of skirmishes, and blame was laid squarely at the feet of the Floridians.

"I hate Florida but I suspect the media wants everyone to think that they're starting everything," he said when he realized I was watching with him. "I'm not even sure those are really Florida troops. Their gear is a little too polished and they fight a bit too well. It's like we're taking a giant stick and poking the Florida bear with it. And for what? Isn't the idea to avoid all-out war?"

The Emperor's sleepy voice came from behind us. "They're trying to get Florida to tip its hand. How badly do they want to hang on to that compound? It's one thing to bomb an unaware city, a whole other thing to have to fight hand to hand. It took no courage for them to lay waste to Chicago, but do they have enough to defend what they want when it means seeing the blood up close?"

"Does the First Minister even care about the blood of his people?"

The Emperor sat down on the sofa next to Drew, and pulled me onto his lap. "I doubt it, but they care about themselves and each other. If they see this, what personal combat can look like, maybe they'll think twice."

"Or maybe not."

He nodded. "Those most loyal to Munson will fight, no matter what."

Drew didn't understand that. Surely they had to grasp that with a single order, Jax could wipe them off the face of the earth. One blast, that's all it would take. He could obliterate them all.

"It's possible," the Emperor agreed. "But it's also not a step he would take lightly. He would wind up killing not only those from Florida, but some of Midlam's citizens as well, and any of our military who didn't retreat in time. The stakes would have to be far higher than they are right now."

"His daughter—"

"Is one life. You're talking the destruction of hundreds of thousands. That's not an order a ruler recovers from. It would define his monarchy and change global politics. It would change who he is. Levi Munson is every bit as aware of that as Jax is."

"I don't think I would have the restraint needed. I want Oz back, at pretty much any cost. I was serious when I said I would choose her over hundreds."

The Emperor was quiet for a few moments, pondering. "There will come a time when you'll have to make a decision that will define your character and determine the kind of man you want to be. Not just in that moment, but from then on. It might serve you well to work on that kind of restraint."

"But Oz…"

"I know."

"I feel nothing but selfish, Will. I'm not sure I care about all those other people out there. It's like I have tunnel vision, and all I can see is getting to her and then killing that bastard."

"Imagine how Jax felt throughout the negotiations. He knew what Munson did to Aubrey when she was just a girl. He knows all the little details, the layers of terror she would never allow anyone else to see, and yet as badly as he wanted to, he didn't kill Munson on sight. And for years—I know the thought has crossed his mind more than once that he could rid the world of Munson with one quietly placed order to his most trusted military advisors. Or a simple request of his best friend."

"Why not?" Drew asked. "What would be so wrong with ridding the world of that kind of evil?"

The Emperor shrugged. "Sometimes it's a matter of accepting the devil you know over the devil you don't."

Or becoming him.

"All right. So we need to get to the devil we know. Any ideas?"

"I intended to think about it, but oddly enough, I fell asleep."

Drew had thought about it while he tossed and turned. "We have the van, if we can get gas. Even without the tags, it's obviously a Florida vehicle. Let's just drive up to the compound and ask for Redmond."

"We would have to get through Pacifica and Midlam soldiers and then through a line of Munson's men, just to get to the gate."

"So when you talk to the King in a while, tell him to make it known to our troops that we're coming, and we're pissed."

*

The Emperor pulled a kitchen chair up to the wall of monitors and sat for a minute before booting up the computer system. He was still tired but unwilling to go back to bed, excusing it as not wanting to wake Zed by going back into the bedroom.

Drew apparently had no problem with it, because he stomped his way through to get to the bathroom, and then stomped his way back out. Zed never flinched; he stayed curled up around a pillow, his blanket pulled up halfway over his head.

"A freaking bomb could go off and he wouldn't wake up," Drew said. "I'm beginning to think Zed would be able to fall asleep on top of an active volcano and stay asleep right through the eruption. Hell, I could probably pee on him and he wouldn't budge."

"Why would that even occur to you?"

"I dunno. Why did Zed think about licking his mom's toes? Stupid stuff goes through your brain when you're tired."

When Drew came back into the living area, the Emperor had maps of Kansas on all the screens. He was comparing them to the map Drew pulled out of the van, and then he called up several satellite images, looking for signs that Drew's map was either correct or a diversion. He paid particular attention to the compound where Redmond Munson was holed up. It looked like an old church surrounded by long stretches of grass and trees, and outbuildings dotted around the church in a horseshoe shape.

He punched in the code to call Jax, and showed him the images he was looking at.

"Saint Theresa's," Jax told him.

Redmond's compound was formerly a Catholic church and rectory with a small parochial school, and the land was used for religious retreats. Most of the buildings dotting the land around the chapel were dormitories where Redmond's people were residing.

The land extended around the church for nearly a half-mile in all directions, and was protected by a six-foot-tall wall. The King believed the wall was less for security than it was for seclusion, and would not be difficult to traverse if needed. The church had used it to keep their activities from prying eyes and to give their parishioners privacy, but it was never meant to keep people out.

"Red's people patrol inside the wall and it looks as if they're basically penned in by Munson's men. Few people enter and few leave, but we've had reports of the front gate being opened by Munson's people to allow others to go in, and there hasn't been any fighting on exit."

"Supply delivery?" the Emperor asked.

"It's been mostly vans and trucks, so that's the most likely reason. Munson's not stupid. He's not going to starve his own people, even if they are more faithful to Redmond."

"Can't turn them into martyrs otherwise," Drew muttered.

"General Myers has facilitated a change in troop rotation, which will leave you with a window to get close to the gate without calling attention to yourselves, but getting past Munson's people and inside will be trickier."

"Is there a way to alert Redmond that we're coming and just want to talk?" Drew asked.

"Not without tipping off the First Minister," Jax told him.

Drew considered it for a moment and then said, "So we just do it. Drive up and ask to be let in, as if of course we're expected."

The Emperor did not share his confidence. "The attitude might work, but being expected? Not likely."

"Yeah," Drew sighed. "That's where you come in. And I'm sorry, but you're going to have to touch someone."

The van was where we'd left it, in the parking lot. The Emperor checked it over carefully; the King had assured him that by the time we left the safe house it would be refueled and inspected, just to be sure that it had not been found overnight and tampered with, but he wasn't letting any of us get in until he had seen for himself that there was nothing clamped to the underside of the van or planted inside.

Because they weren't sure when they would have access to real bathrooms, they all showered again after breakfast, and Zed was weirdly thrilled at having clean underwear until he put them on, and then whimpered "Holy freaking chafing…"

You think you're disturbed? I'm in a room with three naked people.

The Emperor had no sympathy for my dilemma, reminding me that I was naked all the time and no one complained. He walked from his bed to the bathroom without putting his pants on and poked around in the drawer there, and when he came out he tossed a container of baby powder to Zed.

"The cat is offended by nudity," he told them. "Go figure."

"Yeah, well, I never thought I'd be this comfortable around you," Drew said as he got dressed. "And I've seen a lot more of both of you than I ever want to again."

Zed was staring down into his own underwear. "I no longer care. I just don't want any of this to, you know, fall off because I picked up some weird fungus along the way."

Drew snorted. "We need to make a Zed list. Toe-licker, mushroom d—"

"Drew," the Emperor said sharply.

He laughed anyway.

Once we were in the van and on the way, the Emperor cautioned them to keep their weapons in the waistband of their jeans, but well covered by the sweatshirts. Using them was a measure of last resort; they shot well with the light guns, but these had a faster response rate from the time the trigger was pulled until the laser fired. It was milliseconds, but enough to startle someone the first time they shot one.

"We want to appear friendly…and more importantly, faithful."

Drew was in the front passenger seat with me on his lap. "I've had absolutely no exposure to religion. I have no idea how to do that."

Zed leaned forward in his seat. "Yeah, and the way Mom taught us…it won't jibe with the way they were taught, I don't think. She makes God out to be like some super cool old man who loves everyone, and they act like he's a mean son of a bitch out to send them all to some abstract spot in Hell."

"Just defer to me," the Emperor said. "As far as they're concerned, you're both unmarried young men traveling with their father. If they believe that, I'll have the right to speak for you."

Dude, there's no way anyone will think Drew is your son. He's not as pink as you.

"I've considered that, Wick."

"Considered what?" Drew asked.

"Wick is concerned about how different we look from each other. In his head, people are pink, not as pink, very not pink, or not pink at all. And he seems certain that we all either have black hair, blond hair, or occasionally orange. He's curious, but racial diversity is not his strong suit."

"My mother is half Persian, Wick," Drew said to me as he scratched under my collar. "My dad is mostly white, but he's also got a strong Native American line. I'm kind of a lighter version of my mom with a bigger nose and a lot more facial hair. But yeah, I don't look like these guys."

What happened to your hair? It used to glow, kind of.

"Drew's hair color came out of a bottle," the Emperor said. "He actually does have black hair."

You all do.

"In this car? Yes. But you don't really see the difference in dark hair colors, do you? Aubrey has brown hair. So does my father. It's very dark, so I can see why you thought it was black."

Jo has black hair.

"Yes, she does."

She's pink.

"To you, yes. You know, most people are fairly diverse, Wick.

Your notion of pink? It hasn't been that way for a few hundred years. There are far fewer…pink…people than there are those of multiracial heritage."

You all look pink to me.

Drew started muttering to himself. "What did we talk about along the way, Oz? Well, aside from the aforementioned ways the Emperor gets off, we talked about your brother's fungus-laden junk and then racial diversity as viewed through the cat's eyes. You know, normal stuff."

"Oz won't have any trouble believing I talked about my junk," Zed said.

Drew, tell her it was cold. To explain what you saw.

The Emperor snort-laughed hard enough that he had to cover his mouth for a second. "I swear, the longer I'm with you all, the more immature I'm becoming."

"Oz says you're pretty much a teenager," Drew said. "At least when comparing your life span against your age. Maybe you've been immature all along, but now you have people your own age to hang with and it's just oozing out."

"I'm not a teenager."

"Keep telling yourself that. You might even start to believe it."

"Could you really live as long as a hundred eighty?" Zed asked.

"Had I stayed in my own When, perhaps," he said. "I suspect I've shaved a few decades off that by remaining here. Which I'm fine with."

"I'm not sure I wouldn't head for the When where I'd live the longest," Zed said.

"I prefer to stay where I've been happy. I was never happy before, at least not that I recall. I suppose I was when I was a toddler, but once I started school…" He took a deep breath, hesitating. How much to tell them about himself? Oz knew but wouldn't share any uncomfortable details. "When you can't touch another person without invading their thoughts, you quickly become someone of whom others are very much afraid. I survived school for two years, until my mother realized how bad the taunting and bullying had become. She witnessed what she thought was an especially ruthless afternoon, when I sat on a playground bench as classmates threw the remains of their lunches at me, screaming that I was a freak and should go home and die. I never had the heart to tell her it had often been much worse. She'd been there on a fairly easy day."

"Holy hell," Drew breathed out.

"So, yes, I will happily trade thirty or forty years off the back end of my life in order to stay here. I was happy to remain even when I thought my life would end next February. Quality over quantity."

"But you still can't really touch anyone," Zed started.

Drew cut him off. "Let that go."

"It's all right," the Emperor said. "Oz has been incredibly helpful with that. I can maintain contact for several minutes without letting anyone hear inside my head, and for the most part I've learned how to not listen. I still don't like unexpected touching, but she's made it possible for me to relax when your mother insists on kissing my cheek, and when any of you try to hug me."

"So I can just do that?"

"I would prefer to not be caught by surprise, but yes. I would welcome it from you, Zed."

Zed considered it for a moment and then asked, "So you think you'll ever get to a point where you can, you know, have sex?"

"Damn, Zed," Drew said. "It always comes back to that with you lately. That's really none of our business."

"Just curious. And admit it, you want to know, too."

I wanna know, too.

"It's all right," the Emperor said. "But I don't know. It's not the number one thing on my list of priorities. And even if I ever thought it possible, I doubt I have any clue how to truly function in a relationship."

Before Zed could open his mouth, he added, "And yes, I would require a relationship. I'm not going to do it just to do it."

"Not every woman wants a relationship."

"But *I* would," he said. "It's a matter of trust, and I would need to be able to trust someone, quite literally, with my life."

"I guess," Zed said. "I suppose instead of worrying about a broken condom, you'd have to worry about a broken brain."

"Indeed. Well, both. I don't think it would be a good idea for me to reproduce."

"And you know what else we talked about, Oz?" Drew muttered. "If and when the Emperor ever decides to jump some poor, unsuspecting woman, he wants to be in *love*."

"Use my name," the Emperor said.

Drew turned Zed. "Third or fourth thing on my to-do list when we have Oz back home and safe is finding him that poor woman who'll put up with him."

"Why third or fourth?"

Drew raised an eyebrow. "Really?"

"Phfft. I thought you were saving yourself for marriage."

The Emperor looked back at Zed in the rear-view mirror. "Then why were you so upset that they shared a sleeping bag?"

Zed shrugged. "Maybe because even though they're not having sex, there's a lot of inappropriate touching going on. You know he was groping her boobs in that bag. Who knows what else."

I know.

I heard them talking.

They were playing baseball, sort of. No one scored, though.

"I'm willing to wait," Drew said, "but I'm not the only person in the equation. Still, if she suddenly decided that's what she wanted, I have no problem putting it off. I haven't had sex for twenty years, what's a few more months?"

"Yeah, I don't think she's giving you that option," the Emperor said.

"That's fine, too," Drew said. "I mean, she said yes, so…"

"Wait." Zed reached over the back of Drew's seat and slapped the back of his head. "You freaking *proposed?*"

"I freaking did. She freaking said yes."

The Emperor's joy was like a bubble inside his head, and it popped. "Congratulations, Andrew. And I won't say a word about her age. Or yours."

"Hurt her and I'll still break your fingers," Zed said, though he didn't sound angry.

"If I hurt her, I'd expect it."

Hurt her and I'll pee all over your things.

He didn't need a translation. "I know, Wick," he said. "We just need to get her back, and I swear, I'll spend the rest of my life making sure I never do anything stupid to hurt her."

Good. Because I'd do it, you know.

Plus, these guys would help me.

"Indeed, I would," the Emperor said.

He slowed the van down as we approached Topeka, and called General Myers to let him know where we were and how soon he expected to reach the compound. Drew and Zed stopped talking when the Emperor turned onto the road that led to the compound, and we watched as a line of soldiers wearing Pacifica's battle uniform filtered off, leaving only the Floridians to stand in the way between us and getting inside the gate.

"Next troop rotation won't be through for fifteen minutes," the Emperor said, mostly to himself. "And that wasn't suspicious at all. Dammit. If they noticed..."

He drove toward the gate slowly, hoping the age and condition of the van was noted, and he opened the window, sticking his hand out to wave. He stopped when ordered to, a good thirty feet from the gate, and leaned his head out the window, smiling.

There were guns leveled at the car, but he didn't flinch. He called out the window, "Just here for a meeting with the Second Minister."

A large, very pink man with sunburned cheeks and short blond hair that stuck straight up, wearing the all-black of Florida's guard, stepped toward the van, but he didn't lower his gun as he ordered everyone out. Drew carried me to the side of the van where the Emperor was and Zed followed, and I hoped they remembered to not say anything.

"We're fine walking in if the van is a problem," the Emperor said. "My boys aren't afraid to sweat a little."

"Wish mine weren't," the guard muttered. "Names?"

"I'm William Mor. These are my boys, Andrew and Zealand."

When the guard looked at Drew twice, the Emperor said, "Yes, I know. His mother came from a long line of Florida natives, God rest her soul." He sounded very sincere, and very not Scottish.

"I'm sorry," the guard said. He sounded as if he truly meant it, too.

"Thank you. I do miss her, but seeing him every day? A part of her is still here."

"Amen to that," the guard said. He was no longer focused on his men, who were still crawling around the van. "I wish I could offer more than my sympathies."

"If you could remember her in your prayers, I would be grateful."

"I will, Brother."

The Emperor offered his hand, and the surprised guard shook it.

"They're good," he called to his men. "Minister Munson left orders this morning that they were to be let in."

While the gate was being opened, the Emperor leaned out the window again, and said, "Have a blessed day!" as he drove the van forward.

When the gate closed behind us, Drew sputtered, "I can't believe that worked."

The Emperor nodded and said, "I'm not sure it's a good thing I know that I can do that. He will swear until his dying day that he received orders from Munson himself."

We drove almost all the way to the rectory before being stopped. Less than fifty yards away a short man with little round glasses, wearing neatly pressed black slacks and a white dress shirt, stood in the middle of the driveway and held his hand up to signal the Emperor to stop.

He wasn't armed, and didn't seem particularly upset to see that we'd been given entry to the compound. He simply gestured for everyone to get out, and then asked politely what we needed.

"We need to see Redmond Munson," the Emperor said.

The man's gaze flicked toward the gate.

"I realize you have absolutely no reason to trust us, but please, just ask him to speak with us. If he refuses, we'll leave."

"All right," he said. "Whom shall I say is calling?"

"Tell the Second Minister that the Emperor of San Francisco wishes to speak with him on behalf of his sister, the Queen of Pacifica."

23

"I'm Daniel Kimball," the man said, waving for us to follow him. "I honestly thought you were just a myth, another one of the Minister's scare tactics."

The Emperor fell into step next to him. "I'm not sure why. Redmond Munson has seen me. I've never exactly been threatening."

Don't lie, Blackie.

Daniel walked with his hands in his pockets, which made me think he was comfortable, and yet he glanced sideways at the Emperor. "From what we've been told, you're Satan's bastard son, and even the devil himself is careful around you."

Pretty sure Satan is afraid of him.

"Then why are you even talking to us?"

"Because Levi Munson is always looking for a scapegoat and Red will definitely want to see you. Anyone who can tell him even the tiniest things about his sister, he'll be interested in."

He took us through the front doors of the church. It was old but pristine, with colorful spots of light dancing on the floor where the sun beamed through the stained glass. We followed him up the center aisle and then through a door on the right. It led into an apartment with a large and darkly decorated living room; everything seemed to be some shade of red. Blood red. Even the wood trim had a red highlight to it.

Sitting in an overstuffed chair, watching a video, there was a little girl who was all of six or seven years old. Her legs were sticking straight out and she had tucked her dress under the sides of her legs, and her feet ticked back and forth like a metronome. I'd seen Oz do something like that, moving to the beat of whatever was playing in her head. I'd also seen her do it with Drew, and it was nauseatingly sweet.

"Run and get your daddy, Bree," Daniel told her. "He has guests."

She flashed a grin that was missing four teeth and then did what he told; she ran from the room, slamming open a swinging door, and when she was past it she yelled "Daddy!" at the top of her lungs.

Redmond Munson didn't need an introduction; he clearly recognized us all, and started to offer the Emperor his hand before he thought better of it. "Sorry, habit. I recall you're not a hand shaker."

The Emperor thanked him, but didn't offer an explanation.

"You look well," Redmond said to Drew and Zed. "All things considered, anyway. And I'm sorry, we don't have Oz."

But he knows.

"Her presence here was not our expectation," the Emperor said.

Redmond ushered us into the living room to sit. I stayed on Drew's lap, and we were close enough to Zed on the sofa that I could hit his legs with my tail. So I did, because, why not?

"You tried to warn us," Drew said. "Why?"

Straight to the point.

"Because I refuse to play my father's ludicrous games. I took a chance and I'm sorry you weren't able to leave in time."

Drew wasn't letting go of anything. He wanted answers. "How did you even know where to find us? Or your father, for that matter? We were well hidden."

"Indeed," the Emperor said. "How?"

"The morning after Isaac attacked you in San Francisco," Redmond said. "I wanted to say more, but... Oz's guard, the one who failed to intervene? He'd been on my father's payroll for at least a year. He wasn't positive, but assumed that's where you had taken her. When none of you were there on the second day of negotiations—"

"He'd been her guard for nearly a decade," the Emperor said.

"Loyalty can often be displaced with the right amount of money." He looked directly at Drew. "You had a revolving door where your security was concerned. I know he bought off at least one of your guards when you were younger."

"And Will killed him."

Zed twitched. "What?"

"Munson has been trying to kill me since I was a kid," Drew explained. "The Emperor took care of it."

"Damn," Zed breathed.

The Emperor looked a little displeased. "Zed. Language."

Zed apologized, but Redmond waved it off. "I hear far worse on a regular basis from my own family. I am not offended."

"Not around his kids," the Emperor stressed.

Redmond still wasn't bothered by it. "Most of my children are adults. They've heard worse, too, and probably from me. But my youngest daughter, Bree…yes, I would appreciate it if you watch what you say around her. She has no idea why we're here, or who sent us. To her this is a vacation."

"Are you aware of the scope of the situation, Redmond?" the Emperor asked. "The most likely reason why your father installed you to lead this compound?"

He nodded. "Just Red, please. And I'm acutely aware. He wants Jackson to level Kansas and take me with it. He'll leverage Oz to make sure it happens. Her trial will be farce, but most of Florida will trust in the outcome, after which my father will make the offer to your King—destroy the compound, hand Aubrey over, and Oz lives."

"That's insane," Drew snapped.

"So is my father," Red said. "But if he claims that God commanded it of him, they'll believe anything he says. After all, he's the prophet, through whom God speaks, and God doesn't lie."

Drew's anger began to bubble. "He'll never free Oz, even if he gets what he wants. Even in the most ridiculous scenario, if you were dead and he had Mrs. B, he'd keep her just for the mental torture."

Red wasn't as sure. "He has a bigger game to play. Ultimately, he wants control over most of the continent, and he won't take the chance that Jackson will destroy it all in a fit of vengeance."

"Yet he wants the one thing Mr. B would go to war over no matter what the cost."

"He doesn't understand," Red explained. "He can't conceive of the kind of love and loyalty Jackson feels for her. To my father, Aubrey is a possession that he lost control over. He never gave her away. There was no dowry. In his eyes, she isn't duly wed. She's a nearly forty-nine-year-old runaway and he wants her punished."

"Yeah, we know how he punishes little girls," Zed grumbled.

Red wasn't expecting that, and it rattled him. He looked at Zed sharply, as if he expected to be hit, and then looked at both Drew and the Emperor. "I am truly sorry. If I'd been a little older and quite a bit less afraid of him, I might have been able to do something. But it began when I was barely nine, and I had no idea how to stop him. He has this notion that the girls under his roof are his to do with as he chooses, and he has such an overwhelming need for power—"

"You got her out," Drew said. "We know that."

"Not soon enough." He had more to say but the door swung open with a bang, and Bree ran into the room, jumping into his lap. "You're interrupting, sweetheart."

"I'm sorry. Mommy wants to know if your friends are staying for dinner. And I wanted a hug."

He hugged her, and then set her onto her feet. "Tell Mommy I said yes, and that they are very special friends who will be staying the night."

Before the Emperor could protest, as Bree ran back, Red insisted. "You'll need a place for the night, and in spite of my father's men outside, it's safe. And there's more to discuss. I have a video recording of my father's latest sermon that you need to see. He's passing it off as having been made in our new church near Miami, but something about it is…off. I've seen the blueprints and was there when construction began. I have my doubts."

*

Drew and Zed wanted to help with dinner, but the offer was met with a look of horror from Red's wife and older daughters. Darlene shooed them into the dining room and Drew was confused—was she really offended that he wanted to help, or was it just because he was a guest?—but Red thanked them for being considerate and told them to sit and enjoy a drink while they waited.

"And now you have an idea why Aubrey owns the kitchen," the Emperor told them as he took the chair between Drew and Zed. "She grew up purchasing the rights."

"I imagine it's different for her now," Red said. "I assume she has a choice in the matter, where our mother never did. Granted, it's still customary to divide men's and women's work outside the home, but in my family...I have done my fair share of dishes and laundry, and have often been ordered to redo it when I failed to meet Darlene's standards." He chuckled. "My wife is particular and rules the roost. Does your mother require you share in household chores, Zed?"

Zed nodded and Drew said, "She requires it of me, too."

"Seriously," Zed snorted. "We actually have a dishwasher, but using it is *so* much against the rules. She cooks, we clean up. But I have no idea why she's dead set on hand washing every freaking thing."

"Because you talk to each other when you're cleaning up," Red told him. "Some of the best conversations we had as children were in the kitchen while Aubrey and Mother did dishes. I sat in there to keep them company and they both made sure I knew how to clean even if my participation wasn't permitted. It was a bonding experience and I regret that none of my brothers had that chance because they missed so much. They never got to know Aubrey well, and they have no idea what it took our mother to manage the household and still feed us three times a day."

"Huh. I hadn't even thought of that. Yeah, Oz and I talk a lot when we're doing dishes. If we're in the kitchen when Mom's cooking, she lets us help—and I really mean she lets us, we don't have to and I think we get in her way—and that's when we tell her the most about how our day went."

The Emperor's expression softened. "Aubrey has turned many things that could be construed as busywork into her personal labor of love. She might only slap peanut butter on two pieces of bread, but she *will* feed you. Often, whether you're hungry or not."

Red laughed and then asked, "Is she truly happy?"

"The King adores her. He believes that she's his soul mate, and completely treasures everything about her."

Zed agreed. "So yeah, she's happy."

"I was impressed and absurdly proud at the reception," Red said. "My baby sister turned out so elegant and fierce. You should know, her message was heard, even if most of our people attending found it to be a bit scandalous. Still…the whispers have already begun, and those will turn into stories, and the stories will give hope to girls suffering under fathers such as ours. Too many had no idea that your Queen was the First Minister's daughter. Emperor, when you escorted her in and then *bowed* to her, I thought my father was going to have a stroke."

"That would have solved a few things," Zed said.

The Emperor turned to him quickly. "Zed."

"He has a point," Red said. "I'm under no illusions about my father. It would do the world well if he had his final come-to-Jesus moment."

"Does he really want to usher in the end of times?" Drew asked.

"That's what he'd like our people to think. What he especially wants is to possess and control as much of the world as he can in the last years of his life, and I don't think he's concerned with what God thinks."

"And you?" the Emperor asked.

"Ultimately, what God thinks is all I care about. Our church was never meant to be this, and if it continues the way my father wants? I don't think Noah would have survived the flood we're liable to get."

As Darlene and her daughters began bringing food to the table, the Emperor told Drew to put me on the floor. Red, however, pointed to a chair near the wall just behind Zed and told him to pull it up for me.

"I'm still not sure why, but I don't think Wick is an ordinary cat," he said.

"He's family," Zed told him.

"Then he has a place at my table. There will always be a place for true family."

Little Bree put a small plate on the table in front of me and said I was cute.

I think I like this place.

Well, other than the whole notion of it getting blown off the map. The sticky person is sweet.

When the family reached for each other's hands to pray, the Emperor took both Zed's and Drew's; I don't know what he whispered to them inside their heads, but they both took side glances and him, and then smiled, and at the right time both said, "Amen."

I said it, too, but I don't think anyone noticed.

*

The monitor that Red turned on was old and its screen displayed a lot of static, but he was still able to play the video of Levi Munson's most recent sermon. We sat in the living room, bunched close, and watched as he pounded his pulpit, calling for God to smite Pacifica and those who supported it. He told his congregation that once the holy days were done and they had given suitable thanks for all their blessings, the heretic Oz would be given a fair trial—but he had faith that she would be found guilty. She refused to see the truth. She refuted his place at God's right hand. She thought herself to be equal to a man, and had taken lives in her misplaced desire to prove that which could not be proven.

He attacked everything about her that he could. Her physique was proof that she thought she was equal to the brethren of the church; she sweat like a man, trying to build an impossibly strong body, only to offend the Lord by toning herself with muscle that no woman should ever have. She'd cut her hair to an offensive length, wore men's clothing, and believed herself to be far more intelligent than was possible for any woman.

Her very nature, he argued, was an offense to the Lord, whose church was founded on his principles and laws, and she would pay for her arrogance.

"God's will be done," he said solemnly.

Zed wondered out loud if the Minister even knew Oz's real name, but Drew was paying closer attention to the church and the few people in it. Several times, he asked Red to rewind a bit, until he had seen the same five second loop a dozen times. On the last time through, he asked Red to pause the recording, and then pointed to a lighter spot on the wall behind the congregation.

"That window. Look outside. That's Chicago."

"Are you sure?" the Emperor asked.

"It would help to see a clearer image, but I'm almost certain that the building in the distance is the new Hancock."

"How can you be sure?" Red asked.

"I lived there. I know what it looks like inside and out."

"I can't clean it up any more than it already has been," Red said. "Even with my best equipment, I don't have anything to enhance something in the background like that."

"I do," the Emperor said. "I would need my backpack, and it's still in the van."

The van had been moved close to the rectory; once Red knew we were there, he told Daniel to bring it closer. We weren't there to harm anyone, and he wanted us to feel more like guests than intruders.

The Emperor sent Zed and Drew out to bring all three backpacks in, but once the door closed behind them he turned to Red and said, "Understand, I'm ninety per cent sure that you're truly on our side, but I'm reserving room for doubt. And if anything happens to either of those boys—"

"I'm not a fool, Emperor. You'd kill me where I stood. I know it was you who took Isaac Young down. I know what you're capable of. You'd end my life before I could utter even the most rudimentary of prayers."

"Know that I will destroy whomever I must in order to protect them and to save Oz."

"Including my father."

"Indeed."

"I don't blame you for your doubt. The Minister *is* my father. And don't get me wrong, I would never end his life myself…but I also won't stop you."

"You can live with that?"

A lifetime of Levi Munson's abuse pinched Red's face. "Exodus and Deuteronomy tell us to honor our father and mother, and I believe that. I truly do. When he's gone, I'll mourn him, if only for everything he could have been. But I can live with it, Emperor. Evil exists in this world and should be destroyed, and it sadly exists in the soul of Levi Munson."

Using his tablet, the Emperor was able to clean up and enhance the video. He honed in on the window, and agreed with Drew: it was the new Hancock building. He ran the image of the window and the location of the building through his software, and a new map popped up: Munson was preaching in a church just a block and a half away.

"That's a newer building," Drew said. "It used to be a really old Presbyterian church, but it was rebuilt a few years ago, and I have no idea who owns it now."

The Emperor flipped through several pages on his tablet and then said, "It was abandoned following a bankruptcy three years ago. It also sits in the center of a long swath of destruction in the city." He pulled a new map up. "The Hancock stands, as well as half a block to its east, half to the north and south, continuing across Michigan Avenue to a court just past the church. The roads leading up to it are damaged, and he's surely got it heavily guarded."

"So Midlam lost all control of Chicago?" Drew asked.

"Your mother did not return—"

"Yeah," Drew huffed. "I got that memo."

"Your people are fighting," Red told him. "They didn't just run. Our army has less control of the city than the Minister wants the world to think. That he's suggesting he's still in Florida tells me he's confined to that area and doesn't want our people to know. I mean, who could possibly pin God's prophet into one place without suffering divine retribution?"

The Emperor was still looking at his tablet, and didn't look up when he said, "I think your father has more control over Chicago than you give him credit for. The bombing was strategic, meant to inflict as much emotional pain on Midlam's queen as he could muster, with the dual effect of driving its people away. It left the seat of Midlam's government there for him to take. There's fighting, but it's being done by what remains of the military."

He turned the tablet so Drew could see. "This is why she thought your father was dead."

Drew didn't want to look, saying he'd seen the images. He knew what part of the university had been bombed.

"Grandpa is a raging douche," Zed said under his breath.

The Emperor did not chastise him, and Red shrugged and said, "Not really, Zed. He's more like the condition one might need that douche for."

"That's an insult to yeast everywhere."

This time, the Emperor spoke up. "Zed. That's his father."

"In name," Red offered. "I'm not insulted."

"That's not the point."

Drew took the Emperor's tablet and flipped back to a larger map. "Get me to Chicago," he said. "I know the area, Will. I'll get us into that church."

"You're too well known in Chicago, Drew. If we get close, someone could give you away."

"I'll take that chance. He has Oz."

"And I'm going with you," Red said. "You might be able to get in, but I can get you to my father."

Zed balked. "Nothing personal, but I don't fully trust you."

"All right, that's fair. But wouldn't you rather have me with you, where you can keep an eye on me, than here after you're gone, possibly warning him?"

"You have a hundred people who could do that for you," Drew countered.

The Emperor clapped Red on the back. "Give me an hour or so to discuss it with them, Red. There's a bigger picture they need to see."

I see what you did there, you and your wandering pinkie.

He has no idea, either.

The Emperor's new trick. I like it.

*

Darlene Munson came into the living room and apologized for the disruption, but wanted to know if the boys would like to see their room and get settled. I don't think it was what they wanted, but the Emperor told them to go ahead, take some time to relax and perhaps just lay down to rest and complain about him behind his back, and he would be with them shortly.

He told Red that he sensed there was more, something he didn't want Drew and Zed to see. Red thought he was amazingly perceptive and the Emperor told him it was a matter of the sideways glances he gave them, and a pain in his eyes that needed to be relieved; I knew better. When he touched Red, he listened.

"When Drew asked King Jackson for his consent to propose marriage to Oz, I admit, we all thought it was staged," Red started. "It seemed inappropriate for the occasion and none of us could figure out why, even though it's clear he loves her."

"Indeed. And the reason is simple. The reception was broadcast around the world. The King wanted it known that Pacifica and Midlam stand together firmly, and he wanted to give Midlam's people a reason to understand that their unifying would happen sooner or later. If not under him, then under his daughter."

"Giving them hope. There's no way my father would have understood the extent of Pacifica's alliance with Midlam. He was blindsided when Jackson announced their purchase agreement and I don't think he believes it to be valid at all. He railed against it— how can one just purchase an entire country? He's not looking at the bigger picture, and if he had he would have seen long ago that Pacifica and Midlam are far more intertwined than most realize. The agreement was just a formality." He sighed hard, and then told the Emperor to fast forward to the end of Munson's sermon. "There's a ten second delay, and then more video. I didn't think the boys should see it."

We watched as Oz, shackled to a large wooden chair, was subjected to a litany of questions, one after the other in rapid-fire succession. She wasn't given the chance to answer, and her anger at her treatment was clear in her eyes. This was the defiant Oz, the girl who would break you in half if she could; this was the face the Minister wanted to show to his people, the boiling rage and refusal to admit to his truths.

Parts of the recording would be edited, and what aired in Florida would be video of a girl trying desperately to break free and hurt someone while being calmly asked perfectly reasonable questions.

It got worse.

When Munson's lackey got close, placing himself nose to nose with her as he asked her why she refused to listen, because listening would open her heart and save her soul, she head butted him. He collapsed, out cold, blood streaming from his nose, and a second later she was contorted in agony.

"He uses electric shock to control," Red told the Emperor. He looked every bit as horrified as I felt. "Pain to punish."

Taken from the chair, still shackled, Oz was kicked repeatedly; she endured blows to her legs and stomach, and when that was over, she was battered with a leather strap, taking strikes to her back.

She didn't waver and refused to fall.

Before the recording cut, she spat out blood and mouthed, "You'll never break me."

"My father doesn't want to break her. He wants to torture her until he gets what he wants."

The Emperor stared at the dark screen, barely breathing, and his fingers dug into my fur. When he could swallow past the lump that had wedged into his throat, he took a deep breath. "How many family members are here with you, how many others of your faithful, and is there a secondary gate?"

24

Church bells rousted the members of the compound at three in the morning and rang again at four to call them outside. The Emperor hadn't slept, and he woke Zed and Drew at two-thirty to give them enough time to wake up and prepare to leave. While they repacked the bags and dressed, the Emperor tapped away on his tablet, glancing every few seconds at his phone.

When Red knocked on the jamb of the open door and said everyone was outside and ready, the Emperor shoved the phone into his pocket, the tablet into his bag, and told them to head outside.

It was cold out, freezing even, and a mass of people were huddled together near the entry to the church; their collective breath rose like a cloud of smoke that thinned out the higher it went, until it disappeared. I could feel my own breath freeze inside my nose, and wiggled against Drew for warmth. He zipped his jacket until it was at my chin, trying to keep the heat in while letting me see what was happening.

The Emperor stepped away from them and stared up into the early morning sky, waiting. He stared at the stars as Red kissed his wife and daughters, and he pretended not to hear them cry, and only twitched when Red told them to be good and then asked them to pray for the Emperor, Zed and Drew. When Bree sniffed and promised that she would, he reminded them to pray for Oz, too.

He never asked them to pray for him, and I wondered if that was because he assumed they would, or because he didn't think he deserved any.

I heard the whine of air engines before the Emperor spotted the seven shuttles he'd been watching for. At ten after four they pulled into the air space over the compound, landing one after the other. The doors slid open quickly and "Move! Move! Move!" was shouted above the din of the engines and confusion; the reflex of obedience caused the people to run toward them and scramble inside. The shuttles took off, two and three at a time, until there was only one.

It took less than three minutes to load eighty people and send them away.

The Emperor pointed toward the remaining shuttle and we rushed in; it was in the air and blasting away at full speed before everyone was strapped in. Red was pale and his hands were shaking, but he did everything he was told and refused to cave into the gnawing fear for his family.

As we sped away we passed a military fighter heading for the compound, and seconds later heard the first of the blasts that would, within minutes, level the compound to dust.

It was King Jackson's first real warning to the First Minister.

He would take his people and destroy his stolen property, and there wasn't anything Munson could do about it.

"Pacifica and Midlam troops moved out during the night," the Emperor explained when Drew and Zed looked at him with complete horror. "Everyone from the compound will be taken to safety."

"And everyone who was outside?" Zed asked.

He didn't answer.

"What, they're all gone? Even the guy who promised to pray for the dead wife that you don't even have? Just like that?"

Any of the guards outside the gate would have shot them on sight, had they suspected who they were, Red told him. The Minister wanted war, he was getting war. Every man guarding outside the compound knew what they were there for, and understood the odds of their survival were low.

"They had ample time to retreat," the Emperor told Zed. "Only the compound was destroyed."

He wanted Zed to feel better about it, but no one in that car believed it.

King Jackson had struck, and the odds were high that it was not going to be the last time.

*

An hour later, the shuttle landed in a snow-covered field near an old green barn. It was still dark, moonlight tumbling over the crust of the snow like thousands of tiny laser-pointer dots that I knew better than to try to catch, and my breath began to freeze in my nostrils again.

There's an inside, right? One with warms?

Drew stumbled out, stretched, and then realized where he was. "We're in Dayton. That's my dad's lab."

The Emperor hoisted his backpack up, and then reached for me. "Indeed. So lead the way."

The barn door creaked with age, the rusty hinges angry at having been woken in the middle of the night. Inside there was dirt everywhere and it smelled like mildew and old ice, but it was otherwise empty. Red was confused, turning in mild starts, trying to grasp how this was anyone's lab. It was an old barn five miles from a military base. He expected sleepy cows or horses, not cold stale air and frozen spider webs.

Drew took us into a stall near the center of the left wall, and once we were bunched inside he closed the door and opened a panel that was just behind it, revealing a well-worn keypad. He punched in numbers, and then the wall dividing it from the next stall slid out of the way, exposing the staircase down.

There's always a downstairs, isn't there?

Lights came on as we descended the stairs, and when we got to the bottom step the overhead lights popped on one by one, revealing a room that had only two cluttered tables butted up against the far wall. There was a doorway with no door off to the left, and on the wall under the stairs there were several doors, but Drew didn't take us through any of them. Instead he was looking for a way to turn the air on; without it, he said, there was probably only enough air in the lab to last for a few minutes.

I like breathing.

They spread out, walking along the walls looking for the controls, until Zed went through the doorway with no doors and called out, "Found it!" and then, "Whoa…"

The ventilation system hummed to life as the lights in that room turned on, and he called for them to come look.

It was a long and narrow room, maybe only twenty feet across but a few hundred feet long. Halfway down, there was a metal frame bent to fit a circular path, and it ran all the way around the walls and ceiling. Across the floor was a platform that looked like the wall that surrounded the roof back home; it was clear, thick, plastic, reflecting the lights from above, and at the edge of the platform was a roundish hunk of white and cement-colored plastic.

"Don't touch anything," the Emperor warned.

"What the hell is that thing?" Zed asked.

The Emperor peered at it closely, and then said, "Inside out bowling ball."

"I knew he was working on some of the same things Finn was, but damn…he's got a gate." Drew turned to the Emperor. "Did he have this before or after, do you know?"

"After. The hope is that my father will open a more stable gate on his end, and send things through to yours here. The bowling ball was one of the first attempts. They have a bit more work to do."

"So transporters, not time machines," Drew said, a little amazed.

"Excuse me, what?" Red asked. "Time machines?"

The Emperor turned to inspect the control panel built into a counter that ran along the side wall. "Sure. I'm from two hundred years in your future. My father has a giant egg-shaped time machine that he used to poke holes into the fabric of time, and then he built portals around those holes. So that we could time travel. Of course."

Red laughed and said, "All right. For half a second I thought you were serious."

"It would be nice if this thing was already functional," Zed said, getting closer to the gate to get a good look at it.

"Indeed." The Emperor motioned for them to go back to the other room. "And hopefully they'll be able to work on it without distraction soon. Andrew, your father said you would know how to access his transit system. He's given me the codes to get into the tube, but you'll have to show me where it is."

"Yeah, no problem. Under the stairs."

He pushed open the first door we came to, and flicked the light switch when he stepped through. It took us to a small room and another door that was locked; the Emperor tapped the code onto the panel and pushed the door open—it led to another small room and a bigger door.

"I hope he gave you all the codes," Drew said. "He's kind of picky about security. There's another door still."

*

Richard Van Hoff's transportation system was a small bullet train that could carry up to twelve people. It resembled the public transit at home, but was significantly shorter; the trains ran underground across the city and under the bay to Oakland, then up to Sacramento and could carry several hundred people at a time. This, Drew said, went in a straight shot to his father's lab at the University of Chicago.

"I'm not sure we can get to the stop," Drew said. "The tube ends somewhere close to where his lab was bombed."

"There are exit ports along the way," the Emperor said. "Richard said we need to bring the train to a stop a mile or two out, but we can climb out through the maintenance port and use the first ladder up that we see."

"This runs all the way to Chicago?" Red's face pinched. "No stops?"

"It's only three hundred miles," Drew said. "A little over an hour."

"But it doesn't stop for anyone else?"

Like the Prince is going to give rides to all his little engineering friends?

Oh, wait. He might.

"As the Prince Consort, Richard has had some privileges others might consider overblown luxuries," the Emperor said. "Truthfully, this was necessary for his protection while working on military projects."

Red stared down the length of the tube. "If the Minister had ever thought this was possible…"

"You were offered the technology," Drew pointed out.

"We were offered technology to create new transportation infrastructure. Air and hover craft. But this? He would have been all over this."

"This is a fairly simple subway," the Emperor said. "Underground transit systems have existed for hundreds of years. In terms of technological advances, it's not very impressive."

"To you," Red said. "I've had some exposure to hover cars and the like while traveling, but understand, I grew up with cars and trucks on the road, and trains on tracks. I've never seen a subway, much less a personal one."

As we buckled in, Drew leaned over to the Emperor and whispered, "Please let me tell him you weren't exaggerating. Please."

"Play nice," the Emperor said just loud enough for Drew to hear.

Tell him how old I am.

Oh! Tell him where Finn found me!

Don't forget to mention the hippies. It was the nineteen sixties. There were hippies.

"Is Wick all right?" Red asked.

"He's very vocal at times," the Emperor said. "He's probably hungry."

The train was picking up speed, pressing everyone into their seats. I sat in Drew's lap and he held me close, trying to make it bearable for me.

"It'll stop feeling funny in a minute," he told me. "Just hang on."

When the pressure eased up, I took a breath and then curled up on Drew's legs. Red watched me pat his legs down, trying to make a soft spot—which was no longer possible, because his whole body was hard and not squishy—and then asked, "Was I right, at the negotiations? Wick was bugged, wasn't he?"

Zed and Drew glanced at each other and then looked away. The Emperor said, "In a manner of speaking. We learned enough to understand that getting Oz and Drew out of there was a good idea."

"And look how well it turned out," Zed grumbled.

"Zed, I'm sorry," the Emperor said.

"Oh, man, no, I didn't mean—"

"I know. But understand, I have had that thought a thousand times. I failed to protect her again."

"Again? Wait…you didn't fail anything." Zed turned to Drew. "Do you know what he's talking about?"

"You know, I've about hit the point where I don't even try to follow what he means. You know, being a two-hundred-year old guy and all. He can go off on tangents."

"I never said I was that old," the Emperor said. "I said I was from two hundred years in the future."

"Ah." Drew snorted. "That makes all the difference."

Red reached across the aisle and scratched between my ears. "They don't make a lot of sense, do they, Wick?"

I understand them.

"I love how he talks back. Like he's having a conversation."

The Emperor was probably about to tell him the truth—he could understand everything I said—and Red would still think he was joking, but his phone pinged. It was a news alert pushed to him from the King, and he read it carefully twice before putting the phone back in his pocket.

Taking a deep breath, he turned in his seat so he could see everyone else. "Before I tell you, keep in mind there were no populated areas involved. Great care was taken to avoid them."

"What?" Drew asked.

Red waited.

"Jax ordered a blitz over Florida. Sixteen strikes, around but not in cities or suburbs."

"Blitz?" Red looked frantic. "They bombed Florida?"

"Not bombed, per se. Energy strikes, anything in the path of the hover was burned."

"So for sure no cities?" Zed asked.

He shook his head. "Not yet."

"There are no completely unpopulated areas in Florida," Red argued. "If we'd had any place to expand—"

"Great care was taken to minimize casualties. I'm sorry, Red, but he's sending a message. He's not waiting any longer."

Red didn't blame the King.

Red blamed his father for every soul lost in that strike.

*

For the next forty minutes, the only sounds in the train came from the whine of its engines and the breathing of people. My bladder was stretched painfully but had nowhere to go so I didn't even bother telling the Emperor that my back teeth were floating. Zed leaned his head back and fell asleep, hands grasping at the shoulder belt keeping him secure in his seat. Drew started bouncing his foot up and down, which made me slide off his leg and onto the seat next to him.

That was all right, because if I'd stayed there, I probably would have peed on him.

Every mile that took us closer to Chicago made him more anxious; when both feet started bouncing, the Emperor noticed.

"Half an hour, Drew," he said. "That's all."

"And then what? What's the plan? Do we even have one?"

Really, we didn't. But the Emperor told him that the first order of business was getting out of the train and up one of the maintenance ladders to see where we were. Once we were oriented, we'd look for a place to hold up for the night, and would work on the next move from there. He needed access to electricity in order to charge his tablet and phone and to contact the King, and he preferred not being out in the open, so if Drew could start considering where that might be, he'd appreciate it.

"We stay in the train," Drew said. "Find the closest way up and check it out, but we come back here to stay the night. There's power, there's heat, we have food, and we can sleep on the floor."

I need to pee, dude.

"There are personal care concerns here, Drew."

He unbuckled and went to the back of the train. There was a long seat along the back wall, with a hinged panel on the floor just in front of it. He pulled the panel up, and waved to the hatch in the floor. "Here you go. It won't be pleasant, but it's doable."

The Emperor pointed to me.

Drew closed the hatch, then turned to the wall to his right, and opened a supply panel. From it he pulled a shallow pan, and then asked the Emperor for his knife. He sliced open the back seat and pulled the batting out of it, dropping it into the pan.

"For fluid drainage," he said when the Emperor asked him what it was. "The reserve brakes on the train have to be bled every now and then. My dad does it himself most of the time. He figures he knows more about how it works than the military mechanics. He's wrong, but it makes him feel useful." He set it down near the closed hatch and said, "Here you go, Wick. We can rip more stuffing out of the seat as you need it, and dump it all down the hole."

I jumped down and ran to it.

"You should have said something earlier, Wick," the Emperor said, ignoring the quizzical look on Red's face.

I really didn't care if they watched me pee.

I knew that the Emperor and Drew and Zed didn't care if someone saw them pee. They'd been peeing outside in front of each other for days.

I had a feeling it would be an issue for Red. He would be more like the King, who sometimes grumbled, "I don't need an audience, Wick."

He didn't *need* one, but he often had one.

Someone might want to warn Red that there might not be any working toilets for a while.

The Emperor's eyes crinkled at the corners. I suppose he figured Red would either get used to the idea or explode from holding it all in.

Drew's feet were still bouncing. I jumped onto the Emperor's lap instead.

Tell him it's okay.

He wasn't going to answer me. It was one thing to converse with me in front of family, a whole other thing in front of Red. He didn't need to know what the Emperor's talents were.

As I curled up on his lap, the thought occurred to me: he wants to get Red close to Oz, so that she could tell him whether or not Red was telling the truth. No one could lie to Oz, except perhaps for the Emperor, because she could see sound and people's sounds changed when they lied.

I wondered if mine did.

Then I wondered if I could even lie.

Drew's feet stilled, but now he was shaking. It wasn't cold in the train, and he had a sweatshirt on, anyway, but his hands were trembling like he'd been stuck outside on the balcony on a foggy night.

He's losing it.

The Emperor carried me as he moved from his seat to sit next to Drew. "Tomorrow," he said gently. "Just one more night, and then we go after her."

"I know," Drew said in a voice he fought to keep steady. "Tomorrow."

"We find her, we get her, we take her home. And then you have a promise to keep."

Drew's head snapped to look at the Emperor.

"I hear more than you'd like," he said lightly. "Futuristic ears, you know."

Drew wanted to smile, but couldn't manage it.

"We end this war, take her home, and you marry the girl," the Emperor went on. "I swear, the day we get back...the King will celebrate and officiate himself, if that's what you want. Focus on that, Andrew. We're taking her home, and you'll be able to marry her."

"You're forgetting a step," Drew said, his face stony. "We get Oz, and then I kill that son of a bitch. Munson is a dead man."

25

The train came to a stop less than a hundred feet from a maintenance hatch that let out onto a snow-covered park. Drew pulled himself out of the tube and took a few steps to look around, and then laughed.

"Of all the places we could have stopped…we're in Jackson Park," he told the Emperor. "This is the far southern end of it, but it's not far from my dad's lab."

"I'm sure the King has convinced himself the park was named after him," the Emperor said dryly. "How far from here to the Hancock?"

"Ten miles or so. Normally I'd grab a taxi, but…"

"I don't suppose your parks have public bike kiosks?"

"Not a chance. We're not quite as organized as San Francisco. You either have your own ride or take the bus or a cab."

Nearly a quarter mile head of us, and possibly far beyond, was nothing but snow-capped mounds of rubble and the fragile structures of buildings so damaged they only needed the right impetus to crumble. There was no more smoke, but my brain imprinted it from the images I'd seen on the King's giant video monitor, and I imagined tendrils of ashy fingers rising in the distance, waiting to reach out and crush us in one frenzied grip.

The odor of rotting flesh stung my nostrils; it was up ahead, lingering in the air. There was nothing dead and delicious about it;

this was the smell of lives wasted and of uncared-for remains. I tried to not inhale too deeply, and hoped I was the only one who could smell just how much death was all around us.

Moments after he pulled himself up out of the hatch, the weight of it all slammed into Redmond Munson and he dropped to his knees, choking out, "I never imagined…"

Drew ignored him. "We're only about a mile, mile and a half from dad's lab. If we can get through, it might be worth the hike to check it out and see if we can get in."

The Emperor looked pained; he'd seen pictures of the crater left by the bomb that targeted the building Richard's lab had been in, and he didn't want Drew to see it up close.

There's always a downstairs.

"How much of his actual lab was in the science center?" the Emperor asked him. "Is there an underground bunker?"

Drew grinned.

"Do you know how to get in?"

"Not exactly, but I know my father. I know how careful he was, and given the things he worked on? Look at all the access hatches we passed in that tube. He had a dozen avenues of escape. If we can find one closer, past this crap, we might be able to get in."

"Passcodes?"

"I know all his usual ones."

"We still need power. And air."

"Dad worked on a lot of military applications," Drew reminded him. "That lab was built to withstand earthquakes up to a ten, and could theoretically hold up to a nuclear blast. It had to be. Whatever was directly under where the bomb hit is probably gone or sealed off, but the rest of it might be all right. If there's power, there's air, and if the main part of the lab is intact, there's a generator."

And toilets for the delicate.

The Emperor looked at his watch. "We have time to get there and back, if necessary." He had Zed and Red walk backwards, toward the street, and then return, making sure they set their feet in their exact footprints while he pulled the backpacks up, and then he covered as much of the impact they'd made in the snow as he could. It wasn't perfect, but anyone passing by wouldn't think anything other than someone had walked across the park.

He hoped.

Once he had all the packs up he dug into his to get Red two sweatshirts—he wasn't prepared for that kind of cold, wearing just a flimsy windbreaker, and having lived his entire life in Florida it felt cruel to him—and then secured my plastic tomb on Red's back. Drew eased me into his sweatshirt so that I would stay warm, but if they had to, I was going to be shoved into the tomb to bounce around while they ran.

Red was not prepared for winter walking; he was slow and his shoes slid on the wet snow, and before we even reached the first mound of rubble he slipped and nearly fell. The Emperor walked behind him, and even though I couldn't see his face, I could picture it: annoyance and frustration, because simply getting a single mile was going to take an hour with him, and he'd have frostbite before we found the entry to the lab.

Bet you're glad now the Emperor worked your asterisk off.
Also bet you're sorry that this feels like a crawl now.

"I know you're cold," Drew said to me. "I'm sorry."

He put his giant hands around me for more warmth. I was all right, but snuggled against him so he would know I appreciated it.

We reached the first mound of rubble and he started to climb, apologizing when he had to let go of me. He pulled us up easily, but when we got to the top he turned to Zed. "You're not going to have an easy time with this."

Zed was pulling himself up just fine, and he balked at the idea.

"That's not what I mean."

The Emperor scrambled past them to see what Drew was concerned about, and then grumbled that there was no choice and no protecting Zed from the sight.

It was Red who nearly fell apart.

Sticking out between two large boulders of what might have been an apartment building, or even a store or a school, was a tiny, perfect leg. It was frozen there, red sneaker peeking through a layer of frost, jeans bunched up and iced over. Red sat down hard, breathless, and muttered in a thin, weak voice, "Dear God…forgive us."

26

Drew was not kind in his reaction to Red's distress. He snapped, "Get up, we have to move," and then began the climb down, skirting around the tiny, frozen leg. The Emperor might have been a bit less harsh, but he followed without saying anything to Drew about it, and Red scrambled after them.

They wouldn't have left him there, but he had no way of knowing that.

Zed made a determined effort to not look, but when he reached the bottom he looked back, and then told them to go on; he would only be a minute. He scrambled back up, and picked away some of the ice, putting his warm hand on the cold flesh of a child buried under rock. We waited and watched; for this, Drew was less worried about making time than he was of understanding what Zed was doing, so he said nothing.

It only took him a few minutes. Drew and the Emperor moved on without a word, but Red fell into step next to Zed, and I could head their voices from behind.

"Your mother taught you to pray?" he asked Zed.

Zed sounded harsh. "Of course she did. She prays, Red. She believes in God and wants us to as well. She just has no stomach for religion."

Follow your heart to faith, she'd told both Zed and Oz, *but never follow a zealot with an agenda.*

"I can understand that. I hope one day she won't feel like the church is something to keep running from."

"Seriously?" Zed stopped, and after a few more steps Drew and the Emperor did, too. "Why in hell would she ever give your church another chance? It doesn't love her. It doesn't even *like* her. Your church thinks she's second class at best, instead of the completely wonderful woman that she is. Your women are *property*, Red. And no one owns my mother."

You gonna stop him?

"Not at all," the Emperor whispered.

"Women are not property," Red tried to argue, "but—"

"There are no 'buts.' You either cherish your women, or you don't. And unless you can see just how amazing they are, you don't. They're better than we are, and my mother's kindness and refusal to let my dad blow yours off the face of the earth is proof of that. He could have destroyed the First Minister years ago, you know that, right? One sniper, one minute, and boom, he's dead. She's the reason he didn't."

Zed stomped off, pushing past Drew, not looking to see how helpless Red was.

"He just doesn't understand," Red said to the Emperor.

"Yes, he does."

The Emperor fell into step next to Drew, calling out to Zed to slow down a bit since he didn't know exactly where we were headed. I heard Red behind us; he fell twice, trying to keep up, and he mumbled to himself, but he didn't try to explain what he meant.

No one would have listened, anyway.

*

It was only a little over a mile, but between having to climb over the destruction, Zed wanting to stop to check on every body part he saw—and sadly, not all of them were attached to their people, so he didn't hear a lot—and Red's slow speed, it took almost an hour to get to the edge of the bomb blast crater. Drew was less disturbed by it than expected and more anxious to find a way in.

"It'll look like the same hatch we left the train from. We're basically going back into the tube, but hopefully it will end at the lab entrance and not be buried."

Red stared at the crater and muttered, "There's not a chance anything survived that."

You're a cheery dude, aren't you?

"Look, either help us find a way into the tube, or not, but don't try to convince me it's not possible. The underground bunker is there. We just have to get into it."

They lined up next to each other and walked from the crater's edge, scanning the ground ahead for any sign of an access hatch under the snow. I hung out of Drew's sweatshirt pouch, and looked for it, too; it would be big and round and flush with the ground, but it might be warmer than the dirt, so perhaps less snow covered it.

Or, Red discovered as his dress shoes gave out from under him, it would be slick with ice.

He didn't hurry to get up, instead he laid on the ground while weariness settled on him like tiny, tired snowflakes. No one offered to help him up. Drew looked at him with pity and Zed with amusement, but the Emperor was angry. Every minute spent outside was a minute they were vulnerable, and every ounce of energy depleted from Red was a warning that traversing the distance to the Hancock building put us all at greater risk.

"Get up," he finally said. "And once we're in the lab, if you don't think you can keep up, we're leaving you there. We don't have time to coddle anyone at this point."

Red rolled over, got onto his knees and slowly got up. "You need me to get to my father."

Icily, the Emperor said, "No, I really don't."

Zed pulled his backpack off and knelt in the snow, feeling for the release on the hatch. "You know what?" he said, not looking up. "I am seriously sorry for how I acted in the safe house. For every time I gave you crap about running and sparring, and for making you drag me out of that field. Yeah, very sorry."

"How about for calling him a dick?" Drew asked.

"Maybe not that. Not yet." He found the latch and had to force it, but it slid and he was able to pry the hatch open. "All right, you're not a dick. But I was really mad."

The Emperor peered down into the tube. "I know." He slid his pack off and started down, but before he was past his hips, he reached for Zed and planted a kiss in the center of his forehead. "I know you love me."

Then he dropped straight down.

We waited. Zed and Drew stared into the black hole, listening for any sound the Emperor made. His footsteps sounded crunchy as they faded away and then came close again, and a few minutes later he called for them to lower their backpacks down to him.

After Drew gave him the last pack and my plastic tomb, he laid on the ground on his belly, and carefully handed me off. It was warmer in the tube than it was outside, and if there was enough air, I was willing to stay down there for the night if we had to.

Going back to the train was an option, if Red could pick up speed.

I wasn't sure he could.

I was pretty sure that he was spent, and would stay behind willingly if it meant not walking back over the piles of rock and debris.

Drew took the lead ahead of the Emperor, and Zed walked behind Red, mostly so that there was someone forcing him to keep up. There was a lot of rubble in the tube, and their feet made crunching sounds along the way; the closer we were from the hatch, the thinner the air felt, and the Emperor told Drew that they had maybe five minutes before he was going to make them turn around.

"That's all we need," he said.

He ran his hand along the smooth wall of the tube, fingers squeaking against the metal. At the four-minute mark, when the Emperor was about to tell him to turn around, the squeaking stopped and he said, "Bingo. Found the door."

He fumbled around a bit more, until he found the code box, and when he lifted the cover, the numbers on the keypad lit up.

"We have power," he said absently.

Ten input digits later, three sets of doors, the final one slid open and the lights inside came on. The Emperor gestured for them to stay put, handed me to Drew, and pulled his gun from the waistband of his jeans. He entered apprehensively, listening for any other signs of life, and when he was sure there was no one else inside, he relaxed and told us to come in.

The air smelled stale, but Drew had the circulator turned on within two minutes, and adjusted the temperature so that we'd all be comfortable. The entry was a small room, and after he'd gotten things set he led us into the next, which was the actual lab itself. There were rows of tables laden with equipment, and he cautioned everyone to not touch anything. "Especially you, Wick," he said. "Don't jump on any of these tables. Some of these things bite, and other things blow up. Okay?"

Not a problem.

He was looking for the part of the lab that was under the crater; he thought it was probably the office, or even the break room, but everyone searched and all the rooms were intact. If Richard had been caught down here, he would have survived.

In the break room there was a refrigerator and he opened it carefully, not wanting to sniff too hard in case everything in it had spoiled, but it was loaded with unopened bottles of soft drinks and sealed containers of lunch meats and cheeses. Next to the refrigerator was a cupboard and long counter, and he opened all the doors, finding unopened jars of peanut butter and boxes of cereal and crackers.

"My dad eats like an eight-year-old," he explained.

There's cheese. I like cheese.

"There's salami, too," Drew said to me. "And probably ham and bologna. You'll get bites."

Dude, did you understand me?

What the Emperor wanted first was access to Richard's office and his computer system; he wanted to boot it up and check for any possible functioning security cameras, making sure that we were safe from intrusion.

What Zed wanted first was the bathroom.

Drew showed the Emperor where the computer was and then showed Zed where the bathroom was, and I followed, hoping he would grasp that I needed a litter box of some sort. After all, he'd left the pan in the train, and I was going to need it again soon.

He rooted around in the lab until he found a box shallow enough that I could easily get into it, and then shredded toilet paper for litter. He warned that it might not be all that comfortable to use, but it was the best he could do. I didn't care; it worked, and I even had privacy.

After he put the box near the restroom, he went about digging into closets. There were air mattresses and blankets that his father and colleagues used on nights when they worked too late to go home, and in a room near the restrooms were a washer and a dryer. He shoved the blankets into the dryer to freshen them up, and then finally went into the break room to sit down.

He hadn't been off his feet for three minutes when Zed came in to tell him the Emperor got the computer booted up and had found a news broadcast. There were reports of renewed fighting in Kansas, but more importantly, in Chicago.

At that, Drew jumped up and went into the office to watch. A few miles west of the Hancock building, there was a small band of Midlam troops in Washington Square Park, and they were fighting hand to hand with a half dozen of Florida's military. The video footage was taken from a drone that moved over the soldiers and dipped between them, capturing agony in every splatter of blood, and the twisted grimaces of men who fought for their lives.

It was brutal, and the drone never moved away; whoever operated it—from a safe distance likely hundreds of miles away—waited to capture the breathless and pain-contorted face of the last man standing.

Drew sucked in a hard, sharp breath.

It was Carter.

27

He wanted to bolt, run to the tube and outside, and then run to the park to find his brother. He also understood when the Emperor pointed out all the things that were wrong with that notion: he had no idea how many other soldiers were out there, and how many would shoot before asking any questions; he had no clue where Carter would run to; he had no idea what Carter's orders were and the risks he would expose his brother to if he ran into the middle of something Carter already had under control—but that didn't keep him from pacing.

"We find Oz first," the Emperor said. "She's our priority. When she's safe, then we find him."

Finding Oz meant getting her away as fast as possible; Drew knew that, but allowed himself to be placated for the moment. His hands went to his head, fingers laced together, and he began walking the room, back and forth, taking long, deliberate breaths.

"He's supposed to be in Europe," Drew said. "Backpacking. Being the selfish prick he always is."

"He was probably trying to protect your parents," Zed pointed out. "Joining up just as the country heads into war? Yeah, he didn't want them to panic."

"What if something happens to him? What if he gets caught in the middle of everything and dies?"

A long breath in, a long breath out.

"What if he doesn't?" the Emperor offered.

That made Drew stop pacing.

Carter was a jerk, but he was also crafty and strong, and he wasn't stupid. The Emperor told Drew to trust in Carter's training as much as he trusted in his own. And if given the choice, who would Carter prefer he concentrate on?

"For you, there is no choice," Red said.

Drew was puzzled.

"You've committed to Oz, haven't you? You've accepted that she's God's gift to you? Then there is no choice. You're marrying her, not your brother, not Zed, not the Emperor, not your parents. She's the one you're meant to protect, above anyone else."

He thought about it a moment and then asked. "So if you had to choose between your parents and your wife?"

"I will always choose Darlene."

"Your kids?"

"I will *always* choose Darlene."

"And yet," the Emperor said, "were you to make that choice, she would never forgive you."

"That would be my burden to bear."

"Honest question," Zed said. "If she's your priority, why are you here with us and not with her and your kids?"

"I'm here *because* she's my priority. Zed, she's not my property, no matter what you think. If I can help remove my father from power, her life becomes measurably better. So do the lives of my daughters and every other female in Florida. I'm here and I'm willing to die, because she does deserve better than the life she's been given."

"Doesn't that fly in the face of your church?" Zed asked.

"Yes, it does. But it doesn't fly in the face of my religion, and I hope to one day change the church. I'm not my father, Zed. I have never believed that God wanted his daughters to be cast aside."

"Is that why you helped my mom run away?"

"There are so many reasons, but the least of them may be because she would have always been treated as less than a man." Red turned to Drew. "You've seen the way King Jackson looks at my sister. Tell me he wouldn't choose her every single time."

He would, and Drew knew it.

He also knew that Red was at least a little bit right—there was nothing getting in his way of getting to Oz. Not Red, not his father, and not his brother.

*

Zed fell asleep easily, curled up on his air mattress that was half under the break room table. Red slept just feet away from him, and Drew was on the other side of the room, wide awake, while the Emperor sat in the office poring over any new information that he could find.

After tossing and turning for half an hour—I watched him from a chair near the table because I didn't trust that he wouldn't accidentally elbow me if I got on the bed with him—Drew slid off the mattress and sat on the floor with his back to the wall. He folded his arms over his bent knees but his eyes were closed, like he couldn't make up his mind whether to stay awake or not.

I'd seen the Emperor like that often enough, usually when he was in his workshop late at night. He wanted to sleep but couldn't, so pretending had to be enough. Once in a while he sat on his bedroom floor the same way, back to the wall, legs bent at the knee, arms folded on them. He'd slowly breathe in and slowly breathe out, silently begging the sleep fairies to come spend the night.

It never worked.

I wanted to tell Drew that, but I didn't think it would matter. I wasn't sure sleep was what he was truly after, anyway.

He was still sitting like that when the Emperor came in. Instead of getting into his own bed, he sat next to Drew, legs stretched out on the floor, arms folded at his stomach. He seemed far more relaxed, but had a lot of sympathy for how tightly coiled Drew felt.

"Are you all right?" he asked, quietly so that he wouldn't bother Zed or Red.

Drew's eyes fluttered open. "I'm terrified," he admitted. "I'm trying to focus on just getting home and getting to my mom's communications center so that we can use the surveillance equipment, but I can't make my brain stay on that idea. I'm one stray thought away from a full-blown panic attack."

"If that happens, we'll deal with it," the Emperor said.

He wasn't going to talk him out of his panic; Drew was going to feel whatever Drew was going to feel, no matter what.

"Tell me I shouldn't worry. You're proof that everything will be fine, right?"

The moment the Emperor created the gate and sent Finn home through it, he changed the timeline. He still existed, but that didn't mean that he would again, and he couldn't lie to Drew about it simply to make him feel better. "If the timeline hadn't changed, I wouldn't have been able to make this trip. I would be home, getting sicker every day, and very nearly dead."

"You've been sick," Drew said, the realization just hitting him. "And you've actually been sleeping. That worries me."

"Stress response," the Emperor said. "You're not the only one who's terrified."

Maybe it was your cooking. You cooked right before we left, didn't you?

I miss the Queen's cooking.

If things were normal and we were at home, the Queen would be getting everything ready for Thanksgiving. She started prepping two or three days before, and let everyone help. Oz and Zed ran between their kitchen and the staff kitchen, loading both refrigerators with everything that could be cooked ahead. She put the King in charge of baking little rolls, and while he waited for them to be done he sat at the counter tearing bread into tiny little pieces for her stuffing.

She even allowed the Emperor to help. She liked his cherry pie, and always asked him to bring one.

One day, I want to tell her that his cherry pie came from a box that he bought at the grocery store and stored in the freezer until it was time to shove it into the oven.

The Queen loved Thanksgiving, because it meant the start of the winter holidays, and that was her favorite time of year.

I doubted she was even going through the motions this year.

Thanksgiving would come and go, and its lines would be colored in by ugly, empty markers thrown at her like poisoned darts by her own father.

That occurred to Drew as he sat with the Emperor in the dark.

"What the hell is that monster doing to Oz?"

"Don't let your mind go there, Andrew."

"I have to. Because if he did—if he does—I have to figure out how to help her pick up the pieces. There's not much that could break Oz, but that…how would we even begin?"

"I'm not nearly qualified enough to process that," the Emperor said sadly. "I understand pain, but not pain wrapped in cruelty such as that. I certainly don't understand a violation that huge."

Drew turned his head to look at Red. His mattress was bathed in soft light coming from the office, but his back was turned to us and we couldn't see his face. "I want to hate him for the things his father has done. I know it's not fair, but there it is."

The Emperor thought that Red would understand. "His own belief system assumes that mankind bears the sins of Adam. He would grasp the notion of the son bearing the sins of the father."

"Yeah, I don't know a damned thing about his beliefs, not really. When you touched him, did you get anything?"

"He's telling the truth, I think. But I admit, I would be far more certain about that if I had Oz's capabilities. I was limited to a very quick glance, and he was distracted. Oz would be able to look at him and know as soon as he opened his mouth."

"Once she got to know him a little," Drew said. "It's not automatic. Did you know that she can't tell with you? Your colors never change."

"Perhaps because I don't lie to her."

"Come on, everyone has those tiny untruths that slip out. Like early in the summer when Mrs. B made that weird chicken casserole that tasted like gym socks and you told her you enjoyed it. I know you were lying. We *all* lied. Oz just can't tell with you."

The King told her the truth, later.

We owe him for that.

"I spent my childhood controlling the feelings I allowed people to see. Perhaps the result of that was becoming an extremely proficient liar."

"Your childhood sucked, didn't it?"

"Indeed. It's why I don't particularly want to return to or even briefly visit my own When. I'm happy now, but I was miserable as a little boy. Those are people I would prefer to never see again, even if they have grown and changed."

"If the timeline has changed, maybe that will, too. Maybe the next incarnation of you will be happy."

He considered it for a moment, but then said, "My childhood misery is what made it possible for me to come here and want to stay. It's why I was here to send Finn home—which, as has been pointed out so indelicately, may be why I exist in the first place. I needed to be here in order to be born. A necessary loop in time."

"You got the transponder that made Finn's gate work from Wick, right? Did Finn have the same kind? The one that he fried and sent himself to null space with?"

"It was similar."

Drew stared at nothing, the same way he did when he was seeing things that sped around inside his head. His eyes ticked back and forth as his brain sifted through all the notions he considered, and he started to speak, but then closed his mouth because he wasn't done thinking.

Here he goes.

Cough it up, brain boy.

"Okay. So for it to work…the transponder has to emit some kind of signal, right? Some indicator that lets the ship find Finn, grab him, and then move him."

"Keep going."

"Look, I kind of understand how Oz's transponder works in the portals. The portal locates it and then moves her based on what she's thinking, because it's also wired into her brain. But the main thing is that it can locate her, right?"

"Basically."

"Okay. So Finn's transponder had a limited range to his ship, but having it meant the ship could find him. And it would be too far for his ship to move Oz from here to home, but could it just find her? Let us know for sure where she is? I mean, we're guessing Chicago because of where the Minister was preaching, but what if we're wrong?"

Every portal jump Oz had ever made was stored on a computer two hundred years in the future; Finn's ship had access to that computer, which meant he could also access her transponder codes. If he could get to his ship, he might be able to locate her.

"Now I understand how you motivated my father to go back and change the trajectory of the gates," the Emperor said. "We need to get to the Hancock, Drew. I need to access your mother's communications array. Get us in and I'll contact my father. If he can do it, he will."

Drew finally relaxed. His feet slid on the floor and he rested his hands on his thighs. The tension around him loosened; it didn't disappear, but he could at least breathe better.

"Does Finn know who he is?" he asked after a moment.

"He knows. Well, he didn't—when we sent him home in August his memory was still full of holes and he had no idea how closely related he was to the people who had helped and cared for him. It wasn't until he understood how the portals worked and that it was up to him to invent them that it dawned on him to look at his own genealogy and connect the dots. He was both overwhelmed and elated that the grandfather named Andrew he loved so much was the Drew he had met. But even then…it got complicated."

"So you've said. Is that how you go visit your grandparents? Pop through a portal and then go to Scotland?"

He shook his head. "When my father was relocating people, he brought my mother's parents here, and Oz's grandfather helped them get everything they needed to settle in Glasgow. And now my mother can just pick up a phone and see them. Hopefully she'll be able to visit soon."

"And your other grandparents? Did they stay in your own When?"

The Emperor chuckled. "Don't ask me about them, Drew. I won't tell you anything."

"It was worth a shot."

The Emperor got up; he wanted to shut everything down in the office, and wanted Drew to go to bed. "Try to sleep," he said. "Tomorrow, Oz."

28

Morning for the Emperor began at four o'clock. He rolled off the air mattress and crept into the office, closing the door partway so that the light wouldn't wake anyone else. He looked for more news, listening with the volume down as he watched soldiers in Richard's shiny exoskeleton suits move toward a line of poorly armed men dressed in the black uniforms of Florida's military. Bullets pinged off the Pacifican soldiers' armor, and they marched forward without drawing weapons, not until it was clear that Florida would not retreat and would not cease firing.

Arms were then drawn in a movement of practiced ballet; every soldier in an exosuit pulled a laser pistol from their side holster, aimed forward, and shot. It was a bright-white burst of energy that dropped every enemy soldier where he stood, with gaping chest wounds that smoldered but didn't bleed.

The talking head asked what everyone was thinking. "Why have they not given up? This is slings and arrows versus flamethrowers and rocket launchers."

"Indeed," the Emperor whispered.

They would fight until ordered not to, it was as simple as that. Until the First Minister had what he wanted, he would throw whatever, or whoever, in front of the firing squad.

He didn't care.

"He doesn't want Florida to be great. He wants greatness for himself and has no idea how pathetic and small it makes him."

Still whispering to himself.

I jumped onto his lap to let him know he wasn't alone. We watched the news in silence for another hour, when Red and Drew were awake and trying to decide if they should let Zed sleep or not. The Emperor heard them rustling around and made the decision for them; he went into the break room, reached down to the end of Zed's air mattress, and pulled the plug.

Half a minute later, when his body met the floor, he opened his eyes and grumbled, "I really hate you."

"That's fine, but get up. We have eight miles to cover and it may not be a walk through the woods."

I don't want to go back to the woods. I didn't like sleeping outside.

The Emperor started to deflate his mattress as Drew and Zed headed for the bathroom, and rolled his eyes when they began bickering.

"Zed, I swear, if you spray all over the bathroom you damn well better clean it up."

"It's a boner, Drew, not a shower head."

"Jesus, just…"

"Like you don't have the same problem every morning."

"At least I don't parade around with it."

Red began to fold his deflated mattress. "You know, I have brothers, but…I've clearly missed a few things by only having girls."

You're a dude, dude.

You should know these things.

The Emperor rolled his mattress to get all the air out. "They're often crude, but they're good men. I barely think of them as boys anymore. Except, perhaps, when they start talking like that."

Drew came back alone and said, "He'll be a few minutes. He's cleaning the toilet. And the floor. And the wall."

And my litterbox?

I don't think anyone remembered to empty my box, which was probably a nasty surprise for the next people to enter the lab.

We left the same way we'd gotten in, through the tube hatch. It was bitterly cold, with wind blowing hard and snowflakes falling so fast that they drilled into flesh like little frozen darts. Drew wrapped me in one of his t-shirts, then eased me into his sweatshirt pouch and then zipped his jacket up to my chin. If I felt cold, he said, duck down. He'd find a way to keep me warm.

The Emperor gave Red his jacket. He thought he would be fine in just layered sweatshirts, as long as he could keep his head covered and they kept moving at a decent pace.

He's telling you to not slow us down, Red.

Drew led us north. He wanted to get within a few blocks of the Hancock, but because they didn't know if the building was under guard or empty and locked, it seemed too risky to just walk up and try to go in, even though Drew knew the key codes to unlock the doors. Just east of the building—which was huge, its footprint taking up nearly an entire city block—there were manholes in the street, and some of them dropped into an old sewer system that went directly underneath the Hancock.

"You want us to walk through the sewer," Red sputtered.

"It's an old sewer. Like, a couple hundred years old. It's not functional. My brother and I used to sneak out through it all the time. I figure it's a stupid simple way to get in. Drop down the manhole, walk until we see the ladder that has half a dozen old pieces of rope tied to it, and we're there. It'll get us into the basement parking garage."

The hardest part was going to be the trek to get there. He wanted to follow loosely along Lake Shore Drive, because it seemed to have less structural damage than the more direct streets, but he warned everyone: this has the feel of a blizzard starting. If the winds shift and start coming at us from over the lake, it's going to get bad. Once we get going, there may be no turning back if it does get bad. And the closer to the water, the colder it might feel.

"I'll take the cold over the obstacles," the Emperor said. "Just keep Wick warm."

"Two and a half to three hours," Drew said. "It's a little over eight miles from here, but the wind is going to slow us down a little."

"Not to mention anything we have to climb over," Zed pointed out.

They walked quickly, keeping Red in mind; he was nearly running to keep up but he wasn't complaining and he didn't have as many problems with staying upright as he had before, not until we came to the first block in the road. There was a wide seam blown out of it, and to get across they had to climb down one side and then up on the other, avoiding chunks of metal and rock that jutted from the dirt.

Drew, Zed, and the Emperor scrambled up on the far side; Red slipped back three times before his feet found solid enough ground to push off from.

Without trying, they found a marching cadence. They fell into step, one after the other with Drew leading the way, all but Red, who was still at his limit. He took three steps for every one they did, and his breathing reflected his effort.

I kept my head down in Drew's sweatshirt unless I felt like I had to see where we were going. I listened, though: to the sound of Drew's heartbeat, to his breath going in and out, and to the air around us.

Three miles in, I heard a whine coming from the distance. It didn't sound like a car or a van, and I didn't know of an animal that made that noise. I stuck my head out and tried to see but failing that, I butted my head into Drew's stomach to get him to notice.

Hey. Hey. Hey.

He stopped and turned to the Emperor, unzipping the jacket just enough so that he could hear me.

Something in the air is wrong. The sky is crying.

His head jerked up and he scanned the sky. He could hear it, too, off in the distance, and yelled "Run!" as he pushed Drew and Zed toward the next break in the road. They ran at full speed, Drew's giant hands protecting me, and as Red dove in after us, the world exploded and the sky tried to eat us in one big bite.

29

My ears hurt.

One was ringing, and the other felt like it was plugged up. I was protected by Drew's giant hands; he curled up on his side to make sure that his chest and legs provided an extra layer, but the sound still got through and slapped me upside the head. He was breathing hard and fast, and when everything stopped shaking he yelled out, "Is everyone all right?"

It sounded a little like, "Izzy un aw ite?" to me, but I understood the context.

Red groaned and Zed managed a tight, "Yeah," but the Emperor took a beat too long to answer, which made Drew scramble to get up before he was really ready to.

"I'm fine," he finally said. He pointed to his ears. "Give it a minute."

Me, too. My head is eating itself from the inside.

"Look at me, Wick," he said, crouching. "Let me see your eyes."

I opened them wide so he could see, and they were apparently pretty enough for him, because he scratched the top of my head. "Good job. We might not have gotten to cover in time if not for you."

He told them to stay put, while he tried to look over the side of the ditch. Dirt skittered down from under his feet, but he managed to pull himself up enough to get a good look. "There's a long burn mark about fifteen feet ahead," he said. "But it also broke up a huge blockade that was in our way."

"Are we under attack?" Zed asked. "Or was it coincidence?"

He didn't know. It was definitely friendly fire, but they had no way of knowing who we were if they had seen us, and might have struck as a warning if they thought we were the enemy.

"Mr. B knows we were headed for Chicago," Drew said. "Surely he would have issued an alert."

Maybe they did it to make it easier to get over that giant pile of bombed out building that was in our way.

"Don't know." The Emperor started to climb out, and when he had gotten all the way up, he reached down to help Drew. It was tricky, because Drew still had me in his sweatshirt, and he didn't want to slam against the side of the ditch and squish me. Once he was up, they reached for Zed and Red, and then stood up to assess where they were at.

The burn mark was only a few feet wide, but tendrils of smoke and steam rose from it, and as we got closer and felt heat licking toward us, the Emperor didn't think we could get across, not yet.

"We try to cross, and our boots might melt. We wait, we freeze. We jump, we might land in the burn."

Grab snow and throw it across the hot stuff.

"And that is precisely why we need you around, Wick," the Emperor said.

"What'd he say, Will?" Drew asked.

"To start throwing snow onto the burn. And he's right. Scoop up as much as you can, and we'll try to cool down a path wide enough to cross over."

It sizzled when the snow hit the ground, and they kept throwing it down until the snow was slower to melt. The Emperor was the first to cross—he went quickly but did not run—and told them to go one at a time. Red was last, because the Emperor was worried about the thickness of the soles of his shoes and reasoned that by the time he went, it would be cool enough.

"Thank you, Wick," he said to me when they were all on the other side.

"You're actually talking to your cat," Red muttered.

"I'm from two hundred years in the future. Of course I talk to the cat. What else would you expect?"

Red had no answer for that.

*

He picked up speed.

When Drew noted that we were at the six-mile mark, with only two more before we could start looking for a manhole, Red began walking faster. He was breathing hard and sweat was freezing on his face, but he managed to find something inside that let him move faster.

I thought it might be the sound of gunfire in the distance, but I could be wrong.

The others kept their cadence, with Drew taking the lead. He was putting off a lot of heat for me, so I was able to stick my head out more often, and I didn't like what I saw. Snow came down sideways, and the wind hurt my ears and my eyes. When I looked up, Drew's beard had grown little icicles and his nose was beet red.

We need to get inside. You're too cold.

He didn't stop to ask the Emperor what I said. He either got it, or was ignoring it.

We stopped suddenly when a loud boom cut through the air. The Emperor started counting, 1...2...3...4...5, and then the ground shook. It wasn't hard, but I could feel the vibrations move up through Drew, and it startled Red so much that he wanted to run.

"That wasn't close by," Drew said. "Just keep up, we'll get there."

I took one more look ahead before ducking back into the sweatshirt, and hoped more than anything that the sky didn't start crying again, because ahead of us, there was no place to hide.

*

When we reached the two-mile endpoint that Drew had promised, Red said the first thing off the bad word list that we'd heard from him. He looked around at all the snow piling up in huge drifts and the dense white blanket across the street, and groaned, "Dammit."

"What?" Zed asked. "We're here."

"But look at it! We'll never find a manhole cover under all of this."

"Maybe you won't," Drew said. He marched across the street to the entry of an abandoned drug store and then turned to walk back, counting each of his steps. When he got to twenty, he stopped, and said, "Start digging."

He was on his knees trying to push snow from the street before they could react.

Hey. I'm still down here. Keep it off me, okay?

Snow is evil.

It took five minutes, but they cleared enough away to see the surface of the street, and only a few more for Zed to uncover the manhole.

"How the hell do we lift it?" he asked. "Those things weigh like a hundred pounds."

"The real ones, maybe," Drew said. "This one? Thirty if I overestimate. And it's hinged."

He stuck his finger into a hole drilled at the edge, and lifted. It opened with the squeal of the unused and unwanted, but it opened. He reached in to find the ladder, and then began the climb down, carefully so that he didn't bang my head into it.

"It's not exactly pleasant down here," he said when the Emperor was closing the manhole cover, "but it is safe. It's just stale air, not the remnants of actual sewage."

Red gestured to the manhole cover. "We just scraped all the snow off that thing. Won't that serve as a big 'we are here' announcement?"

"You want to go up there and cover it back up, and then walk the rest of the way outside?" Zed asked. When Red didn't answer, Zed said, "Yeah. I thought so."

The Emperor used the screen of his phone for light, and we slowly made our way down the pipe. There were bugs and other things that might eat me, but Drew's hand was on my back to reassure me, and the things scurrying by didn't seem to bother him at all.

I thought they should all be frozen to death, but the rats were apparently immune. Or maybe it was warmer in the pipe than I thought, but it seemed to me that they should all be furry little blocks of ice.

The ground rumbled, and Red yelped.

It scared me, too, but when he squealed the Emperor laughed and told him it was fine. We were safe where we were.

I thought you didn't lie.

Oh, that might only be to Oz.

Drew's heart rate had gone up, so I don't think he believed the Emperor, either.

It took ten minutes to go two blocks. We were slowed down by the darkness and the narrow passage in the pipe, but Drew wasn't going to speed up in case he missed seeing the rope he and Carter had tied onto the ladder that led to the basement of the Hancock building. He was feeling his way, too, which worried me because of the critters that could bite, but when his hand brushed it, I saw the rope move.

Bingo?

"Bingo," he breathed.

Zed looked up, trying to find the top of the ladder. "If this thing doesn't open because someone has put furniture over it, I'm gonna be pissed."

Drew gripped the sides of the ladder. "There might be a car over it, who knows? If this one is blocked, there are a couple of others. Let me get all the way up and get the hatch open. It'll be easier when you have a little more light to see by."

I made sure my head was poking out, because I wanted to see the basement of the giant building. When he got to the top rung, he used one hand to hold on and one to push the hatch open, and then scurried up until he was all the way out and standing on the floor.

He didn't realize we weren't alone, not until he heard the click of guns being aimed at him.

We were surrounded.

30

Drew raised his hands quickly and blurted out, "Don't shoot the cat!"

Smooth, dude.

How about telling them to not shoot anyone?

I tried to raise my paws—if it was important enough for him it was important enough for me—but wound up falling forward and was caught on the edge of the sweatshirt pouch. I hung there, half in and half out with the fabric digging into my hindquarters, and there was no uprighting myself without digging my claws into Drew's stomach. Six rifles were pointed at us, six soldiers dressed in dark blue pants and shirts, with black boots and black armored vests, and they were all staring at me.

Haven't you ever seen a cat?

Don't shoot me. I'm adorable.

"Holy…" The soldier in the middle lowered his gun. "Stand down. It's my baby brother and his girlfriend's weird little cat."

Drew didn't move. He kept his hands in the air and I'm certain his gaze was fixed on the rifle of the soldier right in front of him, watching as lowered slowly. When the gun was no longer pointed anywhere near him, he exhaled and looked up.

His voice squeaked a little. "Carter?"

"Yeah, you little freak. What the hell are you doing here? And with the damned cat?" He moved to see down the hatch and yelled,

"Whoever's with him, come on up. It's safe."

Sure, that'll convince them. Trust that I won't shoot you because I said so.

"It's fine, Will," Drew called out. "It's Carter."

There was movement from below, and as the Emperor and Zed came up, Carter pulled Drew into a tight hug, and then called him a freaking idiot for being in a war zone, though he didn't actually use the word "freaking" and instead plucked one right from the top of the bad word list.

The Queen would not have been amused.

Zed climbed out of the hole, took one look at Drew's brother and then said, "Douchebag, I never thought I'd be so glad to see you."

"Yeah, me either, dingleberry."

Red was reluctant to come up, but the Emperor was in no mood to put up with anything else. "You can stay down there, Red. You'll freeze, but it's your choice."

Carter looked down into the hole as well. "What, you're dragging along a little girl or something? I can jump down and carry her out for you."

"It's the Second Minister of Florida," Zed said. He startled when the guns were snapped up and pointed at us again.

The Emperor was not bothered by their reaction and didn't even look. "He's with us. Like it or not, he's more on your side than he is Florida's." He yelled down the hole, "Thirty seconds and I let the big guy with the gun come down and drag you out, Red."

Slowly, Red climbed the ladder and poked his head out of the hole. When he saw the guns pointed at him, he started to duck back down until Carter said, "Don't give me a reason to drop a grenade into that pipe with you. Either get out and face us, or drop down and die."

Drew put his hand on Carter's chest, and pressed him back an inch. "He really is on our side. And the First Minister wants him dead."

Carter grunted. "The Minister already thinks he's dead. Pacifica torched his compound. Munson uploaded a video to all of the news sites, blubbering about it being unfair and blaming the King for killing his son."

Red's eyes went wide, and Drew shot a look at the Emperor, who seemed wholly unconcerned by that news.

"He knows you're not dead," the Emperor told him. "He knows damn well that we evacuated the compound. But he also knows the rest of the world is likely unaware of it and will use it to garner sympathy. His announcement of your death in no way makes you any safer right now. Perhaps less so, because now he needs you dead."

Red's sense of impending doom was more immediate; he was less concerned about his father than he was about the armed soldiers eyeing him like coveted fodder. The rifles remained trained on him until Carter told them to stand down and then continue their patrol while he took their new guests upstairs.

He took us to an elevator on the far side of the basement and up several floors to his family's apartment. It was spacious and richly decorated, and reminded me more of the guest suite at home, which was overblown and a little pretentious, meant to cater to visitors in a way that the King and Queen had chosen not to live. This made me think that the Van Hoffs were trying to impress themselves, though I couldn't figure out why.

The message was obvious: we're rich, and you're not. Even though they weren't really rich. It felt like taxpayer money misspent, but it was not only not my business, it didn't seem to bother the Emperor or Zed. Maybe all they saw was a place to rest that wasn't the ground or the floor; no matter how stuffy it felt, it was still kind of like home.

I wondered what their Queen would think, seeing it turned into military quarters. There were dirty boots heaped by the door and jackets slung over the backs of chairs; the white carpet was streaked with grime and there was a mound of gun parts and cleaning supplies on the thick glass coffee table.

White carpet.

I wondered if Carter and Drew had even been allowed on it when they were small and dirt followed them like a little cloud. Jax almost had a meltdown once when Zed dumped a potted plant onto the middle of the living room floor, but Aubrey just scooped it all up, repotted it, told Zed that wasn't nice, and then made him vacuum.

It was kind of like home, but very much not. I wanted to be back where I could hock up a hairball and not worry about ruining the décor.

"What's left of my squad stays here since this building has the best surveillance equipment in the city," Carter said as he led us into the living room. "And don't worry, Drew, no one's messing with your junk. Your room is just a place to crash. Except a couple of the guys asked if they could read some of your books. I told them it would be all right as long as they didn't dog-ear any pages or get them wet."

"It's just stuff, I don't care. How many people are left in the city?"

Carter didn't look happy. "Yeah, not many. After the first bombing run, people started booking it to Pacifica and Canada. There are a few holdouts, but they're mostly in the southern suburbs where nothing was hit. We were originally sent to protect them, but—" he shrugged "—can't protect people who aren't here. So we're trying to corner as many enemy fighters as we can and take back the city. Chasing the First Minister has become a game."

"How many are here?"

"Floridians? About seventy per cent fewer than a month ago. We're holding ground, but we don't have the manpower to seriously go after Munson, just enough to keep him moving from spot to spot. Pacifica has burn runs several times a day, and that at least keeps him locked into the city. He can't get out yet. His people can't get in. They haven't had any supply trucks making it past the state line, and there haven't been any more of their planes coming into our air space…Pacifica's doing a damned fine job keeping them out. Though I'm not certain they know he's here. Just his men."

Drew sat next to Zed on the sofa, and slapped at his legs when Zed put his feet on the coffee table. "Munson was broadcasting from the Presbyterian church. That's why we decided to come here."

"Yeah, we know. He broadcast on a time delay and was gone before we could get in there. That's just it—we don't have actual proof he's in the city. If we did, we would report it, then evacuate and let the hovers just burn what's left to the ground. It's like we're chasing a rat. You know the damn thing is there but getting to it?"

"How many of your squad are left?" the Emperor asked him.

"Three dozen, maybe a few more. I'm guessing Munson has twice as many men still, but they're not well armed. The guns they have are old and fire actual bullets, and I figure they're running low on ammunition. Most of our encounters have been hand to hand, a lot of knife fighting. Pacifica's hovers have handled the more gruesome take downs. Man…it's brutal when they catch someone in a burn run." He held up his hands, splaying his fingers. "Poof."

"You know about Pacifica and Midlam?" Drew asked. "I don't know where you were when the news broke. I thought you were hiking through Europe, but now I'm guessing you weren't."

"I know about it. I was just getting out of basic training when the King made his announcement. And yeah, as far as the parents are concerned, I'm still there. All right?"

"That won't hold," the Emperor told him. "They deserve to know."

"Come on, Emperor, you know my mother—she wouldn't be able to handle the idea of what I'm doing. They don't deserve to worry."

"They kind of do," Drew said. "Man up, Carter. Mom's already given up her country and her crown, and she needs to know you're here, fighting to keep what's left of her life out of Munson's hands. And what if something happens to you? She'll be blindsided."

Carter's jaw clenched.

There's the angry little man I know.

"Fine," he conceded. "I'll get word to them. But you—you're all right with losing the crown? I mean me, if it had happened a year ago, I'd have been pissed. But when King Jackson made the announcement, we went from feeling like we only had a slim shot at holding this city to knowing he could level Florida and end it before things got too bad. It sucks for you but for the rest of us, it's a major win. All we have to do is hold on."

"It doesn't suck for me," Drew said. "You know Oz and I always planned on merging Midlam with Pacifica."

"Yeah. Dreams of a couple of kids. You still sweet on her?"

He was teasing, but Drew was deadly serious.

"It goes way beyond that."

Zed snickered. "It goes a disgusting amount of way beyond that. Now there's drooling and inappropriate touching."

Carter was not as amused and the look he gave Drew was pained. "We don't know where Munson has her, Drew. We've looked, we're still looking and won't give up, but, yeah, haven't found either of them."

The Emperor slapped at his legs and got up. "And to that end, I need access to your mother's secure channels. Drew figured out how we're going to find Oz."

*

"It's become the de facto war room," Carter said as he led us down one corridor into another, and then through thick metal doors that he opened with a long code. "We have an eye on almost everything in the city from here."

But not enough of it to find the Minister. Or Oz.

Their war room was smaller than the one we'd sped through at home: there were rows of theater seating and tables with computers, and on the far wall there were a dozen video monitors, with a giant one in the middle. The room didn't buzz with the sound of a hundred voices the way Pacifica's did. On the main screen, they had a good view of the blizzard outside, but not of much else. There was one other person in the room; he sat with his back to us, and never looked up.

"Hakim," Carter said. "Our boy wonder. All he does is keep our lines scrambled and secure. You can safely contact anyone in the world from here. No one will be able to back track your calls."

A few minutes later, the big screen had Pacifica's logo on it, and a minute after that Finn and Richard Van Hoff answered from the Emperor's now-former workshop under Union Square.

Before the Emperor could get to the point, Richard honed in on Carter. He was surprised and pleased to see him there at first, but then realized what his presence and the uniform meant. He exploded in a flash of anger because Carter wasn't safely wandering around Europe with a backpack and credit card. What the hell was he thinking? Leaving a perfectly safe place to come back to a war? How could you do this? Especially to your mother?

Carter tried to apologize in between Richard's questions. He'd never gone to Europe; he went to basic training, and kept it a secret to keep them from stopping him. "It was important, Dad. And it was before all hell broke loose—but I wouldn't have changed my plans. You know I need this."

Not much you can do about it now. Not unless you beg Jax to boot him out of the army.

The flash of anger fizzled; if anyone needed military discipline, it was Carter. Richard sucked it up, telling him he was proud of him. Proud of both his sons. But, "Keep your head down. I don't want you to be a hero."

Sensing the Emperor's annoyance at the delay, Finn jumped in. "You need something, Dash, I can tell."

He explained Drew's idea of using Finn's ship to locate Oz's transponder signal and reminded him that if not for Drew's nonlinear thinking abilities, he might be dying a slow and painful death in a room a few floors down from the King, and Earth would be destroyed in two hundred years. Paying attention to Drew's random thoughts might be well worth the time.

Carter nudged Drew and whispered, "What the hell? What'd you do?"

Drew said he would explain it later. "But, yeah, I totally saved the planet."

"Well," Finn said, "I can see where you're going with the idea. The transponders do emit a signal unique to the person it's embedded in, and the transporters that the portals are built around respond to those signals. Without it, the portals wouldn't activate at all, and—"

"Can you do it?" Drew interrupted. "Can you find Oz by locating her signal?"

"I don't have my ship here," Finn said. "But…I could go to it. The work to restructure the honing system to search for her specific signal and DNA code would take me about three weeks, but it's definitely doable."

"Three weeks," Drew groaned.

The Emperor folded his arms, and considered it. "All right. So go do it. Call me back in about five minutes?"

"Better make it ten. Maybe fifteen. Your mother will want to help, you know how that goes."

The Emperor chuckled to himself as the screen went dark.

"We don't have three weeks," Red blurted. "We don't even have three days. It's not a matter of Oz's trial—it's what he'll do to her in the meantime. He's trying to make an example of—"

"He'll call back in ten minutes," the Emperor said flatly. He turned to Carter and asked, "Who's in charge here?"

"No one, really. Our C.O. is dead. We're basically just hanging on until reinforcements get here."

"Highest ranking officer?"

"Emperor, we're all grunts. All fresh out of training except for the boy wonder and he's strictly data infrastructure. No one thought the Minister would hide in Chicago. They just thought they were sending us to a quiet, safe place to watch and guard a few people. Like, who would come back here? There's not a lot left."

From the other side of the room, without looking up, Hakim said, "Scumbucket is the Prince. So, really, he's in charge."

Drew snorted a laugh. "Scumbucket?"

"You should talk, freak." He called down to Hakim, "I'm not a prince anymore, so drop it."

"Fine. So now you're just an entitled ass. Got it."

The Emperor turned to Red and asked, "Now aren't you glad you've just got girls?"

"I'm not sure. Either way, I'm learning that I've certainly been sheltered my whole life."

They endured the next ten minutes, while Drew and Carter and Zed picked on each other. Red was uncomfortable, but the Emperor took it in stride; it was what he wanted, even for those few moments. Just let them be the same kids he used to watch on the roof while they played.

When the screen lit back up with Pacifica's logo, they stopped picking on each other and paid attention. Hakim pushed the call through, and Finn was there with his back to the camera, hunched over and messing with something, and Jo was looking right at the Emperor.

She didn't even bother saying hello. "William…that hair is being cut the day you get home. And that beard—"

"I know, Mom," he said, resigned already.

"Moms," Drew snickered.

Finn turned around, waving the small computer tablet he held. "I've got you a two-block radius, Will. I pushed the coordinates to your phone, along with the satellite images we took. It appears to be a fairly stable location downtown. It's right on the edge of a crater, but the buildings are intact."

He held the tablet to the camera, so everyone could see.

"That's about a mile out," Carter said. "School of broadcast journalism at Northwest. It's a news studio. Right across from the hospital."

"Dad," the Emperor said when Finn lowered the tablet. "Don't get Jax's hopes up, all right? Just in case she's not really there."

"We won't," Finn said. "Haven't seen him lately. As far as I know, he's locked up in the war room and isn't accessible anyway."

"Boys?" Jo said, looking past her own son. "Is there anything you want me to tell your mothers? They're so worried."

"Just tell them we're all right," Zed said. "And since she'll ask, yes, the Emperor is making us eat."

"Use my name, Zed."

"All right. *Uncle Willie* is making us eat. It's gross food, but we're eating."

Jo smiled. "And you, William? You look thin."

"Mom. Really." He shot a look at Drew and Zed when they laughed. "Yes, I'm eating. Wick is eating." He took me from Drew and held me up so she could see. "We're all fine."

I haven't had shrimp in forever. I am not fine.

"What'd he say, sweetheart?"

"He says he's having a lovely time and wishes you were here."

"You liar," she laughed.

He ended the call then, wanting to keep the image of her laughing in his head. He handed me back to Drew and was about to say something, but Red said, "I'm starting to think you actually do understand that cat."

"Honestly, Red. Have you not grasped it by now? In two hundred years, people will be able to converse with their cats. How does that not make sense to you?"

Carter led the way out of the war room and across the hall into a brightly lit break room that had tables and chairs and a refrigerator. "Eat. So I can report back to your mommies."

"Bite me," Drew said.

"No, seriously…eat something, Drew. So *I* don't worry. After that, we'll head out and find your girl."

The Emperor did not want the attention that a military escort would bring, and after thinking about it, Carter agreed.

"Just me, then. I'll change out of uniform. But I insist, because if nothing else, I'm not facing my mother and telling her I wasn't there for Andrew."

"I can hold my own," Drew said.

"Yeah, I'm getting that about you." He lifted the collar of his shirt and spoke into it, asking someone to get three media kits from storage. "I'll be back in ten. The fridge is stocked, just take what you want."

Drew opened the refrigerator and started grabbing bottles of water, and he handed them out. "Apropos to nothing, this part of the building used to be the Danish consulate. My dad brought me down here once, and I was disappointed because there were no sweet rolls."

"Special snowflake," Zed laughed.

"I was six, I think. Tell a six-year-old it's a Danish place, and he's gonna want sweet rolls."

The Emperor took a bottle of water from him and sat at one of the tables. "And in your crushing disappointment, how many water balloons did you start throwing at people?"

"In my head? A lot. All the ones you never had a chance to take from me." He pulled me out of the sweatshirt and set me on the table. Based on how his face clenched, Red obviously didn't care for a cat on the table any more than Jax did, but it felt good to be on my feet yet not on the floor. I stretched, making sure Red got my full moon view until Drew tapped me on the head and said, "That's rude."

Yeah. I know.

We ate; I got a foil pack of the food I was very tired of, and they ate lightly, not wanting to be weighed down by anything more than a snack. It was the ice-cold water they wanted more of, something not filtered in a canteen that left a metallic taste in the mouth, and not the lukewarm tap water they'd gotten from both labs. Zed drained his bottle and drank half of another, but stopped when he realized the result of drinking so much.

"Probably not going to have a place to stop and pee," he said as he capped the bottle.

"You could, if you want to pee outside in a blizzard," Drew said. "I don't recommend it."

Carter walked through the door just then, and said, "Yeah. Drew would know." He handed tiny square black boxes to Drew and the Emperor, and told them to clip it to their shirts, shiny side out. "These will record everything in your path. Flip that tiny switch on top, and as it records it will auto-upload to secure servers in both our war room and in Pacifica's. Once the start of the upload hits, they'll be alerted and can watch in real time. I suggest you flip that switch once we're inside."

Drew grimaced. "Why, so that Mom can eventually see if and how we die?"

Carter took the box out of Drew's hand and clipped it in place, leaving his hand on Drew's chest for a moment. "No. So that there's proof we did everything we could to get to Oz, and proof that we didn't act outside the scope of the law."

"We're at war," Zed said.

"And that widens the scope, but we're still bound by rules of engagement."

"It also proves the conditions under which Oz is being held," the Emperor said. "Your mothers will not see any of this unless Jax determines that they can."

"But Dad will see," Zed realized.

"That's right, dingleberry," Carter said. "The King has access to everything we do and say, so don't screw up. You'd stay here if it was up to me."

"She's my sister—"

"Yeah, and you're the heir if we don't get to her in time. So keep your head down, Zed. You're last in and first out if it comes down to it."

After he clipped the camera to his sweatshirt, the Emperor got up. "I appreciate this, but I also want it understood. This is not a military mission. It's Drew's."

"I got it," Carter said. "I am not in charge. I expected you would be, but if I have to take orders from my little brother, fine. Just let me get you there, all right? I've been patrolling the underground system for weeks and know this five-mile block cold. I can get you from here to there a lot faster than you'd find it on your own."

No one had a problem with that.

They stowed the backpacks in the corner and filed out the door, but as Drew put me into his sweatshirt he leaned close to his brother and said, "Heads up so there's no question later. The Minister is mine."

31

We went back into the sewer, down the same hole we'd come up from. Drew and Carter headed in first, then the Emperor, and Zed went last to make sure that Red didn't lose his nerve and stay behind.

Red's presence wasn't required in getting to Oz, but he could be useful and the Emperor wanted him to come along. This time he had adequate clothing; Carter liberated a winter jacket from his father's closet, and warned Red to not bleed all over it. He was grateful for it when he slid down the ladder into the pipe; after being in the heated apartment of the House of Van Hoff, the cold underground bit back twice as hard as it had before, and it was hard to feel anything but a persistent, biting chill.

Once we were all in the pipe, Carter turned on a head lamp, and looked at me. "Seriously, Drew, why'd you bring the furball? He's only going to slow you down."

"He's kind of an appendage now," Drew said.

Before Carter could tell him to take me back up, the Emperor said, "Wick is not up for debate. Where we go, he goes."

Carter grunted, "Yeah, whatever," and handed the head lamp to Drew. "Lead the way, boss."

I thought the scumbucket was going to lead us there.

The light from the head lamp bounced with each step Drew took. It lit the pipe for twenty feet ahead, the curling bits of rust that had peeled away from metal created shadows that looked like a swarm of bugs, and in the silence of the walk, breath bounced around us like whispers.

As we neared the manhole where we'd entered the pipe earlier, there was a clicking sound. Drew held a fist up to signal the others to stop, and he cocked his head, listening. The click rode on the sound of a groan, and Carter nudged him forward, telling him it was just old metal. The ground was beginning to freeze, lowering the temperature of the pipe. "It's just contracting."

"Like my intestines," Zed grumbled.

"Nervous back there?" Carter asked.

"Don't tell me you aren't."

Carter turned, walking backwards. "Hell, dingleberry, I'm terrified. No idea what's ahead. I'd be an idiot to not be scared. As long as you stay focused, there's not a damned thing wrong with a healthy dose of fear. It keeps you from letting your guard down."

"Who are you," Drew said, "and what have you done with my brother?"

Carter turned back around. "Traded that piece of crap in on a new model. But don't get me wrong. I'm still an asshole. I just know it now."

Drew kept walking, the light bouncing, and everyone was quiet for the next five minutes, until Carter told Drew to take the next right.

"We saw video of you fighting in Washington Square," Drew said. "A whole group. No guns. You were the only one who walked away."

"I know. I was there."

"For what? There were five or six men in that park, Carter. Fighting for what, Munson's little freak show?"

"No idea why they were there. We were looking for a girl, wanted to find her and send her home."

"Oz," Drew whispered.

"Oz. I don't care if she still doesn't fracking like me. But we picked up footage from one of the servers, the security tapes from her abduction, and I know how deadly she is. She could tear me in two. A girl like that, I want on my side."

A girl like that had to be in a lot of trouble to not have been able to break free.

He didn't have to say it for Drew to hear it.

"Count off," Carter said. "Third ladder up is the one we want. It runs under the building and should come up in the parking garage."

We passed the first, then the second, and then Drew stopped. Ten feet ahead, the pipe had caved in and was filled with dirt and rock, large chunks of the street that had been forced underground by a bomb.

Go ahead. You can say things off the list. Even the number one word.

I won't tell.

"All right," the Emperor said, the first time he'd spoken since we started down the pipes. "We go back to the last ladder. It should open up onto the street."

"How do we get in, then?" Zed asked. "Walk up to the front door, knock, and say hello?"

Red let out a surprised *huh*, and then said, "That's exactly what we do. I'll go in first, and unless the first person I see is my father or one of his soldiers, it's likely that I'll be welcomed in. He'll have civilians with him, people who can run the studio equipment."

Carter didn't trust him at all. "So you go in, dive behind the protection of your people, and they what, open fire on us?"

"They'll either welcome us, or kill me outright," Red said.

The Emperor nodded to the blockage in the pipe. "Unless you want to dig through that—"

No one wanted to dig. They all turned around and Zed wound up leading the way back, mostly in the shadows because Drew was the very last and had the only light, and no one thought to have him hand it forward. It only took a few minutes to get back to it, but opening the manhole proved to be an entirely new exercise in frustration.

"It's either frozen or buried under a ton of snow," Drew speculated.

They each tried to push it up, except for Red, who understood that on his best day he wasn't as strong as any of them.

"Heat it up?" Drew asked. "Fire a laser pistol at the seam all the way around and hope that it melts the ice and snow?"

"And heats up the entire cover," Carter said. "We wouldn't be able to touch it."

Zed lifted a foot. "My boots have inch thick soles."

"Yeah, so? You gonna kick it open, short stack?" Carter sneered.

"I'm not short. I'm as tall as you, douche."

The Emperor sighed; he was running out of patience. "Warm it up," he told Drew. "We'll use Zed like a battering ram."

Red was horrified, but stopped himself from speaking when the Emperor glared at him.

"We'll hold you upside down," he told Zed. "Keep some bend in your knees, and when we lift, the moment you make contact, push. If you yell 'stop,' we stop. Understood?"

Zed nodded. When Drew had fired his laser around the entire seam, they lifted Zed and he pushed. It moved a little on the first try, gapped on the second, and on his third push, the cover lifted.

"All right," Carter said. "Your boots smell like burning crap now, but you definitely kicked it open. Kudos."

The snow was coming down hard, and the wind whipped it in stinging bites sideways. The Emperor warned that we had fifteen minutes to get inside, otherwise we'd be in trouble. "If we're not through that door in ten, we run. Get back to the hole. And mind Wick."

Mind Wick.

Yeah, totally mind me.

I understood he didn't want them to obey me; he wanted Drew to realize that I likely had less than fifteen minutes out in that cold. Carter immediately got it; he reached down deep into the leg pocket of his cargo pants and pulled out a small white packet, bending it with a snap. He nudged it toward Drew and yelled over the sound of the wind, "Stick this next to the cat. It'll keep him warm."

Drew slid it into the pouch with me, and instantly his sweatshirt felt like it had just come out of the dryer.

I hope you don't need this again, because you're not getting it back.

They stood in a small circle, less than a foot between them, but Carter still had to shout to be heard over the wind. "Emperor! We get five feet from the hole, there's no going back. This is a white-out. Once we're moving, we stay moving. Anyone who tries to find their way back underground will just wind up lost in the blizzard."

"Then we have to make it to the door," Drew said.

"Form a chain," Carter said. "Red at twelve, I'll take the six. And if anyone drops a hand and gets lost, keep moving forward. If you stay true, you'll get to a building. Break a window and get inside no matter where you are."

"What about Wick?" Drew asked.

The Emperor bent over and shouted to be sure I could hear him. "You keep your head down, Wick. Dig in with your claws if you have to, Drew can take it." He stood back up. "Zip up all the way, that will hold him in tighter."

"But if he falls out—"

"He won't."

Drew tucked my head down, until I was all the way into the pouch, and he zipped his jacket closed. I tried to stay perfectly still, with my back to his stomach so that I could grab onto his sweatshirt with my claws, and after a few seconds felt him begin to move.

It felt as if he was walking off center, and I was afraid he would fall down. There was a tug and pull cadence to his steps; they were holding hands, pushing and pulling each other through snow that was getting deeper by the minute. With Red in the lead, it was slower than it would have been if the Emperor had taken it. And then I wondered where he was in the chain; he had to be where he could bark orders into Red's ear, just to make sure we wound up going in the right direction.

Fifteen minutes, that was all the time the Emperor thought we had. Carter didn't think anyone could find a way back to the sewer entry. Red was not speedy.

Sweat leeched through Drew's shirt and I felt it on my ears, but he was also beginning to shiver.

How long have we been walking?

I wanted to stick my head out to see and if he hadn't zipped up his jacket, I might have taken the chance. I was warm where I was, but if Drew let go and drifted away from everyone else, I wouldn't stay warm long enough for him to find his way back. Carter's magic hot pad wasn't going to last forever.

Tug and pull. I tried to feel for that, using the rise and fall of his steps to tell me that he was fine, that he still had the hand of the man ahead and the man behind, and I hoped that he was holding onto Zed and the Emperor. They would never let go of each other. They would fall together before letting go.

Drew was starting to shiver hard. I rolled over in the pouch, pushing the warm white square that Carter had given me against his stomach. We could share the warms, at least long enough to get across the street. As I pressed hard against him, there was the sound of a hand slapping hard on glass, and then Red's voice shouting.

"Open up!"

Unzip me. Unzip me. Unzip me. UNZIP ME.

Vibrations from Drew's arm filtered down to me; the Emperor had popped him on the arm and was telling him I wanted to see. Drew unzipped just far enough for me to get my head out. Carter was to his right, blocking the wind from my face, and Zed was between them, keeping snow off me.

Red took his glove off and pounded on the glass.

He lowered the hood of his jacket so that his face could be seen, and pounded again, frustrated. A man wearing slacks and a dress shirt—not the soldier that he'd feared—zipped around a hallway corner not far from the door. He scrambled to let us in, more worried about leaving people out in a blizzard than he was about letting in potential intruders. It took him a moment to realize who Red was, and he went from concern over people freezing to death to excited babbling because Redmond Munson was not dead after all and, praise the Lord, it felt like a miracle. Everyone thought Red had been caught in the burn run at the compound. The prayers that had gone out, all for his soul and his family—he stopped gushing when Drew and the Emperor lowered their hoods, and he recognized them.

His joy at seeing Red flipped and dissolved into terror. Zed moved behind him, to keep him from running for help, and when he opened his mouth to yell, the Emperor struck him with the heel of his palm, right in the center of his face.

He went down without uttering another word, blood trickling from his nose.

Red wanted to know if he was dead, and without looking the

Emperor said, "Probably not, but if he is? The fewer alarms raised, the better."

"But he did nothing—"

Drew stepped in close, so close that all I could see was the color of Red's jacket. "We're here to get Oz. Don't get in the way of that."

Dude, back up. I can't see anything and he needs a shower.

"Where do we go from here?" Zed asked, ignoring them.

While Drew was growling at Red, Carter checked the directory sign next to the elevator door. "First floor is classrooms. Second is rehearsal and broadcast studios. Third is offices."

"Second floor," Red said, backing away from Drew. "It's Thanksgiving." He glanced at his watch. "It's nearly ten o'clock. He always broadcasts a sermon at ten on Thanksgiving, and he'll have Oz with him. He enjoys staging things—she'll be his main attraction."

"A freaking sermon? Why?" Zed asked.

"To show the people what he's thankful for, and I guarantee, today he's thankful because he thinks he's about to destroy Aubrey's life on his way to grabbing half the continent."

*

Red wanted to go up the elevator; he didn't see a reason why it might be a bad idea. Just go up, get out, and walk right into whatever room his father was using. The Emperor had to point out the security cameras, and not only the people who might be coming for them already, but also the risks of being stuck between floors if the elevator was stopped.

"Drop a grenade in and boom," Carter said.

Drew pointed to the stairwell door at the end of the corridor. They would at least have room to maneuver if confronted there. "There are two doors down this hall. One is closed and the window in the door is dark. One is open, lights are on."

The Emperor told them to walk against the wall, and for Drew to stop before passing the open doorway. Just wait and listen.

Red shrugged out of his jacket and dropped it to the floor, muttering "trust me" as he stepped around Drew. While everyone else walked close to the wall, slowly, he took a few quicker steps and stopped right in the doorway.

He waved and said, "Good afternoon, fellas," and then kept walking, but lifted his hand and held up three fingers. Within seconds, as he was reaching for the handle on the door to the stairwell, came the sound of scrambling footsteps. Two men bolted from the room and turned in his direction, calling out his name.

The surprise wasn't over for them.

Carter and the Emperor ran at them, and Drew ran after Red, because someone had to protect him from himself. He was as useless in a fight as I would be, though to be honest I have claws and I'm not afraid to use them, whereas Red could make a fist and have no idea what use it could be other than to pound a pulpit. Drew wanted him out of the way, where no one else would have to defend him, so he pushed the stairwell door open and shoved Red inside.

"Stay," he ordered. "Don't get in the way."

Once Red was safely behind the door, Drew turned around, intending to help. We watched through the window in the door to see all the help the Emperor and Carter didn't need. The Emperor was graceful in his attack, waiting for his opponent to come to him with arm cocked back awkwardly and fist held at his own head height. He let the lanky man with orange hair make the first strike, which from where I was looked like the slowest punch possible. He aimed for the Emperor's chin and was visibly shaking hard enough that he couldn't have hit his target if the Emperor had stood still. Will slapped his arm out of the way and drove his palm into the man's chest. I could hear his breastbone crack through the closed door and flinched when the Emperor was suddenly painted in flecks of blood that erupted from his mouth.

To be certain that the fight was done, before the man hit the ground the Emperor slid forward and wrapped his arm around that impossibly orange head, and when he was done twisting, dead eyes looked back at us over his own shoulder.

Carter's fighting style lacked elegance, but he didn't need it. He whipped his rifle from his shoulder and slammed the butt of it into the face of the man who had turned when he realized there were people behind him, and when he wasn't sure that the blow had done the job, he slapped it across the man's neck and pulled tight, one hand on each end of the rifle, until there was no movement other than one last twitch.

They ran for the stairwell as Drew shouted that there was one more person in the room. Zed had been at least thirty feet behind them, and as he ran to catch up, hopping over the body the Emperor had dropped to the floor, the last man in the room bolted out. The stairwell door clicked shut behind Carter, and Drew tugged on the door handle frantically as Zed ran toward him, but Red was half in the way and it only opened a few inches.

Zed was still running, with no way to get past the door, and Red didn't seem to understand Drew's demand to move his ass out of the way. He took another step back, further blocking the door, and Zed had no clear way out. The man on his tail was brutishly large, taller than either Drew or the Emperor, and his weight was wrapped around him in tight muscles.

It didn't matter how well the Emperor had taught Zed to fight; he wasn't going to punch his way out of it.

He had a name tag on.

Preston.

Preston looked like someone who ate steroids for breakfast, and washed it all down with a glass of growth hormone.

The door was not going to open fast enough, and Zed had less than three seconds before the last man reached him. He picked up speed and aimed himself just left of the door, where there was two feet of wall space. When he reached the end of the hallway, with Drew still pulling on the door as Carter joined in on shouting at Red, he scrambled up the narrow wall; his feet found purchase, and he went partway up, arching his back as he flipped over his surprised assailant.

The Emperor watched Zed without speaking; Carter grabbed Red by his hair and yanked him out of the way. I couldn't see the Emperor's face but I heard the air he sucked in and was sure he was thinking the same thing I was: there was no tree branch to grab onto, and Zed always landed on his back.

Drew pulled the door open just as Zed hit the floor, his boots planted squarely on the white tile.

There was anger in Preston's eyes as Drew stepped toward him, but that quickly turned to surprise when Zed grabbed his shoulders and forced him back, plowing his knee into the back of his head. He dropped with a resounding thud, sprawled out on his back with his arms flung to either side.

He was still breathing. Zed looked at the Emperor for help, not knowing what to do.

Carter stepped back into the hall, put his rifle to the man's chest, and pulled the trigger. The sound of the laser engaging was muffled by clothing, and was no more than a dull pop that could easily be mistaken as the sound of footsteps.

No blood pooled underneath him, but a wisp of smoke curled from the crater in his chest.

"You get in the way again," Carter growled at Red as they slipped into the stairwell, "and I'll shove this rifle up your nose and pull the trigger. You do *anything* to get my brother or Zed hurt, and you're dead. You got it?"

Red got it.

The Emperor's eyebrow lifted, just a little.

Carter's a big boy now.

"Wick," the Emperor said before we began to climb the stairs. "Not a sound out of you now, all right?"

I would have answered him, but that required sound.

"Keep to the walls again," he said quietly. If there's a window in a door, only the first in line looks in. The rest of you, duck down as you move past."

Zed asked, "What if the door is open?"

"Then chances are that's the room we want. These are student broadcast studios and no classes are in session, so I'm counting on only being one in use."

"Unless he's spread throughout the building," Carter said.

"We take the chance." The Emperor nodded to Drew to start up the stairs, and had Red go after him. "Quietly."

They took the steps slowly, trying to minimize the amount of sound they created. Boots squeaked on the tile, and the butt of Carter's rifle banged on the hand rail and pinged loudly. Drew paused at each sound and waited for a response, signaling them to stop by raising his fist.

Halfway up, just as we made our way on the turn to go up the last ten steps to the second-floor door, Drew raised his fist again. There were footsteps coming from above, the dull thud of rubber-soled boots on tile. Carter tapped Drew on the shoulder and motioned for him to move back. He pressed his hand against the wall—everyone, get back—and he pulled the rifle from around his shoulder, pointing it up the narrow space that rose to the top of the stairwell.

Red began to speak, and Zed jammed the side of his fist into his mouth before he could utter a sound.

I wanted to tell him to not even breathe, but I was not going to break the Emperor's command of silence.

The footsteps grew louder and sounded heavier, and the closer they came the more sounds we heard. The static of a radio. Metal slapping against metal. Creaking leather. Carter's head was cocked to the left as he listened carefully, and he slowly disengaged the safety on his rifle.

The noises all started coming from right above us, and a tired voice said, "Roger that. I'm taking fifteen in the lounge."

He made it halfway down the short section of the stairwell when Carter pulled the trigger. There was a tiny pop and a bit of a whine as the laser shot out from the rifle, and what was left of an older man fell face first to the landing by the door. A puff of smoke curled away from a hole in his back, and it smelled like someone had burned a pork chop.

"We have fifteen minutes," the Emperor said as we reached the second floor. "Someone will come looking for him."

Drew pulled on the door slowly, cringing when the hinges squealed.

The Emperor pushed past Red and reached over Drew's shoulder, yanking the door open quickly. "Just get it over with," he whispered. "And move quickly."

The door opened to a long and brightly lit corridor. There were three doors on each side, and all the doors to the right were closed and the lights were off. To the left, light bled through the window in the center door, and Drew nodded toward it. They approached it the way the Emperor had instructed: close to the wall and quietly.

When Drew stopped, the Emperor nudged Red's shoulder. "Yours is the face that needs to be seen," he said. "Don't count on a warm welcome, because your father is probably in there, and the men who are with him may know his plans."

Red nodded, but he didn't look happy about it. He moved past Drew stiffly, like he had a broomstick shoved up his asterisk, and looked in the window. "Two cameras with operators," he said. "My father is in front of the cameras, speaking. Oz is to his left, seated. There are six armed guards standing at the wall behind him, all within the view of the cameras. The back of the room, toward the door, is dark, and where my father is standing is under the studio lights."

He waited, watching, and then said, "She has at least a dozen wires leading from the base of the chair to her temple, chest, and arms. Brace yourselves. She doesn't look good."

"There may be guards close to the door where he can't see them," Carter pointed out.

"So I go in first, alone," Red said. "If there's anyone behind the cameramen, they'll react and you'll know. I'll draw them forward, toward the cameras."

Carter stopped him before he could open the door. "Describe the cameras," he said. "Floor model, hand held, chest harnessed? Do the cameramen look military or civilian?"

"Floor cameras. About six feet tall on wheels. They have black lens hoods, extending about twelve inches out. They aren't military, they're my father's usual cameramen. Old and out of shape. And they don't particularly like him, they stay because he pays them well."

Carter unclipped the little black box from his shirt and put it on my collar so that it dangled at my chest. "Wick obeys well, right? When we get close, stick him on top of one of the cameras. Cat, you just sit there and watch. Let that camera record everything in front of you, all right?" He flicked the switch on it, and I felt it hum. "All right, then. Upload and alert has begun. Flick your switches, too."

Taking a deep breath, Red pulled the door open and stepped in. He kept his arm bent toward his back so that the door didn't click closed, and he waited. No one moved toward him from the side, and when he felt the weight of the door leave his hand—the Emperor had taken it—he started moving toward the cameramen.

Drew followed, and I heard the others behind us, feet soft on the tile floor. When Drew saw Oz his breath caught, but he stopped himself from calling to her.

Red walked up to the cameramen casually, and put a hand on each of their backs. It was congenial, like he was greeting old friends. There was a moment of surprise, but when they saw who it was, they both reached out to shake his hand. It was hard to tell from behind, but I sensed relief. Their Second Minister had returned from the dead.

The First Minister hadn't noticed anything; he was busy smiling for the cameras, extolling the rewards of faith, even in the darkness of mourning.

He knew about mourning; he would be mourning the loss of his son for the rest of his life.

"And how does that work?" Red asked loudly, stepping between the cameras. "How do you mourn for the son you wanted dead? How do you pray for the person you personally set up to die in your twisted little war game? Exactly what rewards will you reap for trying to have me assassinated?"

Munson's mouth opened, but nothing came out.

"Do you ask your people to do it for you? Recite the prayers you can't, because you not only know that he's *not* dead, but you did everything you could to make it happen? Do you beg them to pray for his soul, all the while hoping that the people you manipulated will finish the job?"

The Minister recovered and blurted, "Good God, Redmond! He spared you!"

Drew and the Emperor moved to the sides of the cameramen, and while Drew eased me out of his shirt and onto the black hood of one of the cameras, the Emperor growled, "Don't make me kill you."

They stood behind the men in the dark, where they couldn't be seen from the studio stage. I didn't have to see them to know what

Drew focused on: Oz was shackled to a large wooden chair, her arms cuffed at the wrists and her ankles chained to the legs of the chair. There were straps over her chest and thighs, and she struggled against the bindings and the gag that was jammed into her mouth, jaw working hard as she tried to push it out.

Her arms were a bloody mess of bruises and burns, and there were wires running all over her body. Thin filaments were jammed into her temples and through a dozen or more holes in her ripped red shirt. Thicker wire jutted from her chest, lines that didn't seem to be connected to anything else. Her jeans were torn up to the knees, and her shins were red and raw, knees skinned with bloody rashes.

There was a bruise running from her chin to just under her left ear, and her right eye was slightly swollen and black. Blood stained the front of her shirt, a splotch than ran from her shoulder into her armpit and down her chest.

Red turned so the cameras could see him, so the people would know who was there. "King Jackson of Pacifica spared me. He spared my wife and children. He spared every single person you locked away in that compound to die at his hands. God may have guided him, but we live because Pacifica showed grace when you did not."

Red looked directly into the camera to his right. "Are you listening, Florida? Your First Minister wanted his own son, his grandchildren, and his faithful, dead. Your brothers and sisters. He was willing for them *all* to die. There was never a temple to be built. This had nothing to do with faith and service. It was only a war to be waged so that he could rule over it all."

The Minister's face went red, and he yelled for the cameras to be shut off. His guards moved; four trained their weapons on Oz, and the other two on Red. Behind me, one of the cameramen muttered, "Is he insane? This is live. Keep it running."

Drew stepped between the cameras, his weight shifting front foot to back as he made his way carefully into the light. He pulled his pistol from his waistband as he moved, slipping the safety off with his thumb. As he pointed it at the Minister he called out, "Tell the truth, Munson. Tell the world what you've really done."

The First Minister squinted against the bright lights, trying to see who was there. When he realized that it was Drew, he rolled his eyes.

"Prince Andrew. Tell what to whom? The cameras are off. There's no one for you to perform for." He gestured to the guards, ordering them to step closer to Oz. "Now what do you really want?"

"Then tell *me*," Drew said. "Tell your son. Just tell the damned truth!"

The Emperor stepped out of the shadows, and Carter followed. I couldn't see Zed, but I guessed he had a gun on the cameramen, to make sure they didn't try to run. He was staying back, where Carter had told him to.

"I'm told confession is good for the soul," the Emperor said.

Red sucked in a deep breath. "If you can't be honest with our people, then at least be honest with your Lord. Confess to *Him*, Father. At least confess to God."

"God." Munson snorted. "There is no God, you pathetic little tool. God is a myth we perpetuate to keep the lesser of us in line. God is the lie we tell the poor in order to give them hope that there's something beyond their wretched little lives. The hopeful downtrodden are generous, Redmond. They believe whatever lies we tell them and they open their wallets to us, all because we promise them *God*."

Red took a confused, staggered step away from him. Sounding like a small child, he stammered, "Wait. You truly don't believe in Him?"

"I don't believe in Santa or the Toothy Fairy, either. If you'd been a better son, more of a man, the truth would have been handed to you soon enough. God is for the weak."

Drew inched closer. "Then what's your reason for raping little girls, Minister? Wasn't God your excuse for abusing your own daughters over and over? Because God gave them to you as your personal property? You hid behind your religion to force yourself on your own children."

He was growling as he spit the words out; the guards trained on Oz flinched, and one after the other, they each took half a step back.

The Minister wasn't paying attention to them. He was focused on Drew. "Girls are chattel. Women are here to serve us. My daughters *are* my property, Prince Andrew. I'm free to do what I will with them, until I convince someone else to take them off my hands. It's not abuse, it's service. How else will they learn to serve the needs of their husbands? My responsibility is to show them."

"You sick son of a bitch."

Red fell to his knees, dropping like he'd been handed a heavy weight, and began praying.

"Get up," Munson snapped. "You look like a fool."

"He has faith, Minister," Drew said as he inched yet a little closer. "Isn't that what you teach your people? To have faith in God?"

"What do you know of God?"

"I know he's not an ass."

The Emperor was slowly moving toward Munson from the side, and Carter was shadowing his movements on the other side.

Drew stepped right up to the Minister, and Munson flinched. His guards still had their weapons pointed at Red and Drew, but they didn't try to stop him. "Just say it," Drew insisted. "Admit what you did to your daughter. Admit that you sacrificed your people all for the sake of taking control of Midlam." When the Minister didn't bite, Drew put the gun to his forehead and shouted, "Admit it!"

The Minister looked cross-eyed at the gun jammed to his forehead. "Fine, it's not as if you'll get out of here alive." He folded his arms, but instead of looking at ease, he looked like he was trying to hold the pieces of himself together. "Yes, I taught my daughter how to serve men. It's why women exist, you idiot. And yes, I will use this holy war to take every inch of the continent. Your Emperor? Surely even he realizes that the title is rightfully mine. My people will gladly die for me, because they're too stupid to do anything else."

Red was still on his knees, but had stopped praying. "Your people believe they're sacrificing themselves for God."

"I *am* God!" Munson roared.

Drew pressed into the Minister's forehead harder. "Give me one good reason to not blow your head right off your neck."

"Do it and you'll die where you stand."

The Emperor's gun was leveled at Munson; he lowered it just an inch and said, "Look around, Levi."

Every guard had lowered their gun and they were staring at him. He went pale, ordering them to protect him, first quietly, and then shouting. "Do your job! Kill them!"

First the guards near him backed away, then the guards near Oz followed.

"You deserve to die," Drew seethed. "And it would only take one twitch for me to do it."

The Emperor stepped close to him. "Andrew, stop. Think back. This is it. Who do you really want to be?"

Carter was near Oz, but hadn't touched her, and Drew's eyes flicked in her direction. She was straining against the shackles, trying to shout past the gag.

"Everything he's done to her," Drew sobbed.

"Pathetic," Munson huffed. "Crying like a little girl. You don't have the stones to kill me."

Drew lowered his gun, flicked the safety, and slipped it back into his waistband. "I have the stones, Minister. But I don't need to kill you. I have witnesses. Look over my shoulder at the little red lights. The cameras were never shut down, and we have personal video recorders that have been uploading all of this to King Jackson's private servers. You're live around the world right now, and they've heard it all."

The Emperor placed his gun close to Munson's head, while Drew went to Oz. He unwound the chains from her legs while one of her guards unlocked the cuffs around her wrist, and then he gently pulled the gag out of her mouth before Carter helped him carefully pull out every wire, and he didn't flinch when she screamed in pain.

Drew helped her stand, bearing all her weight as she tried to get over to the First Minister. She tried to speak, but the only thing that came out of her mouth was blood and spit, so with the last bit of energy she could muster, she cocked her arm back, and punched him square in the throat.

32

Drew carried Oz from the news studio to the hospital across the street. He wrapped her in his jacket and held her close, running for the door as Carter shouted directions to the emergency room. The Emperor plucked me from the camera and followed, leaving Carter and Red to guard Munson while they waited for Pacifica's Royal Guard.

The grinding sound of the tank-like treads of a winter emergency vehicle—it was a Snow Cat but I didn't think there was anything cat-like about it, not as loud as it was—came from the far end of the street as we bolted outside, but we weren't waiting for them; the Emperor knew they were coming for Munson, and the quickest way to get Oz help was for Drew to carry her across the street.

Zed ran alongside the Emperor, kicking up wads of snow. It was still coming down and the wind was abrasive, but they had abandoned their jackets and I don't think they noticed the cold.

We were covered in snow by the time we got across the street. My whiskers had little drops of ice on the tips, and it hurt. The Emperor's beard had an icy sheen to it, but he wasn't complaining and didn't try to wipe it away, so I sucked it up and said nothing.

My pain was nothing compared to Oz's.

Drew took her in through the emergency entrance, his screams for help bouncing off the corridor walls. It was quiet inside and I had begun to worry that the building was as abandoned as everything else seemed to be, when a man in blue pajamas darted out of a room down the hall and sprinted toward us. He grabbed a bed on wheels and Drew placed Oz on it gently, while a dozen more people popped out of other rooms and raced toward her. Orders were shouted until it was all noise that made me flatten my ears, and the smell of medical things hung in the air and assaulted my nose.

He stayed with her, while the Emperor called the King.

He stayed while the doctor and nurses debated on what to do, because she was the Princess, after all, and there were protocols. There were things she needed but there was no royal guard nor approved witness present, and what if they touched her without permission?

He yelled at them to just do something, that his word was all the permission they needed, and we heard his terror slap at them from where we sat in the waiting room.

After the Emperor talked to the King, he took me back to the room she was in; Zed wasn't ready to see her, not yet. He was shaking from the cold and didn't want her to notice and then think he was scared; the Emperor agreed it was judicious, not wanting to give her a reason to assume she was worse off than she was. He suggested that Zed pace the waiting room, expend some energy to warm up.

He understood that Zed was terrified.

So was he. He swallowed the fear whole, and refused to allow it to drive him to his knees.

Drew was in a chair near the head of the bed, and Oz's eyes were closed. Quietly, he asked if Mr. and Mrs. B had been told; the Emperor said they had taken off from the transport bay in a military shuttle moments after the upload began to play in the war room, and it would only be an hour or so.

The Emperor stood at the foot of the bed and set me on his shoulder. While we waited, a nurse came in to add medication to the tube that had been jammed into Oz's arm, and told Drew it would help take the edge off her pain. Within seconds, her eyes fluttered, and the Emperor moved to stand behind Drew, so that she wouldn't have to move her head to see more them both.

"Hon, you're in the ER," the nurse said loudly. "We need to cut your clothes off. It'll hurt, but the drugs I just gave you will help with that."

The door popped open and another person in blue pajamas entered, and she had scissors and a metal sheet that had gauze pads and shiny tools and tubes on it. Drew kissed a bare spot on Oz's arm, and told her he would be right outside.

"No. Stay."

The nursed nodded her okay.

The Emperor leaned over Drew's shoulder, and told him to put two of his fingers into Oz's hand so that she would have something to squeeze when it hurt. "Don't give her your whole hand or you'll regret it. Just two fingers. I'll wait with Zed."

"No," Oz cried. "Stay."

"Ozzie, they're going to cut off all of your clothing, and you'll have no privacy."

Tears rolled from the corners of her eyes. "Don't leave me."

*

Drew refused to watch what they did to her; he turned the chair so that he could only see her face, and he let her squeeze those two fingers as hard as she could while they cut away her clothes and pulled the remnants out from under her. He breathed in and out deliberately while they cleaned her wounds and moved her body around to examine every inch of it, and when it seemed unbearable for her, he leaned in close and whispered in her ear.

If I had strained, I could have listened, but I didn't think anything he was saying to her was for anyone else to know. His voice seemed to calm her, and that was enough for me.

The Emperor watched it all, for no reason other than she needed a witness to her pain and someone who could later tell her the truth about what they did to her. He also satisfied the doctor's concern about a royally approved witness; when he growled that he was both the Emperor and her damned uncle, and then used some words I can't repeat because they were that offensive, the doctor agreed; he was officially royal enough to be official.

He stood near the bed, back ramrod straight, grinding his teeth together as they sealed wounds and moved her arms and legs out of the way to get to everything; he flinched when they rolled her over to seal a long and deep cut on her back, and he sniffed when she was rolled onto her back and a deep slice on her chest was attended to. He watched it all quietly, until just before they were about to seal the fractures in her legs, when he cleared his throat and said, his voice breaking, "Her parents will want to know. The man who did this… she may have been raped."

Drew sobbed, quietly, but he still didn't look.

When they were done checking every inch of her body, fixing what they could and photographing everything, and she had been covered in a sheet from her chest to her ankles, he bent over to kiss her toes and then told Drew he would be outside waiting for Jax and Aubrey. He slipped out the door and stayed next to it, his back to the wall, and he leaned his head back, gulping for air.

She'll forgive you for looking. You had to.

"That's not my concern, Wick," he murmured.

Zed got up and started to ask how she was, when the door to the ER slammed open and two royal guards stepped in ahead of the King and Queen. Before they could get a word out, Zed flew into his mother's arms, and then Jax grabbed them both.

"She's heavily sedated right now," the Emperor told them after they'd had a moment with him. "She won't let go of Drew's hand, and he doesn't want to leave her side."

"How bad?" the Queen managed to squeak out.

He tasted the words on his tongue before he spoke. "There's no polite or considerate way to tell you any of it. She was brutalized. Where she isn't heavily bruised, she's burned or cut. Both legs have fractures. Her torso is covered by puncture marks where wires were pushed into her skin, and there are a few deep cuts. She's been beaten with multiple objects and from the neck down there's little skin surface that isn't badly bruised. On her face, there's a large bruise running from her chin to her ear, and she has a badly blackened eye. Her lip is split, as well as one ear."

Jax's eyes flicked toward the closed door. "Did he—?"

"No."

Aubrey fell against Jax with a relieved whimper. "It shouldn't matter because she's alive. It shouldn't matter." Then barely on a breath, "It shouldn't matter."

"It matters, Aubrey." The Emperor's voice was soft and kind. "She has enough to get through, and not having that as an additional burden—it matters."

Zed's face was still buried against the King's chest.

"Have you been in to see her yet?" Jax asked him. "Are you all right?"

His voice cracked as he replied, "I can't."

"She'll understand," the Emperor said to him. "Give yourself a little more time."

When they entered the room, Drew tried to stand up but Oz still had a death grip on his hand. Jax quietly told him to sit. Being polite was not a concern, but keeping her calm was.

"She's sedated," Drew said. "She's not hurting a lot right now."

Oz's dulled sense of pain didn't spare either of them from the sight of how battered she was; Aubrey had to grab for the foot rail on the bed as she was racked with sobs, and tears streamed down Jax's cheeks.

"How…?" Jax choked out.

"She's strong, you know that," the Emperor said. "And the doctor is confident that she'll make a full recovery. There's a long road ahead of her, but she'll get there."

Oz's hand moved from Drew's and without opening her eyes she touched his arm and whispered, "Wick."

Carefully, the Emperor set me on the bed near her pillow, and I settled down gently, my front paws touching her cheek.

I'll stay and purr for you, as long as you need.

The Emperor stroked my tail and whispered, "Help her dreams, Wick."

You can help that, too.

"I know." He touched a finger to her forehead, and planted in her mind the image of Drew curled around her in the sleeping bag in the forest, the fire crackling as Zed snored softly and the Emperor pretended to sleep, while they talked about their future and promised each other forever.

He wanted her to remember that.

Drew was right there, waiting, and none of her real-life monsters would creep out from under the bed or slither out of the closet, because he was never letting them near her again.

*

Hours later, when it had been night for a long time, Drew finally needed to take a break. Thanks to fatigue and pharmaceuticals Oz was sound asleep, so he kissed the tips of her fingers carefully and told me to keep an eye on her while he went to get something to drink.

I know the truth. You need to pee.

"You're a good man, Mister Wick," he said as he got up.

That beat being called a good boy.

A good man, that had nothing to do with being a dog. I could accept that.

A few minutes after Drew left, the door creaked open and Zed slipped in. He froze for a moment, taking in all the tubes that ran from little bags on poles into her arm and the machines that beeped, and saw how fragile she looked, but then he sucked in a deep breath and sat in Drew's chair.

He wanted to touch her; he lifted his hand but didn't know where it wouldn't hurt, and when he couldn't figure it out he started to cry.

"This is my fault," he choked out. "If I hadn't been such a pain in the ass, the Emperor wouldn't have felt like I needed to take that long hike, and we wouldn't have been gone when Martin Smith dropped dead near the safe house. The Emperor would have seen him on the security camera, would have gotten to him in time to get the warning. Maybe even to save his life."

He set his forehead on the edge of the mattress. "I am so sorry, Oz. This is my fault, and I'll never be able to make it up to you."

She didn't open her eyes, but as he cried harder, her hand found the back of his head and she ran her fingers through his hair, the best she could do to comfort him.

33

A week later, after her bones had been set and sealed and the cuts and puncture marks were healing, when she could sit up and talk for more than a few minutes at a time, she was allowed to go home. A convoy of the King's air service waited on the street just outside the hospital, and Oz rode home on a bed that was bolted down in the official hover car, with Drew and the Queen in seats placed on either side of her. The King rode in the car behind them with Zed and the Emperor, and there were guards in cars just ahead and behind.

No one said so, but I was pretty sure that the air had been cleared of all but the military, and off to the sides, where we couldn't see, were fighters ready to bring down any intruding aircraft. It was a first, the Emperor told me quietly as Oz was being wheeled out of the hospital; the royal family never traveled together, not all of them at once. The King usually left ahead of them, and Oz was never with him in the same car, and rarely left on the same day.

He wants to keep an eye on her, even if it is through a windshield.

Any other time, the Emperor would have been with Oz. This time, he left her care to Drew.

She still needs you, dude.

"Oz doesn't really *need* either one of us," he said, watching as she was moved from a wheelchair to the bed. "However, she wants him by her side, and that's as it should be now."

She needed you both to save her.

"Truly, she saved herself, Wick. She only needed us to remove the straps and chains."

When she was comfortable enough, the King ordered the door to her car closed, we got into our car, and no one looked back.

Carter had come to see her twice, but had to report back to duty; the war was over but his service was not, and he had been assigned to help clear out the city and protect it while plans to rebuild were drafted.

Red stayed long enough to see that Oz would survive, and long enough to have a lengthy conversation with Aubrey. By the end of the day that we'd found Oz, he was in a hover car on his way to be reunited with his family. They had been taken to an air base in Ohio, and by the next morning everyone who had been rescued from the compound was on their way home, to Florida.

The hover cars landed on Geary Street in front of Union Square instead of landing on the roof, because Oz couldn't handle getting down the stairs even a single floor, and from the street she could ride up in the elevator. She was not on her feet; she rode uncomfortably in a wheel chair all the way up, until she was in the living room.

Once there, she asked Drew to help her to the sofa; she didn't want to lie down in her own bed until she had to. Until she was too tired sit up, she wanted to be in the living room with everyone else and pretend that everything was normal. No one argued with her about it; instead, the King and Queen went into the kitchen to get drinks and snacks, because it was something they could do and still feel like they were hovering over her. Zed told her to sit tight; there was something he needed, and he had to run to his closet to get it.

He came back with a shiny red bow and he taped it to her head, laughing at the sight of her curled up on the sofa, decorated like a present. She squinted at him—what the hell are you doing? —but then her eyes flew open as she understood.

When Aubrey came out of the kitchen with a plate of fruit, Jax behind her with drink glasses, Zed grinned and said, "Happy birthday, Mom. I was pretty sure this was the only thing you wanted this year."

It might have been, but she cried anyway.

No one questioned it when Drew dragged a mattress from one of the guest rooms and put it on the floor in Oz's bedroom. He wanted to be there if she needed anything in the middle of the night, even if it meant just being there to get up and wake the Queen if Oz needed her instead of him. Jax reminded them that the doctor had suggested hiring a nurse, but Oz hated the idea—enough people have seen me naked already, thanks—and Aubrey and Drew wanted to care for her.

He didn't want to let her out of his sight any more than he needed to; it didn't matter what the Emperor said—he felt like he'd let her down in the bunker, and he wasn't letting her down again.

He read to her when she was bored, helped her eat and drink when she was too tired to manage it herself, and made sure she moved when she'd been still too long. She drew the line at letting him help her bathe or with other personal things; only Aubrey was allowed to help her then, which was fine with Drew.

I spent nights curled up by her head; I wanted to give her happy dreams, but she mostly had nightmares, until the Emperor came in to plant thoughts into her head.

He left orders with me: if she has a bad night, wake Drew. If he's not sure what she needs, pat his phone with your paw. He'll get it.

And he did, almost every night. I woke Drew, and if I pawed at his phone, he called the Emperor. If I went to the door, he padded down the hall and woke Aubrey. He slept in fits, but it didn't seem to bother him, and the better Oz got, the happier he was.

Ten days after she came home, Drew's parents went back to Chicago as a sign to the people that planning and rebuilding would soon begin. Jax went with them, because Redmond Munson was returning. Together, they held a news conference from the top floor of the Hancock, where Jax announced that—while it was unified with Pacifica and its citizens were and would continue to be citizens of Pacifica—Midlam would autonomous, governed under Prime Minister Shazia Van Hoff. "We will be the new United Kingdom," he said, "and we will continue to honor the freedoms of all our people, and welcome those who may choose to join us in the future."

Florida wasn't joining the new United Kingdom anytime soon, but it was headed in a new direction under First Minister Redmond Munson. He wanted open borders and freedom to travel, and to begin a formal and ongoing relationship with Pacifica. Isolationism was not working; they needed fellowship with the world to help maintain their foundations and strengthen their faith. "Faith shared," he told the world, "is faith renewed."

He believed that the church should continue to be the keystone of their government, but stated publicly that transformation was necessary. He wanted private sector equality, and for the church to step back from the individual lives of its citizens. "Your daughters will be required to meet the same academic standards as your sons, with all the opportunities that education brings. They will have the freedom to vote. To work. To decide the course of their own lives. If any of you choose to not participate in this new rule… you are free to leave. Our nation is God's dominion. We are still the Church of Florida, but we will honor the women God has gifted to us. We will be the land of the faithful, and the land of the free. Every one of us. Get used to it."

Jax spoke of Levi Munson's upcoming trial; an international tribunal would preside over the proceedings after the start of the New Year. Florida waived its first rights to sole judgement of his crimes, maintaining that they could not promise a lack of bias, but would guarantee a conviction and execution. He had admitted his atheism, which by the laws he had crafted, was a capital offense.

Oz watched the news conference on Drew's computer while he sat on the bed with her, and when it was over she grunted, "Just kill the bastard already."

*

Five days before Christmas, when it was cold outside and the sky was a watercolor gray, Oz asked Drew to help her out to the balcony. She wanted fresh air even if it was cold, and promised him she would say something when she felt chilly. He carried her out there, and when he set her on her feet, she realized there was a new seat waiting, a padded bench meant for two.

"Will made it for you," Drew said, helping her sit. "He thought you might be tired of trying to grope me with all that metal from the old seats between us."

That made her laugh. "He's not wrong."

He sat beside her, sliding his arm around her shoulder. "Not too cold?"

"Not yet." She patted her lap, inviting me to jump on it. "Don't let Wick get chilled."

"Wick's a big boy. If he gets cold, he knows where the cat flap is."

You might be the first person in the history of people to understand that.

They watched the people on Union Square; the holiday ice rink was open and there were a dozen skaters trying—and failing—to navigate around it. The giant tree was lit up and all the buildings and lamps had holiday decorations with twinkling white lights, and it all made Oz very happy.

"You know," she said after a bit, "you made a promise to me when we were camping with my brother and the Emperor. You still haven't done anything about it."

He hadn't forgotten. "That's probably going to have to wait a while. When you're completely healed, we'll talk about it again. But make no mistake, I still want to marry you."

She looked at him with mock horror. "Oh my God, you want to wait until then."

He shrugged and smiled.

"You're a horrible, evil little man. But I love you anyway. And I know, I'm nowhere near ready for anything more than a kiss or two. It's going to be a while."

She kissed him before he could say it back because she already knew, and it was long and sweet, the first decent kiss they'd had since she was abducted. I was ready to stand up and pat their faces with my paw to remind them where they were, but then the Emperor opened the balcony door and stepped outside.

"I'd tell you two to get a room, but I already know he's sleeping in yours."

"On the floor," Drew said.

"For now," she snorted.

The Emperor grabbed another chair from behind them and set it next to Oz. She pulled Drew's arm from behind her to hold his hand, and then reached for the Emperor's, too.

"I won't listen," she promised.

Drew leaned forward to look past her. "If it has a chain effect, I will."

"Interesting idea," the Emperor said. "Let me know if you hear anything."

There was a pretended quiet for a minute, then Drew said, "Yeah, you are a horny, perverted old man. But I already suspected that about you."

"I still don't own any porn, Andrew."

"Not that you'll share."

"No need for it. I have a hell of an imagination."

Oz scrunched up her nose. "Oh, gross."

"You're a big girl, Ozzie," he said. "Don't think for one minute Andrew doesn't have one as well. You should have heard him in the middle of the night, sleeping under the stars, moaning 'Oz, oh Oz.'"

"Shut up, old man."

She wasn't sure what to say and before she could think of anything, Zed pushed the door open and told Drew he had a call. He got up and kissed her again, said he would be back in a few minutes, but told her Will would help her go back inside if she was cold.

"Nah, I won't," he said when the door closed. "I'll leave you out here to freeze. I'm awful that way."

"Says the man who walked hundreds of miles to get to me."

"Maybe a bit over a hundred. It was fun. I bet Zed and Drew would like to do it again."

They probably would.

As long as there was real food.

And showers.

And toilets.

And clean underwear.

He kept holding her hand, until he had been touching her for longer than I had ever seen him touch anyone. He wasn't even thinking about it; he was comfortable, and didn't look like he was concentrating on keeping his mind closed.

"Drew knows who he is to me," he said after a while. "Sooner or later he'll ask questions."

"The box in the back of my brain is taped shut, Emperor. He won't ask me to open it."

"Use my name. But *not* Willie."

She laughed and then set her head on his shoulder. "Fine. Uncle Will."

"Thank you. I love the idea of being your uncle, but I don't think I want to be the Emperor anymore."

She considered it. "I don't think I really want to be the Queen someday, but it'll still happen. This city needs its Emperor, like it or not."

He sighed. "Fine."

"But…at home, with us? Bonus dad. Uncle." She snorted. "Great grandson."

He lifted her hand to kiss her fingers. "Just Will."

*

On Christmas Eve afternoon, while Oz took a nap, Drew went downstairs to his apartment to call his parents. They missed him but hadn't expected him to come home—and they really didn't want him to, not while the city was a broken, frozen wasteland—but Carter had a few days off and was there with them. They planned on spending the evening together at home, and in the morning they were going to a community celebration at city center. There weren't many people left in Chicago, but those who had hung on were gathering, and his parents wanted to be behind a table, serving food instead of being served.

Shazia said she might not be their queen anymore, but they were still her people, and she loved them. She thought she owed them.

When the call was over he scooped me up and set me on his shoulder for the ride upstairs. I thought he'd be a little bit sad, not spending the holidays with his family, but he was happy.

This is home now, isn't it? You're where you're supposed to be.

Oz was still sleeping, so he sat at the kitchen table with Zed and helped shred dried bread for stuffing, and when they finished with that he chopped vegetables and sliced cheese and salami, and accidentally dropped several chunks of each onto the floor when I patted his leg.

Aubrey noticed me waiting under the table and told me I was being a bad kitty, but she dropped a piece of salami, too, with an exaggerated "Whoops."

I heard movement from down the hall and tried to tell them, but Zed was laughing and Aubrey was talking, and no one heard me. Drew noticed, though. He saw Oz's door open and got up, stepping around Zed to go help her, but she held up a hand and told him to wait.

She walked slowly, every step weighted with effort, until she was more than halfway across the living room. She probably would have gone all the way no matter how much it hurt, but Zed and Aubrey were out of their chairs, too, and it felt a little too much like performing, so she smiled and asked Drew for a little help.

She managed to stay awake and upright through dinner, and then sat in the living room with Drew and the Emperor, until he left to spend the rest of the evening with his parents. One by one everyone else found their way into the living room, and they listened to music and talked, until it was nearly ten o'clock and Oz admitted she was fading fast.

I followed her into her bedroom, trying to avoid Drew's giant feet because he wasn't paying attention to where I was, and I waited with him while Aubrey helped Oz in the bathroom. He scrolled through a list of books on his tablet, looking for something they would both enjoy, because Oz decided that's how she liked to end the day now, with him reading to her. I liked to listen, because his deep voice was soothing and made it easy to drift off.

What are we reading tonight?

I pawed at the tablet so that he would understand.

"This one? It's a story about an entire city of people that live underground, and they don't even know it."

I think I would know it if I lived in the sewer or the tubes.

He fluffed the pillow on his floor mattress and waited. After Aubrey helped Oz get into bed and kissed her goodnight, he started to pull the chair away from her desk to sit near the bed while he read to her. Sometimes he sat there, other times he laid on his mattress while he read out loud, but this time she patted the empty side of her bed and told him to sit there.

"I want to cuddle up to you while you read."

He turned the brightness up on his tablet and then turned the bed side lamp off. "Promise you'll tell me if I move and it hurts?"

"I swear."

He sat gently on the edge of the bed and then carefully scooted back until he was sitting against the headboard. "You still want me to read? You look sleepy."

She set her head on his chest and put her arm over his waist. "Maybe just talk tonight. If you read I really will just fall asleep."

"Hey, the sooner you go to sleep, the sooner Santa will come."

"Funny. I don't think Santa is stopping here this year. We're not doing gifts, remember?"

"I got the memo." He kissed the top of her head. "We don't need more crap. We got you, that's all any of us wanted."

"Hey. You get to want more."

Drew slid on the bed, until his head was next to hers. "I do want more. But not tonight."

"I know." She was almost whispering. "I'm still not quite there. Everything still hurts, and I can't fall asleep without it all rushing back—I feel like I'm drowning every night, until suddenly I'm breathing under water."

"I'm sorry."

"He's coming in at night and changing my dreams, isn't he?" she asked.

He didn't have to ask what she meant. "Wick listens to your dreams. If they're bad, he wakes me, and I call Will. It only takes him a few seconds...he just doesn't want you to have to fight the nightmares yet. He knows that you'll have to at some point, but—"

She stopped him with a long kiss.

"He blames himself, Oz. Zed thinks it's his fault. Half the time, I think it's mine."

I stomped up the bed, and draped myself over his hip.

You're all idiots.

She didn't blame any of them. She was just grateful they didn't give up trying to find her. She was grateful they weren't too late.

"He would have killed me, Drew," she whispered. "I would have been dead before his so-called trial, and he was going to tell the world it was divine justice. If you hadn't shown up when you did—"

Her breath caught, and for the first time since she left the hospital, she cried.

He didn't tell her it would be all right. He didn't promise her anything. He just held her and let her tears soak his shirt, until she couldn't cry anymore.

"I don't know what I can do," he said quietly, when he was sure she was done.

"You're doing it."

I'd suggest smooching, but I think her nose is stopped up now and she won't be able to breathe.

"Will you tell me if there's something I can do? Because I feel kind of helpless here, not knowing for sure what you need. I know I can't fix it, but—"

Her hand went to his face, resting on his cheek. "You've gotten everything exactly right, I swear."

All right. Now...kiss.

Drew scratched the top of my head and told me I wasn't allowed to repeat anything they said.

I rarely do.

Now kiss.

They weren't listening to me. Her hand went to his chest and she drew small circles on it with her finger.

"Right after," she said, "when you took me to the hospital. I know I wouldn't let you leave but I don't really remember what happened. It's like this giant missing piece and I need to know what happened."

"Nothing happened. I sat with you. They took care of you."

"Tell me what they did, Drew."

He didn't want to.

Tell her dude. She's imagining it worse than it was.

"After we got someone to come help, I put you on a gurney, and they wheeled you into a room...the Emperor and I went in with you. The first thing they did was start an IV. Then gave you something to dull the pain." He pulled her hand from his chest and kissed her fingers. "Are you sure?"

"I need to know."

"They had to cut your clothes off because there was no way they were coming off any other way. You could barely move, so you weren't going to be able to undress, and since they didn't know what damage was under...they cut everything off, and kind of rolled you carefully to pull stuff out from under you."

Don't tell her about the blood. She doesn't need to know it was a bloody mess.

"Oh great, you've seen me totally naked and I didn't even get to enjoy it."

That didn't come out as light as she wanted to.

"I didn't," he said. "I turned the chair so I was only looking at your face. But...Will did. So if you want to know exactly how you looked then, he can tell you. It's why he didn't turn away, so that someone would be able to tell you if you wanted to know, and so they wouldn't skip a step. But once they got your clothes off, it was like the doctor was taking an inventory of all your wounds. She counted every cut and puncture, every bruise and burn. Once that was done, they brought in an imaging monitor and checked for broken bones. And then the doctor started closing all the punctures and cuts...Will said he lost count at forty. But they were everywhere, ribs, stomach, chest, neck, a deep one across your back. After that, she sealed the fractures, which honestly sounded like the most painful part. You barely moaned through most of it, but that...yeah, when the doc had to puncture down to bone to get the sealant in, you screamed."

To be fair, that might have been me.

"That's it?"

He took a deep breath. "Will knew that your parents would want to know. He asked the doctor for a rape exam. And yes, he stayed for that, too. There were a lot of pictures taken...he had to give consent to each one. And he had to look at them."

"Poor Emperor," she said, sniffing against a few more tears.

"Use his name," Drew said, managing a small, light chuckle. "I'm sorry, Oz, but I couldn't watch any of that. But I let you squeeze the hell out of my fingers, and I tried to talk you through it when it seemed like the drugs weren't enough."

"Thank you."

"For not peeking?"

"For everything, but also for not peeking." She rubbed her thumb over his chin, feeling his whiskers. "First time you see me naked for real, I want it to matter."

"For it to count."

"Exactly. And mister…we're not waiting until we get married, because who knows when that will be?"

Holy catnip. Kiss her already. She wants you to.

Wait. I'm supposed to be against this nonsense.

Fine. It doesn't matter. Maybe he can heal you the way Jax heals Aubrey. That would be okay.

He did kiss her a few times, but they laid there on the bed and whispered to each other late into the night. He wanted to know what had happened to her and she told him, all the details she could remember. He cried, but it was that same soft crying that Jax did when Aubrey was sad, silent tears that ran down his face, and he didn't even try to hide them.

It felt private even though they kept their clothes on, so I went over to the window seat and curled up where I could hear if Oz needed anything. Their voices became a lull in the background, and I fell asleep.

My gut said she wasn't going to need the Emperor, so I was close enough. Drew couldn't hear her dreams, but he could get me if he wasn't sure.

Right after the sun came up, I heard the door creak open. Aubrey started to come in, but then she saw Oz snuggled up to him. Oz was under the blankets and Drew was on top of them, but her head was on his chest and her arm was across his waist, holding him tightly. I cringed, waiting for her to get upset, but instead she smiled and crept back out, shutting the door softly.

An hour later, Drew woke when Jax threw the door open with a bang. He sat up sharply, confused at first, and then when he realized he was on Oz's bed, his eyes went wide.

"Really, Andrew? What happened to not throwing it in my face?"

"But I didn't—"

He stayed on top of the covers. I swear.

Don't break him. He's one of the good guys.

Jax tried to look irritated, but didn't have it in him. He nudged the bed with his knee and said, "I know. You're not stupid and wouldn't do anything to hurt her. But wake her up—nicely—because Aubrey is making breakfast and it's not an optional meal on Christmas. We sit at the table as a family and yawn at each other, because it makes my wife happy."

"Uh—"

"Breakfast," Jax repeated. "And Merry Christmas."

After he left Oz opened one eye and whispered, "That could have gone so far in the other direction."

"What, you're awake? You let me hang there alone, in case he was ticked off?"

"Be nice to me. I'm still injured."

"Sure, play that card." He laid back down and snuggled up to her, his head on her pillow as he stole a few long kisses. "Your mom is going to come in soon. I really should get up."

"I'm pretty sure you already are."

"Jesus, Oz."

She laughed and kissed him again, and then sat up. "I am going to walk into that bathroom all by myself, and you're going to put some real pants on and go help Zed set the table. And when my mom yells at you for not going to get her before I got up, tell her I insisted, but she can help me get dressed because I still can't get a bra on by myself."

"I am not discussing anything about your boobs with her," he sputtered, sliding off the other side of the bed. "You need help standing? I'll get you as far as the door."

"I need to start doing for myself," she said.

"Yeah, but—"

Slowly, she pushed herself up, and when he tried to reach for her she jabbed her pointy finger in his direction.

Get used to it, dude.

Her favorite words when she was a toddler were 'I do myself.'

Well, that and 'you not my friend' anytime someone made her mad.

She made it into the bathroom and closed the door, and he looked a bit uncertain about what he needed to do next. "Pants, I guess," he muttered. He did what she asked; when he had a reasonable amount of clothing on he went to get Aubrey, and then helped Zed set the table for breakfast. When she was ready, he forced himself to not rush to help her into the kitchen, but watched as she made her own way.

A part of him was a little bit sad, because he knew it was a matter of days and she wouldn't need anyone to help her at night.

I jumped onto his lap when he sat down for breakfast, and peeked over the edge of the table to see if I was going to get yelled at. Jax noticed and he gave me that *dammit Wick* look, but he didn't make Drew put me on the floor. He pretended to ignore it when Drew snuck bites of bacon and egg to me and I understood the deal: don't actually get on the table and you get bites, even if it annoys the King.

When they were done eating and yawning at each other, Drew told Aubrey that he and Zed would clean up.

She didn't argue.

She stayed at the table and watched them for a few minutes, while they stacked dishes and argued over who got to wash and who had to dry, but then left them to sit in the living room with Oz and Jax. They'd put on Christmas music and Jax was on the sofa with Oz. She was resting against him, listening as he read some of the notes well-wishers had sent, including a letter from Bree. She wanted to meet her cousin, because Daddy said that Oz was strong and someone she should look up to. She hoped they would all have a happy Christmas, and ended her letter thanking Oz because she was allowed to wear pants now and was sure Santa would bring her a pair of jeans.

Oz laughed at that; of all the lasting marks she could make on the world, a little girl getting her first pair of jeans seemed like a pretty good one.

Aubrey watched them, too, feeling how bittersweet it was, because for just those few moments Oz was their little girl again, but she knew that soon enough, the boy in the kitchen who was flicking soap bubbles at Zed was going to offer her his heart for good, and Oz was going to take it and never let go.

34

The First Minister's trial began three days into the new year. Oz reluctantly made the trip to Kansas to testify, and the only thing that made her feel better about it was that she was surrounded by the Queen, the Emperor, and Drew. She was mostly mobile on her own by then—she could walk short distances and was not clouded by the pain medications—but the closer the shuttle came to landing the more nervous she was, and the more nervous she was the worse the residual pain flared.

She didn't want to face him again. She didn't want to tell the world—and the world would indeed be witness to her testimony—all the horrible details of what she had endured at his hands and on his orders. She didn't want to see any of the pictures taken in the ER, though she had been promised they would not be part of the news footage that was broadcast globally and would never be made public. She didn't want the world to see how still bruised and battered she looked, over a month later.

She did want to show them she hadn't been broken, so she entered the tribunal theater slowly, on her own. She left behind the bright red cane she'd been using since the day after Christmas, and took the chance that she would list a bit to the left as she made her way from the door to the witness stand. The Emperor walked with her, three steps behind, and then stood nearby once she was seated. His purpose was clear: when Oz could not bear to look the First

Minister in the eye, he would, and with his practiced glare he would make known his anger and willingness to pull the man apart limb by limb, right there on the theater floor.

I sat in the audience with Drew and the Queen; I was allowed in for Oz's emotional support, but only if I stayed on his lap. We were escorted to a front row seat where she could see me and Drew told me not to speak, not even if I thought they were being mean to Oz.

He might have been talking to himself, but I got the message.
She needs to see us, but she doesn't need us.

The Minister's lawyer stood hunched over with the weight of age and his hands shook continuously, his watery eyes blinked frequently and he breathed through his mouth. When the Emperor took his place near Oz, the lawyer protested, his voice thin and trembling, that his presence was not fair to his client and was an obvious attempt at intimidating him and the panel of judges. He wanted the Emperor removed to the audience, out of sight.

There were seven judges, representatives from countries that were part of the United Nations. There were presidents, a king and a queen, and a prime minister; they conferred briefly, and then made the decision that as a member of Pacifica's Royal House, Oz was entitled to the presence of a personal guard, and it was not up to them to decide who that guard should be.

They had already seen the security footage from the safe house, and there was no mistaking the uniforms of Florida's military. It was clear who had made their way through the tunnels, beaten Zed, and then abducted her, but that in itself wasn't proof that Levi Munson had ordered it.

They began to ask questions of Oz, and she answered each one with an edge of anxiety, stumbling over words as she reached for clarity, until the King of England proposed that she simply tell them what had happened, from the moment she was taken from the safe house, until she was rescued in Chicago. Munson's lawyer argued that it amounted to a testimony of hearsay which allowed no room for rebuttal, and was quickly overruled.

"This is not within the jurisdiction of Florida," New England's President announced. "The tribunal's operational orders allow for its judges to make concessions for witness testimony. For the sake of expediency, this witness will be allowed to give a statement. We will all withhold further questions until she is done. You'll get your chance then, counselor."

With that, Oz sucked in a deep breath, locked eyes with Drew for strength, and began speaking.

*

There was no escaping from the tunnels under the safe house, not with more than two dozen men surrounding her. She knew her only way out was through the open access port they had stormed in from, because there were more men behind her than ahead, which meant there was no chance of running back to the bunker.

So she waited. As soon as she had been shoved through the port and outside, she tried to run, but was dropped to the ground with the butt of a gun to the center of her back. She couldn't breathe and could barely move, so instead she went slack as she was jerked up and then thrown into an air van. Survival over escape, she told herself. Pay attention to the details, take advantage when you can, and just don't die.

It was an ordinary delivery van, with an eight-foot-long bed space inside and only three seats; two up front, one in the back. She counted the number of vehicles in the convoy as quickly as she could, and knew she was in the fourth of ten. Chained to the lone rear seat, she waited to see what options she had. Her feet were still free, and she had a little room to maneuver her arms, so she ripped pieces of her t-shirt off and tied one around the arm of the seat and the other to the seatbelt. She had every intention of crashing that van; she knew she had little chance of escape, not with the convoy, but she was going to try and she could leave a sign that she had been there. She worked the material from her shirt slowly, so that there was little sound, and then slid down onto her back until she was hanging half off the seat, her arms twisted painfully over her head. She cocked her legs until her knees were at her chest, and kicked the driver in the head.

The van dove toward the road, hit, and slid off into a tree. She pushed herself back up with her legs by using the back of the driver's seat as leverage, and realized the arms of her seat had broken, so she was able to slide the cuffs out. It still didn't give her enough freedom to run, but it was enough to jump forward and grab the other guard's head and then snap his neck.

She'd had the tiniest sliver of hope that she could get the door open and then take off into the forest; even barefoot and cold she preferred her odds alone in the woods. That momentary hope, though, was the closest thing she came to earning her freedom. The door was hard to open—her hands were slick with blood and she couldn't get a grip on the handle—and she was yanked from the van and without her feet ever touching the ground. Thrown into another van, she was bound at her ankles, knees, waist, wrists, and upper arms. The metal from the ankle cuffs cut into her skin and bled, but if anyone noticed, they didn't say anything, and she assumed they didn't care.

They wanted her alive, but that didn't mean they wanted her unharmed.

Two hours after she had been taken from the bunker, the van landed in Chicago. It was snowing, and when the door slid open she realized how exposed she was; she'd been barefoot when they invaded the safe house, and was only wearing thin jeans and a torn t-shirt. Once outside of the van, the binds around her ankles and knees were removed, but there was a gun at her back, the safety off and ready to fire as they marched her down the center of the street. They kept pushing her along, and based on speed and time she estimated it to be half a mile.

Without telling her anything about why they had taken her, or for whom, she was dragged into the basement of an office building—she could not tell them which business, but it was not a residential area and she had been dragged past several desks—where she was shackled to a bathroom sink with just enough length of chain to reach the toilet. There was no running water to the sink and no light in the room; she was left on the floor in the dark, with the door locked.

She worked at twisting the links of the chain, hoping to push one open far enough to break it. She kept at it until her fingers were raw and close to bleeding, until the door was opened and she was yanked off the floor by one arm. She was lifted until her feet were several inches from the tile, and then tossed forward with the order to walk. The Emperor's voice was in her head: look for an avenue of escape and then run, but there were ten of them and she was shoved back outside into the cold and snow, and knew she wouldn't get five feet away. If she could, exposure would kill her before she could find help.

So she marched.

She was taken to a church and led into a dimly lit room with a baptismal font, and it was there she realized the full extent of her predicament. Waiting by the font, dressed in an ill-fitting pale blue suit and white dress shirt, was Levi Munson. He smirked when he saw her, but it was lopsided and angry, and when he ordered her placed into the font it was with the warning to leave the cuffs on her. Removing them would only bring a world of hurt to whomever was closest to her.

There were other men with him; she made note of three standing behind him, and presumed—based on the murmuring she heard—that there were more behind her. Munson gestured to a younger man who waited behind him and he stepped forward. He was dressed in all white, and eased into the font with her. He didn't speak, but she had the feeling that this was not a place he wanted to be, and the look in his eyes spoke of sorrow.

Pleading with him was useless; he was as much a victim of the moment as she was.

Levi Munson wanted three things from her: accept his church, accept his rule, and confess her sins. Do these things, he said, and he would baptize her as a child of God, which would save her soul. When she refused to utter even a single word, he nodded to the young man in the font with her, and within a second she was under water. He held her there with his hand on the back of her head until she could no long hold her breath.

He let her up, and Munson repeated himself, imploring her to do it for the sake of eternal life. When she refused to speak, she was pushed back under.

The third time when she was pulled out of the water, Munson's arm was cocked back, and he punched her in the face.

She choked on blood as she was pushed back under, again and again, until she was pulled up for a sixth time. As she tried to gulp down air, the young man slipped out of the font and a someone else grabbed her by the neck and dragged her out, throwing her to the floor as Munson barked, "Punish her."

They were prepared for this; four men with batons swung at her as she tried to curl up to avoid the blows, and they kept going until she had nothing left to fight with. When Munson finally ordered them to stop, she tried to curl up even tighter, but was picked up and thrown into a broom closet, her face slamming against the floor.

Time meant nothing at that point. She wasn't sure how long she was left to breathe in the dust and dirt with her legs pushed up against a metal bucket; she only knew that her clothes were damp, and she was too sore to move. She was there long enough to replay everything in her head, wondering if she had missed an opportunity to fight back, if she'd even had enough strength to stand up and deliver a single defensive blow. The thing she was certain of was that she had made herself as small a target as possible, protected her core and her head, which gave her more time.

It was still light out when the door was opened, but before she could get an idea what time it might be, someone lifted her from behind and tossed her back into the water.

She would not yield, and would not tell the Minister the things he wanted to hear. He ordered her taken away, marched outside in the freezing cold in wet clothing, walking long enough that by the time they reached the last place she could remember being taken, she thought she was almost dead.

She had no recollection of the church, but remembered swearing she wouldn't be broken.

There was no real rest. In the center of the room there was a large wooden chair, and there was no mistaking its intention: it was designed to look like an ancient electric chair, massive and intently foreboding. She was slammed into it and chained at her ankles and wrists while Munson paced the room, extolling the wonders of accepting his divine rule and finding eternal forgiveness. As he droned on, an armed guard placed electrodes at her temples, chest, and ribs.

She felt his breath on her face as he breathed out "I'm sorry" silently.

When every wire was in place, the Minister bent over in front of her, hands on his thighs, his face mere inches from hers. He demanded she deny her mother and her father; she was a bastard child and would burn in hell for their sins, but he could save her. *Confess your sins and be saved.*

She would not speak. Even a single word, she decided, was a gift she refused to give to him.

The first shock, even though she expected it, felt like a spring-loaded, stabbing blow. Every muscle in her body clenched, and the pain exploded around her, bright pinpointed spots of light dancing in her eyes.

Confess.

Shock.

Repent.

Shock.

Give up your goddamned mother.

Shock.

She was sure she had thrown up what little there was in her stomach; she could smell the sourness on her and was half aware of something dribbling down her chin, though it could have been blood. There was a moment of elation, because she could feel the chains being pulled from her legs and then her wrists, and she knew she hadn't given him what he wanted.

Break her legs.

She hadn't even been able to open her eyes; every muscle still felt contracted from the jolts of electricity and she wasn't standing on her own, but was being held up by each arm when the blows came. They broke her left leg first, then her right, and then left her in a heap on the cold tile floor.

She wanted to die. There was nothing but pain, and for a breath of a moment, she wanted to die. It would have been easy; just stop breathing, because it hurt less to not suck air in.

It would have given him a victory, and after the moment passed, she knew she'd never let that happen. He grabbed her by her wrist and dragged her across the floor to another closet, and then locked the door behind him.

It could have been an hour or it could have been ten, but the door creaked open and someone slid in a paper plate with three slices of bread and a cup of water. All she could manage was a few bites of the bread and she sipped at the water, willing it to stay down. She decided she would eat out of spite, because every morsel of food meant the hope of a spark of energy.

She slept in tiny slivers of time that fit between the bursts of pain, until he pounded on the door. He stood outside and taunted her—she might live after all; he would show her beaten body to her father, and he would offer the trade: daughter for wife. He wasn't stupid, he knew Jackson would never agree to it—but Aubrey would. Once she saw the broken image of her little girl, she would come running. Maybe he would then send Oz home, maybe not, but of one thing he was sure: Jackson Blackshear would tear the world apart in his anger and grief, and with it he would destroy Pacifica and Midlam.

It would then be his for the taking.

She wouldn't answer him; she wouldn't give him the satisfaction. The louder he became, the more determined she was to not even whimper, until his anger exploded though his cloud of arrogance. He pulled the door open and kicked her, one blow after another, until she was out cold.

After that, she lost track of the days. The next day, or perhaps the day after, she was dragged from the closet and thrown face down across a desk. She heard the strap before she felt it; the sound cracked behind her, and then she felt it ripping across her back. He was careful, she could feel that. It was a practiced move, just letting the leather slap against flesh until it left a welt. He wasn't ready to split her skin open.

Not yet.

But that would come.

His voiced thundered from behind. He was her grandfather, and she would give him the respect he was owed. She would obey him, accept his rule, and embrace righteousness and salvation.

She didn't answer. She couldn't answer.

The strap cracked twice more, but she couldn't make herself say anything. He ordered her dragged back to the chair, which had been moved into the news studio. There was nothing left inside her to fight off the chains or the wires, and she couldn't remember how many times she had been dragged to the chair, or even dragged from one room to another. She wanted to scream, but refused to give him even that much, and when Munson became frustrated that he couldn't elicit even a whimper from her he pulled the electrodes off, clipped the ends until there was only bare metal, and drove the wires into her skin.

There were wires at her temple, down her ribs, into her arms and legs and chest. He ordered the amount of electricity running through them to be turned up, and when she didn't respond—she wasn't sure it was even working at that point—he began to kick at her, spitting out his anger, warning her that she would not survive until the trial. She would die soon, and he would tell his people that it was divine intervention and poetic justice for all the crimes she had committed.

By then, she could barely follow him. Her strength was gone. Her energy was devoted to keeping her heart beating and her lungs drawing in air. She waited, hoping he would get bored, then hoping she would survive his Thanksgiving sermon. She didn't expect to; she expected that she would conveniently die in the middle of it, to serve as proof that God wanted her dead.

But Levi Munson's sermon had barely started when she opened her eyes, and standing before the cameras, confronting the First Minister, was Redmond Munson. She blinked, and there was Drew. It was then she was sure she would live, and she worked for one last burst of energy, just enough to punch Levi Munson in the throat, hard enough that he collapsed on the floor, but not hard enough to kill him.

35

The room went quiet. I could hear Drew's heartbeat, fast and furious, and I heard Aubrey's breath catching next to me, but the world saw as the Emperor folded next to Oz, unable to hold it in any longer. His fist went to his mouth as he tried to swallow whole the sob that nearly made him double over, and then he picked her up from the witness stand and cradled her close, the way he had when she was little. He carried her across the theater, kicked the door open, and took her out before another question could be asked.

Munson's lawyer objected, and was told to sit down.

"We will hear the next witnesses," England's King insisted. "If, after that, you have a reason to cross, the Princess will be recalled."

He demanded a recess and was denied.

There was a parade of witnesses after that, some of the men who had served as Munson's guards and who were privy to his plans for Oz. Redmond Munson spoke about the lie of the temple perpetrated on the people; the sermon had been shown, and with it his confession about his intentions. He testified that his father had been actively trying to kill Andrew Van Hoff as far back as his early childhood; he had access to the written proof of an order to make an attempt on his life in San Francisco, the summer when he was twelve years old, and could deliver it to the tribunal with a phone call. While it was not what the Minister was on trial for, he thought it was important proof of his intentions to eventually launch a war.

The Governor of Texas repeated his conversation with Munson at the reception, when he said that he wanted and intended to take all of Midlam. There were others, but nothing mattered as much as when Valerie Munson took the stand.

Levi, not grasping that the women in his house didn't automatically go deaf when he spoke to other men, had been very open about his plans. He intended to draw King Jackson out, force him into attacking Florida, and make him the villain in a war over religion. He didn't just want to take Midlam, and eventually Pacifica and the rest of the continent; more than anything, he wanted to bring down the House of Blackshear.

Munson's lawyer argued loudly against her testimony; the First Minister had not given her permission to speak, much less be there. A wife could not be made to testify against her husband. That was clearly the law.

"This is not Florida," Valerie Munson said, "and I have not been made to speak. That man has tortured me and he has tortured his daughters, every one of them for *decades*. He has spoken openly and willingly against his God, and he has admitted to being willing to destroy a nation of people just to get what he wants. If you see nothing else, then see what he did to his own granddaughter. He's a stupid, evil, selfish old man, and has brought this onto himself. He is no longer my husband."

Aubrey let slip a surprised gasp.

"You don't divorce in Florida," she whispered to Drew. "Not ever."

"Well…you do now."

*

We viewed the rest of it on the live broadcast; Drew took Oz and me back home, and we sat in the living room with Zed and watched as the Queen addressed the tribunal judges. Munson had easily been found guilty; his own men admitted he'd ordered Oz's abduction, and he had ordered the execution of Prince Andrew and the Emperor had they been on site. There was recorded proof that he had personally tortured Oz. His wife's testimony was admitted as hearsay, until she was able to provide written proof: Minister Munson's plans were carefully scripted if sloppily executed. She had his own words, in his own handwriting, of his plans to perpetrate a lie upon his people to draw them into war. He fully intended to cause the deaths of millions of Midlam citizens, simply to start the war.

The list went on and on.

His guilt was announced less than an hour after the end of the trial, but the judges allowed a few people to speak their opinion on his punishment.

His son called for his execution.

His wife did not refute that.

His guards were willing to die for their part, and agreed that he should be put to death alongside them.

Then Aubrey took to the podium before the tribunal bench. The Emperor was just behind her, as he had been for Oz, and he looked tired.

Everything, Aubrey said, that her father had done was despicable and the rewards for his misdeeds should be as harsh as the misdeeds themselves. His reach went far beyond what he had done in the last several months; he had a lifetime of abuse behind him. "He stole my youth, calling it God's will, excusing it as moments in which he would teach me my place as a woman. He destroyed my sisters' lives. My brothers had no example of what a good man is, and I can only be grateful to God that Redmond, at least, found his way. My mother will never recover. And yet those are not the things he was on trial for, and not the matters about which he was found guilty."

She reminded them of the thousands of people who died on the day he ordered six ancient military planes to drop bomb after bomb on the city of Chicago. "Thousands of children are now gone because he wanted a war to inflate and satisfy his own ego. Those tiny, fragile souls will be mourned forever. If their parents survived, they will never again be whole. Thousands of men and women disappeared in the time it took the bombs to explode. They were fathers and mothers who will never come home. Sons and daughters who will never grow old. There will be parents who will walk through the doors of the homes that were somehow left intact and see neat little lines of shoes that will never be worn again, and they will enter bedrooms where there are toys that will never again be touched with joy, stuffed animals sit on beds that will never have late night fears and secrets whispered to them. These are people he knew existed, but did not care about.

"And my daughter. His granddaughter. He tortured her for no reasons other than he wanted to hurt me and because he could. He wanted my grief to bury me. He counted on her father's grief to lead him onto a path to the destruction of his own people."

She had no doubt—Levin Munson deserved to die.

His crimes met every criterion of his own laws to invoke the death penalty.

He taught Biblical principles: an eye for an eye—his life for the thousands taken on his command.

"But...if we continue to take an eye for an eye, we will all eventually go blind. Pacifica does not have the death penalty, and I am here to ask you to not give him that release. To die is to end suffering, and he should suffer the same pain he inflicted. To execute him is to take the chance that he becomes a martyr to those who still follow him. So I beg you, spare his life. His justice will be met in the next life, when he answers to his Lord."

She turned to face him. "May God forgive you, Levi Munson, because I never will."

36

Ten days after the trial began, Levi Munson was sentenced to life without the possibility of parole in a U.N. controlled maximum security prison located in the upper reaches of Canada. It was in a generally uninhabitable region, accessible only by air and protected by a climate controlled enclosure; he would be reasonably comfortable but had no hope of escape. His life was spared only because the Queen of Pacifica had asked that of the tribunal; they would have been happy to see him die at the hands of Florida's firing squad, but there was no escaping Northern Canada's finest penitentiary and even so, he was almost 80 years old, so her request was granted. Until he could be transferred, he was to be held at Leavenworth, Kansas.

*

Twelve days after his trial, Levi Munson was found dead in his solitary cell. His throat had been slashed and he was hung from the ceiling by his feet to bleed out onto the floor. He was not known to have contact with other inmates, and there was nothing suspicious on the security recordings. There was no one to blame, and while his death would be left as an open case, it seemed as if no one had concrete plans to determine by whose hands he had died. His body would be returned to his family for burial.

Twenty days after his trial, Levi Munson's body remained unclaimed. His wife did not want it, and none of his sons stepped forward. His church declared him to be an apostate, and as such would not accept responsibility for him. Because Midlam was now under the umbrella of Pacifica's government, his body would be handled according to their customs, and he would be cremated. Following cremation, his ashes would be hard pressed into stone, and turned over to the royal family.

*

One month after his trial, Levi Munson's remains were carried to the Golden Gate Bridge in a small plastic bag. The King ordered the west side suicide field to be turned off for the duration of the family's visit, and each end of the bridge was guarded to keep the curious from bothering them as they stood at the center of the bridge.

Aubrey carried the bag, and when they were standing where they wanted to be—the King by her side, her children and Drew and the Emperor with her—she tore the bag open and turned it upside down, dropping the unpolished, dull black stone into her hand.

There was an entire space in the royal house for the pressed remains of those who had passed on with no family; she placed beautifully polished gems there frequently, and did it carefully, with respect and with love. This one would not be kept with the treasured citizens of Pacifica.

"Many, many years ago," she said as she turned the stone over in her hands, "Jax promised me that my father would never step foot in our home. And while I think it's petty of me, I don't want even this much of him to be that close to our family."

"No one does, Mom," Zed said.

"I know. But I also know that once I was able to say what I needed to in front of the tribunal, knowing that my mother was willing to admit to the world what kind of man he was, a very large and old weight slid off of me, one I hadn't realized was still there. And when it went, I think I let it go."

She placed the stone into Oz's hands.

"This is yours, sweetheart. I don't care what you do with it, just please, don't bring it into the house."

Oz didn't even blink. She cocked her arm back, and as hard as she could, she sent the last bits of Levi Munson into the bay.

37

Three floors above the family apartment, one floor above the guest suites and just under the roof, there was a giant, empty room that was rarely used. It ran the length of the entire building, broken only by the elevator landing near the middle, and the staircase that led to the roof. When Oz and Zed were little, the Emperor often brought them to the empty floor to play when it was raining or too cold to take them outside.

When the old King had the throne, it was where formal events were held; there was a stage on the far wall, with aged, dust-covered blue velvet curtains and opulent trimmings that were supposed to look gold but were probably painted. The wall facing Union Square was largely a mass of windows that had several cushioned bench seats. Depending on the time of day, the floor was either brightly lit by daylight, or brightly lit by overhead lighting. It was a cheery space, and I wasn't sure why it was so rarely used.

On a beautiful day when spring was fading into summer, the Queen opened the room and had it cleaned, and she set about decorating the space. The old blue velvet curtains were replaced with bright, rich red ones, and all the ornate decorations were detailed and polished until they looked new. Three dozen tables were brought in and set up on the side of the room farthest from the stage. There were streamers and balloons in every color that I could see and a few that I could not, and at the center of the extra-long food table there was a giant fountain that I was told was not for kitties. It was going to have fruit punch in it, meant for the kids, which was fine because I'd tried fruit punch once and thought it was at least two kinds of disgusting.

Aubrey wanted to celebrate. Oz was nearly recovered—sometimes her legs still hurt and she had an odd, annoying ache in her back that came and went but seemed to have no cause—and she had started running again. Some days she lapped Union Square with the Emperor and the King while they ran fast, and some days she took long, slow runs along the Embarcadero with Drew. She was teaching Zed and Drew karate forms and coached them when they sparred, pushing them to work hard, because sooner or later they'd be sparring with the Emperor.

Zed had powered through and finished nearly an entire year of school in only a semester, and would graduate at the end of the summer term. He'd gone back to work and seemed to have a greater purpose than he'd had before; he could hear memories echoing in the minds of people he prepared for their final rest, giving him the ability to tell their stories in rich detail. He apologized to Rhonda but did not see her again—she had no interest in him and couldn't understand why he felt like he needed to be sorry for anything; she was just having fun, so why couldn't he?—and then extended the apology to his mother and to Oz. "I railed on Red for not cherishing the women in his life, when I was being a massive jerk and I didn't think how hypocritical it was. I am really, really sorry. I swear, I won't do that again."

Those felt like reasons to have a party, but the thing that made her decide that there would be a major celebration was when Jo let slip that the Emperor had never, from the day he was born until he left home at seventeen, had a birthday party. He'd stopped acknowledging them altogether when he was twelve, and she wanted to know if he had ever even admitted to them when his birthday was, and if he ever enjoyed the day.

He'd never lied about his birthday; we all knew when it was. He refused to celebrate it, though, preferring to spend the day quietly, and often alone.

The Queen wanted to have a party, and he balked.

"You know I don't do birthdays," he insisted when she brought it up. "I just don't. I've never wanted to make any kind of deal out of it—"

Oz, who had been sitting at the far side of the table when her mother told him of her plans, slapped her hand down and blurted, "There! Finally! I know your lie color!"

"I don't enjoy the attention, Oz," he said.

That was true; she could see that, but when he said he never wanted to make any sort of deal over it, the colors around him flashed orange, and she knew. At some point, he had wanted to. Somewhere along the line it bothered him to not acknowledge the day.

Aubrey was not going to let it go after that.

"Your parents are here and your mother at least deserves to celebrate your birth. Knowing how stubborn you are, the poor woman probably went through three days of labor. Give her this, William."

He wasn't going to win, and he knew it. He asked that it not be all about him—have the party, wish me a happy birthday, even bake a cake—but instead he thought it should be a celebration of everything good. Oz's strength and recovery. Drew's devotion and unwillingness to give up on her. Zed's new sense of purpose and joy.

There was an engagement to celebrate.

Ozoo.

He wanted it to be about everyone, not just him.

"Let the kids invite their friends. I'll bring my parents, which is more difficult than it sounds, given that my father has practically taken root in his lab to play with his new best friend. Hell, invite the kids' friends to drag their parents along. Call it my birthday if you want, but I'd be happier if it was meant to just be…fun. For everyone."

"And he's telling the truth again," Oz said. "Come on, tell another lie. I want to be sure."

"You have horrible taste in men," he told her. "He's rude, he's vulgar, and he has zero class. Also, he's lazy and he's mean to me."

"Yeah, your lie is orange. And it's a pretty orange, even. Like candy."

When the guest list was done and everyone had sent an RSVP, there were nearly a hundred people coming to the Emperor's birthday party. Oz and Drew only invited a few of their friends, the ones they were sure the Emperor was comfortable with and ones they knew would be happy to bring their parents. Zed invited three friends and their parents—in spite of his best friend's mother also being his math teacher, which didn't make him as uncomfortable as it would have a year before—and he practically begged Aubrey to invite the Governor of Texas and his family.

It had a domino effect. The guests would include the Governor, his wife and his kids, as well as the families of New England's president and Canada's Prime Minister. It would be Shazia Van Hoff's first semi-official appearance as Midlam's Prime Minister. Aubrey looked the list over and realized she had invited a dozen dignitaries and more than two dozen parents and their kids, and it was going to look like the most informal state dinner ever.

"And that," Jo told her, "sounds like William. Stuffy, but when he lets go—?"

She made him get a haircut, too.

I helped him get ready for the party, making sure he had the right amount of cat hair on his clothing. He was forgoing jeans and a t-shirt for black slacks and a black dress shirt, and because he knew it would matter to Jo, he trimmed his beard into a neat goatee and mustache, and made sure his hair was not touching his ears.

Dude, I told you if she stayed in this When she was going to mom you to death.

"I know. I allow it because she missed those last few teen years, but at some point I need to put my foot down."

Yeah, that wasn't happening.

I knew better, and he knew better.

By the time he dragged himself out of the apartment and upstairs, the party was already underway. Finn and Jo were huddled near the stage with Drew's parents and the King and Queen; the conversation must have been about something fun, because Richard was waving his arms as he spoke, and Finn was just as animated. Some of the parents had already arrived and were milling around the food, and Zed was sitting on the edge of the stage with one of his friends. He looked bored, but I knew he was just waiting, because sooner or later the elevator doors would open and Sophia Lopez would walk out.

The Emperor hesitated at the elevator door. What he didn't want was for everyone to turn to him, and he especially did not want a rush of people coming at him to wish him a happy birthday. He just wanted to get across the floor to where Jax and Aubrey were, say hello, and then fade into the woodwork.

Shazia was the first to notice him. She smiled and as he got closer she called out, "Emperor!" and I could almost feel him cringe from where I sat on his shoulder.

"Princess," he said with fake air of derision as he gestured to the glass she held. "Drinking already?"

"Of course I am, you impertinent little fool. It's a party, isn't it?"

"Well, you're here and reek of vodka, so I guess it is."

Jo grabbed his arm and whispered harshly, "William!"

He whispered back, mocking her, "Mom!"

Shazia grinned over the lip of her glass. "You owe me a dance tonight, Emperor. You do dance?"

"Not well. And I was not aware there would be dancing."

"Oz and Drew," Jax said. "Zed and the Governor's daughter. Their friends. All those horny teenagers. There will be dancing, you know there will."

He sighed, and then Jo put her arms around his waist and hugged him. "I haven't danced with you since you were a little boy. You definitely owe me one."

"And me," Aubrey chimed in.

"Hell, it's your birthday," Jax said. "I'll even dance with you. If you're nice to me, I'll let you lead."

I think he wanted to run, but Zed noticed he was here and came over with a hover cart. "Wick, I have your ride for the evening. Remember how to use it?"

I did. I jumped off the Emperor's shoulder and onto the cart.

I want one of these for my birthday.

"We don't even know when that is, Wick," the Emperor said.

We can pick a date. How about tomorrow? Is tomorrow too soon?

I didn't get an answer, because the elevator pinged and a dozen people got off. Last out were Oz and Drew, and when Aubrey saw them she sucked in a short, tight breath. Drew had nearly matched the Emperor, except he had on a bright red tie that was loose at his open collar, and Oz was wearing a bright red fitted tux, but without a tie and her cummerbund was shiny and black.

"Oh my God, she looks adorable!" Aubrey squealed.

She looks like a ringmaster.

"Think we'll ever see her in a dress?" Zed asked.

"Not even on her wedding day," Jax said.

"How long do you think it'll be?" Jo asked. "I've never seen anyone light up the way Drew does when she just looks at him."

"I don't think Oz will be willing to wait until she's twenty," Jax said. "Hell, they might make it to her nineteenth, but I'm not holding my breath."

"And you're all right with that?" Zed asked. "That's less than three months away."

"I'm all right with it, son. Now go hang with your friends, otherwise they're stuck talking to their parents, and no one wants to do that all night."

Jax was right; within half an hour, the volume on the music went up, and nearly all the teenagers and younger adults made their way to the empty floor space near the stage. He and the Queen circulated through all the guests, trying to meet all the parents they didn't yet know, while trying to make sure other state leaders weren't put off by the informality of the event and the inclusion of, as the Governor put it, "regular people."

Robert Lopez watched his kids—they were all dancing in a line, but it looked like there was more laughing going on than actual dancing—and he laughed along with them. "I wasn't sure I wanted to make the trip for a birthday party, Jackson," he said, "but look at those kids. They're having more fun tonight than I've had in a year."

"Thank the Emperor for being born."

"I'd thank his mamma instead." He nodded toward Jo, who was standing with Finn and a man I didn't recognize. "She does not look old enough to have a boy his age."

"No flirting, Robert. You're both happily married."

"Never stopped a fella from being sweet to the ladies," he chuckled. "Besides, my wife is over there flirting with your Emperor. Doesn't mean a thing."

"And my son is flirting shamelessly with your daughter," Jax said. "You might want to keep an eye on that."

The Governor's laugh was booming and I was pretty sure he could be heard across the entire room. "I'm no fool, I know why she wanted to come to this party so badly. Let the kids flirt, Jax. If he sneaks a kiss or two when he thinks we're not looking, good for him. I know my girl, she's probably hoping he will. He's a sweet boy. It's harmless."

You don't know Zed very well.

I'll go tell the Emperor to not let him borrow the car.

By the time I caught up to him, Maria Lopez had moved on and was instead flirting with Finn, and he had been cornered by people I didn't know. He stood with his hands clasped behind his back, and it made him look like he was very interested in whatever they were talking about, but I was suspected it was just to avoid accidental touching.

He didn't look as uncomfortable as I expected, so I warned him about Zed and the car as I floated on by, and decided to ride the cart around the dance floor. I knew most of Zed's and Oz's friends and even though they probably weren't going to sneak food to me, they liked me and would at least pretend to dance with me, too.

The theme of the night seemed to be *flirt with as many people as you can*, so I decided that's what I would do.

Sophia Lopez squealed when I rode up to her, and after she petted my head, she slowly spun the cart around. It made me drift sideways, until I bumped into Drew. He stopped it from spinning and asked if I was all right, so I head-bumped his arm, thinking he would understand that it meant I was okay.

The music changed; the line broke up and the kids paired off to slow dance, and that's when some of the parents joined them on the floor. I saw the Emperor across the room; he sighed hard, because that meant it was only a matter of time before his mother realized and dragged him out there. If she didn't, Aubrey would.

Oz and Drew were in the center of the dance floor, and there was no visible space between them. I bumped the cart into Drew's back, and without looking at me he said, "You're not cutting in, Wick. This is my dance."

But you're too close. Her boobs can't breathe.

I don't think she cared, because her hands went from his shoulders to his neck, and she pulled his head toward hers so she could kiss him.

Well, now neither of you can breathe.

I turned the cart and headed for the Emperor. Jo was making her way between the tables toward him, which meant he was going to be on that dance floor within a minute, so he might be able to help. I stopped right in front of him, which gave him a few seconds of reprieve.

Drew and Oz are dancing really, really close.

"I can see that."

He's going to suffocate her boobs.

"Oz will tell him if she wants him to back away. If I were you, I would worry more about Drew."

If I were you, I'd run. Your mom is going to make you dance with her in front of everyone.

"I'm aware."

I'll snoopervise.

He chuckled under his breath, and when she was near he held his hand out to her and asked her to dance. The kids had all seen him dance before, but it was this weird up and down hopping thing meant to make them laugh. None of them had seen him slow dance, and not everyone knew Jo was his mother.

There was plenty of space between them, but instead of looking uncomfortable, he looked happy.

You whine a lot but you like this.

Finn needs to dance with her. Maybe he can choke a boob, too.

"Wick," he snorted.

"All right, tell me what he said."

"He thinks you and Dad need to dance together. Closely."

"Somehow I think there was more to it, but all right."

"He doesn't always phrase things delicately. But he's right. I would like to see you two dance together. I can't remember the last time I saw you touch longer than it takes to kiss each other hello and goodbye."

"You know I love him."

"I do know." He leaned back, just a little, so he could see her face. "You know, not too long ago I met the young man who was ridiculously in love with you, even if he was thinking about letting you jump off a bridge. And I still have vague memories of you sitting together on the sofa while you tried to read out of the same book, and those long kisses that made me squirm. It doesn't matter if I'm in my forties now, Mom. It still matters to me and I wouldn't mind seeing it every now and then."

She stretched up onto her toes and kissed him on the cheek. "I promise, we still do that, but the last thing we want is to make you uncomfortable."

"Mom, come on. I'm used to Jax and Aubrey. Trust me, you can't make me uncomfortable."

Take that bet, Jo. I'll tell you how to do it.

Jax once grabbed Aubrey's boob and didn't know Will was there. That made him uncomfortable. Go grab one of Aubrey's boobs.

"Wick, holy hell. Why are you so focused on boobs tonight?"

Zed pushed past them to get to the elevator; his best friend, Jimmy, had finally arrived, along with his mom the math teacher.

"He's what?" She reached over to softly flick my chin with her thumb. "Are you a boob man, Mister Wick?"

"Tonight he—" He stopped, his arms falling away from his mother. His gaze was fixed on the people coming out of the elevator, but I wasn't sure what caught his attention. He knew Jimmy, and his mom was just Mrs. Okuda, Zed's math teacher.

"William, what's wrong?" Jo asked.

If he could even speak—and I wasn't sure he could—it would have been lost to the sound of Aubrey squealing in delight. She shot out of her seat and ran to the math teacher, grabbing her in a tight hug that was normally reserved for Jax and her kids when they did something to surprise her.

"Will?" Jo prodded.

"I know her," he said quietly.

Oz and Drew had stopped dancing and came up next to me. "Why is Mom so happy to see Mrs. Okuda?" Oz asked.

He was still staring at her, and didn't answer. Jo shrugged, and even if they understood me I couldn't have answered. It was Zed's teacher, so maybe she'd given him a really good grade and Aubrey was thanking her. But I had no idea why the Emperor was so tongue tied.

Jax jumped up to greet her, too.

Dude, it's just Zed's math teacher.

He finally blinked. "Um, yeah. Zed's math teacher." He turned his focus to Oz. "How are you holding up? I know you went out to run earlier today."

"Getting tired," she admitted. "We're going to raid the food before it's all gone and sit for a while."

"Oz, your mother prepared the menu. There's no chance the food will run out."

"Are you all right? You look kind of rattled."

"I'm fine."

"And there it is again. Orange."

He's turning into a real live boy. He can't even hide his lies anymore.

"Hush, Wick," he said, even though he was the only one who understood me.

Could be worse. Your nose could be growing.

"Mom." He reached for Jo's hand. "I'm sorry, I got distracted."

She patted him on the chest with her free hand. "It's all right. You go get a drink and figure out what just made your head spin, and I'll go grab your father."

Grab his boobs. He'll like that.

He went to the food table with Oz and Drew, but kept glancing over to where Jax and Aubrey were with Mrs. Okuda. While they grabbed food, he stepped over to the bar and asked for scotch, and then drank it in one gulp. He got another, this one on the rocks, and as he held the glass I noticed that his hand trembled a little bit.

Calm down, dude. You don't need to be afraid of her. You're good at math.

He followed Oz and Drew to their table and sat with them, his back to the rest of the room. I hovered behind him, spinning to see where the math teacher was; she was still with the King and Queen, and it looked like Aubrey was talking as fast as she could think. That wasn't interesting, so I moved the cart until I was hovering over the table. If I was a less polite cat, I could have swiped stuff off Drew's plate.

"All right," Oz said, "be honest. Has the party been as horrible as you expected?"

"I can honestly say I've been enjoying myself. And stop trying to decide if I'm lying. I've been having a good time."

"Keep drinking those and you're not going to have one for much longer," Drew said.

"I can hold my liquor, Andrew. And I have no plans on getting drunk tonight."

Oz laughed. "Just a little bit buzzed."

"Perhaps. Although my plans could change, depending on how much I can get Jax to drink." He took a short sip. "What about you, Drew? Ready to have that first drink? And bear in mind, you are not your brother, and I would only get you one."

"He's priming you, Drew," Oz said. "A year from now he'll get you rip roaring drunk, just to be able to give you hell the next day."

"I'll pass," Drew said. "I have plans tomorrow that don't include a hangover, and for all I know one drink would do it. And heads up, Mr. B is headed this way with Zed's teacher."

The Emperor closed his eyes and the fingers on his hand gripping the glass turned red from how hard he was clenching it. Before they made it all the way to the table he took a deep breath and got up, turning to greet them.

Oz and Drew got up, too, but once Mrs. Okuda was standing in front of him, the King shook his head the way the Emperor sometimes did. It was barely noticeable, and meant 'don't say a thing.'

"Aisha," he said, breathing out her name. "I didn't know you were back in San Francisco."

Jax was right behind her; he pointed at Oz and Drew and then pointed toward the table he'd come from. Without a word, they scooped up their plates and moved, and Jax followed. I think he wanted me to come with him, too, but there was no way I was missing this.

He held a chair out for her, then sat down after she did.

Smooth enough.

Uncomfortable silence.

Then, "You broke my heart, Emperor."

"Will. William."

Oh, dude, no.

He took a deep breath. "That was stupid. Let me start over. I know I did, and I'm sorry. I truly am."

"I know. I am, too. I've been back for five years and thought about getting in touch with you a thousand times, but…do you know how impossible it is to get the personal numbers for a king and queen and their emperor?"

At that, he smiled. "You could have simply walked up to the front door."

And knocked? Who would answer? Even the pizza dude has to be expected.

Her voiced was tinged with a bit of sadness. "I didn't think you wanted to see me, not really. Asking Zed to find out seemed inappropriate and I wasn't about to even hint to Jimmy that I once knew you."

"I had no idea Jimmy was your son. He's been here a hundred times, and I never thought about it."

"You had no way of knowing."

"Yes, but—"

"Just ask, Emperor."

"Will, really. I'm not hiding behind the title anymore."

"All right, Will. Just ask."

"You went to Vegas, I know that. You got married?"

"I did. And then I got divorced. I came back because Jimmy's father remarried and moved here, and I wanted them to remain close."

"I'm sorry."

"Don't be. He's a terrific guy and we're still friends. We simply weren't meant to be together."

"How could anyone not want to be with you?"

Dude. You're not drunk yet, so…dude.

"Aside from you?"

He flinched. "All right, I deserved that."

"Yes, you did." She let him chew on that for a moment before going on. "When we met, James was nearly thirty and still trying to find himself. It wasn't until after Jimmy was born and he met George that he figured it out. And I'm happy for them, so don't judge him."

"I'm not."

"And the woman you were dancing with. Mrs. Emperor?"

"What?" He was horrified at first, but then laughed. "She's my mother. There is not, nor has there ever been, a Mrs. Emperor."

I remember her now! She's the girl!

Kiss her, dude.

"Wick, go play somewhere else."

The math teacher grabbed the side of the hover cart before I could even decide if I would go or not. "This can't be Wick."

"It's Wick."

She lifted me from the cart and held me close, rubbing under my chin with her pointy finger. "How?"

"He's probably older than I am," the Emperor said. "We don't question it. And since he's the only constant in my life…I'm hoping he'll hang around quite a bit longer. I honestly don't know what I would do without him."

Talk to yourself a lot more than you already do is my guess.

She put me back, and told me I was still adorable, and then said to stay right where I was. "And you," she said to the Emperor, "stop avoiding it. After all these years, I want an answer. Why did you tell me you didn't love me, when we both know that you did?"

Ooh. She gets right to the point. I like her.

"We were kids, Aisha."

"And we might have flamed out in another year or two. But I stood there in the middle of Union Square and told you how much you meant to me, and I could see it in your eyes. You wanted to tell me then, but instead you snapped that you didn't love me, and we were done."

"You're still angry."

What was your first clue?

"No one has ever hurt me like that. And yes, that includes my ex-husband. So yes, I'm angry. Because I never got to know the real reason."

Tell her.

No. Show her.

Slowly, hesitating several times, he reached out and touched her arm. This wasn't the same kind of caving into want the way he had when he touched Oz's hand last year; he was afraid. He knew Oz would understand, but he couldn't be sure if the math teacher would run in terror, scream, hit him, or what.

He pulled away when he was sure she had heard him, and he waited.

She didn't run. She looked into his eyes until he was visibly uncomfortable but too afraid to look away.

"I missed you, too," she finally said. "I'm not sure I want to know how you did that."

"I didn't think I could control this," he explained. "And I had more secrets that had to be kept than I could risk."

"Will," she sighed. "I would have kept your secrets."

"They were too big, too many, and more important than anything I wanted. Even letting you learn my name was too much to risk. And it wasn't just that. This is a two-way thing. Not only would you have heard everything in my head, but I would have heard everything in yours. All those stray, private thoughts in every awkward moment… every secret you've ever had, every inappropriate thought about people in your life, or even just those you passed on the street. I had no idea if I could control it well enough to not only shield my thoughts, but to not listen as well."

"And now?"

"I still don't know. There are a few people I'm willing to touch, if I have warning. The longest I think I've ever maintained contact with someone is for half an hour or so." He leaned back in his chair. "It's easier to just not be with someone than it is to live so guarded. I could have never touched you, and it was killing me, because that's all I wanted."

"I would have risked it," she said softly.

"Had there not been so much at stake," he said, trailing off. "The truth is, if I had told you, you probably wouldn't have believed it and would have left anyway."

"But we'll never know. And all these secrets, are they an issue now?"

"No. Well, yes, but only to the world at large."

All right, I don't want to witness you crash and burn.

"Fine, Wick. Go play with the King and Queen."

All right. I kind of wish I would be there to hear you explain why you can talk to me, but hey, you can fill me in later.

I rode over to Oz and Drew. They were at a table near the elevator; their chairs were facing and they were leaning toward each other, elbows on knees, holding hands. I missed whatever the joke was, but they were laughing so it seemed like a good place to wait.

"They're taking bets," Drew said to her. "The Governor of Texas says November, because I turn twenty-one and then I would never forget our anniversary…which he has evidently done and says it gets expensive. Finn says a year from now because we need time to plan. Your mom? If I heard right, she thinks it'll be a big deal if you turn nineteen first, and that we won't want a huge, overblown wedding…so no need for all the planning."

"What about your mom?"

"She thinks we should just live together."

"We could do that, you know."

He let go of her hands and leaned back in his chair. "Is that what you want? To just live together?"

"I haven't gotten what I want yet," she teased. "My totally hot boyfriend has this thing about being sure and all that. I need to remind him that if I've been sure I want to spend the rest of my life with him, then I'm absolutely sure I want to jump his bones."

"Huh." He scooted his chair so that they were next to each other. "Your other boyfriend is just waiting for you to be completely healed, and you haven't told him that you are."

"Ah, yeah, that guy. He's super sweet, but a little slow. More patient than I deserve."

I'm going to barf on you.

"What's up, Wick?" Drew said. He gave the cart a little push so that it spun around slowly. "Hasn't anyone snuck food to you yet?"

No. They have not.

This is not a good party for me.

When I'd spun all the way around, he stopped the cart and then dropped a few bites of roast beef onto it. "I think the Emperor would like you to enjoy his birthday, too."

"Yeah, well he's about to enjoy it a lot less," Oz said. The cart with his birthday cake was being brought out from the kitchen, and it stopped right where the room split in half. "He's going to hate being sung to."

"Then we make it as loud and obnoxious as we can." He stood up and offered her a hand. "Let's make Emperor William squirm. Come on, Wick."

The Emperor's skin turned a few shades pinker when the candles were lit, and then the whole room started singing 'Happy Birthday' to him. He sighed before he had to blow out the candles, but I don't know if that's because everyone was yelling at him to make a wish, or because the smoke from so many of them made it hard for him to breathe. He blew them out in one breath and then refused to tell anyone what he wished for.

"If I tell you," he said to his mother, "it won't come true."

I wished for fish cake, but that didn't happen. It was white cake with chocolate frosting, and as the Queen cut into it she apologized because I couldn't have even a bite.

"It's his favorite," she whispered to me. "He always thinks about what the rest of us want, so you don't mind, do you?"

There were still a lot of dead meaty things laid out, so I didn't mind. While everyone noshed on the cake I practiced making the cart go straight up and down, and then worked on making it go faster, which got the King sprinting across the floor to catch me before I smashed into the back of the Canadian Prime Minister's head.

I know how to stop it, geez.

When the music started up again it was with a nice, slow song. Oz and Drew, and the King and Queen headed for the floor, and then Jo grabbed Finn's hand and made him dance, too, even though he kept arguing he was horrible at it.

"He really is," the Emperor told Aisha. "My mother's toes will be battered and bruised by the end of the night if they keep it up." He dug into his back pocket and pulled out his thin black gloves, the ones he had worn when he escorted the Queen to the reception. As he pulled them on, he said, "I'm not any better, but…one of my regrets is that I never danced with you."

She smiles nice. You should let her boobs breathe.

They walked to the middle of the floor and stopped near Oz and Drew, who had given up actual dancing and were mostly standing there, swaying to the music while she rested her head on his shoulder. He kept whispering in her ear and she was giggling, but I couldn't hear what he was saying; I raised the cart to his face level and stared at him, in case he needed my advice.

"Wick," he said, "you're going to run into someone's face. Be nice."

I'm nice. I won't break a nose or anything.

I rode back and forth, weaving between everyone, but decided the startled yelps weren't worth it, and lowered the cart so that I would only bump into stomachs and backs. I circled Jax and Aubrey, trying to figure out how to zip between them, but he wouldn't back up enough. When he looked away from her to tell me to watch out, he noticed how Oz was holding onto Drew, and watched them not dance.

"They're perfectly content, sweetheart," Aubrey told him when she saw how he was looking at them. "Don't you dare tell them it's not appropriate."

"That's not what I was thinking. It's like they're melting into each other, and I remember dancing like that with you. I never wanted to let go."

"I know what you wanted," she teased. "And we were almost there."

"So are they." He rested his forehead on hers and sighed. "Come on." He led Aubrey to them and bumped into Drew, accidentally on purpose, and then said, "Drew, she's exhausted."

Oz argued that she didn't want to miss the Emperor's first birthday party, but he told her that from the looks of things it was going to go on most of the night, and no matter how good she felt most of the time, she still needed to get off her feet. Then, "Drew, take her downstairs and put her to bed."

Now there was space between them. They both took a half step back, not sure they'd heard him right. Drew stammered a bit until he managed to get out, "Yes, sir," and then put his arm around her as they walked to the elevator.

"Jackson," the Emperor said, "you do realize what you just told him to do?"

"I know."

"Does she?" Aubrey said with a laugh. She stood on her toes and kissed him. "Admit it, you love that boy."

He didn't admit to anything but he made her kiss him again.

What does that taste like?

"What, Wick?"

Kissing. What does kissing taste like?

"Seriously? Wick, I don't know. Ask Jax."

"You can understand the cat," Aisha said, not sounding all that surprised.

"What's Wick want to know?" Jax asked.

He sighed, hard. "What kissing tastes like."

"I need to check again, Wick." He stole another long kiss from Aubrey. "Happiness, that's what."

Ah. So kissing tastes like shrimp.

"I can understand the cat," he said to Aisha, "but I sometimes wish I didn't."

You two aren't really dancing anymore, you know that, right?

"And you don't know what a kiss tastes like?"

"As I've observed, kissing involves touching."

They completely stopped, right in the middle of the floor. Jax and Aubrey were barely moving, waiting to see what was happening.

"How much are you willing to risk, Will?"

He couldn't answer.

I don't think he could even breathe.

She slid her hand from his shoulder, resting it on his chest. "You've had almost twenty-five years to think about it. Is it worth taking a chance?"

I don't think she was really waiting for an answer, because her hand was at the back of his neck and her face was halfway to his before he managed to whisper, "Yes."

*

Half an hour later Zed took me downstairs, when he realized I was no longer on the hover cart but sitting on the floor in front of the elevator, staring at the closed doors. The party noise was starting to bother me and I didn't want to keep interrupting the Emperor since he seemed determined to keep dancing with the math teacher, so I waited for the doors to open and hoped I could get off on the right floor. He offered to take me home if I meowed, so I did and then he told me he would just leave me in the hallway by the living room so that I could decide for myself where I wanted to go from there, but I had to stay in the building. He wanted to go back to the party, because Sophia was still there and had promised him another slow dance. He also thought it was funny because Jimmy wanted his mom to leave the Emperor alone, but no one brought a crow bar to the party, so there was no prying them apart.

Okay, you go have fun.

You don't get the Emperor's car tonight, you know.

I checked Oz's room; her red tux was hanging over the back of her desk chair but her shirt and cummerbund were on the floor and her shoes were on the bed, so I figured she'd changed in a hurry to go to Drew's apartment. I could still hear the party from her room, so I made my way down the stairs; it would be quieter there, even if they were watching a video.

Plus, there might be food.

When I pushed through the cat flap I didn't hear the sound of any video being played on the monitor, but the lights were on so I went in. They were in the living room dancing without music; Oz was in a t-shirt and shorts and Drew had changed into pretty much the same thing, which looked a lot like sleeping clothes, so I reminded them that Jax said she was supposed to go to bed.

They ignored me.

Fine, I'll sit here near your feet and stare at you until you listen.

"I'm fine with waiting," Drew said, still ignoring me. "If that's next week, or next year or even the year after that, or we decide to get married first…it's all right, Oz. You waited for me, I'll wait for you."

She reached for the front of his shirt, grabbing handfuls of it as she leaned her head against his shoulder. "I'm not in pain anymore, Drew. I'm in lousy shape, but I'm not in pain."

"Still—"

"No." She let go of his shirt. "I haven't been putting this off because of the pain, because it's not pain anymore. It's how I feel about…me. I have never been self-conscious about my body before, but I am now. And I hate it. I wanted this a long time ago, but every time we came close—" her voice caught "—all I could think about were all the scars, and how ugly they would look to you."

"Tiny puncture marks. Little scars. How would that bother me?"

"Because you didn't peek," she reminded him, "so you didn't see the worst. The little ones will go away, but the one I hate—"

He tried to tell her that the scars only mattered to him because they bothered her and that got him a long kiss, but then she stepped away and peeled off her t-shirt. "I want you to see what you'd be looking at for the rest of your life."

He tried to take a step toward her, but she held her hand against his chest, and made him step back.

"That bastard didn't just jam wires into me. When the pain from shocking me wasn't bad enough, he grabbed a thicker wire and sliced it through my skin, and he flayed me open like a—" Her breathing hitched again. "I just need you to see. You don't have to like it. And don't pretend."

Very slightly, he nodded.

If I had known she was going to pull the sports bra off, too, I probably would have looked away. It seemed important to her, though. She had a still-angry-red scar that ran from just an inch or so under her right collarbone down to her nipple, and she knew that it might eventually fade a bit, but it was never going to go away.

It took him a moment to let himself look away from her face, and to look at it. She closed her eyes and waited, so that he could look and not worry about what she was expecting him to do.

He took the step that she had pushed him back, and kissed the scar.

"You are beautiful," he told her. "The only thing this says to me is that you're stronger than I am, and I damn well be a better man to deserve you."

"It's ugly as hell, Drew." Her eyes were still closed. "There's another one down my back. I've gained like thirty pounds. I feel like I'm a mess."

He ran a finger along the scar, and whispered, "You're my mess. I don't care about anything else, Ozzie. Other than maybe the fact that I can barely breathe right now, and unless you say no, I am about to start touching things I have avoided touching for a very long time."

Her eyes fluttered open. "I'm counting on it."

Great. This is when the clothes go flying off.

"I'm going to apologize right now," he said while she pulled his shirt over his head. "This is gonna suck for you. Pretty sure if you blink twice, it'll be over."

"You're young. I'm patient. I'll give you five minutes and you can try again."

She dropped his shirt onto my head, and didn't even notice. By the time I wiggled out from underneath it, it was definitely time to leave.

I didn't even get any snacks.

I went into the Emperor's apartment and curled up in the comfy chair and slept until he opened the door at three in the morning.

You had a happy birthday?

"Indeed, I did."

So. Your first kiss.

"First kiss."

Was it worth it?

"It was."

Gonna kiss her again?

"We're having coffee tomorrow. We'll see."

Oz showed Drew her boobs.

"That's none of my business, Wick."

But it was a good night for boobs.

"You're really just trying to squeeze boobs into every conversation you can tonight, aren't you?"

It's an awesome word. Boobs.

"It's not polite conversation."

Fine. But still. She showed him her boobs and then he showed her his, and that's when I left.

"Good for them. My birthday just got a little bit happier."

You knew before they were even born that they were gonna get married someday. You even know when.

He headed down the hall to his bedroom, and I followed. "I know when it happened according to the history I learned as a child. You and I may have changed that. Levi Munson never abducted her in the timeline I was raised, so we can't be sure of anything anymore."

Did you think about going back and stopping it from happening this time?

"Every single night, Wick." He started pulling his clothes off, not paying attention to where he tossed them. "It would have been so easy. Just run back home, go through a portal…I wanted to, especially when I saw how badly she was hurt."

So?

"That ended the war. What Oz went through, and finding her with Munson? It ended a war that otherwise would have gone on for years. So my choice was to spare her all of that pain, or spare the world a bloody war that ended with a horrific bang delivered through a transporter invented by my own father. Which I thankfully did not live to see."

You should tell her that. She would approve.

"No. The choices I make are my own burden, Wick."

Dude. You don't have to carry every burden alone anymore. You have family now. It's even on paper. You're William Blackshear.

"I was that before. They just don't know it."

Well, it's even better, because they chose *you.*

"Indeed. They did."

He stretched out on the bed and I sat on his legs, looking at the tattoo that took up so much of his skin.

This is why you helped take care of Oz so much after you guys saved her, isn't it?

"I helped because I care about her."

None of it was your fault.

"I let my ego get in the way, Wick. I let myself believe that I could protect her no matter what, and because I was sure that I could, I let my guard down. I appreciate that Oz doesn't blame me, nor do Jax and Aubrey, but I know better. I failed her again, and this time it was because of my own hubris."

So what if it was?

"Really, Wick? She was almost killed."

But she wasn't. And you just said, it ended the war sooner than it would have otherwise. So really, not only is it not your fault, but thinking it's your fault is your inflated ego telling you that you have so much power that you should be able to stop just about anything from happening.

"Thank you, Doctor Freud."

I'm right and you know it. So you know what you do now?

"I'm sure you're about to tell me."

Tomorrow you go have coffee with the math teacher, and you tell her you want to kiss her again and then see where it goes, and you stop trying to control everything all the time and just for once, get close enough to the sun to get burned.

"You pretty much have the myth backwards. The idea is to not think you're so good that you can get that close to the sun."

Sometimes a guy has to let someone else be Daedalus, and sometimes he has to be Icarus.

"You know what happened to Icarus, right?"

Yeah, but you know what Daedalus couldn't do but he probably would have if he could? If the circumstances were different? He would have let Icarus push his limits, just to see what he was capable of. He would have gotten a bunch of people together to catch the little freak when he got too close to the sun and fell. So grow a pair and fly and take the chance that you'll get burned. You have people to catch you.

"You're awfully mouthy for a cat, you know."

He laid in the dark, wide awake, and I stretched out across his thighs, waiting for him to admit I was right. I was prepared to wait all night, which really only had about three hours left, but then his phone pinged and I fell off when he rolled over to check it.

"Text," he muttered. "It's Aisha."

You gave her your number. Good job. What's it say?

"Of course I gave her my number. And it's none of your business."

I'll bug you all night unless you tell me. What's it say?

He turned the phone so that I could see the screen.

'I'm worth the risk.'

Whatcha gonna do, William?

He tapped out an answer, and set the phone aside.

"Wick," he breathed out. "It's time to fly."

ABOUT THE AUTHOR

Max Thompson is a feline life coach for *Mousebreath* magazine, and he lives in Northern California with his typist, writer K.A. Thompson, and her Spouse Thingy, otherwise known as The Man. There's another cat running around named Buddah Pest, but Max doesn't like to think about very often and prefers to pretend that his existence is one of a solitary cat.

He can be found online at his blog, The Psychokitty Speaks Out
http://psychokitty.blogspot.com

and on Facebook at
http://facebook.com/thepsychokittyspeaksout